FIRE MARKER MAN

by ANDREW FLOWER

Publisher, Copyright, and Additional Information

Fire Marker Man by Andrew Flower

Copyright © 2022 by Andrew Flower
First Edition published in 2022 by M. Swill Publishing

ISBN-
979-8-9867705-0-5 (Paperback)
979-8-9867705-1-2 (eBook)

Editing by Andrea Robinson and Margaret Diehl
Cover design and interior design by Rafael Andres

CHAPTER ONE

"Papa! Papa! Come quick. It's back again!"

Daisy stood frozen by the edge of the potato fields, her red curls bobbing in the breeze. Robert Gillian dropped the hoe he was repairing and raced out of the barn to her side.

"You smell it, Papa, don't you? It's back again, isn't it?"

She turned to him and began to cry. But Gillian just stood there silently—mournfully—surveying the land as far as he could see. He needn't walk out to observe the rotting leaves. Any nose could detect the stench of decay. He removed his straw hat, held it to his chest, and stood solemnly like a man paying his last respects to a loyal friend.

"*Bloody hell*," he murmured. "Daisy, go and get your ma. We'll have to harvest these potatoes fast, else all will be lost."

"Okay, Papa," she managed between sobs, and then she was gone.

But no one returned. Not Daisy, nor her twin, Daphne, not Mary, nor Patrick, not even Aileen. Gillian was walking toward the cottage when a blood-chilling scream came from inside the little dwelling. He burst into a sprint, and upon entering, he found Daisy covered with blood, desperately struggling to pull Angus off her twin sister. But this was not his beloved Angus, an aging Rottweiler he'd raised from a pup. It was a raging beast, blood dripping from its muzzle, a rabid look in its eyes.

Gillian was too late. Daphne was gone, reduced to a bundle of bloody flesh and bone. He gasped and then tried to scream, but nothing came out. He ran to the next room, seeking help from the others. And there he found them, laid out on their straw mattresses, reduced to skeletons themselves.

But not by Angus... by the famine.

September 1869
NEW YORK HOUSE OF DETENTION
A.K.A "The Tombs"

Gillian awoke with a shriek, his shirt and pillow covered with sweat. He was unsure of the time, but from the angle of the sun he judged that evening was approaching. He was safe in his prison cell, he realized. He laughed aloud at the irony.

Now that he was wide awake, finding a comfortable position again would be a struggle. The lump of hard straw in his mattress found him no matter how he turned about. Then he recalled. An odd position on his right side, his back leaning against the wall. His pillow and rolled-up blanket would keep him propped up—for a while. *This will do.*

"Despite it all, we did make the wise decision... right, my love?" he inquired of the mouse that was carrying out its usual routine, running back and forth under his cell door, as if to make him jealous; escape would be so easy if he, too, were just a mouse. "You were always the wise one, Aileen. Coming to America was our only choice, like you said. I just got too big for me breeches, that's all," he muttered. Then he sighed and smiled. "Well, you would have loved the paddle wheeler to West Brighton, my dear."

* * *

"Stop your babbling, you stupid paddy!" shouted the lead guard while stomping down the dimly lit hallway. The second guard, hobbling on an ill-formed leg, was doing his best to catch up.

"Hey, hey, Maurice!" the second one cried. "Be kind to Mr. Gillian. He ain't a bad man, you know."

"Maybe right, Phinny, but he let those young ones die."

"No, he didn't. You didn't read what the papers said."

"You can't believe them rags."

Maurice slowed his gait as they approached the small window forti-fied by three heavily rusted iron bars. This marked the end of the corridor, and a final turn left brought them to the cell of Robert Gillian, the largest cell in The Tombs. The guards had nicknamed it "the royal accommo-dation." Fit for a giant of six foot four inches, it was frequently the final home of those awaiting the gallows.

"Aileen, is that you, my love?" Gillian cried out. His fever had broken, but he still experienced bouts of delirium. The visiting surgeon had said they would fade as he gained distance from the opium treatments.

"Oh, it is, my darling. I'm here to save you from the rope!" Maurice bellowed in his best impression of a female.

"Don't taunt him no more," Phinny begged as they arrived at Gillian's cell.

"Just having a little fun, that's all. You know, makes the day scoot along."

"We got your grub, Robert," said Phinny, surveying his iron key ring then plucking just the right tool. One hollow click, and the iron gate swung open with a raspy creak, the same creak heard when any of the one hundred twenty cells in the decaying dungeon sprung open.

The opium-enhanced dream had abruptly ended when he'd heard the boots approaching. And he stood to greet his keepers.

The guards had no fear of Robert Gillian, despite his towering stat-ure. Sixty years of age now—and showing every bit of it—his movements were slow and painful, a grimace revealing this truth when even modest activity was required of him. But it was intuition that told these men Gil-lian need not be feared. They'd dealt with their fair share of murderers, and Robert Gillian didn't fit the bill. Perhaps he was just a man caught up in bad circumstances. Still, Maurice cautiously placed the tin tray on the tiny bureau beside the cot while Phinny, following orders, kept watch, club in hand.

"Thank you... Thank you, kind gentlemen," Gillian managed in a soft voice, then conveyed a faint smile. He sat back down on the cot, his tree-trunk torso and head hovering over the tray as he surveyed the fare while unwrapping his utensils.

"You're quite welcome, Robert," Phinny said, chipper as usual. "The galley was fresh out of ham hocks today, but they whipped up some hash and eggs."

"Now is there anything else we can retrieve for you, my lord?" Maurice added in his best queen's English. "Perhaps a brandy? Hot toddy, sir?" He bowed.

"I beg, let him be, Maurice," Phinny pleaded again. He shrugged sheepishly in Gillian's direction, as if it was his burden to carry the guilt for Maurice's conduct.

Gillian gave a defeated smile, then all focus was on his food.

The two guards departed, and once again there was the rasping creak and hollow click of the old iron gate, the exact sound he heard all day echoing through the dark chambers of The Tombs—one hundred twenty cells, one hundred twenty prisoners.

* * *

Now he was keenly aware of his hunger. Mealtime was the highlight of his day—except when gruel was served. But to his surprise, the fare was not all bad in The Tombs. So he dug in.

Just then, a well-timed breeze wafted in from the little window at the end of the corridor. Changing of the seasons, finally, he thought with pleasure. Gillian closed his eyes and immediately sensed the fragrance of newly cut lawn. He slowly filled his lungs with the welcome treat. His nose detected some brine, the salt of the sea, and he remembered, *Of course, New York is surrounded by sea. But it's so easy to forget, with all the buildings, people, and filth.* At once he was homesick for Ireland. His Galway was close to the ocean, and oh so beautiful.

But twenty-three years had passed, and the only thing unchanged was that the Isle was still thousands of miles away.

After a sad sigh, he finished his hash and eggs. Then he reached for his drink but caught himself. "Ugh. Swill milk. Maurice's doing, no doubt. Bloody swine he is," he muttered.

The wall opposite his bed greeted the tin cup with a clang, and he watched the bluish-white excuse for milk drip down the limestone blocks. He suppressed a gag. To make matters worse, the breeze suddenly stilled, and the dank stench was upon him once again. *My punishment for complaining, I suppose.* Then he struggled to break the hard tack with the remaining teeth on the left side of his jaw.

His hunger satisfied, Gillian lay back down. The clump of hard straw in his mattress was instantly poking at his shoulder blade, but he didn't care. He slept until dawn. As the first rays of light came through the little window just outside his cell, an orange glow was cast on the wall just above his bed—the light broken only by the shadows of the rusting bars. He squinted as he gazed in the direction of the sunrise.

Then came a familiar command shouted from the courtyard below. Gillian cringed as he rushed his fingers to his ears, as if plugging them would hush the ordeal.

"Drop him!" came the second command. Then the sharp crack of thunder. Or was it more like a single gunshot? He could never quite decide. Regardless, it was always jarring as that scaffold door swung open. The soft creak of the swaying rope followed, easily heard through the deafening silence of the spectators, their mouths, he imagined, open wide in awe. Sometimes he would hear a desperate gurgle. But not today, which was fine with him. Gillian lay back down and drifted off again.

Chapter Two

"You, Gillian, wake up! You got callers," Maurice barked as he drew his club along the cell gate. "Now, you're a lucky one. Most of these poor sods are forgotten. Well deserved, I suppose."

Gillian experienced a wave of queasiness. Visitors meant he would have to confront his shame again. Could it be bad news regarding his appeal?

The guard opened the cell and tossed a clean pair of slops on the cot, which Gillian felt thankful for; he was embarrassed enough about his appearance, and he didn't want to stink in the presence of his daughter.

In simple iron cuffs—it was obvious to the warden there'd be no daring escape here—Gillian was led down three dimly lit corridors toward The Tombs' main entrance, where the receiving rooms were situated.

"He goes to Room Four, as usual, Maurice," a clerk called out from behind a desk.

Despite his numerous visits, Gillian was again moved by the room's cavernous size. The only item of furniture was a long chestnut table at its center. Darkly lacquered, the intricately carved bowed legs added ornateness, offsetting a plain flat tabletop. Four poorly matched Queen Anne chairs were set around the table. Each time Gillian entered the room, it struck him that this ancient table could have been of service for medieval feasts or perhaps treaty signings concluding great wars of the past.

"Papa!" Mary called out, springing from her seat at the table's far end and dashing across the floor to embrace him. Her Mr. Chang—sitting midway the table's length —opened his eyes wide with alarm.

"Cease!" commanded Maurice as he extended his club. "I'm sorry, ma'am. Eight feet from the prisoner. You must remember that."

Gillian's tear-filled eyes never left his daughter's face as Maurice led him to his customary seat at one end of the table.

"Sorry, warden's rules," the guard said, sounding almost apologetic as he released one of the iron cuffs, leaving Gillian with the whole set dangling from the opposite wrist. Then he pulled the chain of his timepiece, tucked between the second and third buttons of his waistcoat, and studied the dial. "You have until half past the hour. I'll be right outside."

He glanced at Mary, who had regained her composure and her seat. After a seemingly subservient nod, he exited the room. This was not the first time Gillian sensed an almost humble discomfort in Maurice. Could the guard have a genuine soft spot when it came to family visits? If so, who was the sympathy for? Visitor, prisoner, or perhaps both? More intriguing, though, was whether these feelings extended to all prisoners and their families. Or was his situation unique?

"Papa, why don't you at least listen to Mr. Chang? He may be able to help you. His brother has a lawyer who may know a way to locate your witnesses."

"Ah, Mary, this will not work." His freed arm swung up in the air as if warding off a pesky fly. "I don't want to put him out. Besides, my gifts to these Negro charities were anonymous. Even if we find them, they won't be able to put the money to my face. It will be hopeless, my lass."

After a few moments of sad silence, Chang, who'd been sitting quietly, lifted his head to smile warmly. "Ah, Mr. Gill, we find way to help. I read book here," he said with delight as he held up a tattered copy of the King James Bible.

"I know, Chang. Your kindness is well received," Gillian responded with a weak smile, then addressed his daughter. "Mary, why didn't you tell him that's the wrong bible?"

"I know, Papa, but it's easier for him than the Catholic book, and it's not the Buddhist scriptures."

"It's blasphemy!" Gillian snarled.

Chang winced, possibly not understanding the reason for the sudden outburst. And the guard glanced through the little window in the door.

"Is this really of importance now, Papa! Aren't there more urgent matters? And you, talking about sac-religion. What pulpit do you stand on? Chang is bettering himself. He will be a good Christian—one day—and we will be married. And that is the way it will be." She nodded firmly.

Although shamed by his daughter, Gillian had an unexpected burst of pride in Mary's display of confidence and resoluteness. He saw traits of Aileen in her now, or at least of Aileen in her better days. But gloom quickly descended again. He placed his elbows on the table, and massaged his forehead in a rhythmic fashion, not caring for once about the cuff or the chain clanging as it hit the table. "Forgive me, both of you," he said solemnly. Then he looked directly at Chang and forced another weak smile. "These are trying times, and I am most grateful for your care, Mr. Chang. We will speak of this again."

Chang stood and smiled, displaying a remarkably full set of teeth. He bowed and took his seat again.

"Mr. Chang will be establishing his second laundry just off Broadway, Papa, around the corner from the Astor House," Mary said in an apparent effort to lift the mood. "The rent is quite high, but he is assured an up-scale clientele from City Hall. He may seek a contract from the hotel to launder uniforms. And his brother has agreed to assist with the rent until the business is secure." She smiled lovingly at Chang.

"A good situation for you, Chang. A man should only move upward in this great metropolis, take advantage of any opportunity that comes his way, I say... assuming it's above the board, of course." Gillian cleared his throat and fidgeted.

Chang smiled and nodded fervently. It was apparent to Gillian that the man's English was progressing, then it occurred to him that perhaps he'd gained proficiency at faking it.

"You've lost weight, Papa, which suits you well," Mary said as she studied his face.

Her observation was of little surprise. He'd caught his reflection in the looking glass on numerous occasions while traveling down the corridor to the receiving room. In fact, he found the profound changes in his appearance—after nine months of detention—to be quite startling and not all bad. The pudge in his jowls had melted away, once again revealing the strong jaw and well-defined cheekbones of his youth. His salt-and-pepper hair was much the same, although perhaps the salt had taken the lead now, especially in his thick and wiry side chops. And his rooster neck was all but gone. He was not able to capture much of his torso in the glass, but when he looked down, he realized his belly was no longer obstructing a clear view of his feet.

"Well, tis strange, Mary, those festering sores on my ankles seem to be gone, as well the tingling in my feet. Doc McGrath would always tell me to cut out the sugar and syrups and stick to substance. So it was potato and a bit of meat, or potato and fish. But the sores and tingling never went away. Now here, I am doing better," he said.

There was an awkward pause in the conversation.

"And your brother? Do you know his whereabouts?" Gillian asked. "I haven't had his company in weeks. And I don't believe I've seen his lovely maiden for many months."

"It's been a few weeks since I last spoke with him," Mary said. "I found him well, and he reported mother and child were all blessed with good health now. Their flat off Union Square is quite spacious, just fine for a growing family. Oh yes. He did say he was to be moved up in the new fire department this coming year. Assistant Engineer, I believe."

"Oh. That's a bit of news. I hear they pay a good wage now for engineer positions, something like one thousand a year. Perhaps your brother will get his dream of setting roots in Park Slope after all."

"Yes, perhaps he will," Mary said, fidgeting in her chair.

"Well, I'm sure Patrick has his reasons for visiting me so seldom. He has lost a great deal of respect for his father, and rightfully so, I suppose. And I'm certain his Helen looks upon me as no more than a roach on the floor."

"It has been especially hard on him, Papa. You sharing the same occupation and all. The volunteers are done, and it's for the better, I believe.

The city is too big now. But his acquaintances are yours also, and so he has... shame for your actions." She lowered her head.

This stung. He assumed she shared the same sentiments as Patrick. "Yes... of course, that's reasonable," Gillian said softly. "There is certainly no pride in being the son of an arsonist—an incendiary, a fireman fallen from grace." For a moment, his shame was alleviated by a pang of self-pity.

"Time has run out," Maurice blurted as he entered the room. Knowing the routine, Gillian stood, grateful for the interruption, the escape. Then came the sadness. He didn't want Mary to leave him.

"Remember, Papa. Think about Mr. Chang's offer. . . Oh yes, and Patrick did send his well wishes."

The lass was never good at fibbing came to his mind.

Now he saw her tears. *She must still love me.*

"Take care, my lamb. All will be fine for me," he attempted to assure her. Then he turned to Jian Chang. "I will consider your most kind offer, Chang," he said for Mary's sake. "And may the good Lord bless your new enterprise."

Chang stood reverently and bowed. Now he wore a solemn but placid expression.

* * *

As the guard led Gillian out of the room, Mary suddenly felt like a young child whose father was being taken away. Her big strong papa, her first protector, reduced to a shameful existence in The Tombs. She'd desperately wanted to hug him. But she had also wanted to beat on his chest in tantrum until he dropped to his knees, begging forgiveness for hurting her.

Mary attempted to regain her composure while still sitting at the great table. Removing a small glass from her purse, she checked to be sure that her hair was in order. Her eyes were red and tearful, and just then, Chang gave her a cloth to pat away the drops that had rolled down her cheeks.

Well, I do have my Mr. Chang, she thought. *My lovely Jian*, she told herself as she smiled appreciatively at him.

CHAPTER THREE

At first Gillian was surprised that the visit with his daughter had exhausted him. Then, he surmised, shame will do that. It takes its toll on the body and soul. But now, he could breathe a sigh of relief, being back in his cell. He smiled at the irony of it—once again—

He lay down on his side and listened to the stiff wind howling just outside the little window. A bit of that wind managed to funnel through the three rusting bars, making its way across the corridor and into his chamber. Again, cool fresh air and a hint of the brine from the East River replaced dank dungeon air. *Oh, Lord, don't let them take this away from me,* he begged. At any time, they could move him to a cell near the center of the building, far from sunlight and fresh air. In fact, he'd been placed there during his first few days in The Tombs, and he'd felt sure he would not last. The unrelenting stench of old piss, dank mold, and rusting iron would drive him mad in short order. Worse still was the constant bellowing of fellow prisoners, some driven to lunacy.

But he was one of the "lucky" prisoners. He had the deluxe accommodation, the one usually reserved for death-row inmates, the last stop before the courtyard gallows below. Perhaps the warden had a kind soul, granting prisoners a champagne send-off of sorts to compensate for a less-than-sumptuous last meal. Although the gallows were not Gillian's fate, he still had good reason to fret. A seven-year term was an eternity for a man of sixty years and not in the best of health. But it was far from the claims at the time of his arrest, that he'd be facing the rope. This didn't stop him from worrying, given all the time he had to think. *What if I lose my cell to a new death row inmate? Worse, what if some new guards mistake me for a death-row inmate and drag me out to the courtyard at the crack of dawn?* Then it occurred to him, *Maybe that would be a befitting end. A mistake, a mix-up of sorts. Perhaps my family would be compensated.*

Mid-morning. Maurice and Phinny would be arriving shortly with his breakfast. He was certain it'd be gruel. It was Wednesday, and Wednesdays always meant gruel. *Maybe they'll let me sleep through*, he considered. That would be agreeable, as tomorrow there would be no napping. It was the start of work detail for him. He'd be brought to the new stables off Third Avenue and 14th Street. It had been years since he worked as an ironsmith, *but if they need me to make horseshoes, so be it*, he thought. *I've done worse work out there.*

PART II

CHAPTER FOUR

GALWAY, IRELAND

July 1846

How the nightmare really began

"Papa! Papa! Come quick. It's back again."

Gillian dropped the hoe he'd been repairing and raced out of the barn. But before he even arrived at her side, he knew what was awaiting him. The sickening scent of decay was in the stiff breeze, an unwelcome visitor returning from the summer before.

"No. I pray not again, my lord," he said solemnly as he stood at the edge of the field. "Daisy, go find Daphne, and the two of you round up the hogs and get 'em in the barn." Robert Gillian just wanted to be alone now. He had to come up with a plan, something to tell Aileen as soon as she returned from Ma Brickel's place. Then it occurred to him that, of course, Aileen would know of the situation already. Why would it be just their crop and not the Brickels' or for that matter, the Connollys' farm, or the Olsens'?

"Oh, hell!" he shouted into the wind as he threw his straw hat to the ground. His outburst was half about the blight and half to do with Aileen's wrath he'd soon be facing. She'd wanted to leave the farm after last year's disaster. He'd convinced her the crop failure was due to all the cold rain they'd had through the spring and summer. This year had been different. Lots more sunshine and dry weather. Besides, they'd made it through without having to slaughter a pig, and they had the small oat crop to sell.

Gillian heard the cart coming down the path toward their ten-acre plot. He could see Aileen in the distance, wrapped in her shawl, bonnet tied tightly atop her head. The old nag was moving even slower than usual, which appeared fine by his wife. It was evident that she was already broken by the news.

Standing by the edge of the field, he waved. She pulled at the reins as she reached the cottage and, within seconds, was standing by his side. Not a word was said as they stared at the acres of withering leaves. The breeze had shifted, sparing them the worst of the stink. A thunderstorm rumbled in the distance as if foretelling the coming disaster.

"Looks like foul weather again," she said softly. Then, more silence, except for a breeze from behind that lifted the bottom of her frock, exposing fair-skinned delicate legs.

He saw a tear slide down her left cheek as she gazed out at the ruined crop. There was no wrath for him to endure, at least not yet.

"Aileen, there may not be such calamity here. If we harvest the potatoes now, much can be saved. Sure, the lumpers will be small... but that's better than no potatoes, ain't that true, my darling? And we'll store them in the cool bins." He spoke with as much optimism as he could muster, then wiped a tear from her cheek.

"Well... I suppose we'll make it work. I'm sure they'll set up those soup kitchens again," she said, voice hollow, "and the turnpiking projects will come back. You could sign up at the board for that work."

Aileen looked at her husband. Her words may have sounded hollow, but her eyes begged for more reassurance.

After fifteen years of marriage, he knew what was expected of him. He put on his best face, took her hand, and kissed it gently. "Aye, Aileen. We will make it through, my love, to be certain, and we have the hogs and oats as last resorts anyways."

"Sure, Robert," she said softly, then her tear-filled blue eyes returned to the fields that had looked perfectly healthy just a few days earlier.

"Slaughtering the pigs will not be easy for the twins... but starving will be worse."

They looked at each other, both aware that she'd said "*will* be worse," not "*would* be worse."

"Let me round up Patrick and Mary. Daphne and Daisy can help with the sorting through, and Roger owes me a debt, so I'm sure he'll oblige us. Within a week, we shall be done," Robert reassured, his plan giving him a burst of confidence.

As they began the trek back to the cottage, a gentle rain began to fall. Then a chilly rain continued for three days straight—another summer-less summer was upon them.

The blight proved to be worse that summer of 1846. The British Isles cast blame on the mainland, primarily the French. Europe laid the blame on Africa. They were all wrong. The culprit was a fungus, *P Infestans*, carried on the wind from the Americas. It first spread to the European continent, then across the channel to England and Scotland, finally reserving its strongest punch for the Emerald Isle. With astonishing speed on par with a swarm of locusts, it raced across thousands of acres of potato crop. First, it attacked the leaves, but it was the unrelenting cold rains that carried the fungus deep down to the roots of the plant, to the potato. Left in the ground too long, the wonderful lumper was reduced to putrid black mush, acre upon acre of the same.

Chapter Five

Galway, Ireland
December 1846

Robert Gillian was certain that another cold and snowy winter was settling in. The potatoes were small, as expected, but the crop was bountiful, and they had a good supply in the storage bins. Ethel and Rosy were safe—for the time being. Truth be told, the thought of cured pork was tantalizing his taste buds.

His neighbors were not so fortunate. Starvation was setting in across the town, and he'd heard that conditions were worse down in Cork and Skibbereen. His real fear was that the Public Works Project would be shut down if the air got too cold or the snow became too deep to dig trenches and pave roads. Not that any of these projects were actually needed, but it was paying work.

The ground was frozen hard already, and he worried that the old nag—in need of new shoes—would wear down her hooves. In fact, she was moving ever so slowly, and he knew her days of usefulness were numbered. But he didn't want to dwell on that problem now. They had barely any reserves to trade her in.

"Top of the morn to you, Roger!" he called from the cart as he pulled up to his friend's makeshift dwelling.

"What are you so jolly about?" Roger asked with his morning frown as he climbed into the seat. "It's cold and dark, our hopes of work are fading, and your nag looks like she's about to drop right here."

"I can always count on you, friend, to keep me in high spirits. Well, us Gillians have plenty of lumpers, still two hogs, and enough kindling for the stove."

"I guess, but you know they're having that meeting this morning at the work depot. Danny Sullivan is sure they're going to change our wages so we get paid piecemeal rather than daily. The commission don't want a situation like last year, paying us even when we couldn't work cause of the weather."

"That's trouble," Gillian agreed. "Too bad there's no inside work for us."

"There is. The workhouses," Roger said, then chuckled—alone.

"We'd rather die—and I'm speaking for me whole family—than go to a workhouse."

"You just may have your way, friend," Roger said softly.

"You're putting me in a foul mood now, Roger! I might just not pick you up tomorrow. What do you think of that!"

Gillian turned to frown at the vacant seat next to him. It had been two months now since his friend's passing. For the past five years, Roger had rented a half-acre plot of land off the Gillians' farm, complete with a mud hut and potato patch. He was a day laborer, without family and fine with that. "Less worries," Roger always said. It wasn't the famine that laid him beneath, or the fever, or typhus.

"A goddamn sore, Roger! How the bloody hell did you let a sore do you in?" he muttered. These things made no sense to Robert Gillian. Why was the lord so unfair, he repeatedly asked himself. It was just a gash on his leg. A simple mishap with a hoe. One week later, it was oozing pus, then the fever set in. Two weeks later, the surgeon removed his gangrenous leg, which was as putrid as the rotting potatoes now in Roger's little patch. "With no potatoes to harvest, no oats, and no pigs, perhaps it was for the best, old chap," Gillian rationalized over and over again.

Truth was, he was not sure Roger could've survived another winter.

Gillian knew much was wrong as he entered the small work depot. Danny Sullivan was sitting on the bench by the hot stove, massaging his hands and deep in thought.

"Oh, Gillian." He sounded startled as he woke from his trance. "I suppose you heard the news, aye?"

"Actually, no."

"They's ending the public works project, till after winter. We won't be going out after today to turnpike roads till maybe March or April." Danny grabbed a few sticks, threw them in the pot belly, and slammed the iron door so hard that the whole room shook.

"I thought they were going to piecemeal pay?" He was already thinking about having to tell Aileen about this new development. *At some point, her temper will blow. More reason we should have left last year like she begged.*

The other men shuffled in. Some had heard the news already; others hadn't. Then the foreman arrived, making it official by reading the letter from Dublin. "Men, you should know that the soup kitchens are reopening, and London reports a large shipment of Indian corn will be arriving from America... shortly." The last word was almost inaudible. "Your wage for today will be paid upon your return this evening. God bless you and your families." Then he fled the little building, leaving the disgruntled men with no opportunity to voice their discontent.

The sleet and rain set in just as the crew loaded onto the wagon to begin their journey to a road that led nowhere, so they could level hills that didn't need leveling, dig trenches that didn't need to be dug, and build roads that were not needed, then not finish them anyway. The public works project was hastily put together by the powers in London to deal with the crisis in Ireland. "The famine is an Irish problem and should be met with an Irish solution!" was fiercely debated in Parliament. And so it was decided that the landed class of Ireland—and large tenant farmers—would be taxed to pay the wage for the men working on the needless projects.

Robert Gillian dreaded the thought of returning home that evening with the woeful news. But they had their potatoes, and the oats, and then there were Ethel and Rosy.

Chapter Six

January 1847

The balmy break in the weather was a pleasant surprise, sufficiently thawing the soil so they could sow seed for the spring crop.

All except Aileen were outside enjoying the fourth day of sunshine until a shriek came from the cottage. Robert and Patrick were at Aileen's side within seconds. She was sitting on the floor, in tears, sacks upon sacks of the potatoes they'd kept in the storage bins torn open around her. The situation was plain to see—and smell. Blackened rotting potatoes were strewn about the floor, evidence of Aileen's frenzied moments. Many were oozing a mucus-like substance, as though the undersized lumpers were giving one last valiant effort to rid themselves of disease.

"Oh, Robert. We're finished," she was now sobbing inconsolably. "Look at them. They're laughing at us! We might as well get the planks for our coffins. We're never going to make it."

Father and son stood there wide-eyed, taking in the disaster splayed out across the pine boards. *The lumpers do look like they're mocking us. Are they deciding our future, right here?* He knew he had to say something quickly.

"My dear, try and calm yourself. There may be some potatoes that are edible still. Let's go through all the sacks—"

"Shut up, Robert! This is all your fault! We should have left after last year's harvest, but you were certain it couldn't happen again. God is laughing at us now!" Then she paused and settled into a gentle sob. "How could this happen?" She gave her hand to her husband, who gently pulled her up from the floor. "We got them out of the ground so early. They were small but perfect. What evil plague is this? It was lurking there for months, fooling us so."

"Shh, my love." He tried to embrace her as Patrick—rightfully uncomfortable with the moment—fled the cottage to be outside with his sisters on what was to be the last of the warm, sunny days.

She yielded to his embrace for but seconds, then pushed him away. "Why did I listen to you! I'm the one with the strong mind here! I knew we'd be better off leaving!" She proceeded to flail at his chest, sobbing uncontrollably, mucus dripping from her reddened nose. He felt helpless and racked with guilt. *This is my fault. We will leave in the spring... if we make it till then.*

Finally out of strength, her arms fell to her sides. He delivered his cloth for her nose, which she wiped hastily. She couldn't meet his eyes, so she quietly apologized to his chest, which was eye-level anyway. Then she retired to their sleeping quarters.

* * *

They could only save a quarter of the potatoes. Even the hogs turned their snouts up at the peels from the rotten majority.

The snows returned, deeper than usual for this part of the country, and the children could not attend the little Catholic school at the nearby parish. Finally, the weather improved. But when they returned, they found the class half absent.

"Aileen. It's a dreadful situation," the pastor lamented, almost in tears as he greeted her at the entrance to the little building. It was the children's third day back, and she wanted to see the situation for herself. "It's the potatoes. The children are sick with bellyaches and fever. They are eating the cursed potatoes. There's not a choice here for some. The animals have been eaten, even the bones rendered for gelatin. Shipments of grain are due any day, so the powers say, but the weather has hampered the relief operation."

"I know, Father. It's worse than last year. We Gillians are luckier than most, I suppose. And with the Typhus back, many are too weak to work—if there was work to be done anyways."

"Many are planning to leave, Aileen. And your family?"

"I'm unsure, Father," she said reluctantly. "If so, not till the spring thaw. I know some are crossing in the winter now. Bless their souls. I couldn't do that, not with the little ones."

There was an awkward pause, both aware there was no telling who would have the strength for the crossing come spring. Or who would still be alive.

"Thank you for all you do," she said sincerely before fleeing to the cart.

As she wound down the sleet-covered path toward their plot of land, Aileen spotted a small black carriage with a plush, red interior situated just in front of the cottage. "Mr. Gelding, what does he want?" she muttered, pulling the reins. It was evident that Gelding was already inside conversing with her husband. *This can't be good news.*

The two were seated by the stove.

"Ah, my love. Mr. Gelding has paid us a visit, and he was kind enough to bring a sack of coal—a most welcome gift, don't you think?"

"Aye. Bless you, Mr. Gelding," she struggled to feign hospitality. She knew she needed to keep her composure. Land agents didn't just show up at the door with a gift of coal for tenants behind in their rent. Besides, her husband was doing his part. She must be strong.

"Mrs. Gillian. A pleasure seeing you again."

Gelding stood and bowed, holding his stove pipe to his chest. He was a tall, well-nourished, middle-aged man, neither handsome nor homely, perhaps pleasant-looking to some. He made use of a cane, the result of an injury in his youth.

"Well, sir... madam, I best get to the point of my visit. These are hard times for us all. Lord Bartholomew has been patient with the arrears from all his tenants—you're surely in agreement on this, I must believe? But he has debts on his land—funds borrowed in better times, but nevertheless, the bank is far more heartless than he. And then there's the labor tax he must pay to support the works program—you are aware of that, I'm sure."

"Aye. The labor rate," Aileen chimed in. "Are you aware, sir, that the work program has stopped for the winter? There is no wage for my husband or the others." She took a deep breath to stifle her agitation.

"Aye. My wife speaks the truth, Mr. Gelding," Robert said.

"I am aware of the situation. Very regrettable indeed." Gelding sighed and took his seat again. "But we are going on three months, Mr. Gillian. Well... Lord Bartholomew has granted me the liberty to come up with a solution, a fair compromise of sorts. You have two hogs, do you not?"

"Yes... this is true," Gillian replied reluctantly. Suddenly there was a gasp from the next room.

Aileen, who was staring at the floor, quickly glanced in that direction and saw a small curly head pop out from behind—for the briefest of seconds.

"We will take one as collateral. The animal won't be slaughtered just yet. That should cover you for six months' rent. When you make good on the debt, you can have it back. The animal will be sold off or harvested after six months, should the debt remain unpaid. I'm sorry, but I pray you will see this as a fair deal."

All three heard the sobbing in the adjacent room.

"You should know not to let your children grow attached to the farm animals," Gelding said defensively, twiddling his hat. "These hard times are not my fault, nor the fault of my lord. Besides, your people are too reliant on the lumper. It is an unpredictable potato, easy to sow, easy to reap, but easy prey for the blight. And you know the other option, I'm sure."

"Not the workhouse. No, never!" Aileen cried. "That would be a dreadful death for us all."

"Shush, my dear. No, never," Robert said softly, patting her hand.

"Now, perhaps there is one other option," Gelding declared as if he'd just come upon a new idea. "None of us can be sure that the blight will not return next year, or the year after, and so forth. Many farmers are taking advantage of the fine opportunities in America. You can become a merchant in New York or mine for gold on the frontier."

"We have considered this before, Gelding, but to leave our home, all we know?"

"But what do you have, Gillian?" a suddenly impatient Gelding exclaimed in a booming tone as he stood and buttoned his cloak. "A hovel on a ten-acre piece you don't even own. Four children you can hardly feed. And two pigs, or soon just one. Now you have a chance to start afresh. You both still have the strength and optimism of the young-hearted, and there are endless opportunities in the new world for your lovely offspring." He finished with a smile that even the least naive could almost find warm and encouraging.

The room fell silent. There was just the whispering beyond the makeshift sewn rags employed as a door.

"The risk is too great. Too much can go wrong for us, Mr. Gelding," Aileen said, surprising herself. But she didn't want a land agent, or the great Lord Bartholomew, forcing them into a decision.

"Here is where I can help you. Mr. Bartholomew will be generously covering the full fare of passage for all his tenants and their families." Gelding paused, like a salesman assessing the impact of their offer on the would-be buyers. "That's right. One hundred percent of the fare for all of you! And additional provisions for the voyage. It comes to a hefty five pounds a soul for the crossing; that's Liverpool to New York on one of Her Majesty's sturdiest vessels."

"Well, I leave you now. Your family has much to ponder. Of course, the earliest voyage would be after March 15th. Calmer seas should prevail then. Many of the other tenants have taken to the plan. Please consider seriously, but swiftly. Lord Bartholomew can be fickle about these things," he said as he tapped the side of his nose. "I bid you adieu for now."

Gelding nodded, restored his hat, and was out the door.

"I guess we have to do some thinking here, Aileen," Gillian said as he sighed and sat down by the stove.

"What thinking is there to do?" she replied while pacing the room. "Can't you see the situation's clear?"

"Aye, but we can put Gelding off a bit. We'll tell him yes, but we don't want to leave till late spring, maybe early summer. It's too cold for the little ones before that anyway. And besides, we could still change our minds... unlikely, I think."

"Right, Robert," she conceded with melancholy. "You know, when you think of it, the Mahoneys would never send us off like this, even being behind on the rent and such. Like you always said, things were so much better when their clan owned this land."

"Aye. I was thinking about poor Daniel Mahoney just the other day. He was a fine man, even after losing all this to Lord Bartholomew. I pray life's treating him well wherever he be."

CHAPTER SEVEN

GALWAY, IRELAND
March 1847

In late February, the Indian corn finally arrived from America, and shipments of other grains reached the town of Cork shortly thereafter. It required another day just to cart it to Galway. Many couldn't hold out until spring. Most of Gillian's neighbors had already consumed their farm animals during the previous year's crop failure. Now they resorted to eating all the seed they had, along with the rotten potatoes. There would be no seed to sow come spring, assuming they had the strength to labor.

Some went mad with starvation, wandering through the town in search of any scrap of food. Dogs and cats went missing, neighbors suspecting each other. One man killed his own family for consumption. Discovering he couldn't carry through with the latter part, a rope in the barn delivered justice. When the constable found him weeks later, only his torso remained, his legs chewed off by wild animals or a pack of once domestic dogs.

Ethel was the sacrificial pig on the Gillian plot. There would be enough salted pork now to carry them into spring.

"I see Daisy stopped crying about the hog," Robert said, whittling away at a piece of wood as he sat near the pot belly stove. "Hunger will do that, I suppose."

"She's not well, Robert. I think she's got fever."

"I've been sitting here since half past the hour, woman! Why didn't you tell me? Let me check on her."

"Mary and Angus are sitting with her. I think she would have preferred we salted that dog instead."

Her far-away look gave him a visual, too, Angus on a rotisserie. *Could they? Would they?* he pondered, then shook his head in disgust.

Gillian had to stoop down when crossing the threshold from the kitchen to the first bedroom. On occasion, this was forgotten, evidenced by the patchwork of plaster repairs just above the linen curtains that separated the two rooms, as well as by the small scar on his forehead.

"Hi, Papa," Mary said softly as Angus marched over to his master, tail wagging in search of a treat, which had become increasingly seldom of late.

"Greetings, my oldest one," he said, lacking his usual enthusiasm. "How is our Daisy feeling?"

Mary said nothing, wearing a sad expression as she looked up at him from her position on the floor. He let out a deep sigh as he knelt down.

"Hi, Papa," a tiny voice came from under a linen blanket. "I was playing with Angus and got really tired. Now my head hurts awful."

"Oh, my poor, poor lass." Gillian pulled the blanket down just barely, exposing Daisy's tiny head. Her red curls were matted with sweat, and her face was so flush her freckles were almost invisible. "We must get you better for our big trip. Papa will go into town for headache powders. You rest, my sweetheart."

"Papa, I'm sorry me and Daphne cried over Ethel. I know that's what you had to do. I'm a brave girl now. You'll see."

"No worries, my precious. Now you hush." Gillian stood and silently indicated to Mary that they needed to talk in the other room as Angus lay back down on the floor next to Daisy. "Where's Patrick and Daphne?" he asked as they crossed the threshold.

"Mother sent them on an errand to the Brickel place to borrow headache powders."

"That ain't going to do it, I'm afraid. Aileen, we need to fetch the doctor."

"Is she worse?" Aileen asked, darting into the bedroom. When she re-emerged, her expression was grave. "Robert, you send for Doc O'Mal—" She stopped mid-sentence. "I near forgot. Doc O'Malley left for America three months ago."

There was silence in the room.

"Then we shall take her into town to the clinic," Aileen said. "Mary, you wait here for your brother and sister. Robert, prepare the cart with the straw cushions while I wrap her in linens. I do hate moving her, but we have little choice."

* * *

Poor Daisy never had a chance. Delirious with fever, cheeks burning red, in her last moments, she ran outside and collapsed on her back, giggling and pointing at the clouds moving overhead, as it was a beautiful sunlit day. Moments later, Gillian found himself sitting on the ground, rocking back and forth, clutching Daisy's lifeless body in his arms.

Daphne's end was different. The fever came on fast and furious just a day before Daisy passed. Daphne, the smaller of the twins, was tragically lucid enough to observe her sister's demise, perhaps knowing her fate. Aileen lifted her daughter's featherweight frame from the straw mattress and clutched her tightly. Then she caressed her sweat-drenched ringlets as Mary struggled mightily to hold back her tears.

Gillian sat quietly by the passageway between the two rooms, Angus at his feet. He covered his face with his large mitts.

"I'm sorry, Mummy. I let you down," came from the child in almost a whisper.

"Oh no, sweetheart, never, my child," Aileen blurted as she burst into tears. Holding Daphne tightly, she felt the child's muscles quiver and then relax. Daphne was gone.

After God had his way, Gillian fled to the cart. In anguish, he whipped the nag harder than he should've. She turned her head toward him and brayed. "Oh, stop yer complaining, yuh stupid ass!" he barked. She proceeded at her usual pace.

He traveled into town to negotiate with the undertaker for caskets. There would be a small service and burial would be in the church cemetery, providing there was still room.

Gillian stepped onto the porch, and the hollow sound of his boots on the wood planks must have announced his arrival, for a tall, well-dressed elderly gentleman greeted him at the doorway.

"Robert Gillian, I presume." The man presented Gillian his hand and guided him into the premises as if accustomed to the bereaved's reluctance to enter such an establishment. "I am so sorry for your misfortune, Mr. Gillian. Forgive me for having the foreknowledge of the events, sir, but word travels speedily in a small town like ours."

"No offense taken, sir. These are troubled times, indeed. I'm sure business is brisk for you these days, and you have to stay on top of things," Gillian said in a stoic, businesslike manner.

The undertaker lowered his head, appearing contrite as if he were responsible for the starvation and plague. "Tis a tragedy for all. My family hasn't escaped it either." He glanced down at his healthy, well-dressed frame, then looked up at Gillian. "I mean, I have relatives that have fared far worse." He cleared his throat, perhaps anxious to move on with the business at hand. "Well, sir, it appears that you need two child-size caskets. Let me show you two fresh pine boxes that I think will meet your requirements."

And there they were, hanging on the wall, simple, clean, unvarnished. Knotty pine with a nice grain. Gillian felt sick to his stomach. "How much for the two, sir?" he asked bluntly, wanting to swiftly complete this encounter.

"The rate is a crown each, but because of your circumstance of… needing two, I'll do four shillings each," the undertaker said. "Now, included in the fee, we pick up your beloveds, deliver to the church—Catholic, I presume—and bring to the final resting place. We have a fine hearse that will deliver you all."

"Aye, it all sounds very reasonable," Gillian said, feeling almost *upbeat* at the surprising affordability of the whole ordeal. Then a pang of shame hit him for the passing thought. "Very well. Do you have an agreement to sign?"

"Yes, Mr. Gillian. Let me draft the paperwork. We require half up front and half after the bodies are safe and secure in the ground. Rest assured, your family will not be troubled with the details of the agreement, sir. They will witness their loved ones buried securely in the coffins. We retrieve the boxes in the middle of the night, place the bodies in fresh canvas bags, and re-inter at no additional cost to you and yours."

The undertaker smiled compassionately.

Gillian's eyes opened wide, and he swallowed hard. *Ah, that's why tis so affordable*, he thought in horror. He stiffened as a wave of rage coursed through his veins. But he was not sure who—or what—to be angry at. The truth was, it really didn't matter.

Any wavering on the decision to take up the land agent's offer for passage to America ended that day.

CHAPTER EIGHT

Farewell to the Lumper
May 1847

"Gelding was right, my love. The *Nina* is a fine vessel. Look at her."

"Aye, it is a fine boat... I think," Aileen managed from her seat on top of their one small trunk. Still sick and heartbroken, but the fever had gone, and she was on the mend. She squinted at the sun shining through the white, square-rigged sails that had already caught the wind. "Looks like she's ready to pull away without us. Maybe she should," she murmured in a hollow, dreamlike way.

"These tickets are six pounds each, so I say Gelding was generous. It's a newly refurbished barque. They say it'll make the trip in three weeks' time, and you know, it cost more to leave from Galway."

Gillian was unsure why he felt the need to make a sales pitch, justifying what they both had committed to already.

"Aye, but it's a small boat, Robert," she snapped. "The boats out of Liverpool are much larger, better for storms. Besides, Gelding's not so generous. Everybody knows Bartholomew put him up to this. He's saving a boatload sending us all away. Putting us up in the workhouse would cost him far more over time."

"Woman!" Gillian barked. He wanted to say, *You're spoiling everything. This was your idea to start anyways!* But when he took in her visage, he saw not the lass he'd married, the lass with rosy cheeks and a contagious laugh, but a woman, aged beyond her years. Pale skin, the gray outline of her cheekbones and jaw clearly visible, and a frail body that appeared like it might take flight in the gentlest breeze. He gave her a weak smile and patted her hand. "Looks like they're putting out the planks. We should be boarding soon. I'll fetch the kids. You'll be fine here by yourself for a little bit."

He patted her bony hand again, but she had already resumed her pose, squinting at the sunlight pouring through the great white sails above.

* * *

"Attention all paddy men... and ladies," bellowed a little man in a green suit. "Your Captain Ross has informed us that the tide will be in favor within two hours, and so your journey will begin. You are truly the fortunate ones, traveling aboard the newly refurbished *Nina,* the beloved queen of our fleet. She's light and swift. All those traveling in steerage have been assigned bunks, more spacious now at a full twenty-four square feet! Each passenger has been supplied a weekly ration as follows: two and a half pounds navy biscuit, one pound wheat flour, five pounds oatmeal, two pounds rice, half-pound sugar, one pound of pork, and three quarts of water per day. Rations are for a five-week voyage. With this perfect vessel, your captain anticipates an arrival in less than four weeks. Any remaining provisions are yours to keep—a gift from Master Dockery, owner of our fleet."

"Say here! I got an inquiry," called out a tall skeleton of a man. "Maybe the trip goes six, seven, eight weeks? It could happen, you know. I heard stories that—"

The announcer broke him off in mid-sentence as the crowd appeared to be taking in the gravity of this new concern.

"Rest your minds now, all of you," he said with confidence. "This here is a speedy vessel. I'll bet my wife—and throw in my five children for good measure—that in one month, the passage will be history and a great tale for your next of kin. Five weeks' provisions are more than you'll need. In the highly unlikely chance of a delay, additional rationing will be done. But most of you have brought surplus provisions, so no doubt all will be fine. Now, one final note. When you're on the other side, watch out for runners that lack scruples. They'll come on the boat and tell you they'll bring you to the finest lodgings in town if you pay 'em such and such. They'll be your kind of people, so you'll warm up to them." Then the little man in the green suit paused. His eyes opened wide as he scanned the entire group. Waving a finger back and forth in front of the crowd, he continued, "But beware! They're all dirty sharks! They'll tell you they can change your money, but you won't have any, as they picked your pocket already. So, go to the Immigrant Relations building as soon as you leave the boat. Now, I'll pass around these papers that show the proper exchange rate so you don't get fooled. Ye should get five American dollars for one sterling British pound, and four shillings should get ye a dollar, nothing less. Well, bless your voyage and your new life in America."

At that, he bowed to the audience and quickly disappeared into the office behind the arcade area.

Aileen turned to Gillian and said in a soft voice, "Thank the Lord we have plenty of the salted pork to spare."

"Yes, thank you for your service, Rosy," he muttered.

The departure from Galway Harbor was exactly on schedule. Steerage passengers were allowed to stay on deck to sob their goodbyes to anyone remaining who cared. After that, they were only allowed on deck three times a day, to prepare their meals on little coal grills located on the starboard side of the ship. They were also afforded one hour in the evening, providing the weather was calm. Cabin passengers were not to be disturbed under any circumstances.

"Twenty-four square feet in the forward hold is not bad, Aileen. And everything is new. I guess we are the lucky ones."

Robert was lying on the second-tier hammock. Being a loving husband—and because she was still weakened by illness—she received the straw-filled cot on the bottom. Included in their accommodation was a small two-drawer bureau for their belongings. The hold of the small ship was at full occupancy with just sixty-five steerage passengers. Twenty first-class passengers claimed the cabins on the main deck.

"I wonder if that Captain Ross will greet us steerage passengers. We haven't seen hide nor hair of him," said Aileen.

"We've only been on the boat two hours, my dear. I'm sure we'll see him in time."

"Let's pray so," came a voice in the adjacent bunk. "My son made this voyage with his family the summer last. The first post we got from America, he said they never met a captain. Turns out there was no captain on the boat. Sick or something. The first mate pretended he was the captain. But it was an easy trip, so it didn't matter much, I guess."

The man's speech was muffled. Sight unseen, Gillian guessed he was lacking a set of teeth.

"Oh, shut up, old man," came from the hammock above him. "Don't go scaring everybody with your stories. Besides, most of these captains are drunkards anyways. Who needs them?"

Somehow, this woman—his wife, Robert presumed—did not alleviate the worry the old man had cast among the passengers within earshot. It certainly did nothing for poor Aileen, still frail from typhus. She was lying on her back, wide-eyed and staring at Robert's hammock above.

"Now, where's the shit hole?" another man called out further down the hold.

"How should we know?" someone yelled back. "Me thinks the first mate is supposed to show us the situation."

"Well, he ain't, and my kid's got to go bad."

"I can lend you a pot for now, but you got to sneak up on deck to deliver it overboard. We don't want no stink down here, being it's so nice and new and such," came a third gruff voice.

"I have to go too, Papa," Patrick chimed in.

"Me too," claimed several other children.

"Oh, mother of Jesus! We've only been at sea for two hours," lamented Gillian.

He peered down at Aileen on the cot below. She was asleep. Then he began to worry. *How will she ever last this journey?*

Chapter Nine

Two Weeks at Sea

Luck was with the voyagers, as the seas were mostly calm. And with the salted pork, coupled with the rations included in their fare, Gillian felt like things were looking up.

"You know, I do believe we're eating far better than before the journey," he commented one morning. "What do you think, children?"

"That ain't saying much," Aileen quipped before they had a chance to answer. They all broke out in laughter, and Robert teared up, catching him by surprise. It had been months since he'd had his old Aileen. *Could she be coming back?* He had a burst of euphoria and would have given her a giant hug had she not been fussing with the corn cakes over the coal fire. They were even near the front of the meal line that day, only three families ahead of them. That would mean breakfast at the respectable hour of nine a.m.

But as things go, there was a price to pay. That evening, the *Nina* sailed into a wicked storm. Nothing she couldn't handle, but it was a different story for many passengers, especially those already weakened by disease. In the hold, it seemed every stick of timber was creaking— as though the vessel were screaming in agony. *Could she be ripped to pieces? She's not a new ship, just refurbished.* As the boat listed from side to side, the hastily installed pine floorboards would shift, resulting in narrow fissures that exposed the storage compartments at the base of the hull. *So that's where the cargo's held. They use that for ballast. Or perhaps we're the ballast for the benefit of the freight.* The *Nina* was a cargo ship, with not enough cargo to make it worth the trip until the emigrant business made the voyage profitable.

Passengers were sick, not just the ones struggling to recover from typhus, the fever, and all the illnesses that preyed on those weakened by starvation. Some of the crew were as well. By the second day, the hold reeked with the stench of vomit; combined with the fragrance of urine, it was a cocktail so sickening that any passenger not predisposed to sea sickness succumbed just the same.

Now the truth became clear. *This is how the rations last longer than the expected length of the voyage. No one can bear to eat.*

Gillian caught little sleep those two nights. He would lie still in his hammock listening to the groaning timbers as the vessel tossed about. He felt certain disaster was imminent, perhaps a sudden thunderous crack, and the hull would give way to the sea. And then there were the odd sounds as cargo shifted below, sometimes like a giant marble rolling off a table, followed by the clang of iron hitting iron. He felt Aileen's thoughts below him, but nothing was said. He knew she was listening too, sharing his fears, as was every adult passenger. For there was no snoring to be heard.

The only distraction from listening to the moaning ship was his thoughts of those dreadful last two months before the voyage. Perhaps Daisy and Daphne were the lucky ones, he tried to convince himself. If this ship goes down in the storm, they'd have been drowned at sea in the dark of night, perhaps first crushed by iron and timber. He wouldn't have been able to rescue their little souls or hold them tight to alleviate their suffering as the end came upon them. At least with typhus, he could do this for them. Then he chided himself for such thinking. *This boat's not going down. The rest of us will go on to much better lives in America. Daisy and Daphne will forever be trapped in those shallow graves in a land that abandoned us!*

Hour upon hour through those stormy nights, Gillian would reflect upon the horrific events of those last two months, anguishing over the idea that perhaps there was more he could have done. The famine had grown worse. The cats and dogs were mostly gone. Perhaps a collective shame—no one discussed it. Then his beloved Angus disappeared. The work projects were never revived because the government discovered it was easier—and less costly—to let the landlords handle the tenant starvation problem. Besides, the workhouses were poorly run, corrupt, and disease-ridden. Truth be told, typhus was rampant both inside and outside the workhouses.

Now lying in his hammock, the second stormy sleepless night, Gillian made a vow. Should they survive the wrath of the sea, he would put those last few tragic months out of his mind, and he'd make certain that life in the new world was worth the journey—for all of them.

CHAPTER TEN

One Week Out From America

"Ay, don't seem right. We haven't moved in a while. What do you think, Robert?"

"Don't know, tis strange," he said to his new "old" friend, the elderly gentleman lacking teeth.

Gillian came down from his hammock. Strangely, Aileen and the children were gone—for that matter, many of the steerage passengers were gone too.

Well, they didn't jump off the boat, and it's too early for breakfast.

Just then, he heard the patter of children's feet above, followed by excited chatter. "Papa, Papa!" a boy's voice called from the top of the steep staircase. Patrick and Mary were in the lead, several young children following behind to retrieve their parents. "You have to see this on deck, Papa! Mama's already there!"

Gillian presumed they were in sight of land—they were approaching four weeks at sea now.

"What's all the fuss?" asked the toothless man. He was ignored in the excitement as every remaining adult who could stand now stepped lively to see the source of the commotion above.

Upon reaching the deck, the monotonous view of sky meeting water was obscured by a tremendous mountain of ice, as if God had just deposited it there. *Perhaps some ice, for a drink to quench his thirst.*

"You see, Papa!" Mary cried out. "It's a glacier."

Three-quarters of the passengers were huddled starboard side near the bow. Despite the excitement, Gillian became troubled that the boat was listing slightly with the lopsided human cargo. Then he spotted Aileen, far in front, clutching the iron railing. Her expression of awe was a sight Gillian had never witnessed—he felt so glad for her.

"Will you look at that!" cried the second mate. "They's people! Right there, hanging on to the side of the berg!"

Suddenly, the awestruck passengers grew silent. Then a murmuring, gradually increasing in intensity as the understanding of the situation set in.

"Look at that!" a woman called out. "Three, no four, no, no, five or six people coming around from the other side of that rock. They must have heard us."

And then he arrived on the scene. The great Captain Ross. A beefy man with a ruddy face and thick white mutton chops that failed to hide his sagging jowls. He'd staggered out of his sleeping chamber—no doubt interrupted from his drunken slumber—and was carrying a brass spyglass, as if this was necessary to assess the situation.

"Ladies and gentlemen," he called out. "Go back to your chambers. All will be fine." He took a moment to clear the gravel from his voice and spit his nighttime phlegm on the deck. "Now, where is my first and second mate and the rest of the damn crew!"

"Ay. You down there!" called a man clinging to the highest elevation of the iceberg. "Please help me! I can't hold on much longer. Me hands, I hardly feel them no more."

"Yes, help me, please. I don't want to die!" cried out a raisin sitting on a pile of snow. Or, no, a young boy dressed in a black shirt, black breeches, and a black cap, none of which could possibly provide much protection from the cold. But as he moved about, he appeared nimble. As Gillian watched, the boy climbed up through a small crevice and found himself a little shelf to rest on.

Then a shriek, followed by two splashes. Two women, side by side on an icy edge, lost their fight and were devoured by the frigid Atlantic.

Their screams faded in less than a minute. Several passengers started weeping and turned away. Parents hugged the youngest children and whisked them off to the hold.

"We're going to risk our ship for... what?" said the first mate. "Three paddies? We need to let them go, Captain! We beg of you, sir, let them go!"

Captain Ross, sobered up by the ordeal, was deep in thought. Then he abruptly looked at the first and second mates. "No! It's the seamen's code of honor. We'd be derelict in our duties by abandoning them. I order you to maneuver our ship for rescue. I'm sorry, men... it's a risk we'll have to take."

As the first and second mate fled to the bridge, Captain Ross stood still, clearly marveling at his own bravery.

Two of the three survivors—one, the boy—leapt off the iceberg into a hastily rigged netting, which succeeded in breaking their fall. The third lucky soul was able to step onto the boat.

Their story was harrowing. *The Little Shamrock* had set sail out of the harbor near Cork, just one day earlier than the *Nina* had begun her journey. The barque was an almost identical vessel, the manifest listing eighty passengers and crew. But the boat had been moving too swiftly for a moonless night.

"The captain had to know that ice was out there," one of the survivors scoffed. "He didn't give a hill of beans."

"They was always fighting, the captain and the mates. Never could agree on nothing. I was in earshot whenever I was on deck," said the second man as he shivered under a linen blanket, his lips and fingertips tinged blue, his nose a purply red.

Then the nimble boy chimed in. "The captain was a drunk. Even when we was going down, 'e was taking a swig. 'E was trying to get onto that berg before the others. I saw the second mate give him a boost over the railing. 'E made sure the captain landed right in the water, and then 'e was crushed between the ship and the berg. I saw the whole thing with me eyes."

The boy chuckled, earning stares from the other survivors and Captain Ross.

This would be a story for all of them to remember, but especially Mary. She knew her best friend, Eileen—and her family—had been aboard *The Little Shamrock*. She never said a word about it to the rest.

After five weeks of monotony, land was on the far horizon. The captain reported that they were just one day out if the weather held. Rations had only been reduced a bit during the last two weeks, but the drinking water had gone rancid. They had survived on grog, even the children.

"This water tastes nasty, Papa," Patrick declared as they ate their supper on deck.

"Well, you'll get used to it, lad," Gillian replied. "You might even start liking it in a while."

He smiled at Aileen, who managed a faint smile in return.

"I know what it is," Mary chimed in. "It's rum. They put rum in the water so we can bear it."

Gillian downed the contents of his cup. "Right you are, lass."

On the last day of the voyage, Captain Ross announced that a celebration would be held on deck that evening. He delivered the news in person, paying a rare visit to the steerage hold.

"Ladies, gents, and children of all ages, tonight we will make merry, celebrating your successful voyage to the New World. The lord's hand was kind to us, not to neglect mention of the fine skills exhibited by your crew... this speaker included." Then he pinched his nostrils and winced. "We are setting up several tubs on deck, with fine cakes of soap. A bath is required of all as a condition of attending the affair. Cured meats and salted herring will be available for a nominal fee. Libations are provided, courtesy of the ship's owner. Now I must tend to other business of the day." Winded by the end of his speech, the man huffed and puffed his way up the steep staircase to the ship's deck.

"I ain't wondering what his business of the day is, but I'll bet whatever it is, a bottle of his finest will be right at his side," Aileen quipped.

The celebration began just as the sun dipped below the horizon, a perfect early July evening. The sea was calm, and a gentle breeze caressed the tired and beaten faces of the passengers, many looking far older than their years. Gillian and Aileen were at the railing near the bow of the vessel. He'd just brought up a linen shawl for her. There was a chill in the air, which greatly affected her, still weakened by disease and near starvation.

He held her tightly as they both squinted at the faint outline of distant land just below the red sunset.

"It's hard to believe, Robert. Here we are... a new world, a new life. I wonder what God has in store for us."

"I don't know. But it will be just fine. You'll see, Aileen," he offered in the strong but kind tone he'd always used to reassure her.

Aileen managed another half-smile, and then she looked back toward the eastern sky, the dark sky, the sky in the direction they came from. She started to cry, gently though. "We left our babies, Robert. Will the Lord ever forgive us? I don't know if I will ever forgive myself or have peace again."

He grabbed her shoulders and looked lovingly into her eyes. "We did what we had to do, Aileen, for Mary and Patrick. The Lord will know this, and we will have his grace."

And then they were silent, just as the lively accordion music in the background was replaced by a lone fiddle playing a melancholic Celtic tune.

Aileen wrapped her arms around her husband and hugged him hard in the chill breeze. And then she pressed her face into his sturdy chest and resumed her sobbing.

CHAPTER ELEVEN

A Seaman's Tale

"Okay, children!" called out one of the seamen. Burly and middle-aged, he had a graying unkempt beard and matching side chops. Both failed to disguise a severely pitted face. "I've entertained you with me juggling and a few card tricks. Now we end the night with a tale never to be forgotten. Gather round me chair here, quick, quick. No dawdling!"

Many of the children, victims of the grog, had already dragged their pillows and blankets from below and were fast asleep on the deck—some perilously close to the railings. The handful remaining, Patrick and Mary included, were already seated around the storyteller.

"Under where you children sleep, this ship holds many wonders," he said slowly, his eyes bulging wide for effect. We carry every type of cargo to and from the new world, things you've never laid eyes on. Sometimes it's a giant tank of moaning mermaids, sometimes captured sea monsters. Mostly, it's farm equipment, printing presses, and planks of lumber. You never can be sure until ye get down there and see for yourselves. So... let's see what we got today. Who here is brave enough to follow me into them bowels of the ship? Now mind ya, I can only take two of yous."

Eyes still bulging, he surveyed the little group, slowly moving his finger back and forth over the outstretched hands. "Take me please, sir!" called out a small boy in the back of the group, his raised hand almost crowded out by the others. With little enthusiasm, Mary's hand was far from outstretched. A bit silly but possibly fun, she was thinking.

"Looks like I'm gonna have to decide meself." Within an instant, he picked the small boy who'd called out with grand enthusiasm. His index finger again moved back and forth over the little group. And then he pointed at Mary, who looked behind her to see if he was pointing at somebody else—but nobody was there. "Aye, you lass, an older one, you probably don't believe in sea monsters no more. But we'll make a believer out of yuh." And he gave a firm nod. "I'm sorry, the rest of yous."

"This ain't no tale," Patrick cried out.

"I'm sorry, lad, but rules are rules."

As the dejected unchosen shuffled off, the seaman quietly led his group of two down the stairs to the steerage hold so as not to disturb the few who were already fast asleep. Most were still up on deck, merrymaking.

The little party crept to the far rear of the hold, where they came upon a short spiral staircase. Then a descent into cold and clammy blackness. At the base, the seaman reached for a lantern attached to a hook on the hull. He quickly lit the tiny wick, which provided scant illumination, but enough for the three to see... nothing.

"There ain't nothing here," said the little boy.

"Shush, little one," whispered the seaman, his breath swirling like smoke around his head.

"I don't see nothing either," Mary whispered loudly. "I don't like this at all. It's too cold and dark. It's like a dungeon." Though she had never been in a dungeon to know what a dungeon felt like.

"Don't you see, young ones? There's no cargo on this voyage. You know why?" Turning around to face the children, he lifted the lantern to his face, illuminating his smile filled with rotten teeth. "You see, when you're holding such a creature as is on this ship, you can't afford other cargo. If it gets loose, it'll devour everything down here."

He resumed walking, then stopped just shy of the front of the cargo hold, where he put the lantern on the floor. The light bounced off cobwebs in all four corners of what appeared to be a wall of flat timber planks, separating the main hold from another room just below the captain's quarters.

"You hear that?" he whispered urgently.

Mary cocked her head, her bonnet shifting to a lopsided position. She listened intently to what sounded like iron chains scouring across wooden planks. Then came a muffled thudding noise from the opposite side of the wall. She contorted her face, not out of fear but skepticism. *This is just plain silly.*

"It must be a sea monster in there," the boy rasped. "I'm no part of this." And he dashed off through the darkness, back to the stairs that had brought them down.

Mary turned back to the seaman. He was smiling again, rotted teeth on full display. "I don't believe there's a sea monster on the other side of that wall, sir. This is another of your games, and you scared that poor boy half to death," she chided.

"Perhaps. What's your name, lass?"

"Mary, sir. Now I want to leave here," she commanded. "I don't like it. It's cold and dark."

"We will... shortly. First, I must have my way with you. Think of it as my wage for entertaining you tonight." With that, he slipped behind her back and cupped his hand over her mouth. "A peep out of you, and America will be less one," he whispered in her ear.

He forced Mary on her back. The cold, hard timbers of the hull were underneath her, the seaman's weight adding to the pain.

"Get off me!... Papa!" she cried out as she struggled to wiggle out from under the beast's frame. Her heart was racing now. He grabbed her neck and muffled her attempt to scream with kisses, thrusting his thick tongue into her mouth.

"You'll never do better than me, lass. You're such a homely thing. You must know that. So, keep quiet."

Covering her mouth again, he worked to undo his breeches with his other hand. She bit his fingers, and he winced. Then he slapped her hard across the face. Her head hit the floorboards. She was stunned but still felt the ache from the blow to the back of her head. And now she was thinking that her heart might burst forth from her chest.

Despite his threat, she managed a loud shriek and dug her teeth into his shoulder.

"You bloody whore!" he cried as he grabbed his shoulder and looked at the blood on his shirt. Finally came the sound of feet shuffling above, and then on the staircase.

The seaman started laughing maniacally, and he began to roll off of Mary just enough for her to pull herself out from under his mound. But he firmly grabbed her leg as she tried to stand. Still laughing, he rose to his knees then let go of her in an attempt to lift himself off the floor. But he was unsteady, as he was still clutching his blood-soaked shoulder. He fell back down, and his hand knocked over the lantern. Mary gasped and quickly righted it - averting disaster for them all.

She twisted just in time to see Patrick, wearing an expression she'd never seen before—fearless rage. In his hand was an iron pipe already raised high. And just as he was bringing it down, a large hand grabbed the weapon in mid-air.

"Allow me, son," said a froggy voice.

The second mate crashed the pipe down on the seaman's head. The man screamed in pain, then oddly resumed his maniacal laughter.

"He's always been no-good vermin as well as off his head." The second mate raised the pipe once again. This time, success. Blood gushed from the seaman's skull.

There was silence for several moments as they all stared—horrified— at the bloody, lifeless heap.

Pulling her knees up into a ball, Mary began to sob. She was clutching her bonnet, which had come loose during the attack. It was soiled with the seaman's blood.

Patrick sat down next to her and put his arm around her shoulders.

"Okay, here's what we need to do," commanded the second mate, keeping his voice low. "You sit with the girl, lad. I'll fetch another ship-hand to help me find a barrel large enough for this... I can't say it with mixed company and all." He stopped speaking, gazed at Mary, then lowered his head. "Anyway, we gotta get him overboard before those up top quiet down. I'll leave this here lantern for you."

Patrick turned to the man, "Thank you... sir."

Mary forced herself to turn her tear-soaked face upward. "Yes, thank you," she said almost inaudibly.

The second mate seemed uncomfortable. "Well... you're paying passengers, I suppose." He fled into the blackness toward the spiral stairway.

"Not a word of this to Mother or Father," Mary said softly as the two moved away from the spreading pool of blood. They both stared at the seaman's gaping mouth and bulging eyes, an image likely etched in their minds forever.

"Okay, Mary."

Wandering a short distance from the lantern, she sat down and raised her knees, clutching them in the near darkness. She shuddered. "This is not the way it will be in the New World... I should hope," she muttered inaudibly, as if she were all alone now.

Part III

A SHAMING FROM PATRICK

CHAPTER TWELVE

THE TOMBS
October 1869

Hmm. Eggs, sausage... and gruel. At least no swill milk today, so I suppose it's a good day.

As Gillian was finishing his breakfast, he became aware of the rain pattering on the rusting bars of the little window at the end of the corridor. From his position on the cot, he could see the water dampening the floor. It was the second day of off-and-on rain. As the refreshing breeze sailed through the little opening, he closed his eyes and imagined he was back home in County Galway. But one where there was no famine or land agents calling on him. In fact, the Gillians owned hundreds of acres of fertile land, a barn with a few well-fed cows that rendered only the freshest milk, and several plump swine. All was as his father had once described it. "We Catholics had a better lot back then."

Then the breeze died down, and the claws of the dungeon gripped him. How swiftly the stench of mold and rusted iron was upon him, he observed. The crushing hand of the law back to swat him down, to remind him of his whereabouts. In truth, the Tombs were an engineering disaster, an overweight edifice constructed upon a poorly designed landfill that once was a vast freshwater pond. The *collect*, as they'd called it, was trying to reclaim its rightful place on Manhattan Island.

"Gillian, whatcha daydreaming there?"

He was startled from his thoughts by Maurice's bark.

"You got callers. So, get yourself dressed. I'll give you three minutes. I usually give two, but with your aged state, I'm feeling kindhearted. No doubt this will come back to bite me one day." He gave his mischievous smile, the one that revealed a lone gold tooth. *Just come and try me*, the smile said as Maurice tapped his baton in his hand. Only a fool would take him up on the offer.

"Thank you," Gillian said, not sure whom to expect on this rainy morning.

"Usual room, Maurice," said the elderly man at the reception desk.

They progressed down the long corridor toward the oversized receiving room, stopping for a few moments near the door.

"I need to make note of the attendance first. Wait here."

Gillian found himself standing in front of the ornately framed looking glass. Again, his reflection startled him. Who was this aged creature? Unkempt beard, pitiful frown lines, and bags under his eyes so large they could hold tears like a cistern. He thought it strange, considering that he felt that his health had improved since his incarceration. The sores on his feet had practically vanished, he was peeing less frequently, and there was less huffing and puffing upon exertion.

"Okay, you know the rules, Gillian," Maurice announced as he returned. The guard unlocked the right iron cuff but left the device dangling from Gillian's other wrist.

Was this a new way of shaming him? Gillian thought. It had been customary until Mary's last visit for the entire apparatus to be removed for these encounters. *Hmm. New rules, Maurice taunting me again. Or is the guard becoming lazy? I shall inquire—next time, maybe.*

To his surprise, seated at the ancient table of imagined feasts and treaty signings was Patrick. It had been several months now since he was last privileged to receive his son's shaming. *Is this Mary's work? I should have left well enough alone, kept silent about the whole thing. I'm sure the boy has gathered more ammunition to throw my way.*

"You have half an hour, gentlemen." Maurice withdrew the watch tucked between the second and third buttons of his waistcoat. He noted the time and then left.

"Greetings, Father."

"Greetings, Patrick. You look well these days."

Had this been a meeting of business acquaintances, all would have sounded normal. Gillian seated himself, feeling self-conscious as the iron chain dangling from his left wrist struck the chestnut table with a clang. At least he wasn't one of the poor sods who had to greet visitors fully cuffed and shackled like a trapped animal.

"You look... well too," Patrick said with obvious discomfort, his eyes on the cuff.

"Mary tells me you've been promoted to engineer at Company Seven. Good for you, lad, good for you. Better at an engine company than those hook and ladder companies, aye?"

"Yes, I agree. And the pay is strong, one thousand a year with lodging. Things have changed so much, Father. The volunteer force is almost gone. No more riffraff loitering at the firehouse, showing up at fires to commit thievery. We have order and respect now, as it should be. And I had to sit for the merit test to advance into my position."

"I'm sure being an acquaintance of Tweed didn't hurt?"

"What are you getting at? Things have changed. I've earned this on my own, and Helen is very proud of me."

"Yes, I suppose things are different," Gillian said pensively. "But . . .?"

"But what, Father?"

Gillian could have stopped there, or he could have lied about what was to come. But he couldn't resist the urge to vent his disapproval, even though Aileen would surely have stopped him if she were in the room. "Still not becoming a druggist? All the schooling and working at Hennessey's, mixing the potions and powders." Gillian looked down and shook his head. "And becoming a shipwright, designing those intricate wood carvings. You were set on that since you were a child." The words were tumbling forth despite the little voice asking what right a father in prison had to lecture a son on his chosen path.

Patrick dropped his head. "Well, you know that wasn't going to happen. Sailing ships are giving way to the iron steamships, no fine wood carvings there. And you know, I'm moving on in years, with a family and such. Next week, I'll be thirty-four."

There was no mention of a druggist career.

"I see. I suppose it's a shame," Gillian said, lapsing into awkward silence. He had so much more to say. He'd hoped Patrick would be furthering himself with something grand. But with his own situation being as it was, he decided it best to allow the conversation to go elsewhere.

"Have you heard?" Patrick said after a spell. "Tweed's in a real mess, maybe worse than a mess. The natives threw their Orange Day Parade, marched right passed the Catholic neighborhoods on Eighth Avenue. They asked for a row, and they got one. It was mayhem. Bricks, stones, lit torches. City Hall demanded that Tweed control 'the paddies,' but he couldn't. Now they're onto his crookedness, and the city's almost broke. They're not sure how they're going to pay our salaries."

"Ha. It figures!" Gillian interrupted, almost delighted at the news. "Tweed's a swine but a smart swine. I'll give him that. He'll wriggle out of this, I'm sure. But what a shame, lad. You just start making good money... and they can't bloody well pay you."

"Yes, a regrettable situation. But there's some good news here. There's movement on raising funds for a bridge over the East River. The Brooklyn Bridge Company is issuing shares. The word is out; they'll be offered at five dollars each. It's to be a toll bridge, operated as a private enterprise. The posters are up, and it's advertised in the papers—'Brooklyn Bridge for Sale! Own a Piece of Our Future!' But it's a farce, Papa."

This piqued Gillian's interest, and he was relieved that Patrick just called him "Papa" again.

"You see, there's no plan for a private endeavor here," Patrick continued. "The state Senate is going to command the city to buy up the shares after the engineer's plans are deemed sound. So, you see, the shares will greatly increase in value. The usual big investors are going to swell their bank accounts. I'm going to put some money into this too." Patrick cocked his head, appearing to be contemplating something. "I suppose I should first inform Helen of my plans."

"How do you know the shares will return profit?" Gillian asked. "These things can go the other way. I've seen it firsthand, as you are aware."

"Because Tweed still holds a big stick in the state Senate. And neither the city nor the state wants privateers controlling the East River Bridge. It's a sure deal," Patrick said with such confidence one might think he personally put the entire venture together.

"Hmm. Interesting," Gillian responded. He was unsure what to say. On the one hand, he felt proud of his son for demonstrating some business acumen—and for building a bit of wealth. On the other, he was concerned about all the unknowns, like men blinded by greed, not to mention Tweed's involvement.

Patrick cleared his throat, signaling that the good-natured chat was over, and it was time for another round of shaming—a talent the boy had perfected. "I know Mary paid a visit to you last month and presented an offer of charity through Mr. Chang."

"Well, yes." Gillian fidgeted in his seat, the iron cuff knocking against the table, causing an embarrassing distraction. "Chang says his brother has a lawyer who can do some detective work, you know, help find the Negros I assisted."

"...And?"

"And what?" Gillian pretended.

"And are you going to take his offer?"

"I don't know, Patrick." His son's insolence was grating on his nerves.

"This could be your only chance to get your sentence reduced. Do you really want to be moved to Sing Sing? That's what will happen, you know."

"I hear Sing Sing is clean and new, out in the country. Maybe it won't be so awful."

"Are you mad?"

"I don't want to be indebted for the rest of my life to a Chinaman who plies the opium trade!" Gillian cried. "Does that suit you, boy?"

"You're a foolish and sick old man! Can't you see? This seven-year prison sentence may be all the time you have left. This is not the time to be prideful or to show prejudice!"

"I understand, but I'm sure Clancy will be back. He can help me. He knows exactly how to find those I gave charity to."

"Papa... Clancy's been gone for years now," Patrick said quietly, his anger seemingly replaced by pity. "Even if he found his son alive, I'm sure the war found them both."

"But the war's been over for four years now. Slavery is done."

"That's a load of malarkey, and you know it. The rebels are seething over this. If anything, there are probably more lynchings now. Point is, you can't rely on Clancy's return."

"I suppose..."

Gillian was cut off by Maurice's return.

"Time's up, gentlemen," he said as he studied his watch dial.

The two men stood simultaneously. Gillian took a hard look at his son, and for the first time, he saw him not as his boy but a man making his way in the world. Then he noted that Patrick was becoming a mirror image of his younger self. Curly, reddish-brown hair threatening to recede, blue eyes, and the meaty Gillian nose. Except his son's had a slight crook in it, the result of a schoolyard brawl.

Same on the outside, world of difference on the inside.

Gillian smiled. "I am proud of you, lad. Send your good wife and child my love."

Patrick appeared uncomfortable again, his eyes back on the handcuffs. "I will let them know your thoughts, but please... strongly consider Chang's proposal." Then he looked at the floor while Maurice re-attached the cuffs and quietly led the inmate away.

* * *

After Patrick's visit, Robert was sent to his work detail at the new stables on Third Avenue and 14th Street. With the cool autumn days here to stay, being near the furnace was very tolerable. He would whistle away the hours, sometimes old Gaelic tunes, sometimes Catholic hymns. He felt certain that the horses were calmed by his whimsical sound.

Beef pie and corn was the evening meal. Again, he noted the irony that he was eating better in prison than when he had first arrived in the Five Points. *How odd life can be.* But then he looked at the substance in his cup. A habit now, he tossed the tin at the stone wall opposite his bed. Still no good milk.

The days were getting shorter, seemingly at a rapid pace. Phinny lit the candle in the sconce just outside his cell at half-past six. "Why do they give me the ones still with the candles?" Robert had heard him complain to Maurice. "Because you're so dimwitted, they don't trust you with the gas!" Maurice barked in return.

Gillian was tired and ready for sleep, but he was a bit fearful of the nightmares he'd been having of late, nightmares of so many fires experienced during his twenty years with Engine Company Five. Small ones, false alarms, larger blazes, and then great conflagrations, the ones that were talked about for generations, at least among fire laddies. It was becoming hard to tell which were memories of real events and which were complete fabrications of his mind.

One thing he was certain of, though—the specter he had seen in some of those fires was not a dream. It was the figure of a man, or an insect, or both, but from beyond this world. A black torso, black legs, black feet, and a face like the head of an insect, with huge round black eyes and a proboscis for a nose. The image in the flames appeared to be seeking his attention or trying to convey something. In time, he learned to ignore it while tending to his firefighting duties, assuming one day he would solve the mystery. But now it occurred to him, this would never happen. When would he be fighting a fire again?

Twenty years at Engine Company Five. *They surely would've had a celebration for my retirement.* He laughed aloud. It occurred to him that perhaps now, he sounded like the other raving lunatics in The Tombs.

PART IV

A BETTER LIFE?

Chapter Thirteen

Manhattan Island
July 1847

On July 5th, 1847, the *Nina* safely anchored at the South Street Seaport. First to disembark were two rats. "Always the non-paying passengers first," muttered the first mate as he continued laying the planks so passengers wouldn't have to jump down to the dock.

One final address came from Captain Ross, who appeared out of character, in that he was sober. He honored himself—and the first and second mate—for making the voyage in a span just five days beyond the original estimate. He concluded by wishing the passengers God's grace in the new world and warning them to be heedful of the sharks on land: the runners, the thieves, the pickpockets.

Later, when the seamen lined up for their pay, Captain Ross was baffled by the extra funds left over, equal to exactly one man's pay. He scratched his crown, shrugged, then declared an early holiday bonus for all. After reserving a tidy sum for himself, he divided the remaining funds among the seamen. Then he retrieved his flask from his waistcoat, took a swig, and departed the vessel.

"I would never have imagined a year ago that here we'd be in America," Robert said, dumbstruck, as the four Gillians followed the crowd off the dock and toward Lower Manhattan.

"It's amazing," Aileen said.

"Why's it so hot?" asked Mary, as her head darted in all directions, scouting for some shade.

"Oh, summers are hot in America. You won't be needing many clothes for sure till October," replied Robert as they reached the dusty curb along South Street.

"I've never seen so many people in one place!" exclaimed Patrick, narrowly missing being trampled by a man balancing wood crates on each shoulder. "Look, Papa, fruit! Can we buy some apples?" Patrick pointed to a streetside market, almost a block long, which appeared to sell every type of fruit imaginable.

"Not now, lad. We have to change our money first. Aileen? You have that paper that gives us the proper exchange rates?"

Aileen reached into the front pocket of her frock, but nothing was there. "Oh, no!" she cried out. "I tucked it into me frock, all forgetting about the hole in the pocket."

Robert felt a tinge of annoyance, but he let it go, mindful of all she'd been through. Besides, what would he do without her? She was the wiser half of their union; her gift for numbers had saved him from trouble on more than one occasion. She was the guardian of the four pounds, one crown, and three shillings safely stored away in a small wooden box in their one suitcase.

"Okay, Robert. You need to put this to your mind," Aileen ordered. "One pound equals five dollars, one crown equals one dollar and a quarter, and one shilling equals a twenty-five cent piece. I figure we have twenty-two dollars in total. You need to remember this."

"I'm not dimwitted; I know what we have!" he shouted, not unaware of the glances his children were exchanging. "Now, I need to consult with a map here." Gillian pulled a neatly folded map from the back pocket of his breeches. He'd obtained it at the docks before the start of their journey. He began studying while wandering through foot traffic, concluding that the exchange was several blocks away.

"Step back, Robert. You'll get run over by the crowds," cried Aileen.

"I be fine," he responded as he knocked into a man carrying rolled-up carpets.

"Watch where you're going, you stupid paddy," the man barked as he caught his balance and re-secured the carpets under his arms.

"Who you calling a stupid paddy!" Gillian barked, but the man was already well on his way.

Aileen grabbed his arm and pulled him back a distance from the curb. "You best keep your mouth shut, husband. We've no time for fights in a strange land. Now, I saw privies near the dock. You children need to go?"

"Yes, Mum," came in chorus.

"I'll stay here with our belongings," Gillian said.

"Fine, but no trouble, pray?" And she looked at him warily.

"You have my word."

And with that, Gillian sat down on a bench and returned to the map. He thought perhaps they could save some money by walking the distance to the exchange. But then he considered the heat and Aileen's condition. *No, we'll have to take a horse cart, like I saw many of the other passengers do.* Then another revelation. *We don't have the American money to pay the driver. We'll have to walk... unless there's a place to change our money much closer.*

Carrying their one suitcase, he walked back onto South Street and meandered to the end corner of the block-long fruit stand, where he spotted a clean-cut boy in a white shirt arranging apples into a pyramid.

"Top of the morn to you, lad," Gillian said with a smile, tipping his cap. "Can you tell me if there's a place to exchange money close by?"

"Oh, that's an easy one. Right over there, across the street." He pointed. "There's a little office in that storefront. Can't see it quite from here, but it's behind that horse."

"Thank you kindly, lad," he said with a slight bow of the head, then returned his cap and made his way across the busy intersection. Then he abruptly stopped and turned back to the clerk. "Pardon again, how much are these apples?"

"Oh, three pennies each, sir."

Seems fair enough, he thought. "Thank you again, lad." *I shall surprise them with some apples.*

Gillian was greeted by the jangle of a bell as he entered the storefront. An elderly bespeckled man standing behind a rather tall counter looked up. He was smartly dressed in a pink shirt with a white bowtie and possessed a strong odor of talcum. *He must have just returned from the barber.*

"What can I do you, young man?" the elderly man asked with a smile as white as could be.

"I've been informed that you change money here."

"Yes, we do indeed, sir, among other services for our newly arrived Americans. Ireland, I presume. I can tell from your accent, sir. And not to be disrespectful in any way, but you're wearing a wool cap in the month of July."

"I suppose I am." Gillian chuckled with mild embarrassment as he removed his cap. "I imagine that's why I was so warm in the street." He coughed. "I just need to change enough money to have the fare to take the cart to the government exchange. There be four of us. So, what's that going to cost?"

"That costs twenty cents, almost one shilling in your money. We can do that easily, but why don't you change all your money here? Surely you don't want to wait on a long line at the exchange, then take another cart to the boarding house... I presume. That's where most of you stay before finding a flat."

"Hmm. True, sir. Maybe not a bad idea."

"Well, then, how much do you have?"

"Four pounds, one crown, and three shillings."

"You're almost a wealthy man, sir! Many show up here with barely nothing. Well, all that converts to twenty-one dollars even. I'll give you twenty even, only charging you five percent.

"Oh, I think you made a mistake. Should come to twenty-two dollars."

"Hmm. Let me refigure that." The man took out a piece of paper and pencil and started jotting down numbers while humming a tune. "Right you are, sir. Please accept my humble apology, no excuse except perhaps my age is catching up to me. Twenty-two dollars to be exact." Then scribbling more numbers, he started to mumble, "Okay, our five percent fee, and the fifty-cent overhead, got it." He put the pencil down and looked up at Gillian. "All comes to twenty dollars and a fifty-cent piece to you, my good man."

Gillian opened the suitcase on the counter, took out the small wooden box, and removed all the contents. Soon, the transaction was complete. Robert Gillian had successfully exchanged twenty-two dollars' worth of British currency for twenty dollars and fifty cents of American currency. The fifty-cent piece came in handy to buy a few apples on the way back to the South Street docks. *Aileen will be happy with this convenience*, he thought. *Now we can take a cart straight to the boarding house.*

"Where have you gone, Robert? We've been waiting here since noon."

"Good news. I exchanged our funds and bought apples for us to enjoy!"

"Yeah, Papa!" Patrick blurted. Sullen Mary just took an apple from the bag.

Pale Aileen turned an even whiter shade of white. "You exchanged all our money for a bunch of apples! Are you mad, Robert!"

"No. No, dear. I exchanged our money, then bought a dozen apples here, three pennies each, that's all. Now we can just take a cart to the boardinghouse."

"So, you got our twenty-two dollars proper?"

"Well, not exactly twenty-two dollars. You see, there's an exchange fee, so we received twenty dollars and a fifty-cent piece."

"You paid one dollar and fifty cents just to exchange our money! You imbecile! The exchange charges nothing!"

She grabbed the bag of apples and hit him on the head, the bag ripping open and the apples scattering about the dock plaza. Immediately, Mary and Patrick dropped to their knees, grabbing all they could. Regrettably, two went over the edge into the water.

"Aileen, calm yourself. We don't have to pay fare to get to the exchange. You're tired. You need your rest. We need to get to the boardinghouse. I'll call a cart right now."

"Robert," she said softly. "You forgot what we were told. The exchange provides free cart service to the boarding house. Now we'll have to pay full fare ourselves. This will cost more than the fare to the exchange. All you needed to do was change enough money to get us to the exchange."

She looked at him forlornly, too drained to maintain her anger.

Gillian felt shame at what she left unsaid. And he certainly wasn't going to remind Aileen that it was her idea to hold off exchanging any money until they arrived in America.

CHAPTER FOURTEEN

The Beautiful Five Points?

"You see, my dear, two weeks and I'm already situated! This never would've happened, say I left New York and sailed to Galway for a job, nope never would've happened, even with no blight."

"Aye, I'm sure you're right, husband. And fifteen dollars a month, that's almost three pounds!" Aileen said with an enthusiasm he'd not seen for a few years. "So, with the rent at five dollars, we still have ten for food and such."

"And Saturday afternoons and Sundays, I'm free to rest. Oh, and church... sometimes... of course," he added reticently. "And I'm certain I can walk to the docks most days, so I'll not need to pay for the horsecar."

Gillian was proud of his decision to sign with the Democratic Party the day after they secured a flat in the Five Points neighborhood. The agent who had steered them to a second-level flat in a tenement building at the corner of Bayard and Orange Streets had also brought Gillian to the headquarters of Tammany Hall. There, he was provided with job references and was registered to vote in the local elections. Then he was transported to three separate polling places to sign up for a ballot. "Such power given to one man for a vote here!" he said to Aileen.

He'd be working on the loading docks, one pier away from their South Street landing. The foreman had explained that he would be unloading the packet ships that traveled up the coast from the Carolinas carrying pressed bales of cotton. Some of the cargo would be set aside for delivery to local textile manufacturers, some was to be further processed then shipped to England. *All and all, not bad*, he thought.

And Gillian was right. The work was fine, except on the steamiest summer days, and he was told there would be winter gales off the East River. However, there was one aspect of the job he'd not been forewarned of, and thus he was quite shaken near the end of his first week of employment.

The final packet ship had landed at half-past four in the afternoon. Upon reaching the rear of the cargo hold, he was overwhelmed by a horrific stench. Under a towering mountain of pressed bales lay a Negro man—more likely a victim of suffocation rather than death by crushing. Alarmed, Gillian raced to report this to the foreman, who happened to be standing on deck, downing a swig from his flask. Gillian had quickly surmised that this was the way the man celebrated the end of every workday, and sometimes assorted points during the day.

"Mr. Denny, sir. I have something you must see. It's awful, it's in the rear hold." Gillian was winded, more from shock than the marathon run through the cargo hold and up to the deck.

"What's it? We all want to get home, ye know?" the foreman barked as he quickly tucked his flask back into a pocket of his breeches.

"It's a dead man, sir; come see for yourself."

"So that's the foul odor that came to me senses all the way up on deck. I was sure it was the harbor again—with all the shit they throw in there, we could walk across to Brooklyn." It was clear to Gillian that the nuisance of the odor was more concerning than the cause. "Okay, let's take a look... er... what's your name again?"

"Robert Gillian, sir."

The man grumbled his way down the stairs, following Gillian to the rear of the hold.

"There *it*... I mean, *he* is, Mr. Denny."

Pinching his nose closed, Denny bent down for a closer look. Then he walked them back a distance from the corpse.

"I thought you said it was a man, Gillian.

"I did, sir."

"But it's a Negro, Gillian. Poor fellow, a horrible way for anybody to go." He sighed as he put his hands on his hips. "You better get used to it. Usually, these runaways make it alive. We here have a habit of ignoring them as they dart off the ship when we land. First the rats, then the Negros, then the paying passengers, as they say. But I ain't in the slave-catching business, nor do I want to be. Besides, mostly they get caught later by paid slave-catchers or the black-birders. Those scoundrels make a good living on the bounty."

Gillian stood tall, hands on his hips, pretending he wasn't shocked—and disgusted. "Now sometimes, this being the case, they show up dead, maybe disease, a wound, or the heat gets them. These ships can sit for days in Carolina before making it up this way."

"Well, what now, Mr. Denny?"

"It's our job to clean out the cargo hold of everything, and he's considered, well... cargo of sorts." Denny shrugged. "It's actually your job, Gillian, not mine, but I'll get a dockhand to help you. He'll bring a barrel down. Looks like a little guy, shouldn't be too difficult to get 'im up the steps. Then you take the barrel to the dockmaster, who seals it up. Used to be they'd take 'im to the Negro cemetery, but I think it's full now. I don't know what they'll do with him. Sometimes the medical college takes them. Anyways, I want to get home, so I'll fetch that dockhand for you."

"Thanks, Mr. Denny," Gillian said, still unnerved at the idea of calling a dead man *cargo*.

"You'll be back tomorrow, Gillian?"

"Aye, certainly will, sir. Seven on the dot."

The foreman gave Gillian an approving smile, and the two climbed back up to the deck in search of fresh air.

* * *

The heat set in with a vengeance by the end of his second week at the docks, and this made for a dreadfully long day. Gillian climbed the steep and narrow staircase that led to their second-floor apartment. Saturday afternoon, mid-July, the light from the blazing sun poured through the front window of their flat—in fact, the only *true* window in their flat.

They'd been fortunate enough to secure an apartment in one of the newer tenement buildings, a "dumbbell building," the agent called it. "This here is the latest design in tenement building under the new building codes," he'd said with pride, as if he'd built it himself. The three-story dwelling was built flush with the buildings in the front and rear but was tapered in the middle to allow for an airshaft between buildings. A window in the middle of the apartment was supposed to allow more natural light but regrettably only provided a clear view of the brick wall of the adjacent tenement. In fact, the airshaft was little more than an oversized chimney flue. Breezy days brought an updraft that carried the unwanted fragrances of refuse and human waste throughout both connected buildings, and the airshaft had the sound-enhancing qualities of a poorly constructed concert hall, sans music. With the window open, the Gillians were treated to the augmented sound of babies crying, spousal altercations, and occasional pig squeals.

Still, it did provide them with a place to dispose of garbage, effluvia, and such, since a trip down the dark banister-less stairwell at night was both inconvenient and potentially deadly.

"It don't seem to matter if this front window's open or closed, Aileen. Just as hot without the breeze," Robert observed as he stared out onto the street, watching a drunkard negotiate a rather large pile of manure.

"I know. That's why I made our supper this morning. I couldn't bear the thought of standing over the stove in the afternoon with that sun cooking me."

"I hear you, wife," Gillian said as he took his accustomed spot on the daybed under the window. There was a rip in the fabric, but at fifty cents, he was certain they'd received good value. Patrick slept here since Mary needed the third little room to herself. "Now, where are the children?"

"Patrick is scouting for coal chips with some of the other boys. Mary went off with another Mary. The Bowery, she said. Something about arcade games."

"I don't like this already. She shouldn't be running off to places we're not yet sure of. I can see there's a lot of bad characters in this town, maybe worse than Dublin."

"Maybe so, Robert," Aileen said while patting the perspiration on her forehead with an old linen. Then she sat down on the opposite side of the daybed, stretched her feet out, and yawned. "I suppose I should have stopped her, but she's been so out of sorts lately. She needs to have companions, you know, to replace what she lost."

"I suppose, and with them out, it gives us a chance to talk about their futures here."

"Aye, it does... I think," she replied. He wasn't sure if she was just exhausted from the heat, suffering the nagging effects of her malaise, or the topic was uncomfortable. Perhaps all three, he concluded. After all, the only other time they had broached the subject since arriving in America, it had resulted in more than a squabble.

"Well, you know my feelings, Aileen. If the boy brings in some money now, working with me on the docks, we don't have to consider taking on a boarder. He can go to the Catholic charity school in the evening to finish his education. We can't afford no private Catholic school anyways, and I ain't sending him to the public school to learn the King James Bible!"

"Not with me here, Robert! He's only twelve years old. He must finish day school. He can get a job after school. And we ain't taking on a boarder! We can afford the five dollars a month just fine with your wage. Besides, where would they sleep? We only got three rooms."

"They're going to taunt him, you know, at the free school. How will he mind his studies? Maybe he even takes a beating," Gillian added, figuring he'd appeal to a mother's sense of protectiveness.

"Well then, he'll have to learn to fight. You can take him to that boxing gym down the block. Besides, I already talked to a few ladies in the building, and they said there are free schools less harsh on Catholics. Those have Jews to pick on. Maybe we can get him in one of them, and he can pretend he knows the King James Bible. Then when we save a little money, we can move him to Catholic school." With that, she gave a firm nod and again dabbed some perspiration off her forehead

Gillian was impressed that she'd figured this all out, that she'd had a plan. "Okay. Okay, woman, maybe you're right this time. After all, he's still saying he wants to become a shipwright. I think he'll need more schooling for that, and he's too young for an apprenticeship anyways."

"Fine. So, it's settled then," Aileen said with a surefire conviction. "Now, what about Mary?"

"I hear a lot of girls get situations as domestic servants. It's good, safe work, and she'll have the opportunity to meet gentlemen at the church dances. In time, someone will take to her, and she'll have the training already to be a good wife," Robert stated.

Aileen sighed and looked up at a small crack in the relatively new ceiling. "I suppose you're right. But she's so intelligent, Robert. There must be something more she can do?"

"Aye. Make us grandparents. That's what she needs to do," he said with a wide grin.

"She will in time, I'm certain. But she's good with the numbers, like me. Maybe she can get a job in a counting-house, you know, like a book-keeper." Aileen smiled at this prospect.

Then they heard the creaking sound of the building's front door reverberating up the airshaft, followed by a thud that grew louder with each stair. Less than two weeks at their flat, and they could identify all the odd sounds, as well as the gait of their children marching up to the apartment.

Patrick burst into the room carrying three burlap sacks of coal chips, his face and hands covered with sweat and soot.

"There's the boy! Looks like you hit the mother lode, Patrick," Robert exclaimed.

"Aye, but this is nothing, Papa. You should have seen what the other boys collected. They said we better start squirreling away for the winter. It'll be slim pickings then."

A most valuable lesson for the Gillian family.

Chapter Fifteen

Engine Company Five
July 1848

"Gillian, come up here. I need a word with you, lad!" Foreman Denny called down into the hold of the packet ship. "Those bales can wait a few minutes. Not our fault the ship docked early anyways."

Gillian was back on deck in a flash. "What's the trouble, Mr. Denny, sir?"

"Gillian, you've been with me a year or more now. You don't have to call me 'Mr. Denny.' Brian, my Christian name, will do."

Apparently, Denny had a congenial side. "Okay, Mr. Denny... er... Brian. What's the trouble?"

"No trouble, here at least. Let me ask you. Have you ever thought of joining the fire department?"

"Not really, with the children, you know, and my wife ain't completely well... no, never gave it a thought."

"Well, Gillian. I'm a volunteer—Assistant Foreman—at Engine Company Five, been for over ten years now. We got a big problem, biggest I've seen. We lost one fireman. His ticker just went like that one day." Denny raised his arm and snapped his fingers. "Just shy of his fifty-third birthday. Then we lost another one, didn't die or anything, just burned bad at a conflagration a few months ago. I'm not sure he's coming back.

Real shame, a good lad too. So, you see where I'm getting to? We have an opportunity for you."

He impatiently pushed back his sweat-saturated salt-and-pepper hair, revealing his receding hairline. Though Gillian still had many inches on him, Denny was a tall man with a sturdy frame, apart from a slight belly. When he grinned, he revealed a remarkably full set of teeth, yellowed but not rotting.

"I'm not sure, Mr.... Brian. Like I said, I got a bundle on me shoulders."

"Can I call you Robert?" He didn't wait for an answer. "Robert, listen here. This is a great opportunity. It don't pay, I mean with money, but there's a lot of extras you come to appreciate. No serving in the militia or jury duty. Loads of respect around town, and sometimes you get to meet the bigwigs in this city, like His Honor the mayor."

"I don't know," Gillian said slowly. "I—"

"I know. You need to talk it over with your lady. That's fine. You're going to make a lot of acquaintances—folks just like yourself. We got a lot of your kind the past few years, and sometimes we have chowder parties and dances on the Saturday nights. You'll see. Think it over, chap, but don't wait too long. Other men in the company might be trying to recruit also."

With that, Denny hopped on the dock and moved toward a vessel arriving in port, needing to be unloaded. Just as it anchored, a young black man darted off the boat. Denny looked down, pretending not to notice.

* * *

"Okay, woman, you made your point, but I'm not in agreement with ya. It won't be too risky, and thirty-eight ain't too old anyways. Some of the laddies are older. Brian's forty-seven."

She joined him at the little table by the stove, tea for both in hand. "Oh, so now you're using Christian names. You shouldn't be getting too close with your boss, Robert. It could bring trouble on you—and us. What if you get into a tumble with him at the firehouse? He'll fire you.

And maybe he's forty-seven, but he started as a young man, knows what he's doing."

Her scolding was not meant to insult him, but it did.

"That's right. He knows what he's doing, and he never got hurt all these years." Gillian didn't know that as a fact, but he'd not observed any scarring from burns or any limp or deformity; that was proof enough in his judgment. "And you should see their latest apparatus: scaling ladders, metal helmets, and pumps that get the water all the way up to the second floor, even the third floor sometimes. The leather fire buckets still come in handy, though, for 'small events,' as he calls them. Besides, I'm going to get apprenticed. They don't just send ya into those big conflagrations, ya know." Actually, she didn't know, and neither did he.

"It's just... you can't afford to go lame, husband. Mine and Mary's needleworking together won't cover our living costs, and Patrick needs to finish school." With that, she drew a deep sip of her tea and offered a fragile smile.

"But Aileen. This is what a man does here to get ahead. It's a noble service. You get respect all around the town, don't have to serve in the militia or do jury duty. Fireman Gillian of Engine Company Five will get notice of the best jobs in town for an Irishman. The ones that pay strong, but you have to be *connected* to get them." He smiled, then gazed dreamily at the ceiling, imagining all the grand opportunities awaiting him.

"Well, I suppose it wouldn't hurt to try, I guess, as long as you get trained and such," she added with a mild sound of defeat.

"No worries, my dear. I'll be going down to the company with Brian after work tomorrow, to meet the other laddies and start the training."

Aileen gave him a sharp look, her brow creasing. "Dammit, Robert! I should've known you'd decided this already."

She stood up and grabbed his unfinished tea along with her own and went to dump them down the airshaft. Gillian smiled again. *It could've gone worse,* he considered.

CHAPTER SIXTEEN

Fire, fire everywhere, but none to keep you warm
January 10, 1849

"Robert, you must wake up," Aileen hissed as she shook him from his slumber. "I thought you said those fire bells would wake you up."

"It did wake me, woman. I was just listening to see if it was the right one for me. Like I told you, the bell's different for each ward. Our sixth ward is five bells, then he waits a few seconds, then a final bell."

"So, which is it?"

"It's me, I mean us," he said, then grunted his way out of bed onto the cold floor. "It's stone-cold in here. Shall I put some more coal in the stove?"

"No. We have to save, and I'll have to fire it up anyways when the children wake up."

Gillian's uniform, boots, and helmet were placed under the bed for these exact occasions. He'd already learned that most fires take place in the dark of night, and on the coldest of nights. This one was no exception. After struggling with his boots, he grabbed the lantern and went out to the hallway to lace up. Then he was crunching through the small accumulation of snow and ice, the swinging lantern periodically casting light on the brown and yellow patches of horse manure and urine.

He was greeted outside of the firehouse by six other men, all waiting for the foreman who held the single key to the wood-frame building. Frankly, the custom struck him as stupid, though he felt it was not his place to say anything with just six months at the company.

"You smell that, Gillian? This is gonna be a bad one, yup, I'm sure," said a tall, wiry man nicknamed Stretch.

"You're always sayin' that. And you're wrong most of the time," Moses scolded.

"I don't know, Moses," said a short Negro man. "He may be right this time. Smell that?" he asked as he studied Gillian head to toe. "That's oil tar. That burns hot and mean. Now, which way's the lantern pointing? Sorry, I forgot your name."

"Robert Gillian, and who am I making the acquaintance of?" Gillian placed one hand on his stomach and bowed.

"My, my, fancy sir. And my name's Clancy. Clancy Carver." They met with a hearty handshake. "You're probably wondering what a Negro's doing in this engine company."

"Oh, no, not at all," he said, though he was surprised to see a mingling in the fire company. He'd never given it a thought, but it made sense. He knew there was a sizable Negro population in the sixth ward, including a scattering around the Five Points.

"A fire's a fire," Clancy stated. "You just want some bodies to put it out. We got a lot of green men like yourself now, them snooty natives, us coloreds, and we even have an Indian—Lenape tribe, he says. He says they owned this whole city before any of us was here."

"Stop your yapping, Clancy," barked Moses. "I thought you was giving him a lesson."

"Oh yeah, sorry. So, what was I saying... I mean, asking?"

"You asked me where the lantern's pointing, Clancy." Gillian quickly scanned what little horizon was in their view. "But I can't see no bell tower from here, so I don't know where the man's pointing."

"Oh, now that makes sense. Didn't any of them tell you? You gotta check the bell tower before coming to this station. We can't see it from Station Five, cause Station Five was built before the bell towers was put in place. Them other companies can see it from their stations, all except us. So they got a leg up on beating us to the fire. At night, the keeper of the bell points a lantern out in the direction of the fire. By day, he just sticks a pole out in the direction. You gotta check that first, then you come to the station. No other way."

"Sounds... strange." Gillian wasn't sure what to say. "Well, now I know for next time." Just then, Brian Denny arrived at the stationhouse with the large iron key.

"Foreman's sick. I had to pick up the key at his flat," Denny said flatly, appearing annoyed to have been bothered in the middle of the night.

Gillian had never seen him so disheveled. His lantern light revealed bloodshot eyes and a flushed face, and when he went over to greet him, it became apparent that whiskey had been his drink of choice that night.

They wouldn't be racing any other companies to this fire. The others were far ahead, and running with the engine on ice-covered snow could result in a bad mishap. The two companies already at the event just needed backup now.

Stretch was right about this being a memorable event. Two warehouse buildings at the corner of Pearl and Centre Streets were engulfed in flames. A third three-story tenement was under protection, with one hose man struggling to deliver a stream of water to its roof to fight off embers that could easily ignite the building. But the stream of water was uneven, as the pressure fluctuated, and most of the spray never reached beyond the second level.

"Oh, lookie here, gents! White Flag Engine Company decided they'd show up for the event!" cried the foreman from Engine Company Three. "I see you're still carrying your pump through the streets, Denny. That's horses' work, not fireman's work, ya ignoramus!" After a quick laugh, he stopped to launch a spitball of chewing tobacco onto a sooty pile of snow.

"If you were here so much earlier, why'd you let the fire get away from you?" Denny shot back.

This got the foreman from Company Three riled up. "Oh, so you're a wise one now. You know, we'll settle this later." He balled his hand into a fist and held it to Denny's face. "Took us fifteen minutes to power up this fucking steam pump. Hand pumps are better, but this is what they want us to use."

The foreman from Engine Company Two, a short rotund man, approached them with a red speaking trumpet. "Are you ladies going to do anything here! If not, I'll send you for a tray of sweetmeats!"

It was clear who was in charge of this event. Gillian and his comrades just stood by their engine, waiting for a hose hookup to a cistern a block away. The wind had picked up, and it was obvious to all that the temperature was dropping sharply. "What do we do now?" he blurted. Clancy and the three other firemen all looked at Gillian, wearing blank expressions. One shrugged and said, "Nothing."

"Nothing?" Gillian repeated.

"Nothing," Clancy confirmed. "What can we do? Those buildings are far gone anyway, and we can't get in there to save any property, probably no people in there either; they're just warehouses. If we get a hookup, three of us will start pumping, and we'll help that hose man get water on those buildings around the corner."

"*If* we get a hookup? You mean *when* we get a hookup."

Just then came a loud explosion from the second floor of the warehouse closest to the tenement building. A ball of fire leaped through the roof, lighting the street below. Closest to the fire, Engine Company Two's horses reared up and whinnied in terror, the glassy image of the orange blaze reflecting from their panicked eyes. Embers rained down on the crowd, one landing on the crown of a young spectator, setting his hair afire. The fireman next to him knocked the boy to the ground and jammed his head in the slushy snow. "You dumb fool! You urchins are always in the way. Now, get out of here!"

The singed boy ran off without uttering a word.

"Like I told you, oil tar must have been up there," Stretch said with great satisfaction.

"So, for once, you were right, Stretch. Now shut yer trap," said Moses as he glanced down the road. "This is real bad. Look, the fire commissioner and the mayor are here."

The coachman had stopped the black carriage a block away so the fire wouldn't spook the horses. The tall and brawny commissioner came out from one side, and the short stubby mayor from the other, both dressed in draping cloaks of the finest quality wools, black leather boots, stovepipe hats, fur-lined sheepskin gloves, and wool scarves. But Gillian could see the hint of their nightclothes peeking out from beneath the fancy outerwear.

Identical sour expressions complemented their identical outerwear, more due to the rudeness of being disturbed in the middle of the night than the impact of the fire, Gillian assumed. They charged toward the crowd like angry bulls, snow crunching underfoot and steam puffing from their nostrils. By chance of position, Robert Gillian was the first to greet them as he was standing by his company's engine—still of no use without a water hookup. "Who's commanding this conflagration?" the mayor barked.

Gillian felt anxious as if he'd already done something wrong. He had told Aileen that he would meet the mayor one day, but he'd assumed under better circumstances. "There he is, sir... Your Honor... the short gentleman with the speaking trumpet," Gillian responded, pointing at the portly foreman.

"Oh, it's you, Spanky!" called out the commissioner. "I should've known. That's why this fire got away from us."

"Greetings, Commissioner... Mayor," Engine Company Two's foreman said with a discomfited smile.

"What's the plan?" the commissioner barked. "Are we going to blow up buildings, create a barrier, and such?"

"I'm afraid we may have to, sir. I've already put the call out for gunpowder barrels, and I got my men marking potential buildings to take down."

"Fine, fine. What's our water situation?"

Spanky hesitated. "Well, sir, the hydrant's holding up fine. That Croton water is really treating us well." The mayor nodded, having been instrumental in launching the Croton Aqueduct project some years earlier. "We're hooking up Engine Company Five's pump right now to a cistern a block away, can't be sure though how much water there'll be."

"And the property?"

"These buildings are a loss, sir, that's why there's no wasting our water on them. We're trying to protect that tenement around the corner."

"Okay, let me know when the gunpowder arrives, and I want the list of buildings to take down for fire barriers," said the commissioner. "This wind isn't helping now, and it's getting colder by the minute. Reminds me of the December 1835 fire, aye, Spanky?"

"Lord, I pray not," the mayor said quietly, appearing deep in thought. "That will make for a very difficult election for me next year."

With that, the important gentlemen returned to their carriage. "City Hall, driver," the mayor commanded. Then he turned to the commissioner. "We shall warm ourselves by the fire and enjoy a cordial before returning to the conflagration."

"Splendid idea, Your Honor," replied the commissioner.

Just as the carriage started to move away from the event, a deep rumbling came from the blazing warehouse buildings. Firemen were shouting, calling for the onlookers to leave the area. A sense of obligation, perhaps, or more about securing the next election—the mayor slammed his walking stick on the floor of the carriage. "Damn fire! Return us at once, driver."

CHAPTER SEVENTEEN

And a Hero is Made

First came the deep trembling. Then the warehouse touching the tenement building collapsed into a fiery heap. Red- and blue-hot embers once again leapt into the frigid dark, then drifted down like ashen snow.

The hookup to the cistern was finally achieved after the hose men had chiseled down to reach liquid. But now, a greater problem was emerging. Standing water was rapidly freezing all around the fire scene. The temperature had fallen so low that even the slow-moving water in the cistern hoses was freezing before arriving at the nozzle. The tenement building was morphing into a glacial mound before their eyes.

"Enough, enough! Shut your hoses down. She's never going to burn now. She's an igloo," cried Spanky through his speaking trumpet, his voice raspy from shouting in the frigid air. "Bring the water onto the warehouses now, or what's left of them."

The two hose men resembled ice statues themselves, encrusted helmets weighing down their heads. The rims were encircled with icicles, even blocking one man's line of vision. Coats, breeches, gloves, were all glittering with ice from the mist of the hose spray blowing back at the men as they fought not just the fire, but the wind.

Denny, who had disappeared for much of the event, was now next to Gillian with a bottle of whiskey. "Here, Robert. Take this to those hose men. Pour it in their boots. The alcohol will melt the ice and help their feet."

"Sure, Brian."

Just as Gillian was approaching the frozen hose men, he heard shouts from several onlookers on the corner. He opened the bottle of whiskey and handed it to one of the statues. "Sorry, laddie. You're going to have to do this yourself," he said.

Walking closer with his lantern, he realized they weren't onlookers; they were tenants from the building now encased in ice. Their outerwear was whatever they had been able to grab from their meager collections of clothes. Huddled together and shivering, they were pointing at the top floor of a three-story tenement, four buildings removed from the one that was an igloo now. Gillian immediately understood the dire situation. *This is how you go from fire to conflagration. It jumps buildings, the dangers of a windy night!* While racing over to the new fire, an awful thought came to him. *What other buildings received these embers to their tar-covered roofs? What other fires do we not know about—yet?*

As he arrived in front of the new Pearl Street fire, he quickly assessed the situation as trained. It appeared the fire was confined to the top floor. Flames were not yet visible, but black smoke billowed from the sole window fronting the street. He shouted up, "Anybody in there! Stay by the window!"

An elderly woman appeared.

"Help me!" she shouted, waving frantically, her voice hoarse from the smoke.

"Stay steady, mum. We'll be right up."

He didn't know why he said that—instinct perhaps. After all, that's what anybody in her situation would want to hear.

The men from Engine Companies Two and Three were now at the scene with a steam pump. They were hooking up to a hydrant that was mercifully close by when a dreadful discovery was made. The water at the head of the hydrant was frozen solid. The new steam pump engines were useless without a water source, and the temperature was still dropping.

Gillian chided himself, kicking a mound of ice. *We'll be right up. How could I have made that promise? Certainly not without water available.*

Just then, two firemen emerged from the building. Gillian was startled, as he hadn't seen them enter. Wearing grim expressions, both were shaking their heads.

"Stairway's blocked on the third floor, and I'm sure there's no fire escape with this old piece of shit."

"Gillian!" called a loud voice from behind. "We have the ladder. I don't see no flames on the floors below her. You should be fine."

He turned around to find Stretch and Moses holding the apparatus.

"Consider this is your induction ceremony into our fire laddies club," Moses said with a smile.

"You can do it... new guy!" yelled Clancy. "You keep talking to her, make her calm while we get the ladder in place. Then we keep it real steady as you go up. Just make sure she don't fight you. They do that sometimes when they panic. One time, I seen them push the ladder away. We grabbed it in time, though—"

"Clamp it down, Clancy. Don't put more fear in him than he already has—if he's smart," scolded Moses. "Now, Gillian, she's a feather of a woman, so this should be easy. Tell her to put her back to the ladder, crouch down, and start moving her legs to the second rung. Then you guide her until she's on the ladder just above you. Keep your hands on her back and tell her everything's going to be just fine; it's just like climbing down any ladder."

"I don't know if I can remember all this. Maybe you—"

"Don't worry. The right things to do will just come to you once you're up there," Moses assured.

"And if they don't, just holler down to us, we'll help," Clancy added. Moses slapped him in the back of the head.

Within seconds, Robert Gillian was halfway up the ladder.

"I'm coming, me lady. Stay by the window!" he shouted.

There was no response. Nor could he see her anymore. Just as his hands reached the top rung, even heavier black smoke began billowing from the window, and he feared the worst. Then he heard a faint cough and a weak cry.

However, his relief that she was still alive was short-lived. The ladder was too short, the top rung several feet shy of the windowsill.

"Oh, shit! The scaling ladder! We forgot the scaling ladder! Hey, you men, we forgot the scaling ladder!" he hollered down to the street.

There were several seconds of stunned silence.

"You nitwits!" yelled the fire commissioner who had reappeared with the mayor. "We paid a ransom for this new apparatus; how the bloody hell can you forget to use it!" Then he looked at the mayor sheepishly. "I'm quite sorry, sir, these new volunteers . . ."

"I got it right here from the hose truck!" Clancy yelled as he pushed through the crowd. "I'm coming up right behind you, Gillian." Sure enough, he was almost there by the time he finished his cry. "You remember how we were learned to use it, don't you?"

"Yes," Robert said as he grabbed the short extension ladder and immediately began pushing the hooked bars up along the wall, using just one hand so he wouldn't lose his balance. He secured the ladder hooks to the windowsill and the bottom of the scaling ladder to the second rung of his own ladder. He began to cough as the smoke hit him square in the face.

Still coughing, he carefully climbed the two steps up to the sill and lunged through the open window. The room was almost black with smoke. Ironically, thanks to the flames licking at the doorway, he was just able to make out the silhouette of a frail elderly woman on the floor under the window. Her eyes were shut, her chest rapidly rising and falling. Small cries came between raspy wheezing and shallow coughing.

No thought was necessary at that point. Screwing his eyes and mouth shut, he grabbed the women's torso and pulled her up into his chest. Then he moved backward toward the window and crouched down to grab the scaling ladder with his right hand, the woman tight to his body.

Her head met the windowsill with a smack, and she groaned.

"Oh, so sorry, me lady!" She didn't seem to be aware of the incident.

He slowly descended. First right leg, then left, wobbling all the way down as he struggled to avoid crushing her with his vicelike grip around her small torso. He arched his back just enough to allow her some respite from his hulking frame as he began down the main ladder, slowly. With each step, the woman's head hit the ladder rungs, and Gillian cringed, but he knew there was no other way to perform the rescue. "Sorry again, mum." *There's gotta be a better way for next time.* "Though I ain't sure I want a next time," he mumbled.

"Right behind you, Gillian!" came a shout from Brian Denny, who was a third of the way up the ladder. "A few more steps, then turn her outward a bit, and I'll grab her."

At that moment, a cry came from below. "Aye. We got water, sirs!"

Gillian was hit by a blast of water.

"Shut that fuckin thing off!" yelled Denny. "You're gonna turn us into ice men—and lady!"

Moments later, they reached the street, where a stretcher was waiting for the elderly woman, who was now breathing heavily and coughing while attempting to mutter something in what Gillian recognized as Gaelic. His grandmother had been fluent in the old language. As they placed her on the stretcher and covered her with linens, she smiled faintly, still with eyes closed, and uttered in English. "Bless you... Bless you all."

Denny followed the stretcher to the cart that would take her to Bellevue hospital. "Mum," he called out. "Do you know if there're any others in the building?"

She uttered something incoherent.

Gillian glanced back at the tenement. The fire was still limited to the third floor and a part of the second floor. The wind had died down considerably, and they could extinguish the blaze, perhaps save a building that should be torn down anyway.

"Hey, Spanky. Water her down!" Denny yelled.

"I'm running this here show, Denny! I make the orders. Okay, hose boys, let her have it," Spanky cried. "I guess two igloos is better than one," he muttered as he broke an icicle dangling from his beard. "Get a fire going for these wretched in the street. Then we gotta get 'em over to an almshouse. Denny, you figure that out," he commanded through his trumpet.

Denny pawned off the job of getting the carts for the newly homeless ones to Moses. The latter grudgingly mounted one of Company Three's horses and took off for the almshouse on Water Street.

Gillian leaned against the steam pump as the men were lighting a small fire in the street. It was after two a.m.; it appeared they weren't going home anytime soon. He received several pats on the back from the men of all three fire companies. He knew that his brave feat made him part of their family now. He would have friends here in America. He would make new business contacts. There would be more opportunity for him. But above all, he'd saved a person's life that night.

This is an experience like no other, he said to himself and smiled. But his smile faded quickly. *Why, Lord, why couldn't you let me save me own little ones?* He walked over to the street fire to warm his hands and feet.

"We're sure to be in the papers tomorrow, Gillian," Denny said as he slapped his back and handed him his flask. Gillian passed it on to another; he wasn't interested in drinking at two in the morning and surely didn't want to share spit with Brian Denny. He just wanted to go to sleep. He'd be seeing Denny again in just a few hours at the South Street docks.

"Well, gents, it was a team effort anyways" was all he could say.

Suddenly, Spanky came from around the corner. "Okay, the warehouses are out. Let's finish up and go home. We're sure lucky the wind died down like that. We might have been out here all night, like in 1835."

The men from Gillian's company started back to their horseless, hand-pulled, and hand-pumping engine.

"Hey, wait up, Gillian," called Spanky. "Good work there. They say you've only been in the department for a half year. Well, you certainly displayed the courage of a fine firefighter here tonight. The fire commissioner wanted me to tell you he was impressed. And that's a big deal, you know. Wasn't your fault the nitwits forgot about the scaling ladder."

"Well, I'd be lying if I said I wasn't scared enough to piss my pants. Probably would have froze solid anyway."

Spanky laughed. "We're just lucky this all worked out. These igloos should thaw out by the spring. And we didn't have to blow up any buildings after all. That's a real thorny issue since you have to make sure they don't have firemarks on them, and more of them do every year."

"Firemarks?"

"Buildings that are insured. We can't just go blowing up insured buildings without permission from the commissioner, who has to get permission from the insurance company, sometimes the mayor too."

"I'm afraid I'm not getting what you're saying."

"Too late to go into it. But Denny will tell you all about it. Now, my cart's over here. Let me get you home. You deserve it tonight. A hero like yourself shouldn't have to ride on the outside of a fire engine—or drag one through the streets like your White Flag Company from General Washington's day." Spanky spat a wad of chewing tobacco on an already yellowed mound of frozen slush, then patted his white Percheron. "A beauty, ain't she. I'll bet she didn't even flinch with all the commotion."

Within seconds Spanky was at the reins, Gillian huddled in the corner of the cart, attempting to shield himself from the wind. Two firemen stayed behind with the homeless tenants, awaiting Moses's return with cartmen from the almshouse.

Chapter Eighteen

"Denny said to sleep in an extra hour or two. I thought I'd take him up on it, me being the hero of the department as I'm told." A self-satisfied smile spread across Gillian's face as he sat down at the little table by the stove. "And think, just six months with the company."

"Well, you are a hero—our hero, too, my husband," Aileen said as she kissed the little bald spot at the top center of his crown. "They're not going to throw a parade for you, I hope."

"Oh no, me lady, but I'm sure it's going to be in the *Herald*'s afternoon paper," he boasted.

"Wow!" Patrick chimed in while gobbling up his corn cake and sausage.

Aileen brought the iron coffee kettle to the table and sat between her two men. Then she refilled Gillian's cup. "I'm keeping your meal warm on the stove until you're ready, Robert."

"Taking me time this morning, like I said. And where's our young lady?"

"She and Mary went to pick up the needlework for the day, mine too. You know, that Mr. Farragut is a real miserly creature, untrusting too. Now he wants all the ladies to bring him security for the shirts they take out of the factory each day. Just because one desperate soul ran away with his inventory. I ought to give him a piece of my mind. Neither my Mary nor me would ever steal his crummy shirts. Nor would the other Mary."

"Oh, my lord, another Mary. That's the third Mary, isn't it? I'm never going to keep record of this."

"Now, with the other Mary and another Mary, our Mary and Mary are going to a minstrel show on the Bowery tonight," Aileen teased.

Before Gillian had a chance to respond, Patrick gagged and spit out his milk on the table. "Yuck! What is this bloody stuff?"

"Hey, watch your tongue, young man!" Gillian chided.

"Oh, damn. It's probably that swill milk again," Aileen said with regret. She looked up at the peeling paint on the ceiling and closed her eyes. "Please forgive me, Lord. I should've known; the price was too good to be true at three cents a quart."

"What is swill milk?" Patrick inquired.

Gillian explained. "It's an imposter for milk. You see, they put a dairy with a bunch of cows right next to a distillery. Then they feed the cows just the mush from the distillery—that's the leftover waste after they make the whiskey. So the feed is free. But the cows get sick, and the milk is all watery. They put chalk in it to thicken it up, and they can sell it real cheap to all of us poor folk." Gillian's deadpan explanation adeptly hid his sarcasm.

"That's vile," said Aileen. "No more milk until we can afford farm-fresh. Just spill it out the window over the alleyway, Patrick."

"Why'd you tell him to do that?" Gillian asked.

"Because that's what everybody else in the building does with their unwanteds."

"No wonder the foul stench never goes away," he muttered.

"Don't you think you better get going to school, Patrick?" Aileen suggested.

"I suppose," he grunted as he popped the last piece of sausage in his mouth. He grabbed his books, one being the King James Bible, and fled to the stairwell.

"Ah! Blasphemy!" Gillian cried out. "Stupid free-school society."

"Alas, but it is really for the best, husband. His reading and writing are coming along well. Math, too. But he doesn't have the gift with numbers like Mary and me. A shame."

"I know, but the King James Bible?" Gillian shook his head and gave the table a knock.

"Robert, he has the catechism classes after school anyways. And besides, he's getting along fine with the boys—they think he's Protestant." Aileen treated herself to a brief laugh. "Don't know how he does it."

* * *

"Okay, me lady. I'll take my meal now," Gillian said as he heard a familiar clomp on the hallway stairs. "That must be Mary for certain."

The door flung open with the usual creak.

"Greetings, Father, Mother. It's a dreadfully frigid morning out there," Mary stated with unusual animation.

"Well, listen to you, my lass!" exclaimed Gillian. "So formal now. She speaks the queen's English, ain't that so, Aileen?"

"It's that class she's been taking in proper grammar at the Five Points mission, ain't it, my dear?"

"Mother, Father, there is no place reserved for 'ain't' in the native dictionary," Mary chided as she dropped the day's needlework projects on the daybed.

"Oh, I see," Aileen replied with the smile of a proud mother. "Now sit down for some breakfast. Soon as we get rid of your papa here, we'll get started with our work."

"Father, look here. I have obtained a copy of the *Herald*'s morning edition. I direct you to page five, lower right corner."

Gillian eagerly took the broadsheet and laid it on the table.

Engine Company Five—the Beleaguered "White Flag Company"— rescues an elderly lady from certain death using the latest firefighting apparatus, a 'scaling ladder,' to reach her third-floor window. Rookie fireman of six months is credited with making the rescue on Pearl Street. Cheers to him, and all the fine fire laddies of New York's Bravest!

"That's the whole thing?" blurted a crestfallen Gillian. "Where am I in this blurb? Not even my surname mentioned! Ah!" He threw the paper aside.

"It is a bit disappointing, Papa," Mary said.

"You're still a hero, no less, Robert." Aileen planted another kiss on his head. "Like you said yourself, you got honor now. More opportunity for you... and us."

"I suppose so, certainly don't diminish me none."

"I have to admit, it's far less than a parade. Maybe there'll be more in the evening paper, Robert." Aileen pouted sympathetically as she patted his hand. Then she brought his breakfast to the table, which he proceeded to gobble down as if he'd not eaten in weeks.

"Well, I should be off to the docks."

With that, Gillian gave the table a fisted knock, stood up, and grabbed his cap, scarf, and outer garment off the rack by the door. He'd booted up before breakfast, his usual routine, as the task of lacing was time-consuming and could make him late. He gave them both a peck on the cheek, opened the creaky door, and stooped down as he left. Unlike the cottage in Galway, there were no dents on the jamb from his head—yet.

"I bid you adieu, Father," said Mary, practicing her proper English.

Now in the hallway, he turned around and smiled at her affectionately, then at Aileen, who smiled back with an expression he hadn't seen in years: contentment.

Chapter Nineteen

"Steppin in the pudding"

Gillian was not halfway down the stairs when a burst of commotion came from the third-floor apartment, just above his flat. *Oh, Abby and Harry Dilway—again.*

"I know where ya been, ye two-timing drunk! You don't even know her name, I'll bet!" The shrill Irish brogue echoed off the narrow walls of the stairwell.

"Might not rightly know her name, but I wish I could forget your name, ya old hag!" Harry tossed back from the top of the stairs. Realizing that he should swiftly depart the premises after that, Harry Dilway clomped down, catching up to Gillian by the main door. An old pro to their spats at this point, Gillian reflexively stepped to the side, facilitating old Harry's escape.

"Top of the morn to ye, Harry!" he called out as the man fled. What Gillian didn't count on was the iron pan crashing down the stairwell, just missing his head. "Takin' it to a new level," he muttered as he headed out.

Proudly reflecting upon his heroic feat of the night earlier—and the reception he might receive at the firehouse this coming weekend—he stepped off a curb and into a pile of *corporate pudding*. That was what the natives so eloquently called the concoction of warm horse manure and slush, spiced with excrement from other animals, including the human variety, and sometimes topped off with slaughterhouse remains.

"Oh, bloody shit!" he cried out as one boot was sucked down almost to his ankle. In his fury, he kicked the muck with his other, almost losing his balance on the slick cobblestone beneath. Wanting to avoid landing on his back in a pile of the stuff, he stepped to the curb with his good foot and carefully withdrew the buried boot.

"Aye, you, sir. I can help with that!" a young boy called from across the street. Coincidentally, he was sitting in a chair with a small wooden table by his side.

"Ah, a bootblack," Gillian called back. "Very clever, me lad," he said, impressed with the boy's industriousness. "I suppose ye get a few of us daydreamers throughout the day, carelessly steppin' in the pudding?"

"It's an honest living. Now, let's see what we can do for ya, sir."

"If it were honest, you would be calling out to stop someone from steppin' into the shit in the first place, young man. Then he'd have a choice if he wanted to step in it or not."

"But then I wouldn't be here in the first place. Why would I be sittin' out in the cold in this fuckin' chair, just stoppin' people from steppin' in the pudding?"

I guess the lad has a point, Gillian considered as he dipped into his breeches to count his change. "You win. How much?"

"I do a spiffy job for six cents, but for you, sir, a five-cent piece for the same."

That's all Mary and Aileen get for one stitching job.

"Okay. I'm coming over."

His boots needed cleaning anyway, and in a short time, Gillian was back on his way to the loading docks. He carefully executed his route, knowing the sunny side of each block as he turned left, right, and left again, an expert now on which blocks were best shielded from the frigid wind blowing off the East River. Yes, indeed, he was privileged that morning, strolling in late for work with Denny's permission. His heroism was likely the talk of the morning.

The bright winter sun reflected off the choppy East River, creating a mirage of shimmering diamonds, a sight that never failed to mesmerize him. A packet ship from one of the Carolinas had just anchored, and he heard Denny barking commands from the deck. No gulls hovering over the boat, a good sign there were no dead slaves in the hold.

"Ah, our hero! Glad you could grace us with your presence today, Robert. Did you catch a good slumber?"

"Yes, indeed, and a hearty breakfast too."

"Good, because we have a full schedule. Already on to the third ship, ye know. I'll bet Mrs. Gillian and your brood were proud of you?"

"Aye, but the wife, I know she's all afeared. Never told her about the Fireman's Fund, should I get hurt. It would just make the woman worse."

"I seen her once. She seems like a worrying sort. No offense there, Gillian."

"None taken. She's had it real rough over the past few years, the Great Hunger, you know, and leaving our twins behind."

Gillian had never revealed the details of the story to Denny, and the man had never asked. Which was just as well. Denny knew of the desperation in Ireland. How could he not, with the stories of so many of the dockhands.

Gillian knew some bits and pieces of Denny's earlier life, but not much, as the man mostly kept quiet about such things. He did know of some sad and tragic events that he figured must have shaped Denny's questionable character. His family emigrated from Northern Ireland when he was a teen. His father became a well-respected cabinet maker but died tragically in a horsecar accident just five years later, leaving Brian to care for his grieving mother and two sisters. There'd be no time for apprenticing in a valuable trade. He had to find work immediately, leading him to a job as a dockhand. He worked his way up to foreman.

Gillian observed that Denny was an angry sort, especially when given to drink. He supposed the man was disenchanted with his lot in life. At forty-five, he lived alone, "just *outside* of the Five Points," he'd claim, "a higher-class neighborhood." He'd been almost married twice, but the women smothered him with love that quickly felt like iron chains. "Didn't like me still palling around with the whores," he would say with a laugh. So he broke off the engagements.

"That old Gaelic you saved, she's going to survive—a tough woman there."

"Oh, bless her then." Gillian was relieved that he hadn't risked his life for nothing. Then he immediately felt guilty. Certainly, it would have been a more agonizing death in the flat than in a hospital. "How'd you find out, Brian?"

"On account of my pal at the fruit market. His lady works at the hospital, wee hours of the morning. I got a bit of bad news, though. Turns out, there was an old man and two children in a back apartment on the second floor. They never had a chance without a fire escape. Engine Company Two found them early this morning when they were bringing down the place. Awful sight, Spanky said." Denny dropped his head, shaking it. "Encased in ice, all three, when the hose men turned that place into an igloo. Their eyes were bulging wide. I'm sure it'll be mentioned in the afternoon paper. Well, we better get moving here. There's probably going to be another packet in 'bout an hour."

Shocked now, Gillian was silent. He knew he was not to blame, but it disturbed him anyway. *Saving an old lady when there were two children in peril.* With the air out of his balloon, he wished there would be no mention of the event in the afternoon edition—or at least no mention of himself by name.

Gillian got his wish—partially. His name was not directly stated.

Engine Company Five—the Beleaguered "White Flag Company"—rescues an elderly lady from certain death using the latest firefighting apparatus, a 'scaling ladder,' to reach her third-floor window. Rookie fireman of six months is credited with making the rescue on Pearl Street. Regrettably, they failed to rescue two children and an elderly man on the second floor. Fire commissioner investigating whether something could have been done to prevent this tragedy.

CHAPTER TWENTY

February and March of 1849 felt like winter and spring had been bundled up into one season. One week of deep freeze, followed by one week of spring thaw, followed by one week of deep freeze. But Gillian had learned the hard lesson after their first winter and was better prepared with a supply of coal gathered through the summer months, although with limited storage, there was only so much one could squirrel away. And fresh coal was so expensive, Patrick and his friends had to venture into the well-to-do parts of the city to scavenge the partially burned and discarded scraps the maids in those fine houses tossed out. Aileen even excused him from attending church one particular Sunday morning in late March, as the pickings in the alleyways were better early in the morning.

"Black as coal himself, there he is!" Robert said as his son marched into the flat, burlap sack slung over his right shoulder.

"I dare say, Father, he doesn't quite resemble Santa Claus," Mary stated in her well-heeled English. The two chuckled while Patrick, exhausted, collapsed into the chair closest to the stove.

"I already have a hot wash basin made for you, Patrick," Aileen said lovingly. "After you clean yourself off, dump the water out the window into the airshaft. I don't want you going outside into the cold all wet like that."

"Okay, Mama." Grabbing the large washbasin and rag, he fled to Mary's room—the only one that offered some privacy.

"This coming week, we're buying soap, Robert, no excuse from you," Aileen commanded. "Gertrude told me there's a deal to be had at Flanagan's grocery, starting Monday."

After checking that Aileen was not looking in his direction, Gillian rolled his eyes for Mary's benefit. Then he stared at the burlap sack Patrick had left in the middle of the floor. It should carry them a few weeks, at least.

"Well, Mother, aren't you going to deliver the celebratory news to Father?"

Gillian looked up from the burlap heap. "Yes, my lady, pray tell?" he asked, poking fun at Mary's new English.

Appearing a bit excited herself, Aileen sat down at the table. "Well, I think it's good news anyways. Last Friday, I went with Mary to Mr. Farragut's factory to pick up the day's job, cause he told her Thursday he wanted to talk to both of us. We were all worried we were in trouble for something. Maybe we'd be getting fired. So I didn't want to tell you—" Patrick returned from dumping the dirty water down the air shaft. "Oh, Patrick, I have a shepherd's pie on the stove. Fetch a plate for yourself."

"The boy can figure that out, Aileen. Now tell me what happened."

"Oh, yeah, where was I?" She stalled, clearly taunting him a bit. "Well, he said the sewing machines are coming. He said he met with a Mr. Singer a few weeks ago and worked out a deal for his gadget. There's going to be a lot of changes." Aileen paused to catch her breath.

"You're killing me, my dear! Get to the part about you and Mary," Gillian barked.

"First he says we both do great work and we're dependable and trustworthy, so we don't have to leave him a deposit for what we take out each day. Then he says that all the needleworkers are going to be called into work at the factory on the sewing machines. I never saw him so excited."

"Get to the best part, Mama," Mary chimed in.

"He says he needs someone to manage all the ladies and handle the calculations for wage payments. And then he said I'm the one. He's seen my number skills and Mary's too. She's to help, like an assistant manager. I'd still be sewing, but I'll be paid more as a bonus for managing the others."

"And me too, Papa. I'd get a raise per sewing job, albeit small, for assisting. And I'll be working on waistcoats, not just shirts."

"What does *albeit* mean?" Gillian asked, now irritated with all this queen's tongue.

"Although," Mary and Patrick said at the same time, earning Patrick a look of shock from the rest of his family.

"So why couldn't you just say 'although'?"

"Why care? Isn't that great news, Robert?" asked Aileen.

"Certainly is, me ladies. Job well done."

"Why can't I earn a living?" complained Patrick.

"All in good time. You have to finish your schooling," Aileen said. "Besides, I thought you had your mind set on becoming a shipwright?"

"I do. I want to design the most brilliant sailing vessels, with intricate carvings throughout."

"'Intricate!' Good choice of words, Patrick. You're learning," Mary said.

"Then you must stay in school, boy, and get better with your numbers, not like your papa." Instinctively, Gillian pulled out his unreliable pocket watch. "Half past three already. I'm supposed to be at the station at four, a celebration for Old Man Voorhees. He's finally retiring—second time, I'm told. Denny's in line to take over as foreman."

"Even with his drinking? White Flag Engine Company's never going to live down their name, now," Aileen said with a light chuckle.

"We'll see." Robert sprung up to get his boots.

"I'm off to Mary's flat," Mary said. "We're meeting the other Mary on the Bowery. There was a street show this afternoon. The last act's a magician, supposedly an acquaintance of Mary's—the second Mary. So too-da-loo to all you three." And she was bundled and out the door well before Gillian finished tying his laces.

"What do they do on that Bowery?" Aileen asked.

"All sorts of things, Mama," Patrick said, saving Gillian from an obligation to respond.

"I don't know what that means, but somehow I don't think I like it," she said, glancing at Robert, who was making a speedy exit for the door.

"You know, like magic lantern shows, arcades, and such. The rest, I don't know."

* * *

She wasn't about to ask her fourteen-year-old son about the "other activities," but she was certain there was plenty of drinking, gambling, and whoring, at least in the back alleys. She'd heard about the Bowery B'Hoys and Gals and the nightly carousing. She just hoped they paid little interest in Catholic girls from the Five Points. Still, this was not a place to be frequented by her daughter, or the other Marys, she brooded. *There'll never be a chance to meet an honest gentleman there.*

CHAPTER TWENTY-ONE

Gillian trudged through the slush covering Bayard Street. At this point, he was quite adept at avoiding the pudding, as he knew where each horse passing through the cruddy street made its deposit each day.

He rounded the corner at Orange Street and began his journey toward Canal Street, quickly crossing to the opposite side of the block to avoid an unwelcome encounter.

"Mr. Gillian, sir, why do you turn away from me? I am clean and ready for you," came a voice from the crevice between two brick buildings. "Let Aggie take away your troubles."

The middling whore stepped out and glanced in both directions, making sure the street was deserted. She ran through the slush until she was directly in his path and then she pulled down her chemise, just enough to expose her left nipple.

"Please leave me be, Miss Agnes," Gillian responded, head down, attempting to negotiate a detour around the woman.

"For such a handsome man as yourself, just a fifty-cent piece would be fine."

He was well past her now. "I told you, that was a one-time thing, ma'am. Never again!"

"Oh, you disappoint me so, Mr. Gillian."

* * *

At four p.m., Gillian drew open the heavy wood door. A cloud of blue cigar smoke greeted him. And there was the familiar crowd.

"Good evening, brother Robert," Moses called from his seat by the keg.

"There's our hero!" cried Stretch. "You need a beer, my lord," he said as he grabbed a tin off the wall hook behind him. "So, what's your next act of heroism, Robert?"

"I've yet to figure that out." Impressed with his own quick wit, he followed up, "Maybe nothing until you boys reach my bar."

"Oh, Robert, don't say that," said Moses, in good spirits already. "You should have seen all the great rescues Stretch made... well, in his younger days."

"Aye, what's that supposed to mean! What have you done lately, Moses?

"I'm an expert now on blowing up buildings to keep the fires from spreading, ain't that so, Clancy?" he called out.

Clancy was sitting on the bench by the new steam engine, and smoking a cigar. "Oh sure, Moses, you're an expert on exploding things. Problem is, you're supposed to make them implode, not explode, like we were learned in the training. Problem with your exploding, you started another fire last year, remember that?"

"Shut your yapping now, Clancy," Moses hollered across the room. "Besides, it takes a lot of practice mixing the saltpeter to make the black powder and such."

Everyone knew the mixture was readymade in the barrels, but no one was interested in fighting—at least just yet. All eyes were on the huge caldron fired up over the makeshift pit in the center of the room. The chowder was starting to simmer, and the aroma of the sea was gradually overtaking the smell of cigar smoke. Katonah and his Lenape friend had gathered the oysters and clams off the Peck slip, and flounder was fresh catch that morning off the Verrazano Narrows.

A half-hour after Gillian arrived, the room was full. In fact, it was more than a full crowd, as old acquaintances came to honor the old Dutchman, second to their quest for free spirit and victual. Soon the rear doors were opened to allow more space and vent the cigar smoke, allowing passage into the dirt yard that was to be the future home of their stables for Engine Company Five's planned transportation. The new steam pump engines were getting bigger, heavier, and too cumbersome to run by hand. Horsepower was to do the work now, as per the fire commissioner's edict. "Any companies caught racing through the streets, carrying their apparatus, will be disbanded!" he'd commanded. But on this night, Hendrik Voorhees regaled the men with stories of yesteryear's firefighting, when leather buckets and scores of people organized like army ants were their only chance to quash a blaze.

Robert Gillian filled his tin bowl with the sea broth, took a thick slice of bread, and refilled his beer cup. Juggling it all, he made his way across the room to the bench Clancy had claimed. In Gillian's opinion, the man was a peculiar sort—friendly to most, sarcastic with some, and demonstrably opinionated on important matters. But at large gatherings, the man was suddenly shy, even to the extent of being a hermit. Tonight's occasion proved no different.

"Evening to ye, Clancy!" Gillian said, carefully sitting down on the bench so as to not spill his ambrosia. The chill in the room augmented the steam that was rising from each man's hot tin. The chowder cauldron resembled a witch's brew.

"Hey, there's my hero. Maybe you be the new boss one day, Robert," Clancy said as he lifted his bowl to his lips and slurped. A few drops landed on the bandana that was substituting for a necktie.

"Maybe... one day. At least that's a paying position, I hear. But Brian's got it now, anyways." Then Gillian felt a tad guilty. "I mean, we all do this for the honor and the other benefits, but a little extra wouldn't hurt if you know what I mean."

"Oh, I know what you mean. They're always talking about doing away with the volunteer department, saying we're too ornery, get away with too much. If they pay us, they control us. Now, I'm not one that needs controlling, but we all know who do." And then Clancy laughed, his narrow brown eyes quickly reduced to slits. The laugh induced a jarring cough, but he regained his composure after a swig from his tin. "Then again, I have to wonder, will they hire us coloreds if they have to pay?"

"Hmm. Never thought of that," Gillian said almost to himself, and then he changed the subject to something less uncomfortable. "You never did tell me how you got into this line of work or how any other situation came your way."

"Oh, so you got time for a long story then."

Gillian smiled, then slurped down some chowder, wondering what he'd gotten himself into.

"Well, I was born fifth of July, eighteen-o-three, yes, siree. Mama died the very next day. Both my mama and papa were owned by the Rutherford family, worked at their mansion on Church and Barclay Streets. Not a bad place for me to grow up. It's still there, but the missus made it into a rooming house since the master died. Any hoot, because I was born after slavery was done here, I only had to work for the Rutherfords until I was twenty-five. My daddy was the butler, so we lived pretty well. Slaver or not, those Rutherfords were a nice bunch, treated us well. I became their main coachman and did lots of odds and ends jobs for them. Then Daddy died when I was twenty, and I took over as the butler. They said I was free to go, even though I still owed them five years' time. Truth is, I didn't want to go. Where would I go anyways? I liked living in that big old mansion—oh look, here comes Denny."

Although interested in the story, Denny's arrival was not unwelcome. Gillian hadn't expected Clancy to start at his *very* beginning in this world.

"Ain't you boys coming out back to toast the departure of our dear Hendrik Voorhees? And to toast my coronation? Besides, we got sweetmeats out back, and Herbert's getting out his fiddle." He took a sloppy sip from his oversized personal jug, some of the beer splashing on the dirt floor.

"Count me in, Brian," Clancy responded. "We'll have to finish my story later."

"Sure, Clancy." Gillian went to refresh his beer tin though he was feeling quite spirited at that point.

Outside in the yard, the tall and slightly hunched-over Dutchman was toasting himself behind a wood podium.

"And so, my loyal fire laddies, it has been an honor—once again—to serve at the helm of our ship. These are exciting times for you brave men. You are blessed with the good fortune of having the most advanced fire apparatus that could ever be imagined at your service! The finest steam-power engines, a bountiful supply of water to feed those monster pumps, ladders that extend to the heavens—well, at least to third-floor windows." This last statement drew a chortle from the crowd. "But most important, my boys, you have the bond of fraternity to each other, the fireman's code, which mitigates the perils each and every one of you face when that bell sounds. So, I bid you adieu, my brothers, for the last time, as I am off to the Caribbean to spend my sunset years in balmy paradise, indulging in mangos and papayas all day through. And if—"

"Enough, ya old windbag!" came from the back of the crowd, likely one of Voorhees's old comrades from the bucket brigade days.

Accepting this message, Hendrik Voorhees jumped to the finish and held his jug high in the air for one final toast, unaware that his jug was tilted and the contents trickling onto his head. It didn't seem to be of concern to him as the crowd laughed. He concluded with the introduction of Brian Denny, the new foreman of White Flag Engine Company. Reception to this was mixed, but all drank up as Brian Denny stumbled to the podium to lay claim to his throne—and to the pewter-plated helmet and black speaking trumpet.

Gillian and Clancy filled a plate with sweetmeats and walked back to their bench by the new steam engine, a behemoth of a contraption with glossy red sides, yellow wheels with black spokes, and two bright yellow hitching leads for the soon-to-arrive horses, once the stable out back was completed.

"Say, Clancy, what did Voorhees do for a living wage?"

"He was a druggist with his brother. Had a place just off Broadway and Rector. He said they did okay after fighting off the competition."

"How did the man end up with so much money? An inheritance, maybe?"

"That's right, you don't know yet." Clancy laughed, his eyes again becoming slits, his composure only regained after a gravelly cough. "No one seems to know for sure, but some say it all changed for him when he met the Fire Marker Man. Or should I say, when he became a fire marker man. You see, I never met the real Fire Marker Man. Some say he's hideous, never comes out much, at least during daylight."

Gillian's face must have shown his confusion because Clancy chuckled again.

"Oh, you really don't know much. You see, a lot of the newer buildings have what's called insurance. That's where the owner pays a company a certain amount every year, and if something happens to the building—usually a fire—the company pays for the damages, or they pay to rebuild it. Most of these companies mark the buildings they's insuring with a sign; it's like advertising but not in the papers. You've probably seen them and paid no mind to it. The marker's a plaque, sometimes iron, sometimes copper. Those turn green over time. It's at the front entrance near the sign that tells you who built it and what year. Now a few of these companies pay money to the engine company that puts out the fire if they can save the building and stuff inside."

"Huh," was all Gillian said.

"That's right. I was told it's the old way the English companies would pay the firemen. And a few of the London companies who insure buildings in New York do it here too. So a fire marker man is the guy who goes around attaching the fire marks to the buildings when the company insures them. It's usually the insurance salesman at the company. But one company, Chelsea Surety, they's different. See, they use fancy brass markers only, real classy looking. It's a very old company based in London, and it's said they've been around since the Great London Fire in the 1600s. It's their adjuster who puts up the fire marks. He's the one I told you about, you know, the one who's hideous looking."

"Not to be rude, my friend, but I need my rest. Can you get to how Voorhees fits into this?"

"That's where I'm at now. You white folk are always rushing things." He gave Gillian a scolding look. "Anyways, where was I? Oh yeah. Voorhees, being the foreman of our company, became the fire marker man for

Chelsea Surety, since like I said, the adjuster there don't get out much himself because of the way he looks."

"So how'd Vorhees end up with so much money?"

"I still haven't figured that out. He probably gets money for putting up the fire marks, but it doesn't seem like it would be so much. Not to buy a classy mansion off Broadway, I don't think." Clancy leaned back against the wall behind them and began scratching the side of his head. It was now apparent to Gillian that the man was re-visiting the oddness of the mystery.

"He has a mansion, too?... Huh." Gillian brushed pastry crumbs off his breeches. Then he yawned and pulled out his watch. "Half past ten already!" he said with alarm. "I have to get home. I suppose Denny will be the new fire marker man, aye?"

"I reckon so."

"After that whole story, you can't even tell me how the man got rich?" Gillian laughed and gave Clancy a weak punch in the shoulder.

As Gillian stood to depart, the fire bell sounded.

"Oh, hell! It figures. Right when we're celebrating my coronation," bellowed a drunk Brian Denny. He stood and wobbled a bit. "Now, which way's the lantern pointing, laddies?"

"How should we know, Mr. Engineer? Clancy asked with more than a touch of sarcasm. "We's all here at the firehouse already."

Murmuring spread throughout the station as the men looked at each other. Then a chorus of laughter engulfed the firehouse.

Vorhees grabbed his old speaking trumpet out of Denny's hand. "Send out the scouts!" the retired man shouted. Shaking his head in disbelief, he handed the trumpet back to the new engineer. "For Christ's sake, I wonder when Denny would've gotten around to making that call," he mumbled as he walked away.

Something's gotta be done about this stupidity, Gillian thought.

CHAPTER TWENTY-TWO

By the time two scouts returned with the location of the fire, ten precious minutes had been lost. They loaded their gear onto the old hand pumper, as the new steam engine was useless without any horses to pull it.

The great wooden doors swung open, scraping loudly against the hardened slush. One man grabbed each of the four corner handles of the platform that anchored their pumping apparatus, and then they were off, running through the dark streets, lanterns swaying, in search of a fire. Thankfully someone had remembered to stay behind to extinguish the fire beneath the chowder cauldron.

This would not be a conflagration; the wind was calm and the night chilly but not frigid, as April was just days away. Smoke was billowing from a basement stairwell below a main-level butcher shop. Gillian was relieved that ladders wouldn't be necessary that night. "Probably a stove fire," he muttered to himself as commands began to bellow out from a speaker trumpet.

Spanky again, Engine Company Two. *Well, they were here first, I suppose. But there ain't no fire markers on a building like this anyways. So we won't lose out on any bounty.*

Moses and Clancy wandered over to Gillian's position on the opposite side of the street. The three knew they'd just be spectators, as twenty firefighters were clearly not necessary for whatever was going on in that building. Besides, their earlier merrymaking had exhausted them.

"I don't see no flames," Moses said, sounding disappointed.

Just then, they observed two hose men attempting to connect the heavy leather and hemp tubing to one of the new city hydrants. The result was a powerful spray, the likes of which none of them had ever seen. Even so, the connection point was faulty, and water was leaking onto the street.

The hose men made their way down the few steps to the basement entrance. The door was ajar, but the acrid smoke was so thick it was impossible to discern any details inside. Though there was no sign of flames, they began spraying water into the blinding smoke. They called out, but the powerfully loud spray made it questionable if they would hear a weak cry for help. Then the lead hose man stumbled over a body. The two immediately turned to exit the basement to retrieve a stretcher and backup support. Now, the smoke was starting to overwhelm them, so both bit down on their walrus mustaches to obtain some sort of filter.

"What do you got down there, boys?" Spanky called out as the men were climbing up to the street.

"What? We can't hear you! Use the trumpet!" called out the second hose man.

"Turn off your fuckin' hoses first! That would help," Spanky called back, then waited a few seconds for them to comply. "I said, what can you see down there!"

"Can't see much but one body," said the lead hose man, who began hacking up sputum as brown as chewing tobacco juice.

"Get the stretcher down here. We're going up to the first floor, see what's going on there. I have a hunch the fire's in the back," barked the second, who seemed much less affected by the smoke.

"Get the stretcher down there!" Brian Denny called into the speaker trumpet he'd just inherited from Hendrik Voorhees, but his command was unnecessary. Four men were already on their way into the basement.

Spanky flashed Denny a queer look, then turned back to his own trumpet.

"One of you men from my company, unhitch a horse and get up to Bellevue," he barked. "They should have responded with an ambulance by now. Lazy bastards, they are." The last bit was said softly, although he'd forgotten to put down the trumpet.

Gillian heard the energetic blast of the hoses once again. They'd located the origin of the fire, he surmised. At that moment, a bizarre sound came from the first-floor entrance.

"What the hell is that?" Moses asked.

"Squawking! That's what it is, squawking," Gillian exclaimed.

Suddenly the two hose men came running out the door, followed by a flock of chickens. The men were ducking as the frantic birds flew wildly in circles inches above their heads, wings flapping and feet drumming on the men's leather helmets.

"Look at them! Five, no six, I think," Gillian said in awe.

"No, I see three more!" Clancy shouted. "And look, those last two are burning up. Holy smokes!"

Now the firemen were swatting the panicked birds, white feathers dropping to the ground like oversized snowflakes. After a minute, the chickens began to settle down, squawking replaced by clucking as they jumped about in the cold street. All except for the two birds on fire, frantically flying in a tight circle. For a moment, Gillian thought this could ignite another fire. But then both fell to the ground, still burning.

As the two firemen went back into the butcher shop, Clancy ran for a bucket and collected water that was leaking out from the poor connection at the hydrant. He doused the poor birds, and another fireman threw a burlap tarp over them—more than they had done for the dead man.

The crowd of firemen and onlookers was suddenly silent.

Spanky said, "What the fuck are we supposed to do with all these chickens?"

"I say we bring these fried birds back to the firehouse for a snack," Denny said.

"It's out!" shouted the lead hose man as the two came back out to the street, both hacking and spitting tobacco-colored sputum. "This was arson of some sort. I didn't see no cause for fire."

"Arson covering up murder," said one of the men that removed the body from the basement. "Hard to kill yourself with a cleaver to the back, I reckon."

"Oh, bloody hell! Now we got to get the constable up here—and some cages for these chickens. No rest for me tonight," Spanky grumbled. "Hey, you, Gillian."

"Evening, Spanky," he said with bounce, although he was unsure what sort of encounter to expect.

Spanky, being almost a foot shorter than Gillian, reached up and put a hand on Gillian's shoulder. "Here, take a look at him. Pitiful, ain't it?" Spanky held the lantern over the face-down body. They both stared at the bloody mark between the man's shoulder blades. "I don't remember his name offhand, but I know he wasn't here that long, just like yourself. You see, this is what happens when you don't vote the right way, if you get what I mean. A real shame, ain't it. Good at his trade, I was told."

Gillian stood tall and let out a foggy breath into the cold night air. "I got it, Spanky," he said, hoping his voice didn't quiver.

"Well, you certainly deserved to sit this one out anyway, Gillian, after your heroic save on Pearl Street. You and the boys should head home. I got to wait here for the constable and the ambulance. Coroner's got to determine the cause of death, as if it ain't obvious." That toothy laugh again.

Feeling unnerved, Gillian walked back over to where Clancy and Moses were standing.

"What was that about?" asked Clancy.

"Oh, nothing important really," Gillian said, but his thoughts were still on the bloody mark in the man's back. "Goodnight, laddies."

As he headed away from the scene, Gillian tried to recollect what he had done wrong or didn't do that he should have done. He was certain that he voted at all three polling places, and for the right candidates. But then, he became confused. *Was that last year or the year earlier? No, both elections I did the right thing. This must've been just a friendly word of caution.*

It was after midnight now. He took a different route home, in case Aggie was still plying the streets. The cold quiet of midnight was a welcome treat. Sometimes the silence was interrupted by a shrieking drunk or the rhythmic moans of the night trade, but he still preferred this over the shouting street vendors and the general cacophony of the day.

In his heart and mind, he was still a farming man from rural Ireland. Nothing would ever change that. But to get ahead here, he knew that he would have to keep pushing that down. *I didn't abandon Ireland. She abandoned me,* he reminded himself. *But I did abandon my little babies, lying in the ground with not so much as a coffin they could have shared. Couldn't afford one stinkin' coffin. Never again.* He would have to make this all worthwhile, if not for Aileen and the older ones, at least to justify leaving the twins behind.

As he rounded the corner of Bayard and Orange Streets, he began thinking of his old friend, Daniel Mahoney, the Junior. *Seventeen years now since I last saw Mahoney. A fine man he was.* Gillian experienced true grief that spring day when Daniel told him that he would be leaving for America. But a twenty-two-year-old man does not cry or show emotion to a thirty-two-year-old man. *A good Irish Protestant landlord he was, always treated us Catholic tenants fairly, so we took care of him when he was destitute. Poor Daniel, humbled by his circumstances, but hardly bitter. I should look him up. Perhaps he lives here in New York.*

Aileen was fast asleep, as were Mary and Patrick. He threw a few more coals into the stove, defying his wife's careful budgeting of their reserves, and retired for the night.

CHAPTER TWENTY-THREE

July 1849

"Mrs. Gillian, can I see you in my office?" barked Farragut from the little glass cubicle he had built for himself along a periphery wall, dead center of the long expanse of the factory floor. This way, his eagle eyes could spot anybody or anything that could jeopardize the day's output.

"Coming, sir," Aileen shouted as the forever-growing group of ladies looked up from their stations, wearing worried expressions. Aileen was hoping this wouldn't be a closed-door meeting. Between the stifling heat and the little man's flatulence, she felt certain she couldn't stomach any bad news.

"Shut the door please, Mrs. Gillian."

"You can call me, Aileen, like ye did before, sir, like when we worked at home." Truth was, the man's addressing her by surname made her feel as though she was about to be reprimanded.

"Great news, Mrs. Gillian! We're expanding again. I just signed a few new agreements, including a very lucrative contract with Brooks Brothers. These Singer machines—a marvelous invention, don't you think?" he said with childlike thrill. "We will have to bring on more ladies, but that's going to take some time."

"Well, if you can offer a little more wage, sir, we have a better chance of getting the more skilled ones. That means less time training."

"I suppose you're right. But I have to invest in more machines right now, and we may need to acquire more space." There was silence as the man turned from his desk to look out the window of their Broad Street factory. After many seconds of contemplation, a loud fart broke the silence. "Okay, Mrs. Gillian, run the ad for two cents more an hour and don't tell the other ladies. We're going to have to increase the hourly quota until we get the new hires on."

Aileen wanted permission to leave at that point, or at least to open the door. "How can they do more in an hour, sir, without making mistakes that cost us more time?"

"That's your job to figure out, Mrs. Gillian, not mine. You and Mary need to solve that issue." Suddenly, he pulled out his timepiece. "My, I'm going to be late to the barber. Oh yes, speaking of Mary, have her come into my office first thing tomorrow morning. There are two women that need to be reprimanded, perhaps threatened with termination."

"Aye, sir... I will tell her," Aileen said, her head lowered.

"Thank you, Mrs. Gillian." She stood and moved toward the door. "Oh, one more thing. Mary and yourself are both performing to my expectations, possibly greater. Thank you for your service," he said with his best smile, which wasn't much.

"Very kind of you, sir."

She stepped out of Farragut's office, closed the door, and heard the man's explosive release of gas, followed by a grumble about his wife's cooking. All the women, including Mary, were staring at her, eyes begging for a story.

* * *

"I can't bear this heat no more," Aileen moaned as she collapsed on the daybed by the window.

Despite her full recovery from typhus, she had never regained the weight lost during the famine years and her illness. Her frame was always somewhat bony, even in better days, but now she looked frail beyond her thirty-nine years. The bounce in her auburn hair had long since vanished. But she did bring her bright blue eyes and remnants of childhood freckles to the New World. And it didn't go unnoticed by Gillian that she was moving swiftly again, going about her daily business just as she'd done before all the calamities befell them.

"I know, my dear, I know," he said as he sat down next to her and patted her lap.

"You never told me it was would be this stifling in America."

"I didn't know myself. Perhaps if we had a fire escape, we could make our beds out there in the evening. They're required now in new buildings."

She sat up. "Then we need to move to a new building. That's what we should do!"

"But our allowance for rent is five dollars a month. It will cost us far more, my dear."

"We can afford to do it," she said eagerly. "You've been raised at the docks. I have a respectable job at the factory, and it appears Mary will be adding to it for a while—unless she becomes attached."

They looked at each other and both rolled their eyes.

"And Patrick will be coming to work with me at the docks," Gillian said.

"Oh, no, he won't. He needs to finish his schooling if he wants to be a ship designer. We can easily afford eight dollars a month now for something better. Besides, I've been putting away money each month. I hide it so if we're robbed, they'll never find it." She leaned in to whisper. "Thirty dollars. But we should open an account at the Emigrant Savings."

"Eight dollars a month! Are you mad, woman?" he cried.

"Then it's settled," she said as if he'd said nothing. "I already have an appointment set for us with an agent on Saturday after we get back from the bathhouse. We can't live like this no more. Soon I'll be jumping in the stove to keep cool."

Gillian was about to protest when they heard the clumping of boots in the stairwell. Patrick burst through the door, slamming it behind him. A gust of hot wind followed, carrying the stench of boiled cabbage that had been lingering in the hallway.

"Oh my, what happened to you, lad?"

"Fisticuffs! That's what happened if you need to know!" he shouted, throwing the empty burlap sack on the floor. The blood between his nose and lip had thankfully already crusted over.

"Oh my," Aileen cried as she jumped off the daybed and rushed to his aid. "Look at that, Robert, what they did to our boy." She buried Patrick's head into her small bosom.

"Mama, stop! I'm too old for this." Patrick pulled away from her, leaving a few spots of blood on her frock.

Gillian laughed, and Aileen glared at him.

"Well, he is fourteen now, Aileen."

"Not one, but two black eyes!" she exclaimed. "Let me run down to the pump and wet a rag for you."

After finding a rag in the cupboard, she was out the door in a flash.

"So, what happened?" Gillian asked.

"I was on Canal Street looking at a sign in a druggist window. They're looking for a stock boy, so I thought I'd ask. Then I was gonna collect some coal bits and come home. But I ran into Scotty and some of the boys from school. They were heading over to that big alleyway off Orange to play stickball. We were there about fifteen minutes when another group came over. One comes up and pulls the stick out of my hand and throws it to his friends. He says, 'Aye, it's the little pope boy here to play, gents!' And they all start laughing."

"Did you put 'em up then, lad, like I learned ye?" Gillian asked. The two had made a few trips to the boxing gym over the past year, and Gillian was impressed that his son seemed to have a natural talent.

"No, I couldn't. He was much bigger than me, so he says he can't fight me, but he makes me fight another kid my size. Scotty tells me to run, they'll back me up, but I can't. I just froze, then got real mad. 'I've seen you going into that Catholic church,' the kid says to me. Then he said, 'My pop says you paddies are niggers in white face. Get it?' And his friends laugh, some of mine too. So, I made like I was going to walk away, then I turned around and charged his belly. Then another kid knocked me to the ground, and we're fighting like pigs in the dirt."

Patrick's lip started bleeding again just as Aileen came through the door with the wet rag.

"Here you go. Why don't you wash yourself off and lie down for a while?" she said.

"I want to hear the rest of the story," Gillian complained.

"You should see the other kid," Patrick said. "I knocked one of his teeth out. Then, some older guys start coming into the alley. I think Bowery boys. I thought they would break up the whole thing, but it turns out they're the older brothers of those fighting us. They start calling out, 'Kill those paddies!' So, we take off like lightning. Last thing I hear, one of the Bowery guys yells down the block. He says, 'Yer niggers in green face, not white face,' and I hear his friends laughing. And that's it. So, I got no coal today."

"That's quite a story," Gillian said, letting out a long sigh.

"Quite a story, aye," Aileen affirmed, with one hand over her mouth in horror. "We have to get him into a Catholic school, Robert."

"Of course, dear," he said to placate her, knowing that Patrick would be finishing school in a year at most. "Ah, that must be Mary now," Gillian said, recognizing her pitter-patter gait on the stairs.

"Greetings all," she said as she burst through the door, thankfully without any black eyes or bruises. "Oh! Pray tell, my brother. What horrid incident befell you?"

Robert and Aileen rolled their eyes. Before Patrick could start his tale at the beginning, Aileen cut him off.

"We need to talk, Mary," Aileen said while attempting to fan herself with an old book. "Mr. Farragut has a chore for you. You're supposed to visit him tomorrow morning in his office. I'd take something along to pinch your nose closed if I were you."

Mary dropped herself on the daybed between her parents. "Just dandy, I guess," she responded while grabbing the book from her mother so she could fan herself. "So you're going to leave it at that... not tell me what's it about?"

"Don't worry yourself, Mary. You did no wrong, but best he explain it to you. The good news is, we're growing again, more machines coming from Mr. Singer, too."

"Oh, so I shalln't miss any sleep tonight," she said with sarcasm.

"Oh, Lord, there she goes again. 'Shalln't'?" Patrick teased.

"It's a conjunction of shall not, my brother. A little less formal, for use in colloquial speech. Now, pray tell, what happened to you?"

Patrick attempted his story again, only to be sidelined once more by Aileen.

"We have a cold dinner tonight. I got a nice chunk of ice from Mr. McKinney, so it'll keep us till tomorrow, I'm sure." She smiled. "Oh, and your papa and I have some good news. We'll be moving to a better flat. Bigger, with a fire escape to sleep on, and maybe Croton water too."

Gillian looked over at Aileen, who had just stood up to prepare dinner. The nonchalant way she delivered the news exuded a confidence and command of the household that had been absent for several years now. And despite his trepidation, he knew they could easily afford eight dollars a month rent.

Patrick's bruised face was cheerful. "Maybe I get my own room then!"

"Maybe I won't have to walk through your room to get to my room anymore," Mary added.

"Well, one step at a time. We have to find a place first at the right price, ye know," cautioned Aileen.

Robert Gillian stood and walked over to the stove. Feeling confident that his wife knew what she was doing, he felt a surge of love for her, and pride that she was his mate. He bent over and kissed the top of her head.

"Whatever makes you happy, my sweet pea," he whispered in her ear.

CHAPTER TWENTY-FOUR

The Great Distillery Fire
February 15th, 1850

No great blizzard that winter, just a steady snow every other day, drifts compacting into glacial mounds that would not melt until deep into spring. But Aileen was determined to forge ahead with her plan, and so the family moved to a new tenement further up Orange Street. She'd found a spacious second-level flat almost twice the size of their first apartment. Even the stove was almost twice the size... which meant it consumed twice the precious fuel.

One Saturday afternoon, Gillian was sitting at their new dining table, fretting. Weeks ago, the docks had shut operations due to the ice situation in the harbor. The packet ships carrying the cotton from the Carolinas were not able to unload, so there'd been no work for him. All he could do was wait for a thaw, which was just now taking hold. Fortunately, business was brisk as ever at Farragut's factory, so making rent was not an issue. Aileen and Mary were benefiting from their new positions, and Mary received additional compensation for training the new hires on the Singer machines. Still, Gillian felt ashamed, sitting idle while they were working.

"Papa, I'm going sledding with Scotty and a few others," Patrick said. "Then we're stopping for a grog at Flannagan's."

Gillian was not in favor of Patrick drinking spirits, but at fifteen, he also knew the boy would not take a scolding well. Also, he'd just caught sight of something disturbing in the newspaper.

"Tell Mama I will be home for dinner," Patrick said as he dashed out the door.

"Really, hmm," Gillian replied again. What caught his attention now was a small article at the lower right-hand corner of page five—clearly not anticipated by the editors to be of great interest.

FIVE POINTS WHORE FOUND DEAD IN SNOW DRIFT

This unrelenting winter has regretfully claimed another victim. Five Points whore Agnes Butterfield was found frozen to death in the alleyway where she plied her trade on a regular basis. Coworkers at the brothel near Bayard and Mulberry Streets identified the body this morning. No evidence of foul play was found. It's assumed that she was prone to intoxication and did not realize that her scantily clothed body was at great risk of succumbing to the elements. A small funeral will be held at the chapel on Elizabeth and Bayard Streets Monday morning. Any person with knowledge of relatives of the whore is asked to contact the local constable's office.

"Poor, poor Aggie," Gillian said softly. He put his head down for a minute, then went over to the new picture window and watched the light snow settling on the slums below. It felt strangely odd that he'd had an intimate encounter with this woman, now dead. And the fact that she would offer her services to him so cheaply. Why didn't he just give her alms?

Then it occurred to him. How would he face Aileen? His remorse might give him away. *I'll have to make up another reason for my sadness. Ah! The story about the Dilways' fate. After all, I am very disturbed by that.*

The Dilways had planned to move into Gillian's old apartment once they had gone to the new flat, since the rent was more affordable. But Abby had discovered that Harry was not spending all his wage on booze and gambling, no—he was also supporting a prostitute he'd grown steady with. No more throwing pans down the stairs. She took care of him at the breakfast table with a bullet to the head, reserving one for herself.

Still, both vacant apartments rented quickly. "Aye, that's what I'll tell Aileen is troubling me. She'll believe that."

* * *

Half past eleven that evening, a fire bell sounded in another ward. Then another after that. Finally, his own ward. *This must be big*, he thought. By now, Gillian had the procedure down pat. Check the bell tower to see the direction the fire watchman was pointing the lantern. Then report to the firehouse.

With the slush already re-frozen, Gillian slipped twice on his way to White Flag Engine Company, his kneecap smarting from one of the episodes.

"I have a bad feeling tonight," said Stretch just as Gillian limped inside. Several of the men were tardy.

"There you go again!" scolded Moses. "What do ya smell, oil tar? I don't smell nothing, except you."

"No, not oil tar; I just have a bad feeling, maybe gunpowder or something. What do you think, Gillian?"

"I don't know. Just too cold to be standing around here. Is Denny here yet?"

"I doubt it, probably didn't even hear the bell," Clancy remarked. "And I'll wager on this, even with our horses and the new engine, Spanky'll still have his crew there before us." No one was interested in taking his challenge.

The horses whinnied in the new stables behind the engine house. Some of the men were getting them ready for the hitch-up.

"Hear that? They probably don't want no bother going out in the cold," Clancy added. "They's smarter than us, I guess." Moses hit him in the back of the head.

Brian Denny, only a bit unsteady, walked in wearing a new wool coat. Surprisingly, he was in good enough condition to be useful that night. "It's the distillery on the west side near the river, off Bond and James Streets.

It's bad, four alarms. I heard the bell tower all the way from the fifth ward. Then a rider caught up with me a few minutes ago. He was scouting for help from the companies in this direction. So, let's move out."

As if on cue, the front doors of the firehouse opened wide, and the men were greeted by two white Percherons already hitched up to the new steam engine.

* * *

Five other engine companies, two hose companies, and one hook and ladder company had already arrived by the time White Flag entered the narrow streets of the old west side. The full-square-block distillery was ablaze, but more disconcerting to Gillian were the flaming embers blowing over blocks of wood-frame tenements to the south and east. He knew the other men were aware of the implications, though nothing was said as they moved through the cold, dark night.

"Ah, there they are!" Spanky called out as the men from White Flag were unloading gear. "What a new engine, Denny. She's a sight for sure! I'll bet Tammany got the city to pay a pretty penny for her, aye. And those are quite the draft horses there, young, healthy." And then the hammer dropped. "Shame it's all wasted on you ignoramuses."

"Go fuck yourself, Spanky," Denny said in a tone colder than the temperature outside.

"I'm just pointing out a simple fact, Denny," Spanky said. "Here you are with all this fancy equipment, and you still show up late. Pitiful, really. And with the city overpaying so Tweed can line his pockets." He tapped the speaker on his chin as if considering. "Or maybe it's the drink. That explains it. You—"

Brian Denny cut him off with a fist to his already crooked nose. Spanky fell on his back, his helmet and trumpet rolling off into the street. Blood was oozing from his nostrils, dripping onto the collar of his woolen coat as he attempted to stand. Despite the traction from his boots, he fell again. Now, he was frantically squirming on his back.

Denny laughed. "Serves ye right, ye little worm. No. No. I think you're a little turtle stuck on his back. What da ya think, boys?

Despite the roaring fire, the relentless wind, and fire bells frantically chiming throughout the city, the row caught the attention of some of the men who were gathering around talking about placing bets.

Spanky sprung to his feet, enraged, and lunged at Denny, who was strangely still standing there. It was only at the last second that they saw the glint of a knife in his large hands. Denny was able to hold him off at the cost of a nick to his middle finger, but not before the blade tore a gash in his new coat.

Denny was moving quickly, undoing the lowest button of his coat, no doubt to access a much larger knife on his belt, when Gillian stepped forward and yelled for them to stop. "Cease, men! What the bloody hell are you doing!" They both looked at him—as did the others in the crowd. Gillian was surprised himself that he'd stepped in to stop a duel.

"Drop the arms, both of you!" commanded the foreman from Engine Company One, who was running this event. An elderly Dutchman, tall and slim, with a sharply pointed nose, stood between the two of them. "You filthy Irishmen! It's not enough that you're ruining this city. Now you're going to let it burn to the ground while you fight like pigs in the street. You're as bad as the heathens that used to own this town. You can bet the fire commissioner's going to know about this. Now let's get to work."

The enraged foreman then held his trumpet to his mustached mouth and began barking orders.

"We got three hydrants in the area. They shouldn't be frozen, and we're close enough to the river for a backup supply. I want eight engines to get down there on the double and start hooking up an elephant line, so you're set if we need you."

Within seconds, men started to argue as to which companies should head down to the river. The old Dutchman quickly stepped in and made the decision for them.

By that time, four hose men were releasing water at the flames, successfully reaching the second floor and the roof. But by now, the fire was too extensive, the source unknown. Their efforts were futile, and they were just wasting the precious resource.

Chapter Twenty-Four

"We have to get up there, somehow," Moses said. "Guide the hose men."

"Let this thing burn is what we should do," Clancy said, giving voice to what they all were thinking. The upper level had been burning for quite some time. A collapse could be imminent. "We need to let this burn and scout for other fires started by the flying embers. That makes the most sense."

"We can't just let it burn," stated Denny, who was standing right behind them. "It's a distillery, you idiots. There're eight giant stills on the ground floor that will explode, blow away everything around here, including us. Besides, the owners are here with the commissioner and the mayor."

This new information was greeted by a cold silence. Before Gillian could ask how Denny knew about the number of stills, their foreman was barking more orders.

"Clancy, Robert, you boys come with me. We're going in to the second floor. Get the equipment and some wet rags for your faces while I tell the lead foreman—Mr. King Dutchee himself—our plan."

"I see what he's up to," Clancy said as soon as Denny was out of earshot. "He's gonna pose as a hero, probably get us all killed, to redeem himself on account of the fight."

"I'm sure you're right, Clance," Gillian said somberly.

"Oh, I know I am. I don't want to go in there. I'd rather scout around for fires from those embers."

"I getcha, but..." Gillian couldn't continue. Clancy was right, but Denny was his boss on the docks, and Gillian was in good favor with him; he had received two raises since he started. He'd also caught the attention of the commissioner and mayor when he made that heroic rescue in the tenement building.

"But what?" Clancy asked.

"Listen here. Go to the engine and get that long probing stick and two hatchets. You stay behind me. I'll poke about, see how sturdy she is in front of us as we move. Besides, the first floor ain't on fire, so the second floor shouldn't collapse anyways. And if we can't find the source of the fire, we're out of there fast."

"Yeah, but if the roof's on fire. Could cave in on us."

"Just stay behind me, Clance. Now get that equipment."

Gillian worked on convincing himself that the risks were manageable while Clancy was off collecting the equipment.

"Come on, men. We got the go ahead. Now let's grab those two hoses while the pressure's still good," Denny said, eyeing the hose men spraying into the smoke billowing from the second floor. "Stupid ignoramuses, wasting water like that."

Somehow Gillian ended up as the lead scout, Clancy right behind, then Denny in the rear. A battering ram had already been employed to break through the heavy wooden front doors. Gillian was surprised to find the smoke less dense than expected. The wet rags tied around their mouths made talking difficult, but from their grunts, Gillian knew the others wanted to head up the stairs. Despite this urgency, he lingered, marveling at the huge fermenting vats and the copper stills mounted over coal-fired ovens. Behind these contraptions, he saw the expansive malting floor.

"Enough, Gillian!" Denny gave him a sharp tap on the shoulder.

Shaken out of his paralysis, he moved toward the smoky stairwell situated smack at the center of the building.

"Must be accounting offices up there," Denny said through his mask.

As they started up, the roar and crackle of the flames quickly grew loud. And then there was the familiar orange glow. They opened the nozzles of the heavy leather hoses, and one spray burst forth with fury, the sound so loud it almost drowned out the noise of the fire itself. But the second hose quickly sprang a leak. Water gushed out in all directions, cascading down the stairwell like a waterfall, drenching Clancy and Brian Denny. But Gillian moved forward.

Just as Gillian entered the cavernous offices of the B&J Whiskey Company, he heard a creaking sound coming from the wood floorboards. Still, he focused the spray on the raging flames that had engulfed at least half of the second level. A gaping hole in the tar-covered roof was, no doubt, the source of the embers they'd seen from the street. Despite the heat of the flames, Gillian felt a cold dry wind racing up the stairwell, providing unlimited energy to the fire and creating a shrieking whirlwind of blaze. It was clear that one hose was not sufficient, perhaps not even two.

As he attempted to move toward the nucleus of the inferno, the creaking sounds escalated to loud groans, like a dying ship about to succumb to the waves. He turned off the nozzle and frantically motioned to the others to reverse course.

They were two steps shy of the ground floor when the groaning sounds grew even louder, then abruptly ceased, as if the building was dedicating a last prayer to itself. Then came a thunderous explosion as a portion of the second floor collapsed onto the fermenting vats and copper stills. Flames instantly engulfed the cavernous room as the long rows of malting barley laid out behind the stills ignited. More alarming, three of the stills fell off their heating elements, spreading hot coals across the floor.

"Let's get out of here!" yelled Denny, who was carrying the heavy broken hose, the water now just dripping from the seam as the pressure had long since been depleted.

"What'd you say?" yelled Gillian through his soot-covered face cloth.

"I said I'll make sure our new steam engine is hooked up to the closest hydrant. That and a new hose, we'll have great pressure," Denny yelled to Clancy, who relayed the message to Gillian.

As Denny took off for the exit, it occurred to Gillian, *White Flag has the newest steam pump engine. Somebody should have thought of hooking our engine up earlier.* But then all thoughts fled as the raging flames near one of the overturned stills began to organize into a tornado of fire right before his eyes.

"You see that, Clance!" he yelled out.

"Yeah, those stills are gonna explode if we don't put this out soon!"

"Not the stills. Look at that!" Gillian watched in disbelief, his spray frozen, as the whirlwind of fire turned black and began morphing into the image of a man, or something like a man. "What in Jesus is that?" he muttered. "It's a bug, maybe."

Gillian, frozen in terror, was still directing his spray at the fire but in an unthinking manner. "It's a man and bug at once!" he yelled to Clancy who'd already moved back from the scene toward the entrance doors.

Maybe it's a fireman from another company. Surely, they're tackling this blaze from another front.

Just then, the creature of fire waved for Gillian to come forward, and strangely he felt a drive to comply, as if he was being oddly hypnotized, even though compliance would mean stepping into the flames—an agonizing death for certain. But he felt an urge, like a need to learn more. About what? He did not know.

Then the first of three explosions rocked the building.

"It's the booze, Gillian! We got to get out of here," Clancy yelled back toward the fire. "What are you looking at? Come on!"

Water pressure was diminishing, almost to a trickle, but Gillian just stood there, staring into the fire while holding his useless dripping hose.

Holding his bandana over his nose, Clancy ran over to where Gillian was standing. "Come on, Robert! This building's gotta burn! There's no being a hero here!"

Just as he completed the last sentence, another explosion came from an overturned still. The force dislodged wood rafters above, and they began crashing down, immediately feeding the blaze. As the men turned to run, a burning log came down upon Clancy, knocking him to the ground. The long torch lit his wool coat.

Panicking, Gillian dropped the trickling hose and tried to use his poking stick to pry the log off Clancy's chest, but his stick was no match for the log. So, he ran to the exit to call for help.

"I need men and blankets to smother a man out!" he cried.

Two men arrived in seconds, and a third went to retrieve the blankets. Now, the main blaze was approaching Clancy's feet, but he was unaware of this, as he was desperately fighting his own fire. He thrashed wildly at the flames that were devouring his coat. A primal response, but he was just fanning the fire.

Then the shrieks began, the excruciating pain of a man burning alive. Gillian had an urge to shriek himself, the pain so close, so real. He felt sure he was living his friend's trauma as the ordeal unfolded before his eyes. Later, he would feel guilty for having such a thought. How could he compare what he was experiencing to what Clancy was experiencing? And the man had come to save him, while he, "the supposed hero," just stood there imagining a specter in the flames and wasting their precious water supply.

"Get to the other end of the log!" one of the men shouted, snapping him into action.

Gillian and the two men used their feet to roll the burning log down past the man's torso, across his legs, and with one final push, the log bounced over his feet and rolled back into the fire. Then they smothered Clancy's torso with blankets, finally extinguishing the flames.

Clancy had lost consciousness, and Gillian was sure this was a blessing. But the stench of burnt skin and hair arising was a certain indication to Gillian that there would be much suffering ahead.

With the fire advancing, there was little time to obtain a stretcher, so the men lifted Clancy by the arms and legs and removed him from the building. A few seconds later came another explosion. The rest of the second floor had collapsed into the inferno.

Flames illuminated the entire block and made visible the cumulus clouds rolling across the windy sky. The normally steady horses began pacing and whinnying in a distressed chorus. But it would take more than this to make these Percherons run.

Even while coughing up brown sputum, Gillian noted that several engine companies had departed the scene. He knew they were scouting for more fires generated by the embers. Then it occurred to him, *What happened to Brian Denny, our fearless leader?*

Clancy was placed on a stretcher, then into a cart for transfer to Bellevue Hospital, all while the White Flag Company's new steam engine was pumping water on the fire. The goal now was to prevent the remaining stills from exploding. Sending some of the engines down to the great North River had been a miscalculation. The elephant train of pumpers and hoses was too long and complicated to maintain a steady flow, despite the unlimited source provided by the river.

The greatly diminished crowd was mostly quiet now. The old Dutch-man leading the show stood with the fire commissioner and mayor, all frowning and shaking their heads.

"I'm sorry, gentlemen," the Dutchman said solemnly. "We failed you on this one. We were a wee bit late in getting started, and ye know, with all the companies coming, we had some confusion. Then there was a squabble between two of the foremen. I can assure you there'll be a disciplining there. And that damn river was just a little too far away for a water source, just by a block or so—"

The commissioner interrupted him. "I still say a paid department would be better organized, fewer people tripping over each other."

The mayor said nothing, just nodded.

After a few seconds of silence, he spoke. "Gentlemen, I believe this was an insured building. See that melted plaque protruding from the rubble over there?" He pointed to a heap of smoldering remains, now partially covered with slush.

The fire commissioner, already gloved, carefully removed the brass marker. Though covered with soot, bits of brass still glistened, illuminated by the lantern. He rubbed the marker clean to make out the name.

Chelsea Surety Company, London and New York.

"I know of them," said the commissioner. "Been around since the Great London Fire. There's going to be a sorrowful adjuster looking at this tomorrow, I presume."

"Well, I'm tired and cold to the bone," said the mayor. "Let's call it a night, Mr. Commissioner."

"Yes indeed," the commissioner responded as he drew his watch from a side pocket of his cloak.

* * *

The fire wasn't extinguished until three a.m., and then exhaustion suddenly came upon him. For the first time all evening, his mind went to Aileen and the children. *Oh my, she must be nerve-wracked as to my whereabouts,* he thought. Now he was anxious to return home. And then his thoughts went to the missing Brian Denny. *Denny's probably in his night clothes already, skipping out on us like that.* Then there was Clancy. *I must visit him tomorrow. Or perhaps not.* He shuddered, as he had a vision of finding him in the morgue.

The men packed up their gear and prepared the engines and horses for departure.

Gillian, standing on the side board of their shiny new steam pumper, noticed poor Spanky sitting alone on the rear board of Company Two's machine, still bloodied from the brawl with Denny. Gillian assumed that the man had brooded there all evening. He wondered as to the reason for the animosity between the two. Maybe a long-standing disagreement? Perhaps one of them welched on a gambling bet? He knew, like himself, Denny wouldn't be standing on two feet if he had failed to vote properly.

As the healthy Percherons were about to draw the engine away, Gillian caught a glimpse of two men conversing in the street, a half block away. He recognized one voice as Brian Denny. *So the man didn't flee after all.* He didn't recognize the second man.

Both men were carrying lanterns, the unknown man's swinging sharply back and forth like a clock pendulum, thanks to his extreme agitation. As the sway of the lantern illuminated the stranger's face, Gillian was startled by the grotesque disfigurement. Even from a distance, he could see that there was something very wrong with this man.

He squinted his eyes, recording each glimpse as the sway of the lantern illuminated the figure for just split seconds at a time. Then his attention was caught by an odd sound coming from the opposite direction, the far side of the smoldering distillery. He thought it sounded like a cow bellowing in distress.

I must be tired, he thought as the engine driver cracked the whip.

With a jerk, they were moving back through the night, and the strange encounter he'd observed was now out of view. As cold as he was, Gillian enjoyed the chilling wind smacking his face. And as tired as he was, he felt very much alive, as he did after every major event. Only this time, it wasn't a gratifying feeling. There was nothing for him to feel proud of. Not only had they been ill-prepared to extinguish the blaze, he was responsible for dropping the ball, perhaps costing his friend's life—all for a reason he couldn't even explain.

Chapter Twenty-Five

The Next Day

"I don't like this no more, Robert. First, I never know if you'll even make it home. We all heard the fire bells ringing throughout the city. We knew this was a *conflagration*, as you men call it. Now, how are you going to get through the day on so little sleep?"

This was all rattled off as Aileen was preparing tea and breakfast for the two of them in the room that could be described as "almost a kitchen" in their new apartment.

"Like I said, I'm goin' in later this morning. So is Denny. With the ice breaking up, they'll be bringing in packets by midday. A short day, better than no day anyways." He wanted to tell her about Clancy and his own strange encounter in the fire. But he held back. She'd immediately think that it could have been him under the flaming log, and she'd want him to quit the department. He didn't know what she would make of his vision in the flames. And he didn't expect the paper to report of a Negro burned in the fire. So, he'd make little mention of it—unless Clancy died. "Oh, I hear pitter-patter. Must be Mary."

"Aye, she went to fetch the paper. Thought you'd want to read about the fire." Aileen stopped as Mary burst into the room.

"Ah, there's my Mary Sunshine," he said, although from his daughter's expression, this was hardly an accurate description for the day.

"I ain't feeling no sunshine today, Papa."

"Where's your finer English?"

"I left it in the gutter."

"What's the matter, sweetheart?"

"Nothing, I just woke up this way. Well, here's your paper, Father." She held it high and dropped it on the table, resulting in a loud thud, then she stripped off her coat and threw it on a chair.

"Okay, dear," he said cautiously while glancing at Aileen, who shared his worry. He spread the *Herald* open on the table. "Here it is, page two, not bad. Well, it was a big one." Aileen joined him in reading the article.

WORST FEARS AVERTED

The night of February 15th, 1850, will not be one for the history books! Blaze at the B & J Distillery fails to ignite city despite the ferocious winds off the great North River. Was it the Lord's blessing, or the might of no less than seven fire companies that confronted the challenge? Even White Flag Engine Company showed up for the occasion in an almost timely manner with their state-of-the-art steam pumper and the finest horses the fire department has ever declared ownership of. Sadly, too many paddy laddies at the party— and the usual fisticuffs—resulted in much confusion and mayhem, possibly hampering the response. Further, "that damn river being just a tad too far away," worked against New York's bravest. The square-block distillery was diminished to rubble, and the owners won't reveal the location of the precious casks that could be of great value someday.

On a brighter note, mothers and children should delight in the fact that the attached dairy was also destroyed by the blaze, where up to thirty sickly cows were roasted alive. No more swill milk, boys and girls!

"Well, they got this one right... mostly," said Gillian, relieved that there was no mention of injuries to firemen. "We were lucky. Only one tenement caught fire from the embers, and scouts in the neighborhood spotted it fast and extinguished it. Funny thing, I did hear a cow complaining as we were leaving the scene. Oh, and Clancy got a bit injured. I'll check on him tomorrow."

"Well, there're still dairies in the city peddling that swill milk to poor mothers. Something's got to be done about that. Maybe a fire wouldn't be so bad," Aileen stated angrily as she went into the next room to get ready for work. "You coming with me today, Mary?" she called from the changing room.

"Yes," Mary said glumly and then sighed. She kicked the open chair next to her as she stood to change into her uniform. "We shalln't encourage a scolding from dear Mr. Farragut," she said, then contorted her face.

Shortly after, they were gone, and Gillian was alone. He began reflecting on last night's experience, not the fire, but the vision in the fire, the vision or specter apparently only he could see. *I must dismiss this ridiculousness. I could have got Clancy killed—and myself.*

Then he heard the main entrance to the building open, followed by Patrick's familiar thumping gait. He immediately felt alarmed since this was an odd hour for the boy to be returning home from school. When the door burst open to reveal a bloody-faced version of his son—again—he jumped up to get the wetted rags Aileen kept by the stove.

"Sit down, lad," he said.

As Patrick seated himself at the table, Robert began patting the wounds on the boy's face. Most of the blood had come from his nose and was now rapidly drying.

"I think your nose is bent, maybe even broken," he said, towering over the boy. "Black eye too, just one of them this time."

Robert shook his head in distress. Patrick said nothing, just stared at the wall, fiercely struggling to hold back tears.

"I suppose you better tell me what happened, lad," he said, though he could guess the story.

Patrick took a few deep breaths, his nostrils flaring, allowing a bloody bubble of mucus to pool just below the right one, then drip down to his lip. Gillian caught it in the rag.

"I'm gonna kill them tomorrow! That's what I'm gonna do!" he blurted. "It's all Mama's fault. She made me bring the Catholic book to school."

"Well, son, she thought it important that you had your prayers with you... Then Gillian stopped. He knew Patrick would not go for this line of reasoning, especially since he didn't either. How could he expect the boy to accept such a trade-off? Now the woman would see the result of her folly. *After all, Gillian could be a Protestant name; there was no reason for the others to know.* But he knew this wasn't true either; somehow, they always did. "Well, you're just gonna have to learn to fight better than those Bowery kids. We'll go back to the gym—"

"I started the fight, Papa! Scotty and I were on line when these two boys in the senior class showed up right behind us. Same ones I fought with when we were playing in the alley, you know, the ones whose brothers own the Bowery or act like it's their territory."

"Yes, I do remember," Gillian said as he sat down. "So then what?"

"So then one of them, John, says to me, 'You're still here, little pope? I thought you'd be getting beaten by the nuns now. I guess I didn't finish you good last time around.' Then I started backing away. But strange thing, Scotty still stands there minding his own business."

"That tis strange. Hmm. Then what?"

"John grabs the book out of my hand and throws it into the street. Then he says, 'You like blackface shows, little Paddy?' I say, 'I don't know, never been.' Then he says, 'I like whiteface shows, little Paddy. That's when coloreds paint their face white and act like Irishmen. Or maybe, that's what a paddy is, yeah, like my daddy says. Just a colored painted white.' Then he and the other one started to laugh, and Scotty's all quiet and has his face down."

Patrick stopped for a few breaths. Gillian, feeling that the air was getting close in the room, went to draw open the front window. A fresh late-winter breeze instantly filled the room.

"Then the door to the school started to open and the two of them cut to the front," Patrick continued. "That's what they always do. So I made like a battering ram and slammed that guy John right in the middle of his back with my head. He lost his balance and fell. His friend started laughing, so John gets up real fast and comes at me hard. Gives it to me in the nose, then shows me his knife while I'm bleeding on the ground."

Chapter Twenty-Five

Gillian shuddered at the thought of this brute killing his son.

"Then he says to me, 'I've seen you with your sister on the street; she's sure an ugly one.' I was gonna lunge at him again, but there was too much blood, and they were all going inside. Scotty gave me a handkerchief and helped me up."

"I can't understand why Scotty never has to deal with this. He's one of us, ain't he?"

"Aye, Papa. I wondered that too, so I asked him before he went inside. He said his papa lets John's father take fruit from his stand. He just turns the other way like he don't see it, but they sort of have a deal. John and his friends ain't allowed to row with Scotty."

"Good thing your mama doesn't see you this way. The Free School Society does nothing to stop this. I wish we could've sent you to Catholic school, lad. Maybe when things get better for us, we can... "

He paused and their eyes locked. Both knew this wouldn't happen in time.

"We gotta get you to the clinic to see about your nose, but I have to head down to the docks in a bit. I'll try and get off early. Meanwhile, take some rags down to the pump and clean yourself off."

Gillian hated to leave the boy alone, but he wanted to hear Denny's excuse regarding his whereabouts last night and see if he could learn anything about that strange figure he was arguing with. Still, it would've been better if he could take the full day off, tend to his son's nose and pay a visit to Clancy. He adjusted his cap and walked out the door. Once in the hallway, he briefly took note of the freshness of the new building, the wider stairwell with a banister, cleaner privies out back. *We Gillians are living in the finest tenement in the Five Points.* Then he stepped outside and was almost trampled by a gang of squealing pigs that suddenly crossed his path.

* * *

Gillian was glad to see that the warmer sunny day was eating away at the slushy mess. Now, late morning, the streets were far less tumultuous, and the absence of cacophony made it easier for him to think. Although he knew a shortcut to work, he decided to take the longer route down East Broadway. He enjoyed treating the hot corn girls along the way to a few pennies. Aileen didn't seem to notice the coins missing from the jar, which surprised him considering her keen attention to all matters of money.

There used to be three little blond ones, their territories carefully agreed upon, and he would give each a penny and take no corn. Now they were down to two. One girl became orphaned when her mother fell down a stairwell in an inebriated state and broke her neck. The girl's aunt sent her off to live on a farm in the Midwest.

"Good morning, Mr. Gillian, sir," he heard.

"Good morning, my little one," he called out, never knowing which one he was speaking to. In fact, in his earlier encounters, he'd presumed the girls to be triplets. "A fine day, a bit warmer and brighter."

He stopped in front of her and considered that something seemed different. *The girl has had a bath, I believe.* Her plump rosy cheeks beamed in the bright sunshine, and the curls in her golden hair, freed at last from grime, bounced in the breeze. Even her dress was clean, he noted.

"An ear of corn, Mr. Gillian, sir?" she asked in her usual sweet voice, knowing his reply would be "Not today, my lass," and he would smile at her, then tip his cap before dropping a penny in her tin. He followed the same routine that day but observed that the girl had but one cob left in her pot and quite a sum in her tin. Business must be brisk, he assumed. Still, he felt something was amiss.

"Thank you, Mr. Gillian, and may the Lord bless you for your kind generosity!" she recited.

He tipped his hat again and began to move along when he saw that his barber—located in a storefront just beyond the corn girl—was open for business already. Again, he realized that made sense since it was half past ten. *So what're a few more minutes. Let me drop in for a quick chat.*

He walked up the two steps to the entrance. There was the familiar jingle as he opened the door, and he was pleasantly greeted by a gust of warm, humid air; Simon was just returning from the back room with a vat of boiling hot towels. Seeing him without a wig for the first time,

Gillian was shocked at the extent of the man's baldness. Tall and brawny, Simon had been a semi-professional boxer in his younger days. Now at fifty years, he'd acquired some thickness around the middle, evident by the slightly tugging brass buttons on his waistcoat.

"Ah, my dear friend Robert! What brings you here at this hour of the day?" the man asked as he placed the hot vat on a round marble table in the center of the room.

"I was passing through late today. With the warmer weather, the docks are back in business. Expecting a few packet ships this afternoon."

"Getting a little gray there, I see, Robert. Those hairs will grow wild soon. I should expect to see ye here more often then?"

Although posed as a question, it seemed more of a command. Then again, he did owe Simon a bit. A month after he started at the docks, he became plagued by a rotting tooth. Too much of a coward to pull it himself, he stopped in at Simon's shop for the first time. As he was short of funds, Simon pulled the tooth free of charge and gave him a haircut at half price once they quelled the bleeding.

"I suppose you're right, Simon. Say, that's new, ain't it?" Gillian asked as he pointed to a bird cage near the window.

"Aye, ever seen an African parrot?" Simon whistled, and the bird came to attention.

"Can't say I have. Nice-looking creature. Can you train 'em?"

"Not this one, I don't think. I call him Peety. Should be able to talk, but he don't. Not sure why. Maybe he's dimwitted."

"Maybe he's got nothing to say to you," Gillian quipped.

"Like me wife." The two of them chuckled. "I let him run around the shop for exercise just before I close up. I'd like to train him to pick up hair."

"Well, I need to get to the docks before the boats start coming in. Looks like we're down to one hot corn girl now, unless the other's just sick."

"Oh, you didn't hear? One of them was killed last week, run over by a trolley. She was helping her brother break up ice on a pathway for pedestrians. You know these children shouldn't be working so close to the damn road." Simon paused, then sighed. "They say she slipped off a pile of frozen muck and fell in the street just as a trolley was approaching. I heard it was a dreadful sight. So, this little one's out there doing a great business—for now." Simon shrugged.

Gillian felt heavy with sadness, and then a shot of rage. "A lass that age should be in school! There's plenty of time for work when they're older!" he barked, unthinkingly, as if he was scolding Simon for the tragedy. They both lowered their heads.

"Aye, I agree," the barber replied solemnly, seeming to understand Gillian's outburst. They passed some seconds in silence.

"Well, best to you, Simon," Gillian said as he stepped outside the door.

"Thanks for calling on me, Robert."

Gillian forced a sad smile, tipped his hat at the barber, and walked back down to the street. At that moment, he'd decided to avoid this route for a while. It was now a street of sorrow for him.

He could smell the sea in the stiff east wind as he approached the South Street docks. He breathed a sigh of relief—lately, particularly during the warm weather months, the stench of sewage would sometimes settle in, making his work less than bearable. The common council had investigated the problem and determined that the night soil crews were shortcutting at their job. The cartmen were supposed to deliver their loads of crap to the dock near 30th Street, where it was hauled across the river for transport to the farms of Long Island. But, as their work was performed in the middle of the night, they'd developed the sneaky habit of dumping their loads off the docks along South Street and other slips further south.

Gillian now recalled a bit from a local paper, addressing the extreme dismay of the new arrivals.

Welcome to America, dear paddies! We know you're weary and sick from your journey, so we want to apologize for the stench that may greet you here. Rest assured, it will pass as the wind changes direction. And if you're seeking employment as a night soil worker, please disregard the N.I.N.A. warning that may still appear in the job advertisement. An exception has been made for you. Our apologies also extend to runaway slaves and all greeted by the foul odor.

He arrived at the designated dock while reflecting upon his past naivety regarding all things American. How much wiser he felt with less than four years in the new world. In fact, the slip that greeted their ship, the *Nina*, was in his line of view almost every day. He felt embarrassed to admit to himself that when he saw the sign posted throughout the port—the sign that said N.I.N.A, or "No Irish Need Apply"—he'd thought it related to their ship or perhaps other ships with the identical name. His journey to work each day also took him right by the little storefront where he was swindled exchanging his English currency. Sometimes, he felt the urge to go in there and pop the man right in the face. He was not sure why he tormented himself this way when just a slight detour in his route could avoid the memory.

Predictably, even though it was eleven thirty, Denny was nowhere to be seen. Gillian figured the first packet could arrive shortly, especially considering the backlog of boats due to the recent ice closures. Luckily, Sean and Elmo were there, gobbling down their lunch as they waited.

Sure enough, at noon, the first packet tied up at the dock. Sean and Elmo quickly jumped on board to survey the cargo. But within seconds, the two climbed back onto the docks, wearing looks of disgust.

"Uh! I can't do this!" Sean cried out.

"It's bloody revolting! I'm gonna retch if I have to stay down there," Elmo added.

Gillian could guess the situation. The first ships in after the closure would have been idling somewhere—perhaps for a month or more—between the Carolinas and New York. He couldn't begin to guess how many corpses lay below. Dehydration, starvation, disease, all were possibilities.

Just then, the captain of the packet climbed onto the dock and patted Gillian on the shoulder, his eyes bloodshot. "Sorry, fellows," he said, then lowered his head.

He'd prefer to believe that the captain felt some shame about the deaths, not just embarrassment regarding his arrival in a drunken condition. Nevertheless, after the man fled, the three dockhands were left standing there.

"We're not getting paid enough to deal with this mess!" Sean barked. "No, siree."

"I've never seen anything this bad," Elmo added. "And ain't it strange that Denny never showed up? He knew what to expect with the first ships waiting out there for months. He's all yellow, that's what he is!"

"Shhh. Keep it down, Elmo," Gillian cautioned as he saw other dockhands looking their way. "Remember, he's our boss, and we don't know for sure where he is. We had a long night with the distillery fire." Gillian felt proud that he was managing the situation, even though he knew his excuses for Brian Denny were horseshit. "I'm going over to the dockmaster's office. They'll order a cart for the bodies and provide us with more help. The job description says, 'all cargo,' nothing about it being alive, or dead, or whatever." He gave them a sheepish smile.

"Okay," Sean said. "Just come back with some wet rags and ties like you use in the fires. Maybe that'll help with the stench."

"Yeah, and a bottle of whiskey," Elmo added.

While walking to the dockmaster's office, Gillian began to plan his visit to Clancy at Bellevue Hospital. He had no idea of his friend's condition, and guilt haunted him throughout the day. But first, he had to tend to Patrick's nose. *Aileen's not going to be happy with another crooked nose in the family. I wonder if Simon can take care of it if we're in a jam. Nah.* He shivered at the notion of bringing his son to the barber for a nose fixing.

CHAPTER TWENTY-SIX

BELLEVUE HOSPITAL
Saturday after the blaze

The trip to Bellevue Hospital would take one hour on the bright but blustery morning. During his journey, he reflected upon the ordeal of Patrick's nose and the satisfactory outcome the evening before, which pleased Aileen and consequently was a great relief for him. Doctor McCleary, the surgeon at the clinic, told them, "Your boy's very lucky, indeed. The nose is broken, no doubt, but the location of the break makes this easy for us to snap it in place. A little pain for a few weeks, then he's as good as new."

"So his nose won't be crooked?" Aileen asked, still needing reassurance that all would be well.

"Well, maybe just a smidgeon, Mrs. Gillian. No one should notice. If you're not happy, we could always re-break it and work on it some more."

"Oh, no chance of that!" Patrick cried out, and he cupped his hand over his damaged proboscis.

They went home.

Ten blocks walking through the slush and two omnibuses later, Gillian arrived at the wrought-iron entrance gates at ten in the morning, exactly as he'd planned. The immense, ornately carved entrance doors to the hospital conveyed a feeling that he was about to enter a medieval English castle.

As he stepped inside to find a cavernous lobby, he realized his assessment wasn't far off. The gaslit wall sconces provided woefully inadequate lighting for a room of such proportions. Warmth was provided by two identical mammoth fireplaces, one on each side of the massive room. The stone floor was covered with immense area rugs, elegant at one time but now showing their age. A motley assortment of sofas and chairs were also tired-looking, and reading materials of all kinds were randomly scattered about on once majestic baroque tables, scratched and scuffed now, but still with good life remaining. The display hinted at the many hours whiled away here by visitors awaiting news of their loved ones.

While crossing to the information desk, Gillian became aware of the sea of heads glancing above their newspapers. He rang the bell on the counter, and within a few seconds, a young woman with blond, bonneted hair and wearing a periwinkle uniform arrived on the spot with a subdued smile.

"May I assist you, sir?"

"Aye, I'm looking for the burn ward. Clancy Carver's the patient. I'm a friend of the man."

"Follow me, sir," she said, maintaining her calm disposition.

Within seconds, she was unlocking a door that provided access to the bowels of the building. She led the way through the first ward, which housed at least thirty children in various splints and casts. Just as they were reaching a set of double doors separating this ward from the next, Gillian's attention was caught by a boy of about ten years of age, who lay there staring at the ceiling with a vacant expression. His head was unusually large, incongruous with his small torso, and covered with red blotches. A line of stitching ran just below the hairline. The escort must have observed Gillian's horrified expression because she explained.

"His father beat him about the head with a walking stick," the escort said with no emotion.

"Ghastly," Gillian responded. *How could anyone do that to their child?*

Her gait picked up as they sailed through the next ward. From the incessant coughing and the escort's obvious haste, Gillian could only imagine what sort of diseases might attempt to ensnare him. Then a quick right after the next set of doors brought them to the burn ward, where a distinct stench overwhelmed him within seconds. It seemed to have little outward effect on the young escort.

For obvious reasons, this ward was relegated to the deepest level of the great institution. A humming beehive of moans and suffering souls. But despite the patients' chorus of distress, they were all staring at him.

"Don't fear, sir, they're not in great pain. It's the morphine, a wonder of modern medicine!" the escort exclaimed. "Now, which one is your Clancy?"

Gillian walked back and forth as he carefully took inventory of each disfigured patient. "He's not here, Miss. There's no Clancy here."

"Are you sure?" the escort responded. "Sometimes disfigurement makes it hard to recognize—"

"No. I am certain. He's not here."

"Well, perhaps you can describe him to me?"

"He's a short fellow. He has small narrow brown eyes and a wide nose. He wears a bandana... usually. He's a man of color, and he should have a big burn wound across his chest from a burning log—"

"You said a man of color, sir?"

"Aye."

"There's your answer, sir. Negros have their own ward up on the third floor. Let me take you back to the stairwell. You can go the rest of the trip yourself."

She quickly reversed their journey. Gillian struggled to keep up with her as her dress swished loudly across the floorboards.

In a short time, they were back in the cavernous lobby, where the escort directed him to the stairwell. He was beginning to perspire, and this would only be exacerbated by the long steep climb to the third level. It didn't help that the air grew increasingly warmer as he made the ascent.

His heart was pounding when he finally arrived on the third floor, but he was unsure if this was due to the climb, the anticipation of seeing Clancy in a state unknown, or perhaps both. He decided to visit the water closet, still a novelty to him. An ingenious contraption, he thought. Just pull a chain and gravity would do the rest.

With no other excuses for delay, Gillian swung open the set of double doors to the ward. He was greeted by the sound of rats scurrying to safety, and the grunts of men in different stages of delirium, now startled by his intrusion. All Negro men, he noted. But it wasn't a burn unit or tuberculosis unit or ward for accident victims. In fact, the only defining quality of the ward was that its occupants were all colored.

As he began to scan the room for Clancy, a patient yelled out to him, "Hey, you! Are you a doctor? I need help, sir."

Gillian was taken aback by the idea that anyone would mistake him for a physician almost as much as by the man's gruesome appearance. He didn't want to move closer, certain that the smell from those wounds would be nasty. "I'm sorry. I'm not. I can try and find a surgeon... or nurse if that would help? Surely there must be one on this floor?" he said, even as his gut told him there was not.

The man didn't respond; he was apparently asleep again.

"Psst!" came in a loud whisper from the last bed. "That you, Robert?"

Gillian quickly moved to the rear of the ward, a smile breaking across his face. "Clance! That you?" he said in an equally loud whisper.

"Sure is, my hero," came back, followed by Clancy's usual cough.

As Gillian approached the cot, he spotted the familiar grin, but one that happened slowly, evidencing much effort. His battered cheekbones pushed up against his eye sockets.

"How are you faring, my friend?" Gillian asked as he clasped Clancy's hand between both of his own. He was grateful that the wound across Clancy's chest was well hidden, although there were some minor burns here and there around the man's face and arms. As well as the disturbing odor of singed hair.

"Oh, you know me, Gillian. I'll get by. The doc said I ain't gonna die, but I got to change the dressings a lot, so I don't get infection. He said I should keep a bottle of whiskey on hand, a little to drink, a little for the wounds. I told him I ain't wasting no whiskey spilling it on myself only to have it burn like a bitch. He said, 'Well, suit yourself, Mr. Carver.' Then I ain't seen him since. But how do you like that? Nobody's ever called me

Mr. Carver. The nurse comes around in the evening, changes my dressing, and I get my morphine. She don't say nothing."

"Did they tell you how long you have to stay here?" he asked.

"Not really, but the nurse says the burn has to start healing from the inside out, so she washes away the dead stuff on top, which hurts godawful. Then there's the oil and lime water, and new bandages. Then I get my morphine."

The patient next to Clancy suddenly came to life. "Morphine, morphine? Where is it?"

"Settle back down, Jackson," Clancy said calmly. "I was just talking to my friend here. We got several hours before we get more." The man was asleep by the time Clancy finished his sentence.

Gillian really didn't know what to say. Small talk was done, and the events at the distillery were hanging in the air around them. But shame made him want to avoid the topic altogether.

Clancy's eyes were closing as he settled into a gentle snore. Gillian felt relief—he could dodge the subject for the time being. He carefully patted Clancy on the arm as he stood and turned to leave.

"Where are you going?"

He spun back. "You looked like you needed to slumber."

"I was just resting my eyes. You ain't goin nowhere. I need company, that's what I need. This place is a morgue except for the rats, and I'll be lucky if I can get Emmet to visit once a week. That boy's just no good."

"Has he been here yet?"

"Yeah, the first day. He cried like a baby. Don't think it was for me, though. The boy's worried where his next meal will come from, and the rent for sure. He's probably shittin' in his pants that he has to get a real situation now. No more odd jobs for gambling money."

"I'm sure he's worried about you, Clance."

"Maybe. But I'll bet he's already emptied out my cookie jar, and it wasn't to set aside for my funeral," Clancy said, then managed a weak and painful laugh.

"What about your boss at the cobbler shop? He knows what happened?"

"Yes, and he sent word that he'll be paying me a visit tomorrow. He probably figures I'm gonna be laid up for a while. But look at my hands, Gillian. I'm the luckiest man alive," Clancy said as he held both in the air. "See them, they're perfect, no burns at all! I'll be back repairing shoes in no time."

"Meantime, you should be getting a stipend from the Firemen's Fund to help pay for things," Gillian said. "And Emmet will have to step up."

"Don't make me laugh again, Robert. You're too cruel," Clancy said, smiling with his eyes closed.

"I never made you laugh, at least not today. You made yourself laugh."

"Oh yeah. Now tell me something. What did you see in the flames that night?"

Gillian was caught off guard, having thought that, with everything, his friend would have forgotten. Suddenly he felt anxious. He sat down again in the chair by the bed and sighed. "I just don't know what it was. It's like I was under a witch's spell. I wanted to pull away. I knew my hose was useless against the fire. But I just couldn't take my eyes off of . . ."

"Off of what?" Clancy seemed wide awake now as he propped his head up on the pillow.

"Off of nothing. It had to be nothing, just my imagination," he dismissed as he looked down at the floor and twirled his cap. He knew he owed Clancy an explanation, and his friend wasn't going to accept anything less. *Why should he? My actions almost got him killed.* "After one of the stills blew, there was a whirlwind of fire, like a tornado. I've seen that before, but this was different. The tornado turned black and took on the form of a man. Or really... "

He halted, too embarrassed to continue. Clancy would think he'd gone mad, or worse, become a drunken paddy who imagined leprechauns and gold treasures buried at the center of a conflagration. He could still see him, the hybrid man-insect creature that beckoned him forward into the flames. Gillian was figuring out how to proceed when he saw that Clancy's eyes had closed and a gentle snore set in. Gillian felt relieved. He was safe for now. The visit was over. Clancy was going to live, and it was time for him to return home.

The air grew noticeably cooler as he descended to the lobby of the great hospital. The identical majestic stone fireplaces on each side of the great room were devouring their fuel, embers swiftly rising up their chimneys. Just before exiting, he stopped as if to pay tribute to one of these controlled infernos.

"Now that's where a good fire belongs," he said aloud. Then he tipped his hat to the fireplace, gave a firm nod, and left.

CHAPTER TWENTY-SEVEN

Monday after the blaze

Mary had hoped that Lorenzo was back on the corner. It had been two weeks since her handsome Italian newsboy had disappeared, only to be replaced by a ubiquitous neighborhood ruffian. This made her sad and moody, a poor way to start her workday. She had hoped Lorenzo could be the one. His exotic accent, his infectious smile, his attentiveness... she'd felt certain there was interest there. And now, he was gone. Her dream of delivery from the Five Points shattered, at least for the time being. She had learned so much about him in the accumulation of those brief encounters where she exchanged coins for a paper. He had arrived in New York as a boy, just a few years earlier, but not with his parents. Poor farmers from the south of Italy, they had sold him to a man who promised room and board and that he'd be trained as a musician in New York City. The man honored his deal, and Lorenzo learned the harp. But he was required to play that instrument eight hours a day, six days a week, at a designated street corner, and only received a small percentage of the daily take himself. But within three years, the man had died, leaving Lorenzo to fend for himself, which he appeared to do with at least modest success.

Sad as she was, Mary wished the best for him, hoping that he'd secured a higher position in the newspaper business. But getting the paper for her father would not be the same anymore, certainly not the high point of her day. Thus, her foul mood lately.

"Mama, I'm an ugly girl, am I not?" she blurted that morning as the two of them were preparing for work.

Aileen, caught off guard, still had a quick response. "Of course not, my lamb. Though..."

"Though what?" Mary continued.

"You are what they call handsome, my dear. A noble woman. You just haven't come into your own quite yet. When you do, you'll catch yourself a man."

"I suppose you're right. Things will work out in time."

Truthfully, Mary was in no rush to enter into a relationship. Was it the near rape on the crossing to America? Perhaps. She and Patrick's secret haunted her. She knew it was certainly not her fault, but she still felt oddly ashamed, as if she should've known the brute had a plan to trap her. Then rage, sudden as a bolt of lightning, would seize her, and she would see his crazed smile and rotten teeth. *I was just fourteen!* she wanted to scream. Sometimes, she thought it strange that her experience of being violated was hardly more traumatic than the realization that she might actually be "ugly." Could the brute have been right? She'd never been told this before, but she'd never been told she was pretty either. If true, it was a punch in the face, and she felt ashamed that she was not aware of this. Had they owned a looking glass, she might have been privy to this information far earlier.

But now, she was determined on one thing. Homely or not, she would never marry a drunkard Irishman. Or an Englishman, for that matter!

* * *

Farragut's expanding business required conversion of the entire second floor to factory space, so management was moved up to the third level of the building. As much as she hated to admit it, Aileen found the walk up three flights arduous.

"You wouldn't think one more floor would make such a difference for me, Mary," she said, feeling winded. Her daughter climbed with ease. "I suppose the Typhus did something to me breathing."

"Well, maybe we go too fast, Mama. Tomorrow, we'll slow it down. Farragut will just have to wait a few more minutes."

"I suppose you're right. He's standing at the door looking at his timepiece right now, I expect." Aileen let out a long breath as they reached the final step.

Mary tugged at the heavy oak door, which had a glass window at its center. Gold leaf lettering was to be applied to the plate glass in the coming days, identifying this new space as the Executive Offices of Farragut Textiles LTD. Still, not wanting to miss out on any new business opportunity, the "Executives" would soon be sharing this floor with more sewing machine ladies.

Farragut was standing just outside his new private office, wire spectacles pinching his nose as he studied his timepiece with one hand while twisting one end of his handlebar mustache with the other.

"Ladies, late again?" he boomed. His habit of phrasing reprimands as if they were actual questions was unnerving and infuriating. Sometimes Aileen felt tempted to take him up and actually debate the issue at hand. Not today.

"We're sorry, Mr. Farragut. The ice on the streets should be gone soon, so we can walk a bit faster. Plus, we have to account for the extra floor in our travels." Aileen was not sure why she'd added that final piece of information.

"Very well, very well, both of you," he quickly replied, his mind already onto matters of greater importance. Business was booming since the introduction of the Singer machines. Within only a few weeks, Farragut had deals with the finest clothiers in the city. Of course, it didn't hurt that he made promises to the client that most producers couldn't commit to in good conscience. "A promise made is a promise kept" was his motto. Figuring out just how the promise would be kept could always be dealt with later.

"Mary, can I see you in my office after you settle your belongings?" Farragut asked.

"You want me there too, sir?" Aileen asked, not wanting to leave her daughter alone with the man.

Chapter Twenty-Seven

"No, that's quite alright, Mrs. Gillian. You best be getting to your work."

"Oh," was all she said with a nod.

Within five minutes of their arrival, Mary found herself knocking on Farragut's door— with trepidation.

"Enter, please."

Head down, deep into his paperwork, he waved her on to take a seat. .

The new office already carried his foul odors, although the spaciousness of the room seemed to ameliorate the issue—somewhat. Mary did note that after just a few weeks in his new third-floor executive suite, the clutter was beginning to close in.

"Are we meeting with the ladies at noon, Mr. Farragut?" Mary inquired in an attempt to distract him from what she feared was the real purpose of the meeting.

"Yes, yes indeed, but I think I will treat with a lunch. We need to celebrate my success with two new accounts, Mary. All will be pleased. Which reminds me, call down for an errand boy when we are done here. I need you to make a reservation for me at Delmonico's. Mrs. Farragut will be delighted. It's her favorite establishment. Besides my success this week, we will be celebrating our twenty-fifth wedding anniversary. So, make sure a bouquet of the finest flowers is waiting at the table."

Then Farragut giggled strangely, which could have been contagious, had Mary not been wary of what was to come.

"Yes, of course, sir," Mary responded with tempered enthusiasm. "Now, about the lunch? Which caterer shall we call up?"

"I'm not sure. Perhaps ask your mother to choose."

"Aye."

And then there was a pause.

Farragut swiveled to observe the view out the large picture window behind his desk. He folded his arms behind his head, leaned back, and began gently rocking, seemingly deep in thought. "I do believe it's getting warmer each day. Here it is mid-morning, and I can count on one hand the number of fireplaces still going strong."

Mary wondered if counting the belching chimneys each day was a hobby. "Sir, was there anything else you wanted? I believe I need to start on my own needling."

"I know this is difficult, but we have to terminate three ladies," he said. "I believe you know the ones. You reprimanded them twice already. They just don't seem to catch on."

"I see, Mr. Farragut. Can we give them just one more chance?" she begged.

"I'm afraid not. Each order of new machines from Mr. Singer is faster, better, more efficient. But more costly too. I need to get more production out of our women to justify the cost of the machines. Most have stepped up, but those three." Farragut swiveled his chair back in the direction of Mary and clasped his hands over his ink-stained blotter. "Your mother keeps impeccable records on the women's production, and it's always those three that bring the overall numbers down—and inevitably my profits! So, what am I to do?" He sighed, then pulled his watch out and placed it on the desk. "Time is money, you know. With the new contracts I promised, the girls must step up to the mission."

Mary felt heat rising to her face. She had the urge to lunge across the cluttered desk and grab his meaty neck with both hands. The desire was so strong, she feared her thoughts alone would give her away. She bit her upper lip—a habit very unbecoming, her mother would say—and focused her gaze out the great window.

"I quit!" she blurted.

Farragut's eyes bulged, and he sat back hard in his chair. Mary felt certain that, had the man been standing, he would now be stretched out on the floor.

"What do you mean, you quit? This is unheard of. Have you no respect for your employer!"

"What you expect of me is not proper, certainly not for the wage you pay, sir," she said.

"So that's what this is about! You're shaking me down for more money? Is your mother aware of this, young lady?"

A wave of shame spread from her belly to her head, which was now beginning to hurt. In the heat of the moment, she hadn't thought of her mother, or any consequences for that matter. In fact, none of this was planned, at least not on a conscious level. Could she take it back? Could she turn the clock back just five minutes?

"I didn't mean to disrespect you, sir. No, it's not the wage, really. I don't want to fire people. These ladies have so little already. One of them is slow because her eyesight is poor. If she moves any faster on that machine, she'll be stitching up her fingers for sure. Besides, we've already increased their production by twenty percent just six months ago, and for the same wage."

Farragut began drumming his fingers on the dirty ink blotter while staring at his crooked bookshelf on the opposite side of the room. Again, he was deep in thought, and she had no idea what might come next from his mouth. The silence was only broken by his passing wind.

"I suppose I should do the firing here," he said finally. "After all, these women are much older than you. It's a bit awkward, I suppose, to be fired by an eighteen-year-old girl. Okay, I've made up my mind; I'll do it then." And with that resolved, he slapped his desk once, as if the task was complete and it was time to move on to other matters.

Even though it seemed she would not be fired for insubordination, Mary was not relieved. In fact, she was quite dissatisfied. Of course, she didn't want these women fired. She felt it to be an egregious injustice. *He's just a greedy pig. He presses these ladies for more and more on the same wage while spending lavishly on Mr. Singer's machines.*

"Well, thank you for understanding, Mr. Farragut," she said tightly. "I best get to that errand boy for the reservation, and I will tell my mother you need her suggestion for the lunch."

Mary stood to leave, quickly becoming aware that Farragut was staring at her cleavage. *Maybe I should've quit anyway.* As she departed his office, she wondered if he was going to fire the three women before or after the lunch celebration.

That would be mean of him to make them sit through a celebration of his good fortunes, only to find out later that they're terminated. No, being

Farragut, he'll probably do it before to save money on the lunch—three fewer mouths to feed.

CHAPTER TWENTY-EIGHT

Spring 1850

Spring came early that year, and the docks were back in full operation. Gillian saw less of Brian Denny, as Denny was given more accounting responsibilities due to his alleged back injuries. Gillian was pleased with this since seeing Denny at White Flag Company was quite enough.

Twice a week, Gillian would steal away a bit early to Bellevue Hospital to visit Clancy. Often, he'd find Katonah at Clancy's bedside, a friend from his earliest days at Engine Company Five. Katonah was a descendent of the original Indian tribe that occupied the island of Manhattan, the Lenape, and his immediate family used to live just within the boundaries of the Five Points neighborhood. However, after the population explosion in the Points, his family had fled to the Hell's Kitchen neighborhood on the city's west side. A quiet and humble man, Katonah clearly valued his long friendship with Clancy Carver, even though their lives had parted ways several years earlier. And they both shared a similar tragedy, becoming widowers after their wives birthed a single child.

Clancy had often voiced his hopes that Emmet would take Katonah's daughter as his wife. She had remarkable cooking skills and was fine at needlework and other crafts, thanks to the many cousins who trained her well. But Emmet would have no part in this plan. He claimed she was homely and a heathen. "The Lenape don't belong here in New York anymore, Papa," he once told Clancy after the two had a squabble. In the end, this was just as well since Katonah—and his clan—had little fondness for Emmet.

On this particular visit, however, it wasn't Katonah Gillian found at Clancy's side. It was Emmet.

"Mary, mother of Jesus! Tis a miracle! Clance, you're up and about!"

"There's my hero," Clancy responded from the edge of the cot. "Yes, siree. Clancy's coming back," he said with a brief chuckle, then his usual cough. "I was about in the wheelchair this morning too, but they don't let us coloreds leave the floor anyways."

"Papa, you back to complaining already?" Emmet mocked from his chair at Clancy's side.

"What's the matter with you, boy? Where're your manners? A man of eighteen, you'd think he'd know how to greet his elders."

"Oh, sorry, Mr. Gillian, sir. Good afternoon to you," Emmet said with a shamed smile Gillian suspected was just an act for his father.

"Good afternoon to you too, Emmet. But you don't have to call me sir, me lad."

"Take my chair here, sir," Emmet said. "I have to leave for my job now anyways."

"Don't mind if I do, rest my feet a little," Gillian responded as he quickly dropped into the seat. The trek up to the hospital, then the three flights of stairs, had tired him out.

"I'll try and drop by again tomorrow, Papa." Emmett kissed his father on the top of his crown. "Good afternoon, Mr. Gillian."

Gillian smiled and tipped his hat without saying a word. The taller, younger version of Clancy swiftly departed.

"What were you two talking about, Clance?"

"I was just telling him how I got started. I know he's heard it before, but the boy won't listen. He says he's going to work now, but I'd wager the first thing he's gonna do is track down the pretty colored nurse attending us here today. Then it's either a poker game or the cock fights. Depending on how well he does, next is the colored saloon on Pearl Street or the groggery on Centre. I just don't know what to do with him." Clancy lay back on the cot and sighed.

"He needs some training. What about the cobbler shop? Or maybe, he can be a barber's apprentice?" Gillian suggested.

"He could be a lot of things if he wasn't always trying for the easy way out. He knows it wasn't easy for me but look at me now."

They looked at each other and laughed.

"Well, you know what I mean," Clancy said. "The boy don't know how good he's got it, is the problem. I went from being a butler in a mansion, having my own room and three square, to sharing a room in a boarding house and scooping up shit for a living. Do you know what it's like being a night soil man, Robert?"

Gillian shook his head, pretending he hadn't heard this story before.

"You start work at nine in the evening, rain, snow, heat. No weather matters. It gotta get done. First stop, you pull your bottle out before getting off the buggy. You down about a quarter of what's hopefully whiskey, as grog just don't do the trick. Now, if it's the summer, the stench'll be even worse, almost unbearable. So you better drink more. Then you get out your stinkin' shovel . . ."

"I know the rest, Clancy," Gillian interrupted. "How many times you gonna repeat that? Till I gag?"

"Yeah, that's the idea." Then they both laughed. "Say, did I ever tell you the story of how I became a fireman?"

"Don't suppose you did." Gillian settled in for a longwinded tale.

"Oh, good. Well... You know already the Rutherfords released me from duty before I was twenty-five. After Master Rutherford took ill and died, the missus found she had a lot of debts. She couldn't keep me on. I didn't want to leave, but she had plans to turn the place into a boardinghouse. The Rutherfords were all the family I knew, even though they wasn't really family." Clancy looked at the table by the cot. "Can you fetch me that glass of water over there? Whatever they're giving me makes me real parched."

Gillian delivered the glass to his friend, who promptly drank the whole thing in one gulp, then belched loudly, causing a stir among the morphine-addled patients. He handed the glass back to Gillian and continued.

"I asked Mrs. Rutherford if I could stay on as a paying boarder if I got a job. She put me off for several days, seemed real uncomfortable. Then she came to me and said she wished she could, but the other boarders wouldn't be comfortable living with a colored man. Then she apologized and kissed me right here on the forehead." Clancy tapped his forehead where his bandana used to rest. "Never had a white lady kiss me on the forehead before."

Gillian smiled affectionately. "Sounds like a nice lady, but her back was up against the wall."

"Real nice. So anyway, I shared a room at a colored boarding house and became a night soil man for about six months. That's all I could stand. Then I got a job repairing those leather fire buckets, making new ones too. That's when I learned they were looking for a bell tower watchman, night shift, of course. They trained me well, although it was hard to stay awake except when it was freezing cold. Then one night, we had excitement. My first fire. I remembered everything I was supposed to do, you know. I saw the fire, looked like a warehouse building of some type, so I started ringing that bell. But I had to stop to get my stick for the lantern. Everything was fine. I put the lantern on the stick and held it out in the direction of the fire so all the men could see just like I was supposed to."

Clancy stopped and sighed, and then smiled.

"Then the damnedest thing happened, Robert. There was a strong gust of wind, caught me off balance just like that. My stick drooped down, and the lantern slid right off. It dropped straight down, all the way into a pile of garbage, setting it on fire. I started ringing the bell frantically, then realized, what the heck am I doing? I can't even point to the fire right below me. So, I ran down the ladder, which, by the way, was already catching fire."

Clancy started to chuckle, and then he had trouble controlling his laugh. Gillian was smiling in delight.

"I don't know why I'm cackling away; this was bad. But at the time, I was thinking, why the hell do they build these fire bell towers out of wood!"

They both laughed until Clancy stopped for a few deep breaths.

"So, after I got down to the street, the whole tower went up in flames. There was no fireman to be found, but I heard another bell going in the next ward. His lantern was pointing in my direction. Anyway, I was fired for burning down the fire tower, but I met a bunch of firemen from White Flag Company. That's how I started there. Then Moses introduced me to the cobbler I work for now. Phew, some story, ain't it? I'm trying to get Emmet to see things don't always work out, but you keep trying, and somehow you end up where you're supposed to be."

"Well said, my friend. Well said. Now it's time for me to head home. How much longer do you have to stay here?"

"The nurse says just a few more days. The Negro doctor comes here once a week. When he comes by to check me out, I should be goin' home."

Gillian stood and smiled. "Well, thank the Lord all has worked out. You get some rest."

"Amen. Hey, look, there's still daylight and it's half past five already."

"Heavens, you're right, Clance. Perhaps I shall be home before dark."

With that, Gillian took his friend's hand into his palm and patted it, relieved the appendage was healthy and useful, just as Clancy had claimed.

* * *

"Smells like we're celebrating something, Mrs. Gillian!" he said upon opening the door to their apartment.

"Aye, we are at that, Robert! Took me a while to get the potatoes soft," Aileen said, seeming exhausted from beating the lumpers into submission. "Shepherd's pie, with real beef, not that chopped meat that looks red until I bring it home. And minced pie for dessert."

"Did you find a pot of gold, me lady?"

"Right in front of this building!" she joked, feistier than ever. "Now stop being foolish, sit down and take those boots off. You'd think we have a scullery maid to chase after you."

"So, I'm a-waiting," he said while unlacing his boots.

"Well, it all started this morning. Mr. Farragut wanted Mary to fire three of the ladies, the very day he was celebrating two new deals he put together. You would think his good fortune would soften his position, let them stay on a little longer. Anyway, Mary was so angry she was fixing to quit, but she didn't, or he wouldn't let her."

Gillian felt a spot of panic at the thought of Mary being without employment or a husband, but Aileen seemed in a fine mood.

"So, he comes to his senses, I mean about Mary. Decided that shouldn't be part of her job. He was going to do it himself. I was still raging mad. He spends more and more on these sewing machines, then expects the ladies to get more done every hour to justify what he spent. But he don't pay them any more, just drives them harder."

She paused to remove the cast iron pan from the heat. The smell of sauteed beef and onion caused Gillian to salivate as he closed his eyes and drew in a deep breath.

"Heavenly, my dear, heavenly."

Aileen sat down at the table and removed her bonnet, letting her faded auburn hair fall to her shoulders.

"So I marched into Mr. Farragut's office and shut the door. You should have seen his face, Robert. He knew something was up with me, and it was not good. I told him this has to stop. I said, 'You keep increasing the quota on these women, then expect me to hire more of them for the same wage. Then we get girls with the least experience. Then you want Mary to fire them.' That's what I told him, just like that."

"You could have brought about our ruin, Aileen," he said with a shudder.

"Naw, husband. I'm the best he has there with my number skills."

"So, what did you do next?"

"I sat down."

"You know that's not what I meant," he chided.

"I says, 'Mr. Farragut, sir. You're under a lot of weight with all these Mr. Singer sewing machines. He keeps convincing you to buy more every time he makes an improvement. I see the books. No wonder you're so worried about the ladies' output. And what if things slow down? You'll be stuck for sure.' Then I shut up."

"What did he say?"

"He didn't say. He dropped his quill and went to the window. That's when I got a fright. I was sure I overstepped. But there was silence. I couldn't bear it, so I had to speak up. I said, 'Mr. Farragut, why don't you tell Mr. Singer you will only rent the machines going forward, like on a monthly basis? So, when a new model comes out, you get to see if it's really better, if the girls can produce more for the same hour's wage. And if business turns down, you ain't stuck with all the machines. Maybe you wouldn't have to lay as many off.'"

"Brilliant, me lady! Now come sit beside me on the sofa."

"I can't. In a minute, I have to get up and finish the supper. Farragut turns around from the window and sits back down at his desk. He looks at me, stares for a while. I'm feeling scared again. Then he says, 'My lord, Aileen. For a woman, you appear to have a remarkable flair for this! That's an excellent idea.' Then he smiles at me—something like I'd never seen."

"I'm surprised he had no shame that a woman came up with such an idea before he did," Gillian said.

"'Tis true. It could have turned out different. Anyway, he says, 'Just one thing. What if Singer refuses to rent me his machines? After all, less profit in it for him, I would think.'"

"So I says, 'Mr. Farragut, all those trade journals in your office. Look at the ads in them. There's so much more competition now in the sewing machine business. Tell him that if he don't rent the machines to you, you'll go elsewhere.' Then he just nods his head and starts tapping his quill."

"That's it?" Gillian asked.

"Almost. I told him I have to check on Mary about the food for the luncheon. He says to keep it the same amount, any leftovers he'll take home to his missus. Then he says he's only going to let one of the women go for now."

Aileen had stopped talking, her mouth pursed like there was still news behind it.

"I suppose that's great, but what are we celebrating?" he asked.

"Well, at the luncheon, he announces that I'm getting promoted to Assistant Manager of Equipment Acquisitions. Then he tells me after—

you know, in private—that he's raising my salary fifteen percent. I'll be at twenty-five dollars a month!"

Gillian felt giddy with pride. "That's wonderful news, my wife, worthy of celebration!" He walked over and kissed her forehead. She stood up from her chair, and they embraced, his new pillow of a belly covering her fragile bones. "I love you, my dear. And you see, it was worth it in the end, coming to America."

She was silent but continued to embrace him.

CHAPTER TWENTY-NINE

AT THE LOCAL GROGGERY

Spring 1852

"By golly, you moving again, Robert!" Clancy said as he placed his jug down.

"Yes, siree, Clance. Out of the Five Points. We're taking a flat in another new building, north of Canal Street. It wasn't my idea, but Mrs. Gillian's, you know."

"Well, I'll be," Clancy said. "What do you think of that, Katonah?" He turned to his quiet friend, who was gazing about the room. Katonah smiled at Gillian and raised his jug, a congratulatory response.

"Aileen figures these things out, so I believe her," Gillian said. "Even if Mary should find a suitor, we can afford the rent with Aileen's wage from Farragut and mine from the docks. I just have to get the boy out of the place."

"What's his plans for a working wage?"

"He's uncertain. Maybe a druggist, he says, which I think is suitable work. But then, sometimes, he talks about the clergy, which I think is an awful idea. You can't go around this city flapping your gums about the Roman Catholic Church." Gillian put down his jug and leaned back in his chair.

"Fill 'er up, Robert?" the proprietor called.

Gillian debated whether he should have another round. He had to be up early the next morning as the ships were coming in earlier now that it was spring. He also had an uneasy feeling that a fire was due. It had been an unusually long period since the last significant event. "No, I'm fine here," he yelled back.

Clancy sighed. "I wish Emmet would have some ambitions. I just don't know what's to become of him. He'd do better as a slave living in Rutherford's mansion like my daddy did." He chuckled—and coughed. "Well, boys, time for the privy." And Clancy was off to the back of the cellar. There, a small stairwell would take him to the rear yard.

Suddenly Gillian felt uneasy. Making conversation with Katonah was difficult. "So... all is well with you and yours, I suppose, Katonah?"

"Yes, the family is doing well, Mr. Gillian." Katonah took a sip from his jug, seeming content to leave it at that.

"You're a cabinetmaker, Clancy says?"

"Yes. My employer is Schultz Company, German, you know. You've heard of them?"

"No, I'm afraid not. We were never in the position to buy new furniture, but if we ever are, we will surely look them up."

Even as he was still hoping for Clancy's return, Gillian pondered if this man might be a suitor for Mary. *He is a professional craftsman, takes his responsibilities seriously, and perhaps their offspring would be a fine-looking brood.* Then he thought, *How silly of me to think of these things. He has twenty-five years on her, and he's a heathen. But then again, he could become a Catholic.*

* * *

By late June of that year, the heat arrived, and it was punishing. And by mid-July, casualties were mounting in the Five Points, especially among older tenants residing in stifling upper-floor apartments. Some took to the tar-covered roofs; others would sleep on the flimsy fire escapes now required in the newer buildings. The papers reported incidents of tenants rolling off the fire escapes in their sleep or roof dwellers sleepwalking to their deaths. Sure, the newer dumbbell-shaped tenements allowed for more natural light, but certainly no fresh air. And if the heat alone were not bad enough, the excrement on the streets and sidewalks—animal and human—could overwhelm even the hardiest residents. Even the brothels were hurting for business. Few men were interested in fornication, given the discomforts of the heat and subsequent foul body odors.

By the second half of July, several odd fires erupted in lower New York. Dry lightning had ignited a large complex of stables on West Street. Although Hudson River water was nearby, the fire had spread so swiftly, the horses stood little chance. A few were able to escape, frantically galloping through the narrow roadways. The unfortunate ones were roasted alive. The fire burned itself out quickly on that windless, humid night. But a putrid fog—the papers compared it to a biblical plague—hovered over the lower west side, the stench so bad many residents fled in the middle of the night. Another fire engulfed several vessels at Peck Slip. And then another engulfed the slip itself. Arson was frequently suspected, but seldom proven.

As for the Gillian family, good fortune abounded. Their spacious first-floor flat in the new tenement building on Grand Street was "grand," in Gillian's own words. Patrick's nose healed just fine, except for the slightest crook, and Aileen and Mary were the most valuable employees at Farragut's flourishing textile factory. The jars were well stocked with cash, and their account at the Emigrant Savings Bank was growing.

But as life goes, all this was about to change.

CHAPTER THIRTY

October 1852

Gillian awoke in the middle of the night, his gown soaked with sweat despite the coolness of the apartment. He'd assumed his usual nightmare was the culprit: him, in the middle of a conflagration, only to be greeted by a firestorm that morphed into an insect-like creature. In fact, the nightmares were so frequent that it'd become hard for him to separate the real visions he'd learned to ignore from those in his sleep.

That particular night, he rolled over in bed to find himself alone. He lit the lantern and went out to the living area and small pantry. Aileen was not to be found. He checked Mary's room first, then Patrick's. "She must have gone to the privy," he muttered, and returned to bed. Twenty minutes passed as he lay awake. Still, she didn't return. He walked out to the stairwell, which still carried the odor of fresh paint, and went to the back of the building where a door led to the rear yard. He crossed the yard, his swaying lantern illuminating the outline of the new cast-iron water pump that serviced their building. When he arrived at the four stalls, he observed a weak light emanating from under the door of one privy.

"Aileen, is that you in there?"

"Yes," she sobbed. "I woke up with the cramps, something awful. I usually don't go in the middle of the night. But it's the runs I have now."

"Oh. Is there anything I can do for you, sweetheart?"

"No, it's getting better. You best go back to sleep."

He didn't want to leave her there, but truthfully, what was he to do? So, he returned to the flat and half slept until her return.

"Maybe a bad piece of food," Gillian suggested the next morning at the kitchen table.

"I don't know. We ate the same thing. None of you are sick. I think I have to run again." And she was gone.

At least they were lucky to live in this fine new building with clean privies and fresh Croton water. *If you got to be sick and stuck in the privy, no better place, I guess.*

Mary left for work without Aileen that morning. She stopped at the privy herself as Aileen was emerging from a stall. Her mother looked haggard and was trembling. "I really should stay home with you today, Mama. I can nurse you, fix some tea."

"Don't be silly, lass. You go explain to Farragut that I'm sick and will likely be back tomorrow. Tell him it was something I ate."

First hesitant, Mary obliged her. "Okay, make sure Papa or Patrick carries the water for you."

"At least no stairs for us anymore," Aileen said with a weak smile.

* * *

"You can't just lie in bed there, Aileen," Gillian said, brow crinkled with concern. He'd laced his boots up and was ready to leave for work.

"I don't just lie here in bed," she quavered in a weak voice, her face more pasty than usual, and now her lips dry and cracked. "I visit the privy," she said, then attempted a laugh.

"There's no time for mirth," he scolded. Then he made his decision. "I'm not going to work. I'm going to fetch the surgeon."

"We can't afford the surgeon. I should go to the clinic," she said dreamily as if falling asleep.

"You're too ill, my dear, and we have plenty of money in the jar."

"Get me water, Robert. I'm so thirsty, always."

Within a second, he was in the kitchen filling her tin with a ladle. When he raced back, Aileen was standing but teetering, holding fast to the bed rail.

"What are you doing?" Gillian snapped, then felt guilty for scolding her. "You must get back in bed, dear. Patrick?" he called out.

Patrick was preparing himself for work. "I heard, and I'll fetch the surgeon, Papa."

"Thank you, boy. Will Hennessy understand if you show up tardy?"

"Probably, but it doesn't matter. This is the way it has to be." And Patrick hurried out the door.

"Robert, you have to get me to the privy, now," Aileen said, mustering the strength to down the entire tin of water.

They had made it as far as the back door when Aileen collapsed, bloody diarrhea mixed with rice oozing out from under her night dress.

"Oh no," Gillian muttered with alarm. "I shall return in a heartbeat, my dear." Instinct had him running back to the flat to get a blanket to cover her mess. His head made hard contact with the top door jamb, haste causing him to forget his need to duck. For a few seconds, he felt bewildered but quickly got back on task. Upon return, Aileen appeared to be aware of her situation and stirred as if she was trying to stand.

"Lie still, Aileen," he said as he covered her with the blanket and patted her shoulder. "The surgeon should be here... soon," he said, not at all convincingly.

"I'm dying, Robert," she muttered.

"Rubbish, my dear!" he insisted, even as he felt the welling tears. His forehead was throbbing from his mishap with the door frame.

Gillian heard the creak of the main entrance door and two voices, one Patrick's, the other a woman's voice.

"Certainly not a surgeon," Gillian said, and Aileen stirred. Rapid steps grew louder as help approached.

"The surgeon had too many cholera patients, Papa. He said a nurse could assist us just as well unless we want to bring Mama into the clinic."

The nurse, in nun's habit, bent down to Aileen's wretched body.

"Bless you, my child," she spoke sweetly as she stroked Aileen's matted hair.

Then she stood and turned to Robert, her expression grim. "She must have a constant supply of water. And we'll try some quinine. That sometimes helps." She lowered her voice to a whisper. "She really needs to be in the hospital."

She bent down again and checked under the blanket, then instantly cupped her hand over her mouth. Gillian's stomach dropped to the floor.

She pointed quietly toward the back door. He followed her, now intuiting that the situation was indeed grave. As he left, Patrick sat down on the floor and started massaging her shoulders and telling her that all would be okay.

"How long has she been like this, Mr. Gillian?"

"Not more than a day... Sister," he responded, finding it strange that he was speaking of medical issues with a woman of the cloth. "It's confounding. The bloody rice is a new occurrence. We don't eat rice."

"That's not rice, sir. It's the lining of her bowel disintegrating," she said with her head lowered. "She has the Cholera, and I'm afraid it's far advanced already."

"Oh, Lord, no." His body shivered. "First the Typhus, now this. What can we do?" he begged.

"I'm afraid it's too late to get her to Bellevue. Besides, they're overrun with another outbreak of the Yellow Fever. Bed, water, and prayer are all I can offer."

Suddenly feeling weak himself, Gillian fell against the back wall. He heard Patrick crying inside. His mind quickly went to Mary. *The poor girl is completely unaware of what's going on.*

"How could this happen? We have good water here. Fresh from the Croton Reservoir. None of the rest of us have fallen ill, maybe some runs now and then, I suppose."

The nun nurse appeared uncomfortable. "I don't believe so, sir," she stated solemnly.

"What do you mean, you don't think so!" Gillian said incredulously. "This row of new houses has the best water in the Five Points. The agent told us that the new pumps receive fresh reservoir water."

The nurse didn't respond, but she glanced in the doorway toward Aileen, who seemed almost lifeless except for her rapidly twitching eyelids. "She needs fluids, and we need to get her back to bed."

Patrick, composed once again, assisted in lifting his mother's feather-weight body onto Gillian's shoulders. Gillian brought her back to the flat, lay her in bed, and propped pillows behind her so she could be upright to drink.

"Patrick, fetch the bedpan in the back of my cart," the nun nurse ordered, and he was gone in a flash. "Now, here is that tincture of quinine." She drew a vial out of her surgical bag and handed it to Gillian. "Once every two hours, add it to her water..." She hesitated, and he could tell she had more to say. "I'm afraid you may have been deceived, Mr. Gillian. The Croton water doesn't extend this far. Your pumps are pulling up water from the ground, like the rest, and that's probably the source of your trouble. The surgeon says the water is most foul here, near these new buildings. I'm surprised the rest of you haven't taken ill, but cholera usually goes after the weakened. Some say that boiling it first may help." With that, she descended to her knees while removing a bible and a cross from her overcoat pocket.

Gillian stood frozen at the doorway to the room. *This can't be. She's lying to us. No. Why would she be lying? She's a woman of the cloth. Maybe the surgeon's just plain mistaken? What does he know about water?* "Me and the boy will be just outside, Sister," he said solemnly.

The nun nodded, her back to them, all her focus on Aileen now.

Gillian and Patrick retired to the living room, where they sat down at the table, both in their own thoughts.

"Life makes no sense at times," Gillian abruptly blurted as he rested his chin on his fists. "To stay alive, she has to keep drinking the water so she doesn't shrivel to nothing. So, I gave her the water... But drinking the water's been killing her. Dammit, I killed her!" He slammed his fist on the table. Then he picked up a tin cup and threw it at the wall. The tainted, poisonous water dripped down to the floor.

Patrick winced. And there was silence again, except for the murmured prayers coming from the adjacent room.

"You better go fetch your sister, boy," Gillian said, hearing the break in his own voice as he massaged his smarting forehead.

Patrick laced up his shoes, then went to the closet and retrieved his overcoat, the first time since the turn of the seasons. It was his first brand-new coat, one Aileen had just bought him. He paused, the coat draped over his arm, his eyes filled with tears.

"It was not your fault, Papa," he said, the words bursting forth like an unexpected sneeze.

"I know, lad," Gillian said. "It was not my fault, but I was ignorant to believe that bloody lying agent about the Croton water! I could hang myself!" His voice was rising again. "We should have stayed put in the old place; maybe the water was better there. But your mother... " Then he stopped. Was he about to blame his dying wife for this? A pang of shame mixed with his grief and frustration.

Without saying another word, Patrick put his coat on and was out the door. Gillian retrieved the large cast-iron pot next to the stove, which Aileen used for boiling potatoes. How heavy it was, even empty, yet Aileen had hauled it by herself to the rear-yard water pump, then back again, full.

Now he would be collecting the tainted water—the poison for boiling.

* * *

The cold, rainy day was most appropriate for a funeral. Just as appropriate was the simple pine box, one that Aileen would've surely approved of.

They held a small ceremony at the neighborhood church. Clancy attended, and Gillian was very grateful, as he knew his friend must have felt uncomfortable being the sole Negro amongst many strangers. A few of the other White Flag Company firemen attended, including Brian Denny. And of course, Aileen's small circle of friends, along with Mr.

Farragut. Only the immediate family made the trip across the river to Brooklyn for the burial in Gravesend. Robert Gillian found some solace in the fact that this time he could afford a casket, as well as a burial plot in a Catholic cemetery. Only a small donation to the affiliated church was expected.

On the return journey across the river, he reflected upon his last moments with Aileen. Her face no longer revealed the agony of this second disease ravaging her body. In fact, she'd appeared at peace. She hadn't spoken for several hours, as she'd drifted in and out of a mental fog. He was at her bedside massaging her left hand while Mary, Patrick, and the nun nurse sat despondently in the kitchen. In her final moments, she smiled faintly. Her eyelids, closed, were gently quivering. And in the softest voice she said, "I'm coming, my dears. Don't worry, Mama's coming." Then she was gone.

He'd felt an unexpected sense of completion after she uttered those last words. Perhaps that's where she belonged, back with Daisy and Daphne. The others were settled in now, with their life in the New World. Two children were rescued from famine and desperation. Maybe her job was done here? They were grown. There was money in the bank and opportunities awaiting them. Perhaps the beyond was where she was needed now.

Gillian smiled as he looked out over the river. The rain was over, and the clouds were parting. And then came the shimmering diamonds again, sunlight reflecting off the crests of the ripples. Mary and Patrick were standing beside him, both staring at the river, both looking tired and forlorn.

For the moment, some solace for Gillian. But he was not a man at peace. And in the coming days, he'd often reflect upon his misfortunes, how the rug would be pulled out from underneath him just as he was enjoying a bit of good fortune. *Why am I not entitled to a good life? Am I being punished? Is it because I don't attend church often?* Then the anger set in. *This didn't have to happen. If we were not lied to about the bloody drinking water!* Finally, there was guilt. He would think about the lost wages from Aileen's salary. He didn't want to associate her death with lost income, but financial worry was a cold reality.

Part V

A VISIT WITH PATRICK

CHAPTER THIRTY-ONE

THE TOMBS
Fall of 1869

"Drop him!" came from the courtyard below.

Gillian was startled awake. Not enough warning to plug his ears, as if that mattered. Then came the clap of thunder—the scaffold swinging open—causing him to shiver in his damp nightclothes. After the creak of the rope ceased, the murmurs of the crowd grew into regular conversation. Shortly thereafter, he dozed off again.

"Gillian!" Maurice barked, standing outside the door holding a tin tray with one hand. "I got your grub here. I'm earlier than usual on account that you have a visitor in an hour. So, eat up, cause the warden wants me to clean you up real good with a shave." He mimed a slit across the throat—his symbol for prisoner shaves.

"Where's Phinny?" Gillian asked.

"He's seeing a surgeon about that withering leg. Don't worry. I didn't poison you... today." He opened the cell gate and pushed the tray along the floor for Gillian to retrieve, then quickly slammed the door shut. Standard protocol if a guard lacked backup. With a prisoner like Gillian, most guards would break protocol. Not Maurice. Stickler for rules and fearful of all prisoners. "I'll be back in fifteen minutes to take you for the shave." Again, he mimed a slit across the throat, and then smiled.

* * *

"You look well, lad!" Gillian said with enthusiasm. Patrick's visits were a bit more frequent lately, and he assumed Mary had a role in this.

"You also... Papa. You look well-shaven and neat."

"Well, it's not the Astor House, for sure, but the food is very passable and my work at the stables is agreeable—not hard work for an old man, just hammering out horseshoes." Gillian had an uneasy feeling that they were about to run out of conversation.

"Well, I know Mary told you—I'm a junior partner with Hennessey now at the drugstore, which is good for our household. In fact, there is to be a celebration."

He paused, and Gillian supposed that his son regretted spilling the last bit of news. And he felt bad, as it wasn't Patrick's fault that his father would not be attending the event.

"Aye, she did tell me. Congratulations, boy. I know your heart was set on crafting ships, but times change. Not your fault iron is the way to go now for sea-faring vessels. But a druggist is always a fine career, mixing all those potions and elixirs." There—he'd successfully distanced the conversation away from the celebration he wouldn't be attending.

"But I have more good news, Papa."

Gillian's eyes opened wide. "Your lady with child again?"

"Heavens no. It's the bridge to Brooklyn, Papa. It's really going to happen. We've raised our ten percent of the project's cost—five hundred thousand dollars! All the shares to own the bridge have been sold at one dollar each. I'm the owner of quite a sum myself," Patrick said proudly. "And the state Senate has approved Tweed's demand to control the project."

"I thought that scoundrel was in all kinds of trouble?"

"He is, but he'd put this all together. They've agreed to go with the contractors Tammany had picked, so some others will get Tweed's share of the kickbacks."

"But what's in this for you, Patrick? So you own a bunch of shares of the Brooklyn Bridge? It'll be years before the bridge is done."

"What's in this for me? The shares are worth far more than what I paid. You see, the city's never going to allow the Brooklyn Bridge to be in private hands, especially not in the hands of a group of men who invested just half a million dollars. The city's going to want our shares. In fact, they need our shares for the project."

"What do you mean?" Gillian asked, glancing at the door to the receiving room, suspicious that Maurice would be listening in. Fortunately, the man appeared to have disappeared for the moment.

"We own John Roebling's engineering plans. You remember, Papa. I told you about Roebling; he came up with the plans for the wire suspensions—an ingenious design. The city needs that from us."

"Couldn't they just hire another architect?" Gillian asked warily.

"Perhaps, but there's more." Patrick sat back in his chair, a self-satisfied grin spreading across his face. Then he bent forward as if about to divulge a great secret. "You see, the Lenape Indians still own a spit of land in Manhattan that will be necessary for the bridge. It's right by the shore, and it's needed for one of the bridge towers. There's no other place to connect the bridge on the Manhattan side."

"But how does the city get the land?"

"They can't. Except through buying our shares! It's ingenious, Papa! Remember Clancy's Lenape friend, Katonah? He's convinced the rest of their clan to contribute the land in exchange for shares. So, you see, the Lenape Indians own a substantial number of shares in the Brooklyn Bridge Company. And the city and state need those shares. They're going to pay us a ransom for full control of the bridge. Perhaps ten-fold our investment!" Patrick sat back in his chair and smiled.

It occurred to Gillian that his boy still desired his father's approval, his father's support, perhaps? *So, all isn't lost. Maybe we can mend things?*

"This is remarkable news, lad. My son is going to be rich!" he exclaimed. "Only in America!"

He stood to shake Patrick's hand, completely forgetting about the cuff and chain dangling from his left wrist. They clanged loudly on the enormous table, drawing Maurice's attention. He opened the door to check on his prisoner. Gillian had a brief moment of shame.

"Well, perhaps not rich," Patrick said humbly while staring at his father's cuffs. "A healthy profit nevertheless, which will benefit my family."

"Why, this reminds me of my investment in the Broadway Railroad Company. We did quite—"

Patrick cut him off. "This is nothing like your Broadway Railroad scandal!" His words leapt across the table like fire from a dragon's breath. "That was a sham, a get-rich scheme!"

Gillian shuddered like a child being shamed. "It was no such thing, Patrick!" he declared. "It was not our fault the city put the kibosh on the whole thing, and then all attention was on the war—"

"Father?"

"Oh, I see we're back to formality," Gillian said, feeling the heat coloring his face.

"Father, why do you delude yourself here? You all knew an elevated railroad was never going to be built. The lot of you sold your shares to pigs who then went and resold them to the ignorant sods who didn't—or couldn't—read the fine print in the flyers anyway."

Gillian stood tall. The iron cuffs clanged on the table again, causing Maurice to appear back at the door.

"Five minutes, men," he gave as his excuse and then quickly closed the door.

Gillian sighed and dropped back down into his chair.

"Did you forget, my boy?" he said. "The money from that stock holding went to your schooling to be a druggist, among other things. And I didn't hear a complaint from you about our staying in the spacious apartment on Grand Street, meals in the best restaurants, the trips to West Brighton!"

"And what else paid for all that, Father? Hmm?"

Gillian took in Patrick's cold glare. And then he had to look away.

There were a few moments of silence, both avoiding eye contact.

"You think you're better than me, lad, I see that," Gillian said softly. "Perhaps you are... but perhaps you're not. I pray you never have to bury your children in burlap sacks for lack of funds or contemplate sending your family off to a workhouse. But then you'd learn the truth about yourself." He turned his head, and their eyes met. "Maybe it's best if a man never has to learn the truth about himself," he said solemnly.

"Maybe true, Papa. I'm sorry," he conceded, his proud head now lowered. "I just wanted you to know the Brooklyn Bridge project is certain. Sure, there's some chicanery, the kickbacks and all. But, in the end, this bridge will be built. The public will own it, and crossings will be free! My profits are handsome, but all will benefit in the end. That's the difference here," he said sadly.

There was the sharp click of the door handle.

"Time's up, sorry to say," said Maurice.

The two men stood, and this time Gillian managed to avoid attracting attention to the dangling cuffs. He sighed, smiled at his son.

"You've grown into a fine man, Patrick. Your mother, God rest her soul, I'm sure she's very proud looking down upon you." With that, Gillian kissed his free hand and tossed the sentiment in Patrick's direction.

Patrick nodded. "Thank you," he said softly. "Take care of yourself, Papa."

And he quickly brushed past Maurice.

PART V1

FROM RAGS TO RICHES

Chapter Thirty-Two

Spring of 1853

The White Flag Company Spring Chowder Party got off to an early start. The men were eager to drink in celebration of whatever good news Brian Denny was planning to announce. Besides the usual stout and grog, they still had the cask of whiskey that had mysteriously disappeared from the site of the Great Distillery Fire.

The spring night was cool and moonless. Gillian arrived on time, which meant many of the laddies would be there already. He was happy the invitation didn't extend to the wives, so he could just enjoy the camaraderie of his fellow firefighters. He was greeted by Clancy, Moses, and to his surprise, Katonah. The quiet man usually avoided these events after generously supplying a sack of oysters and clams harvested from their little spot along the East River.

"Greetings, boys!" Gillian cheered.

"Aye, same to you, Robert," Moses responded. Clancy just gave him a wave, as the two were vigorously polishing the new steam engine. This latest model required an even shorter start-up period and provided an even more powerful spray.

"Good to see ya again, Katonah," Gillian said. The quiet man gave a quick nod in his direction while hauling a second burlap bag of oysters to the side of the great cast-iron kettle at its traditional spot in the center of the room, ready to be worshiped like a giant Buddha. Gillian closed his eyes and drew in a deep breath. The scent of the cool spring breeze coming through the open doors, coupled with the rich smell of the sea chowder, was intoxicating.

"Here. Take a tin, Gillian. We got that cask out back," Moses said, pulling him out of his trance. "Drink up. There ain't goin to be a fire tonight, at least, according to Stretch."

Not a second after he filled his drink, Gillian smelled cigar smoke. *Gotta be Denny and his cohorts.*

"Evening, boys!" the foreman said as he entered the half-empty station house. A lackey was carrying his lantern, and several firemen trailed behind. His evening attire had improved since his promotion to foreman, and the pull in his waistcoat told that he'd been living quite well. Denny had just finished boasting about the new address he'd taken, uptown on Union Square. He removed his top hat, and handed it to the lackey.

"We have a flutist to entertain us tonight, boys. He'll be along shortly. Now, which way to that cask?" he asked, rubbing his hands together—as if he didn't know the hiding place of their spoils.

The flutist arrived and set himself on top of the freshly polished steam engine. Gaelic ditties were the theme for the night, which unexpectedly drove a dagger into Gillian's heart, not for the land that abandoned him, but for his poor Aileen. All evening, he would struggle to fight off the feeling. *She didn't abandon me; she left to carry out her duty to the twins. She did what was necessary, what was right.* His efforts were futile in the end.

"You, my hero, Robert Gillian. Want to dance?" Clancy called out as he strolled over. The spirits were at work, and Clancy was wearing a huge grin. Beads of sweat covered his unusually bandana-free forehead. He'd finally changed out the dirty piece of cloth for something livelier and more colorful and was using it as a necktie for the occasion.

"I'm not doing no Irish jig with you," Gillian responded, finally cracking a smile.

Clancy laughed. "You don't do no Irish jig with a nig?"

"It has none to do with you being a colored one. I don't make it a habit of dancing with men."

"Fair enough, I got to take a load off anyways. Let's get some fresh air at the stables so I can refill this tin."

"Fine, although I wouldn't call it 'fresh air' at the stables."

"What? Those are the cleanest horses in the city. We wipe those precious asses'... asses." He laughed again.

"Clancy, a horse is not an ass, a donkey's an ass... as are some people," he said.

"Oh, sorry," Clancy said, realizing he wasn't going to change Gillian's somber mood. They sat down on a bench between the whiskey cask and beer keg. "Tough, ain't it, Robert? Give it time, takes a lot of time, you'll move on. You probably need to put some new things in your mind. That's what I did when Emmet was born, when my wife died."

"Maybe true," was all Gillian said. He'd been looking forward to the party all day, but now grief had overtaken him. Many of the Gaelic tunes were Aileen's favorites.

Clancy intuited a change of subject was in order. "You get a load of that outfit Denny was wearing? Wooo. Must have cost a fortune. I'll bet it's one of them fancy department store things."

"I sure did. And he's moved up to Union Square. I hardly see him down at the docks anymore. He's in the accounting office most of the time. I'll bet they fixed him up good with a hefty wage."

"Probably so. But not that type of money he's showing around town. He's like Voorhees now. You don't get rich being foreman of White Flag Company or working at the docks, that's for sure. I'll bet this has to do with the Fire Marker Man. In fact, I'm sure," Clancy said, now appearing sober and staring at the flutist sitting atop the steam engine platform. "That's how the old Dutchman made his fortune before retiring to them Caribbean islands, and I'll bet Denny's holding his coat tails."

"This Fire Marker Man, what does he look like?"

"Like I told you before, he's ugly. Well, I suppose that's not being nice. He probably wasn't ugly until being burned. Poor guy. I remember his name now. John Mahon, it is. He used to volunteer here at White Flag, back around when I started, so before 1835. Voorhees was already foreman back in those days. I think it was the conflagration of 1835 or

36. That's what got John Mahon. Half the city burned that night. Maybe I'm exaggerating. Almost half anyways."

"I heard about that one, probably everybody did," Gillian stated after a hard swallow from his tin.

"It was the coldest night ever in this city. We was pumping water from holes in the ice on both rivers. If you didn't keep it moving, it would freeze up, clogging the hoses if you can believe. The next day, they had to count the igloos we'd made that night. Building after building, encased in ice, many just partially burned. It wasn't till a week later, when it got a little warmer, they could get inside those tenements. That's when they found the ice mummies. That's what they called them. Missing children and ladies covered in ice, in their beds, with their eyes open. Like those people they found in that building where you rescued the old lady."

Clancy stopped for a swig from his jug, then let out a belch.

Gillian didn't want to be reminded of that night—of his initial euphoria, dissolving when he learned of the two children just one floor below, the ones no one knew were there.

"Clancy, get on with it. Where does the fire marker man come into it?"

"There you go again. White folk all the same. I'm getting to that." He shook his head with feigned exasperation. "So, Mahon was a young man then, me too of course. About the time of that fire, they figured out they could make firewalls by blowing up buildings, ye know, to make large spaces between them so the fire can't spread, sort of. They were bringing gunpowder over from Brooklyn, jamming through the ice and such. The river was so frozen they didn't need boats; they were just taking carts across to get the gunpowder from the navy yard.

Gillian sighed, catching Clancy's attention, and getting him back on track.

"Voorhees ordered Mahon to go into a burning warehouse with a fire hose and climb to the second floor, which is where the fire was. No one could understand why they didn't blow the building up. It was marked for that by the commissioner, but Voorhees wouldn't do it. Found out later, the building was insured by Chelsea Surety. It burned to the ground anyway, after they got Mahon out. They never found the brass fire marker in the rubble. The rumor was that Voorhees stole it from the scene. So, Mahon lived, but Vorhees felt terrible about the whole thing. At least the old Dutchman had a heart. Mahon was burned on one whole side of his body and face. About a year later, Mahon becomes insurance adjuster at Chelsea Surety."

"So how is he a fire marker man?"

"That's just part of the job. When his company insures a building, he's supposed to go out and have a fire mark placed on the front. You're a smart man, Gillian. That wouldn't be a full-time job for nobody. But being Mahon's deformed, he don't like to go out in the streets during the day. So, he assigns others to mark the buildings. That's what Voorhees was doing. That's what Denny's doing now for Mahon."

"I think I get it now, Clance."

"So who's really the Fire Marker Man? It's Mahon, it's Voorhees, it's Brian Denny. You see, my hero?" With that, Clancy finished off his whiskey. There were a few moments of silence followed by an even louder belch.

"Hmm," Gillian finally said. "Despite that whole tale, there's still the unanswered question. Where's the loot come from? How did Voorhees get rich? And is Denny right behind?"

"That's what I told you before. I just don't know."

Suddenly, a crowd of firemen invaded the yard area. The stable horses whinnied at the sound of an inebriated Denny's booming voice.

"Attention, attention, my fire boys! I have a few announcements before we return to the festivities." The speaking trumpet was unnecessary, but he was still using it. "First off, two crates of the finest Caribbean rum are now sitting near the front of our engine, all compliments of our dear friend Hendrik Voorhees. There should be a bottle for each of you. Second, we have secured interviews for workman positions at the to-be-constructed Crystal Palace Exhibition Hall." His balance wavered, upsetting his tin and sending whiskey dribbling down his waistcoat. "I don't remember the location for the interviews... or where the Crystal Palace will be constructed, come to think of it. But rest assured, I'll find out." He struggled to suppress a belch. "Anyway, it is an honor that the city, and the investors in this grand project, have considered the men of White Flag Engine Company Five worthy of these well-paid positions." He finally lowered the speaking trumpet. "It appears that we all voted well in the last election."

The men raised their tins and beer jugs and chanted three times, "White Flag Five Stays Alive!" Even Gillian and Clancy, still sitting on the bench, felt compelled to join in.

"Oh, one more thing," Denny continued. "I have three boxes of the finest cigars in front by the rum cases. Compliments of myself."

The men were on their way before Denny had even finished speaking.

"Hmm. Not even a thank you," he muttered as they brushed past.

Just before the festivities concluded, Brian Denny pulled aside three of the men for a most important talk, Robert Gillian included. Gillian had a strange feeling that maybe another opportunity was on the horizon.

CHAPTER THIRTY-THREE

Farragut's textile business—and bank accounts—were expanding at the rate of his waistline. He had purchased a vacant lot and constructed a four-story brick-and-stone building upon which "Farragut and Son, LTD – 1854" was artfully engraved in the granite cornice. A plaque next to the main entrance prominently displayed the architect's name. And just below was a brass fire mark with the insignia of the Chelsea Surety Company. Sure, Farragut paid a higher than typical premium to the elite English Company, but he could rest easy, as his building would take priority should conflagration strike the neighborhood.

The location of his new facility was quite out of the way, which meant a longer commute for the ladies, including Mary, but this was of no concern to him.

"Mary, can I see you in my office after you settle in?" Farragut was in a particularly good mood that morning.

"Of course, sir," she said, even as *please sir, no sir* was what she was thinking.

Farragut's new office was three times as spacious as the one in the former rented premises. A smaller office belonged to his even heftier son, James, who had been brought into the fold a year earlier. Completely subservient to his father, James exercised his muscle and vented his anger at the worker bees, Mary included. And in less than one year, the boy had managed to impregnate two of the workers, forcing his father to pay for two proper abortions to ensure he wouldn't have to hire anew—at a higher wage—should two of his workers die from botched procedures.

"Here I am, sir," Mary said, shutting the door and taking a seat. "My, I'm always so taken with the view here on the fourth floor." To quell her nerves, she looked out at the soothing view of the great Hudson River.

"Hard to believe two years have gone by since... we lost your mother."

You didn't lose my mother. I lost my mother, she thought. But she only dropped her head. "I know. 'Tis amazing, and so much has changed with the new building."

"Well, life goes on," he said with a reflective smile. "Aileen was brilliant with the numbers, and for a woman, she had a sharp business acumen. I mean, her idea of leasing the machines, making the companies bid for my business. We even cut Mr. Singer down to size." He chortled, and his thick, scraggly side chops—now graying—bobbed up and down. He cleared his throat. "Now, about you, Mary." Her heart started racing. "I feel that you are a chip off the old block. I see you have the same sense with numbers and ideas."

"Thank you, sir." She felt a bit lighter now.

"But I can see you're a tad shy with the ladies, not commanding enough. So, I am offering you your mother's position of keeping the books and leasing the equipment as need be. My son will take your position managing the ladies. He is thrilled about this."

"Oh... I see." She quickly chided herself for not being prepared for this. Who else, logically, would be taking her mother's job? But the chubby boy managing the ladies... surely there would be another scandal. *Say something he wants to hear.* "I would be honored to take my mother's position, Mr. Farragut."

"Fine, fine. And from now on, Alvin, my Christian name, will suffice. We will build out an office for you. I can't make it larger than James's. Family, you know. But it will be a fine office right next to mine."

"Thank you, sir. You're most kind," she said.

"Now I take it, Mary, you don't have a beau?"

"No, sir, not yet at least." She felt alarmed. *Oh no. Not James, please. Maybe he just needs me to work late or weekends.*

"I am seeking a mistress at this time in my life. You see, Mary, a man can grow tired of those parlor rooms near the Astor House. I'm in need of somebody with whom I can also converse... at my level of intellect, if you follow. Now you—my dear—are a highly intelligent woman, and trust me, Mrs. Farragut will never catch on." He let out a quick but giddy laugh. "I know the perfect spot for us to meet, and I will always greet you with a gift."

Mary was not sure if she should laugh or cry, or both. She said nothing.

Farragut sat back in his chair, wearing a self-satisfied grin, as if he'd just closed one of his business ventures. "Now, I can't raise your wage just yet to your mother's level. We'll have to see how you perform first... in various ways. But if—"

She abruptly cut him off. "No! I don't want your job! And I certainly am not going to be your mistress! You, sir, are truly a vile man! And I quit as we speak!" Mary couldn't believe this was rolling off her tongue, but she couldn't stop it, not even as her mind chided her that without her mother, her wage was more important than ever.

She stood to leave. He abruptly stood, too, his belly wobbling under loose suspenders. His face was flush. "You can't talk to me that way, young lady! I'll fire you."

"Too late, sir," she said in a calm, cold voice as she headed to the door. She saw that all work had stopped beyond the king's lair. Ladies were frozen at their workstations, staring doe-eyed at the events in Farragut's office.

"You're not going to do any better, you know," he said calmly, a faux sincere tone, which hurt her. She was not sure if he meant any better with a job or a beau. She concluded he probably meant both.

Her hand was still on the doorknob. She didn't want to reveal her tears, but she turned around anyway and looked at him sharply. And there was the face of the deranged seaman, smiling through rotten teeth.

"Then I suppose I'll just have to take my chances."

As she exited, she slammed the door behind her, the glass rattling in its frame. She looked at the frozen workers, all eyes on her.

"Bloody fuckin' beasts, all men are!" she barked at the women, who uniformly went slack-jawed. Seconds later, she'd gathered her belongings and departed for the last time.

Chapter Thirty-Four

The highly unusual meeting was held on a Sunday afternoon. Denny, Gillian, and two other firemen moved swiftly down a sun-filled but windy Broadway, arriving at a strangely narrow building on the northeast corner of Duane Street.

"This is it? The great Chelsea Surety Company you speak of?" complained Moses.

"Shut up, Moses," countered Stretch. Denny and Gillian just shook their heads.

"The main quarters are in London," Denny said. "This is just where they do the insurance adjusting in New York." He pulled his gold timepiece out of the pocket of his cloak. "Almost half past the hour. Looks like we've a minute to spare. He said a Mrs. Grimble will be coming down the stairs to retrieve us. Let's hope she's timely—it's cold as a witch's tit out here."

"You got some nerve complaining," Stretch snapped. "You with that fine wool cloak."

"Aye, and I got a fur hat, too," Denny added. "Just didn't wear it. Didn't want you boys getting green with envy, ye know."

For once, Gillian noticed, Denny was entirely sober. This meeting must be extremely important.

Punctual to the second, Mrs. Grimble arrived at the door, wrinkled and frail looking. Gillian tried to determine if the woman was truly elderly or had aged beyond her years.

"Good afternoon, gentlemen. Mr. Mahon is expecting you." Her voice was unexpectedly strong.

The stairs were steep, but the frail woman moved swiftly. The four men struggled to keep her pace until she arrived at a third-floor landing, where she removed a large brass key from her dress pocket. A sharp click reverberated through the stairwell, and then they were inside a small waiting room comfortably adorned with several plush King George armchairs.

"Wait here, gentlemen," she said and then quickly disappeared behind another door.

After five minutes, Mrs. Grimble returned.

"Just Mr. Denny, please," she corrected when they rose to follow. Denny, comfortable in his plush King George, appeared bothered that he needed to oblige.

Fifteen minutes passed, then twenty.

"I can take my slumber right here," said Stretch.

Gillian and Moses both had their eyes half closed. Then all three were startled by the chime of the wall clock.

"Holy Moses!" Gillian cried, jolted from his trance.

"You rang?" asked Moses.

Stretch was about to respond when the three were startled again, this time by a loud scratching sound as a large piece of wood slid past a partition window, the glass separating the cozy waiting room from what appeared to be a sun-filled interior office.

Gillian saw a familiar sight on the other side of the window. There was Denny, conversing with the same hideous figure he'd observed the night of the distillery fire. But this was different. The body language didn't tell of an argument but a business discussion. Then the unknown figure turned toward the glass partition and came just shy of pressing his nose against the window, studying the three firemen in the waiting area.

Though aghast, all three managed to squelch their gasps. But Gillian's shock was not of revulsion. He had seen his share of disturbing images, enough for a lifetime. *Such awful pain must plague this John Mahon, every day of his life, pain of the body and soul.*

Mahon's appearance was one of remarkable contrasts. The right side of his face was a patchwork of taut and leathery scar tissue—nothing resembling God-given skin. His right eye had been burned out of its socket, he only had half an ear remaining, and something resembling a nose that Gillian was hard-pressed to describe. He was completely bald on the right side, with similar scar tissue from his forehead to the back of his crown. Even if hair could grow there, Gillian thought, it would not want to. And yet remarkably, the left side of his face was perfectly intact, short graying hair included. One blue eye, a plump lip, birthright skin, all enough to remind a man looking in the glass of what he had been, what he should still be.

Gillian wondered. Did a man like this avoid the looking glass? Or did he grow used to his visage as he went about his business? He had ample time to make these observations, as Mahon stood before the window for perhaps a full two minutes, scrutinizing the three men. Gillian was uncertain, but he felt that Mahon was scrutinizing him much more closely than his comrades.

Then the man pulled away, and the loud scratching sound returned as the wood board slid across the partition window. The waiting area was once again in twilight. Fifteen minutes passed, and the wall clock struck half past the hour.

"This is odd, ain't it?" expressed Moses, appearing annoyed.

"Sure is," replied Stretch. Gillian nodded, his thoughts only half there. Mary's issue was on his mind. He'd hoped to spend time with her this afternoon to discuss options. With the loss of Aileen's income, and Mary out of work now, they'd be slowly depleting their savings. And he didn't know why she couldn't just put off Farragut's proposition until she found a better situation.

Finally, the door to the inner office opened with a creak. A ray of light from the late afternoon sun illuminated the waiting area once again.

"Okay, boys," Denny boomed as he mounted his top hat. "Let's march on."

Behind him was Mrs. Grimble. "Let me follow you gentlemen down so I can lock the door. We don't want any drifters coming in to warm themselves up."

Denny was silent until they were back out on the street.

"Sorry, laddies, he ain't interested in any of you. Not sure why."

The men walked in silence, heads down to shield them from the stiff breeze, until each went his own separate way.

On his journey home, Gillian continued to reflect on the bizarre encounter—which he felt was not really a meeting anyway, except for Denny. And then the strange way Mahon focused on him, as the man peered through the glass pane. *Why was the Fire Marker Man studying me?* He supposed he might find out more in time.

Chapter Thirty-Five

A New Situation for Mary

As Mary walked down Vestry Street, a fine but cold mist was hitting her umbrella, the water condensing on top, then dripping off the edge in thin streams. Anxious about the encounter, she was dreadfully afraid of arriving late, even though she had planned her route carefully. But a lot was at stake. Feeling guilty about abruptly quitting Farragut's manufactory, she wanted to replace the lost household income as swiftly as possible.

It had been a few years since she passed through this neighborhood, and she noticed that an increasing number of commercial buildings had changed the character of the area. Now there were just a smattering of the majestic Colonial-era townhomes and Dutch-style residences left. Some had been destroyed by fire, but many were razed in the name of progress. It saddened her that financial gain seemed to be all that mattered lately.

This must be it. Climbing five steps brought her to a stately and towering red-painted door. A polished brass knocker was set prominently just above her eye level. Before she could grab hold of it, the door swung open. Standing there was a short, plump woman in an unflatteringly flowered dress and a hat adorned with colorful feathers. She greeted Mary with a warm smile, as if this were a social engagement. Mary reminded herself that this was just a business-friendly greeting, not a friendly greeting. *The woman is just relieved that domestic help has arrived.*

"You must be Mary Gillian. How wonderfully punctual! Come in, dear." The woman stood aside for Mary in such a way one might assume she'd been filling in quite some time for the vacant position. She extended her hand. "Clara Bidwell, glad to meet you. Tea?"

"Oh. Yes. I mean... if it's no trouble for you, ma'am." Mary was taken aback by the woman's cordiality. Certainly nothing like her initial greeting at Farragut's manufactory.

"Follow me to the parlor. I would have our servant check your coat, but, well, I'm afraid we're short a servant. That's why you're here," she said with a chortle.

Mary, anxious as she was, managed to conjure a polite smile and a nod, which was entirely unnecessary, as Clara Bidwell was already moving swiftly through the hallway to the rear parlor room.

"Now, you make yourself comfortable, dear. You can keep your coat next to you on the sofa, and just place your references on that table there. Let me retrieve Mr. Bidwell." She sighed deeply, and Mary couldn't tell if the woman was annoyed at the thought of searching for the master of the house or was just winded from their journey. "That man's always at the furthest corner of the house when I need him," she added, her voice trailing away, as she was already in the next room.

Perhaps the husband's distant location in the house was no coincidence.

Mary sat on the corner of the plush sofa, now worried about the aforementioned *references*. Of course, she lacked references in the field of domestic service, and Farragut's reference—even if possible—would be of little use. *This wasn't supposed to be a problem. Hopefully, Clancy told the Bidwells that this will be my first domestic servant job. Could he have forgotten?*

She felt annoyed at having to explain the situation. Then, her attention was diverted to a black Siamese cat that had jumped onto the armchair opposite her. Presenting itself regally, it perched tall, right in the center of the cushion, and stared at her, as though it was going to be part of the interviewing procedure.

Clara reentered the room, moving slowly now, carrying a silver tea set that she placed on the table right where Mary's references were supposed to be.

"Nucky... uh, Mr. Bidwell will be along shortly. No need to wait for him, though."

She sat down on a matching loveseat—apparently, she wouldn't dare disturb the cat—and removed her ornately feathered hat. After placing it gently beside her, she proceeded to pour the tea.

Seconds of silence reinforced Mary's anxiety regarding her lack of references, and she felt the need to initiate conversation. "I can see that you have a lovely home, Mrs. Bidwell. Clancy did prepare me, to some degree, all flattering, of course, but he still didn't do it justice. It's spectacular, if I may say so."

"Oh gracious, thank you, Mary! Mr. Bidwell will be glad to hear that—he does so love to show off his collections. Now you jogged my memory. I almost forgot that you're a referral of Clancy Carver. It was a joy to see the boy after so many years. Of course, I shouldn't call him a boy; he must be beyond fifty years by now. But we do remember him as a happy and polite Negro, back in the day when we paid visits to the Rutherfords next door."

Mary knew much of the background from Clancy himself—never one to be shy—but she just smiled and welcomed another point of view.

"Clancy was acquainted with our butler, so we saw him quite often. But with slavery gone in New York, Mrs. Rutherford couldn't afford to keep him on. By law, Clancy was a free man already when his father died. But I know he didn't want to leave. The Rutherfords treated him like one of their own, but she needed rent money to keep the house, so she converted that beautiful mansion into a boarding place. It was really such a shame— "

"Ah, Miss Gillian, I presume," came a booming voice as a stout man made his grand entrance. "A pleasure to meet you," he said and then bowed.

She stood and curtsied, her dress making such a swishing sound that she felt embarrassed.

"Pleased to meet you, sir," she said and then returned to her seat. She noticed that the cat was observing her every move.

"Clancy could not attach one unfavorable trait to your character, my dear," he said as he looked her over, head to toe, with an expression she recognized as less than one hundred percent approval. "I know your experience with paid domestic work is limited, but Mrs. Bidwell will teach you what you need to know, and she has a schedule for you to follow. Besides, it's a fair deal. Your wage is on the low end, as befits your lack of experience, but there's room to grow. And I'm sure you will find your quarters quite satisfactory, as well as the fare. Should you and Mrs. Bidwell have mutually agreeable feelings, I hope you can start your employment within a week or two. We would send for your belongings."

"Oh, thank you, sir." She stood to honor him, then quickly sat back down, again conscious of her swishing dress.

"No need to call me 'sir.' Mr. Bidwell will do fine," he said as he fished for his pipe in the pocket of his smoking jacket. After securing it, he smiled at Mary, then his wife, who was busy refilling both tea cups. "It's nice to see your people moving up in America. This country has certainly treated me well."

"Indeed, it is nice to aid the Irish people," Clara chimed in, stirring the tea she had just drowned with milk. "You've had such a dreadful time these last years with the famine and all."

Mary, unsure what to say, just smiled and nodded.

"Well, I have to return to my work," Mr. Bidwell said. "Had to fire my bookkeeper last week, nice fellow but incompetent."

As he left, voice trailing after him, Mary noticed his peculiar gait, a slight wobble in his left leg. And he was gone, apart from the sweet scent of his tobacco smoke.

"So, tell me about your background, Mary? This is most exciting," she said giddily. "We've never had a servant girl of our type."

CHAPTER THIRTY-SIX

June 1853

"Robert, can I talk with you when you're done with this last load?" Brian Denny asked.

It was an unusually hot spring day, and both men were sweating. Gillian was nearing the end of his shift, having spent the morning hauling burlap sacks and crates of tea from the Orient. Denny had just walked from the accounting office to the docks.

"Fine, Brian. About ten minutes."

Gillian wondered what this could be about. A promotion to accounting? That might be a disaster, considering his numbers skill.

When he finished the work, Gillian found Denny sitting on the edge of the adjacent dock, the dock where the *Nina* had landed six years earlier.

"You remember our meeting with John Mahon last month, don't you?"

"Of course. He's a sight not to forget, poor bloke. Strange how he wasn't interested in meeting any of us."

"Well, that's not true, just what I said at the time," Denny said bluntly. "Truth is, he's interested in you, Robert. He wants you to help me place markers on the new buildings they're insuring. He said Chelsea Surety has plans to grow big in New York. They see the changes in this city. And he's right. The buildings will be growing taller with the Otis elevators and tougher fire codes. But the competition between the insurance companies is fierce now. And these English companies operate a little differently."

"Why does he want me?" Gillian was thinking back to the attention Mahon paid him the day of the meeting.

"He wouldn't tell me. Strange fellow, he is. I wouldn't have picked ya," Denny said with a chortle and gently punched Gillian on the shoulder.

Ah, the softer side of Brian Denny, Gillian thought. He was grateful that the man liked him since Denny was *technically* still his boss, even if he spent most of his time with the ledgers. And in the rare instances when the man was dead sober, he was almost likable.

"I don't know, Brian. How am I going to find time to anchor those brass things into stone? I have this job on the docks, and maybe the Crystal Palace project on Saturdays."

"You trust me on this, Gillian. It's worth making the time. You'll see."

"How so?" Gillian felt defiant. More encroachment on his limited free time was not what he was seeking.

"You'll find out. A lot of extras come along with being a fire marker man."

"Hmm," was Gillian's only response, still trying to figure out how placing markers on buildings could amount to much additional money. But he'd been struggling to replace Aileen's wage, and with Mary in a new situation at the Bidwell residence, she wouldn't be contributing much to their coffers. Nor did he want her to. Should she end up a spinster, he wanted her to be comfortable in her later days. Then there was Patrick, wanting to be a druggist.

"Well, while your mind is going on this, I hear Otis will be having a display of his safety devices right on the first floor of the Crystal Palace. He wants to show that the whole contraption won't come crashing down if the cable breaks. That's the ticket for new buildings that'll reach the heavens one day. Speaking of which, how did the interview go over there?"

"They seemed to like me," Gillian replied. "They said to stop by next week to check, but I feel strong that I'll be getting the work. It ain't easy, you know, getting all the way up to Sixth Avenue and 42nd Street, but it's a sight to see. And they have the drawings posted on the wall of the reservoir. It's to be a beauty. All glass and cast iron. They're saying two hundred thousand square feet with a glass dome too. Welding, that's what I'm going for. They train you and pay well.

"So good luck with that," Denny said. "So did you decide yet, Robert?"

"Decide what?" he said, annoyed.

"You know, being a fire marker man for Mahon. Besides, you can't say no, ye know. Nobody says no to him."

Gillian turned a puzzled face to Denny and cocked his head. "What do you mean, no one says no?"

"Like I said, no one turns down his offer. I mean, no one with a head on his shoulders."

"Well, I guess I'll have to find out what's it about then," he said, slowly standing. "Now, I best be heading home. Since Mary left, me and Patrick have to figure our supper."

Gillian felt stiff. It'd been a long day of hauling in the heat, and he was starting to think his age was getting to him. Not that forty-three was old, but maybe it was for the work he was doing. "Well, good evening, Brian Denny." And in the words of a true fireman, "I hope I don't see ya later."

"Same here," said Denny with a smile.

As he headed for South Street, Gillian already knew his answer regarding the Fire Marker Man.

CHAPTER THIRTY-SEVEN

He took the longer route home that evening, first stopping by Simon's barbershop for a cut and shave. No hot corn girls were out on such a warm evening, which was just as well. He didn't want to think about that poor one being run over by a streetcar while helping her brother chisel ice along the road. He imagined she had long since been replaced, perhaps forgotten.

As he approached the row of newer tenements—even newer than his—on the opposite side of Grand Street, he noticed a sign posted just in front. *Brand New Flats for Let.* Underneath, it said, *Fresh Croton Water.* Then in much smaller print, further down, *Nearby.*

In a fury, he threw his cap on the ground. "Those bloody bastards!" he yelled. "They didn't even honor us with a sign! Bloody pigs, *nearby,* my ass," he growled. "Lying scoundrels, now my wife is dead. Twice the rent we were paying before, for stinkin' poison water," he went on, ignoring the curious just-lit lanterns turning in his direction. *I ought to burn these buildings down. They're no better than the land agents in me old country.*

Still in a fit, he crossed the street to his first-floor apartment and saw from the window that Patrick had lit the gas lamp. *Good, the lad has started our supper.* Visiting the privy before heading to their flat, he noted the facilities were still in relatively good condition. As usual, he avoided the third stall, Aileen's brief home during her brief illness. While sitting on the seat, he conceded, *Maybe the Croton water sign was there all along. We never took the time to read it closely.*

That night the dream resumed. It always started the same. "Papa, Papa, come quick!" Daisy screams, so he drops his hoe, runs to the field, and takes in the smell of decaying lumpers. "Go get your mama, Daisy," he orders. But this time it's different. Now he hears the buzzing of flies, many flies, perhaps a swarm. As he walks toward the source, the stench of dead flesh overtakes his senses. So strong, the rotting potato plants are now odorless. And there, in a heaping pile, the rest of his family. But also his old friend Roger and Clancy. And a third man is there, a short distance from the rest. His old friend, Daniel Mahoney. But he's alive, sitting amongst the potato plants, sobbing uncontrollably.

Grunting, Gillian woke with a start. He was soaked with sweat, not just a result of the nightmare but also because the air in the apartment was close. Daniel Mahoney? Why, after all these years, was he there? And why was he the sole one alive? And why was he crying so?

Gillian heard Patrick stir in the next room. Then he opened the window, but there was no breeze. He walked over to Patrick's room, the first room of his own now that Mary had left. The boy, actually a man of eighteen years, was snoring ever so slightly. His son was looking more like him every day, except for the slight crook in the boy's nose. This irritated him. *Why couldn't I afford a better surgeon! Why couldn't I have a business like Scotty's father? Then I, too, could have bought off the bully who maimed my son! A couple of free apples to the bully's drunken papa is all it would've taken!*

These thoughts loud in his head, he went back to bed. Within minutes, his conscious mind let go. Suddenly, Gillian sat up with a start of rage. *She didn't go back to be with them, our little ones. She's just dead like them!* He wanted to scream. Now, any attempt at sleep was futile.

CHAPTER THIRTY-EIGHT

The Crystal Palace needed to be completed in a tight timeframe to meet the date for the first World's Fair to be held in New York City. Thousands of enameled glass panels had to be inserted into cast-iron frames, the latter produced at the site. Robert Gillian was trained as a forge welder, standing beside a blast furnace for hours at a time. Each weekend he arrived at the site, he was stunned at the progress during the preceding week.

Sixth Avenue and 42nd Street, once near the edge of *'civilized'* Manhattan, had come alive. Businessmen and real estate developers were drooling at the expected opportunities around this new tourism magnet. While Gillian and Clancy—and even his derelict son, Emmet—were working hard on the project, Brian Denny was applying his newfound wealth, joining questionable partnerships to gobble up the surrounding buildings and land. But apart from a large and elegant ice creamery, the businesses springing to life in the area were far from the grandiose imaginings of the city planners. Instead, more arcades, cheap eateries, whorehouses, and tenements were in order. Along with that came the street swindlers and pickpockets.

But this was just a small part of Robert Gillian's life, although the extra wages had allowed him to remain in the no-longer-new tenement building on Grand and Mott Streets. They had to keep boiling their drinking water, but at least they remained out of the Five Points neighborhood.

February of 1854, Robert Gillian received his first fire marker assignment. A postal box had been assigned to him by John Mahon, Chief Adjuster, New York Branch of Chelsea Surety Company. The instructions were simple but explicit. First, a note carrier would arrive alerting him to check the postal box. Inside would be the finely detailed brass marker wrapped in a linen containing a letter stating the address of the building to be marked, the precise location to place the marker, and four brass screws to be anchored in the brick or stone facade. Then, exactly one week after he completed the assignment, he was instructed to collect his fee, in paper or coinage, inside the same postal box.

Despite the chill in the air, Gillian's palms were sweaty as he removed the first package from his postal box and placed it on the large wood counter next to a lighted gas lamp. He carefully unwrapped it so as not to rip the paper carrying the all-important instructions. Under the lamp, the brass marker shone brilliantly. Gillian was startled and quickly became self-conscious, thinking others in the post office would be distracted by the light bouncing off the object and dancing about the room.

He read the instructions and was off to complete his assignment. A new textile building was waiting to be marked.

Boring holes in brick with a hand drill was no easy task, but he got it done. The brass plate featured a fire bell, and just beneath, written in script: *Premises Protected by Chelsea Surety Company London-New York*. To his surprise, Gillian felt a sense of pride. This truly was the highest quality fire mark he'd ever seen. Others he'd seen were weather-beaten, the polishing neglected over the years.

One week later, he returned to his assigned postal box. There, in coinage, was not the five dollars he was promised but ten dollars! "How remarkable!" he blurted. Heads turned in his direction, but he cared little. He quickly closed his postal box and was off to the savings bank to make his hefty deposit. "Strange. This Mahon is so generous, Aileen," he muttered as he walked. "I am a fortunate one, I think."

CHAPTER THIRTY-NINE

In time, the placement of the fire marks increased in frequency. Chelsea Surety was indeed growing its presence in New York City, and New York City was growing outward—and upward with the perfection of Otis's elevator contraption. But despite improved fire codes, buildings were still burning at an alarming rate. Of course, the fire-fighting equipment was improving, too: Larger steam engines, better water pressure at the Croton-supplied hydrants, and superior hoses and ladders. Fire bells were becoming increasingly obsolete, replaced by the telegraph. Still, Gillian felt as if the growth of the city was always more than one step ahead of their fire-fighting abilities.

Nevertheless, he continued to collect the handsome fees paid to him by the insurance adjuster at Chelsea Surety Company. And as the buildings grew bigger, so did the placement fees. Ten dollars was common, but now he was finding fifteen or even twenty dollars for a single job. In fact, one fire mark placement easily covered an entire month's rent on their Grand Street flat. Visits to the local bank became more frequent, and the tellers and managers were recognizing his name. He couldn't help but feel giddy. *I dare say, I'm growing rich in this line of work. Well, not quite,* he would humbly conclude, lest Aileen's line of thinking was right, and he'd be struck down by deserved misfortune.

He knew Brian Denny was also enjoying the benefits of this work, but the two rarely shared information. He couldn't speak for Denny, but Gillian instinctively avoided the topic—knowing something wasn't right with the overly generous pay. *But easy money's good money just the same,* he concluded.

The late-night fires came and went, always difficult to predict. But what Gillian knew with certainty, upon encountering a working blaze— or the rare conflagration—was that he could expect a visit from the specter in the flames. A whirlwind of fire, first turning dark red, then purple, quickly getting darker until it was almost black against the back-drop of orange flames. The whirlwind would grow tighter and tighter as it spun faster, until it resembled a rope-like object. That was when the transformation would occur. The rope-like form would abruptly stop spinning, and it would morph into a figure, part man, part insect with a peculiar proboscis. Sometimes it would beckon him forward into the fire, sometimes not.

He continued to ignore it. What choice did he have? Nobody shared his vision, so nobody could possibly understand. He'd be marked as a madman if he ranted of such. To remain a firefighter, he had to accept this.

Gillian now counted four comfortable years since his first fire marker assignment. Not only had he put a tidy sum away in the bank, but he and Patrick had purchased *non-used* furniture for the Grand Street flat, including the first ever full-length mirror he would own. In fact, it was his first mirror of any kind. Patrick was enrolled in school to become a druggist, and frequently when he returned from his studies in the eve-ning, they'd venture out for supper—sometimes at more than modest establishments. And Mary would join them on her days off from the Bidwell household.

One hot summer day as he'd just finished his last haul at the docks and was walking toward South Street, he was approached by Brian Den-ny. Denny worked exclusively in the accounting office now, sitting on his rump all day. He'd gained considerable around the middle, and his hair was almost completely gray. Gillian felt sure his boss could no longer haul cargo even if he'd wanted to.

"Robert, you have time for an ale?" the man asked.

"Aye, sounds like a great idea," he fibbed.

Truly, Gillian wanted to head home. The hot days at the dock were taking a toll, especially since he too had accumulated some weight around the middle, as Patrick and Mary liked to point out—or poke at. He took pride in this, sensing others would see a well-fed fellow. Still, his wardrobe didn't reflect his comfortable existence. He was mostly oblivious of that fact, though Patrick had suggested Mary assist him in correcting the issue, and he'd agreed.

They settled on a saloon just at the corner of South and Fulton Streets, an establishment several tiers above the basement groggery he still frequented with Clancy and Katonah. Denny slapped a handful of change on the table, quickly getting the barmaid's attention. "Two jugs of your finest ale, my lady!"

"Coming right up, fellas," the tall woman said as she bent over to place drink coasters in front of them.

"Yowsa!" Denny exclaimed as he stared at her cleavage.

The barmaid smiled, unabashed, then took off for their drinks.

"You see them set of apples, Robert? They're for sale, I'll bet. You can afford them now."

"How could I miss them? But she's just showing for the crowd— probably a married woman."

Truth was, it had been a long time. Gillian never had many women in his life. One before Aileen, and neither she nor Aileen had been well endowed in the bosom. Then there was the whore, Aggie, whom he tried not to think about. *Poor dead Aggie.*

"Anyways, let me get to the point," Denny said. "The Fire Marker Man likes you, Robert. lord knows why, but he thinks you're ready to step up for the big work, if you know what I mean."

Gillian had the urge to feign naivety. He had a strong hunch what this meeting was about. Rumors abounded, but all firemen knew. They just kept it in whispers or to themselves.

"I'm pretty sure I do," he said just as the ales arrived and a fiddler appeared in a far corner of the room. He breathed easy when it was a Celtic tune he didn't know.

"Let's take that corner table," Denny said, and the barmaid chased after them with their coasters. "Classy place, aye. Coasters are important here." Within seconds of taking their seats, Denny began. "So, you know what a *good* fire is, Gillian, right?"

"I suppose so." He left it at that and took a swig from his jug. He was curious to hear Denny's explanation.

"You see, a few insurance companies will pay us for saving a building. In a way, it gives us volunteers an incentive, being that we risk our lives and all."

As Denny stopped for a swig of ale, a touch of foam landing on his heavy chin, Gillian was thinking, *When did I ever see Brian Denny risk his life in a fire?*

"Now, it may change some day, but companies like Chelsea use their adjusters to investigate after a fire," Denny said. "The company then lays out money for the damages. Then they pay the spiff, some call it the *reward*. They forward the money to the adjuster's office, then he gives it to the foreman of the first fire company on the scene—assuming they did right, putting it out quickly."

"So that's how Voorhees grew so wealthy. And you, Brian, seem to be doing quite well yourself." Gillian prompted Denny to raise his jug for a toast. "Cheers to good fortune, Mr. Denny!" *Clink.*

"Aye, Robert, I'm fortunate too, but there's more to the point here." He stared at Gillian with one eye as he took another swig. Gillian, feeling a bit uncomfortable now, followed suit. "Wise up, boy!" Denny blurted unexpectedly, and then peered around the room to see if he'd drawn attention. "Or you're just playing dumb, Robert, eh?" he said, bending forward to breathe beer at Gillian.

"How so?" Gillian replied regretfully. He wished the unsaid could remain unsaid. He just wanted to continue collecting the generous pay for placing the fire markers on the insured buildings. But for a while now, he knew this day would come.

"You can't possibly think Voorhees and I grew wealthy on rewards from an occasional fire." Just as he was about to divulge the truth, the barmaid arrived to set down Denny's next ale.

Chapter Thirty-Nine

"Another for you, sir?"

"Hmm," Gillian replied, rubbing his lips in contemplation. "Aye, bring it on, lass." Based on the strength of his Irish brogue in that last statement, the first round was already doing its magic.

As soon as they were alone again, Denny glanced about the room, at the fiddler making his music, at the bartender tending the bar, and back to Gillian again. He leaned forward, and in a whisper, he said, "We can't always wait for a fire, you know." Then he shrugged. He was tentative about continuing, perhaps not sure what reaction to expect.

"Such as I thought," Gillian said, feeling sad and a bit anxious now that the cat was out of the bag. He couldn't pretend anymore that life would stay easy—and lucrative.

"Sometimes there simply aren't enough fires, or rather, ones we can control. Mahon has a detailed schedule. It's all quite organized, you'll see. He'll make you an expert, like me." Denny cleared his throat. It was obvious to Gillian that the man might've wanted to pull back the last part of that statement. "Here's how it works, usually. Mahon chooses the building. He figures out the when and how. You, the stager, relay the information to the closest firehouse—foreman only! It's important that only the foreman's privy to the details. He'll make sure his company's first on the scene. Then, if the event goes well, Mahon gets a hefty reward from the home office. He splits it between the foreman, the special event team—that's you and the fireman who starts the fire—and, of course, he takes a bite himself." Denny, a bit winded, sat back in his chair, licked his lips, and started on his second jug.

"It all sounds well planned... oh, here's my ale," Gillian sat back as the well-endowed barmaid placed the jug in front of him. She was tall and the tables low, so her cleavage was in his face. He drew in her perfume, considering she must be aware of the position this put her in. Then she smiled at him just before turning away.

"So are you in, Robert?" Denny asked impatiently.

"Well, I just don't quite know," Gillian said. "I'm stuck on the 'Here's how it works *usually*,' and the '*If* the event goes well' part of what you said."

"From time to time, you have to expect issues to come up. You can't control everything. Why, I remember a few times the fire failed to ignite, once because the dingbat incendiary used the wrong powders. The foreman was waiting for the bell, which never came. Rare, though. Sometimes we lose control of the thing. Rare, too, but devastating. Becomes a bad fire quickly. You don't want to deal with Mahon after that. His wrath is mean, or worse." Denny's eyes opened wide, as if the fearsome man was the one in front of him, not Gillian. He took a large swig of his ale and appeared to squelch a belch. "You remember the Great Distillery Fire back a few?"

"Aye, of course. Damn near got Clancy killed."

"Oh yes, I do recall that now." When Denny leaned forward, his red face told Gillian that he was back in his familiar state. "It was my fuckin' doing," he whispered. "I botched it good, and Mahon wanted me hide for that." He sat back and shrugged, certainly not conveying any remorse or shame.

"How did it happen?" Gillian asked.

"I prepared the camphene and oil of turpentine mixture early in the night, up in that second-floor office. A few hours later, Mahon's man ignited the fire. In between, I was supposed to reach the foreman of Company Two, ye know, Spanky. His engine was supposed to be first on the scene for that one."

Denny stopped, looked down at the table, and started tapping his fingers on the side of his jug as if having second thoughts about divulging the story. But he went on.

"So, I went to see Spanky at his flat just after I did my part. He wasn't there. My plan was to check back in an hour or so. But I fell asleep. Don't know why. Could've been from making too much merry the night before. Next thing I knew, I heard the fire bells, and it wasn't one or two, if you think back. We had a real disaster now."

"That's why!" Gillian said.

"That's why what?"

"The row you had with Spanky, the two of you almost carted off to jail! Spanky knew you . . ." He stopped before saying *fucked-up*, although the intention to was obvious.

"Aye, Robert," he muttered before finishing his ale. "But there's more. Mahon lets us call it off if we think it's best. I should have called it off. It was a windy night, and the mixture was too strong. In haste, I forgot to dilute the turpentine."

Gillian's mind went to the argument he'd witnessed between Denny and the Fire Marker Man, the lantern swaying back and forth, himself catching momentary glimpses of the enraged figure. Then his mind went to Clancy on fire, the strange specter in the flames, and the sound of the lone dying cow in the attached dairy, the animal no one paid any mind to as they fought the fire. *You bloody bastard, Denny. I bear the weight of guilt for what could've been Clancy's end.* He shook is head in disgust.

"So what did Mahon say?" Gillian asked with trepidation.

"He said that I cost Chelsea Surety a fortune and maybe caused his ruin, which would be my ruin. The owners of the distillery would suspect arson, and he would have to head it off with his own investigation and get them top dollar in a payout. Then he said to me, 'If I go down, it's going to be worse for you, Brian Denny.' He gave me a look, Robert, that I'll never forget or be able to explain. But I knew in my soul what it meant."

"Hmm," is all Gillian said, in deep thought as he tapped the side of his unfinished jug. "The price for growing rich, I guess."

Suddenly more upbeat, Denny said, "Gillian, surely you didn't think you were getting all that money for placing bloody signs on buildings, did ya? He was feeling you out, seeing if you'd do exactly as told. Still, I don't know why he chose you without even talking to each of you boys. But you can't say no, ye know. And why would ya? This is your ticket, Robert Gillian." With that, Denny was done with his persuasive speech. His eyes roamed the room, seeking out the barmaid. "I'm gonna get me some pork and beans for my supper. You in?"

"For pork and beans or for working for the Fire Marker Man?" He was far from comfortable that his own words, "working for the Fire Marker Man," meant, quite bluntly, "becoming an arsonist."

"Both," Denny replied as he snapped his fingers to get the barmaid's attention.

"Definitely not pork and beans. My boy has dinner on the stove. What happens next?"

"Nothing happens next," Denny said nonchalantly, now annoyed that the barmaid wasn't hustling over right away. "A boy will call on you with the message to check your postal box. In it, you'll find a paper with all the details you'll need: address of the building, the night of the scheduled event, location at the site for the ignition point. And that should do it."

"What do you mean, that should do it?"

"Just like I said, that should do it."

"That's not enough, Brian!" Gillian barked.

"Keep it down," Denny hissed. "You'll have us both strung up."

This final statement didn't sit well with Gillian. "What about the *how*? And *if* the situation doesn't look right?"

"I'm gonna teach you the different methods we use, whether it be oil tar, turpentine, a careless cigar, or even gunpowder. If it's a manufactory with high combustibles on site, we can get away with the gunpowder. The cause of the fire has to make sense, depending on the situation."

Gillian shushed him; the barmaid was approaching.

"Another round, boys?"

"Aye, one more should do it. Just one more, Gillian?"

"Oh no, not me. I have to leave," Gillian said as this seemed to be a fine opportunity for him to make his exit. He rose quickly, feeling a bit wobbly. *Two pints, not too bad. Maybe the years are catching up to me.*

"See ya again sometime, handsome," the barmaid flirted and then rushed off, clearly not wanting to stand there alone in Denny's presence.

"Cheerio, Brian." And he tipped his cap at the engine company foreman, dockworker boss, and now, perhaps, partner in crime.

"Same to you, Robert. See ya bright and early—as usual. Hopefully, not sooner."

As Gillian fled to the street, he took in a deep breath and exhaled slowly. Suddenly, he was angry at Denny. *Why couldn't he have left me alone, free from this fuckin charade.* Then he realized he was angry at himself. He'd known something was wrong since his first job placing a fire marker and being overpaid for the pleasant task. He'd felt something was off when the Fire Marker Man chose him above the others for the job. But the money came so easy, and so it was easy to pretend there wasn't more to this affair. And now was the moment of reckoning. A decision needed to be made.

CHAPTER FORTY

"I am an unusually tall fellow, and that's a good thing, I think. It makes for a commanding presence and allows me to carry my belly proudly, under suspenders and waistcoat. What do you think?"

Ever since Patrick had started leaving early for work, Gillian had picked up the habit of talking to his reflection in the full-length glass. Mary had implored him to make the purchase with the other new furniture. "Father, a person must know how he appears to the outside world, so he can determine how best to carry himself among his peers." He didn't necessarily agree, but he did have the means to make the purchase—and end the nagging. Now, he saw value in what he once thought of as a frivolous expenditure.

Sometimes he would observe himself, stark naked, making note of his aging body. Then sometimes he would dress for an outing: high white collar, necktie, waistcoat, trousers, formal shoes, and a top hat. All additions to his wardrobe were insisted upon by Mary, except for the wool cloak, which was Patrick's request. The compromise he made was that he would purchase just one of each item, as outings were rare. Finally, he would dress in his usual slops, boots, and cap, and admire himself as a rugged dockworker and former potato farmer.

This day was different. He stared at his naked reflection.

"Just who are you, Robert Gillian? Are you the humble, well-principled Catholic Irishman, proud husband of the late Aileen Gillian, father of two remaining offspring? Or are you an arsonist, an incendiary? Will you do anything for money?"

His reflection stood there waiting for an answer.

"Perhaps you are the good one in the glass, and I not so," he said in almost a whisper. "I should reason this out, not be quick to jump at the idea, but not be too self-righteous either." *We firemen do risk our lives; why shouldn't there be some financial reward? It's just commercial buildings, empty of people at night. And I'm not lighting the match, just doing my part. "Staging it," as Denny says.*

"Hogwash!" came from the glass. "Who're you kidding, Gillian! All true, but can you live with yourself?"

"Perhaps not, or maybe I can. Just for a little while, you know. Patrick's to become a druggist. The boy still needs help with the schooling costs. Besides, why did we come here in the first place? And look at the sacrifices we've made. We left our darlings behind, near broke Aileen's heart. Then she had her life stolen from her by greedy, lying landlords, filthy water, swindlers. This town's no better than London or Dublin."

The image in the mirror had no chance to respond as Gillian slammed the closet door shut.

CHAPTER FORTY-ONE

January 1857

Half a year after his meeting with Denny at the pub, and a few years since he began placing fire marks for the hideous insurance adjuster of Chelsea Surety Company, Gillian received his first call to action.

With all those months to ponder, now he was having second thoughts.

"Where are you going, Papa?" Patrick inquired, as it was unusual these days for his father to leave the flat after sunset. But Gillian was prepared for this. He had lined up a set of excuses to be used for his whereabouts as need be.

"Clancy and the boys set up a game of cards at the firehouse. I think I'll play a few hands, that's all," he said as he finished lacing his boots. "I won't be gone long." Quickly changing the topic, "Boy, why don't you put some extra coals in the stove. It's gonna be a bear tonight."

Fresh coal was plentiful with their newfound wealth. No more picking the well-to-do neighborhoods on Sunday mornings. He put on his heavy wool cloak and quickly navigated the wooden buttons. Finally, a wool hat with ear flaps.

"Okay, Cheerio, Patrick. Wish me luck," he said.

"Aye, make a killing," the boy said from the dining table, his head deep in the newspaper.

I hope not, Gillian thought as he departed for his first job as an arsonist. *Or just stager for an arsonist.*

The cloak's deep pockets were handy as storage for his incendiary materials. But first, the privy house to pee, and then to retrieve two small cans planted under a deep bed of leaves just behind "Aileen's stall." One, camphene, a mixture of turpentine and ethanol. The other, acetone diluted with water.

He placed one can in each pocket and began his journey to a small manufactory at the northeast corner of William and John Streets. A windless night, perfect for a well-controlled fire. Still, after walking a few blocks, he felt the need to recheck the instructions. His lamp was weak, or Mahon's handwriting was weak, so a match, perhaps. This would have solved the problem had he brought matches with him.

What sort of incendiary are you... idiot! he chided himself. Then again, he thought, *Why would I bear matches? After all, I am just the stager, not the incendiary.* Nevertheless, at that hour of the night, no match girls would be found on the streets, and he didn't want to show his face in any retail establishments. The lantern would have to do.

He knew he was close to his destination when a familiar queasiness arose from his stomach. The same feeling he had the night it became apparent that his Aileen would be leaving him. And now there it was, just as described in Mahon's note. The building couldn't be more than a few years old. Red brick and brownstone. A handsome structure, he thought, but rather narrow. The ground floor was fitted for two small retail tenants, both long since closed for the night. Between the storefronts, at the centerline, was a massive wood door painted hunter green.

He climbed the three steps to view the signage. The gold leaf lettering read, *Claskey And Sons, LTD Fine Printing and Lithography.*

A clever choice, Mr. Mahon. A reasonable place for a fire, plenty of chemicals around. But then again, that could result in an uncontrolled fire, a "bad fire." Then he noticed the brass plaque to the right of the door. Just a few years old, but it exhibited tarnishing already, looking quite different than the brand-new markers he unwrapped at the post office.

The instructions referenced a cellar window at the rear of the building. Work was being done in the basement area, and it was common knowledge among firemen that worksites were frequently the source of fires. Careless workers welding, soldering, or leaving flammable materials and unsealed chemicals about. Mahon had the underwriter's notes from the policy's issuance, which claimed the basement was used for the storage of paper, linens, and printing chemicals. But the underwriting was done a few years earlier. Perhaps the basement was vacant now, no longer put to that use. A fire might not be so likely there any longer. It would certainly be suspicious.

And what if... a vagrant were down there, to escape the cold. Gillian shuddered as he arrived at the cellar window. *No, I can't go through with it. It's just not right.* And the prospect of getting caught caused another shiver. *But you're going to have to, my boy, at least this one time. You're just pouring some weak solutions down on paper mounds. Your fears are suspect. But your job is real.*

He rested his lantern on a grassy mound next to the cellar window. Then he surveyed the area for witnesses, fearfully aware that it was not guaranteed he would remain unseen. He removed his cloak, wrapped it around his hand, and stopped just before breaking the glass. *This will make too much of a racket.* No, he would have to pry the window open with the plyers... the plyers he'd forgotten to bring with him. *Oh hell!* he almost said aloud. *Well, it would probably break anyway, so there's no choice. Just get it done and get out!* his mind commanded. It was cold without his cloak.

He broke the basement window with one blow.

To his surprise, the sound was muffled and even the glass hitting the floor was not particularly loud. He grabbed the tins in each pocket, unscrewed the caps, and proceeded to pour their contents down along the basement wall. Wanting some view of the basement interior, he reflexively reached for his lantern, but caught himself. "You ignoramus!" he blurted. *Twice time over at that. First, you damn near blow yourself up, then you bellow so everybody can hear you.* He shook his head and made a face of disgust, as if he were outside himself, bearing witness to his own amateurishness.

Cloak back on, cans in each pocket, he had an unexpected feeling of exhilaration as he returned to the street, walking briskly. In the distance, he heard a clock chime. Half past ten precisely, he noted. His next stop was Spanky's flat to relay that he'd set the plan in motion. According to Denny, these events were staged in Engine Company Two's territory more often than not. This supported the little man's ego and did no harm to his bank account. Then Gillian could return home—hopefully not to Patrick's questioning—and at half past midnight, two hours hence, the incendiary would do his part. Spanky's gang would be there in a flash and the event over shortly thereafter. *If all goes as planned,* he remembered Denny's words. *What have I gotten myself into?*

A five-block walk brought him to Spanky's seedy flat. Gillian had expected the man to live in finer quarters, given he was responsible for just himself, with a good job and a side hobby supporting *good* fires.

But no matter. He walked down the long hallway that smelled of old cabbage and knocked on apartment 2B. Not a word was said as Gillian handed the instructions to the little man.

* * *

Once you do it once, it gets easier after that. You'll see.

He lay there in bed thinking of Denny's words and listening to the gentle snoring of his adult boy in the next room. He was grateful that Patrick had been asleep when he arrived home. Surely, there'd be questions the next morning. But for now, he could just wait for the fire bell summoning Spanky's company. Hopefully, it would stay at just one bell. *The solution was weak, very weak, so nothing should get out of hand. But what if it be too weak, and the arsonist can't ignite anything? What about the wind? It was kicking up a bit upon my return trip. Not bad though, and the fire's confined to the basement, at least it should be. Did I leave evidence at the scene?*

Gillian never expected to sleep, but he'd not considered how agonizing the wait would be. Surprisingly he started to drift off, only to be awakened by the clock at City Hall striking one a.m. He sprung up in a panic. *What happened? The incendiary should've been long finished with his work by now. The solution must have been too weak. Or maybe he's an incompetent incendiary, forgot his matches or something. What if the fire watchman is sleeping on the job?* Gillian realized there was no end to the possible disasters that could foil the operation. He paced the room. The floorboards were creaking, and he heard Patrick toss restlessly.

The clock struck one thirty a.m., but still no fire bell.

Gillian wondered what Spanky was thinking. The little man might already be at his station house, getting equipment ready for the boys. He'd just tell them he couldn't sleep and had a bad feeling tonight was the night for some action. Some of them would believe him, and some would know the truth but keep their mouths shut. But they all would be relieved and happy when they found out they were first on the scene at a building insured by Chelsea Surety.

Finally, at one forty a.m., the fire bell rang. Gillian leapt back into bed and under the covers and prayed it stayed at one bell.

"Is that for you, Papa, or is that my company?" a hoarse voice called out from the next room. Gillian had almost forgotten that Patrick had joined up with a local hose company connected with Engine Company Three.

"No, go back to sleep, lad. Sounds like just Engine Company Two." No more bells had rung.

"Hope it stays that way," said the half-asleep Patrick.

Me too.

A half-hour passed with no additional alarms. A good sign. Finally, it was a full hour since the first alarm. All was quiet. Gillian sighed with relief. He began to drift off when the city hall clock struck three. Fully awake again, a disturbing question grabbed hold of him. *What if there was a tenement building close to the event, perhaps right next door? How could I do this then? Take a chance of it spreading.* The answer came to him. *I will stay out there if I have to. Bring my own hookup to the hydrant, alert the people inside, control the damn thing from the start!* But the idea was absurd. *No, I'd have to refuse the assignment. But that wouldn't be possible, surely. The only answer is to not do this at all. This will be the one and only good fire I'll participate in.*

CHAPTER FORTY-TWO

The next day brought snow, lots of snow, cutting short Gillian's time at the docks. Brian Denny caught up to him as he was approaching South Street.

"Robert. Wait up," the man called out, his boots crunching in the snow as he trotted toward Gillian. "How are you, chap?"

"Oh, just fine, Brian. You have to love a good snow sometimes," he said, even as his mind raced with questions as to whether Denny had been privy to the plan for last night. Neither Denny nor John Mahon was clear on this matter.

"I wanted to talk about something, Robert."

Here it is, Gillian assumed.

"We have an opening in the bookkeeping office. You might be perfect for it. You must be getting tired of this dock work, I have to think."

"I never thought upon it," he replied, caught off guard.

"You ain't getting younger, my friend, and this will only get harder as time marches on. All that hauling nearly broke my back, and the dead slaves, especially in the summer's heat… I can't get that out of my nose." A huge snowflake landed on the tip of his nose, which he brushed off with what appeared to Gillian to be another pair of new wool gloves.

"Well, you know, me and numbers don't always get along, but you have a point about the hauling and such. Give me a little time to think about it." Then he paused to reflect. "That would've been a great job for Aileen."

Denny ignored that. "I have my carriage around the corner with Fulton and Pearl. You want a ride?"

"Oh, no, thank you, much obliged, though. I love a good walk in the snow."

They had arrived at the corner of Fulton and Water Streets. Suddenly, Denny smiled.

"One bell. Good job, Robert!"

Denny was off before he could think how to respond.

For the first time in a while, Gillian took the longer route down East Broadway. He passed Simon's shop, which had also closed early due to the storm. His ears were freezing as he just had his old wool cap. And his torso was getting increasingly chilled since under his wool cloak he wore only his dockworker slops. He was having second thoughts about not taking Denny's offer of the carriage. *I could hail a carriage. I do have the means*, he thought. But he didn't.

"There she is!" he called out. "My hot corn girl."

"Good afternoon, Mr. Gillian, Hot corn today?" the lone girl asked as she struggled to curtsy on the snow-covered walkway. She wasn't carrying her tin; instead, it lay close by on a small iron grate set atop a pile of hot coals. Her caretaker must have carved out a spot for her in the snow.

"Oh yes, my little friend. Thank you. How many ears do you have?"

"Just two, sir, of course." She'd grown accustomed to their joke.

Gillian let out a hearty laugh. "No, silly you. Ears of corn."

"Oh. Let's see." She walked over to her tin and lifted the lid. A bouquet of steam wafted up into the cold air as she counted six.

"I am hungry for corn. I'll take five of them, lass."

"Five! Of—course, sir. Right away!" she said but paused in retrieving them. "You didn't bring anything to hold them, no sack or such, sir?"

"No worries. I have these deep pockets here. That'll do fine. What do I owe you, miss?"

"Twenty-five cents, that's five cents apiece."

"That's unheard of!" he boomed. "Such good corn is hard to come by this time of year. I won't pay less than two shillings, ma'am."

She crinkled her nose. "Two what?"

"Oh." He cleared his throat. "Sorry, wrong country. I meant a fifty-cent piece." And with that, he pulled such out of his pocket and placed it in her partially gloved hand.

Her face, already flushed from the cold, turned a darker shade as her blue eyes opened wide. "A fifty-cent piece! Bless you, Mr. Gillian. My papa will be so pleased."

"Speaking of him, where is he?"

"He comes back to check on me about every hour. He waits at a saloon about two blocks away. When I'm done, we get to go home."

Gillian smiled at her, a sad smile this time. He dug into his pocket again.

"Here, take this ten-cent piece. I shall keep the last ear for my son."

She quickly retrieved the remains of her inventory, which he managed to stuff into his already bursting pockets. He smiled again and tipped his cap. An inch of white powder fell on them both. They laughed, and he moved on.

Just as he rounded the corner of Grand and Mott Streets, a small break in the clouds allowed a few rays of sunlight to stream down onto the powdered snow. The light bounced off the row of new white tenement buildings just across the street from his slightly older abode. Gillian imagined the cluster of new buildings, viewed together, as a mansion, one that he might be returning to after a long day's work in the financial district. But then his eyes fell on that sign, also reflecting the bright sunlight.

Fresh Croton Water

Nearby

A surge of anger returned, breaking his daydream. "Give it a few years, these buildings will look like the rest of the scum in the Five Points," he muttered.

When he entered their three-room flat, which lately seemed so spacious, he was surprised to find himself alone. He'd assumed that Hennessey would have closed the drugstore and sent Patrick home. Apparently not. *Hmm. Good German work ethic.*

His mood lightened more when he saw two pies sitting on top of the stove. Mary's doing. He was glad she was happy at the Bidwells'. Not a bad wage, he thought, considering she had free room and board. Everything, except a husband.

Not more than five minutes passed when a knock came on the door. A young caller, well bundled up, had arrived with a note.

"From a Mr. John Mahon, sir," the boy said, handing over a small envelope.

"Thank you, lad." The boy stood there, then cleared his throat. "Oh, you want to collect something? Very wise of you." He dug into his pocket and gave the boy a ten-cent piece.

"Thank you, sir."

As he dashed off, Gillian quickly opened the letter. "This is turning out to be a very expensive day," he said.

The message was brief and straightforward.

In your postal box, you will find $250.00 in notes, an advance for your efforts. Job well done. In the future, all payments will be made upon my collection from the company. Regards. JM.

Gillian's hands began to quiver as if what he held wasn't a letter but the money itself. Then he felt lightheaded and dizzy. "Pull yourself together, man. It's just business," he said aloud. But this was the type of money most could only dream about. Now it was waiting for him, real money, to deposit at the Emigrant Savings Bank. Well over a year's rent!

He quickly redressed for a visit to the post office and then the bank, even though he knew one or both may have closed early due to the weather. But he was feeling like a child in his impatience. *I must see the money now. I can't wait.*

He hurried out the door, this time with his top hat. But as he walked quickly through the snow, he thought, *Who can I share my good fortune with? Tis not fair that I must keep this a secret from all.*

The thought brought his mood down—just a notch.

CHAPTER FORTY-THREE

Like Denny had said, it did get easier. Gillian became an expert at rationalizing the merits of his new job. A well-planned fire by an expert was a controlled event. No one got hurt, and many benefited from a cut of the pie. Even Chelsea Surety was making handsome profits, expanding their share of the insurance market in a rapidly growing city.

Still, there were nights he would lie awake tortured by counter thoughts. *What's wrong is wrong, no matter.* Sometimes, it was Aileen's voice saying it; sometimes, it was his old friend Roger, and eventually, it would be Clancy. *I'm putting money away for Patrick's schooling to be a druggist,* he would argue. *And what if Mary winds up a spinster? Surely, she could benefit from it. Then there're the charities I could support, money for the Catholic schools.* This would bring him to thinking about the crook in Patrick's nose. *If I'd been able to pay off that ruffian's father, there wouldn't have been a broken nose. And what about Daisy and Daphne? We left them behind for a better life in America, and all of it destroyed my Aileen. The costs, the sacrifices. I deserve this!*

And thus, 1857 and 1858 were busy and lucrative years, the "special requests" infrequent but highly profitable. As a crowning achievement, a dock supervisor position became available at his place of employ. Now Gillian was managing others for the first time in his working life. With the new, hefty wage, and Mahon's stipend for placing fire marks, he could easily explain their comfortable existence, at least for now, burying the source of the *real* money.

The cellar groggery was a far cry from the saloons off South Street he frequented with his dockworker apprentices. But this establishment accommodated Negros, the small tribe of Lenape, and others considered less desirable by the citizens of New York City.

As usual, Gillian arrived before the others. Halfway through his first ale, in walked the shoemaker, the cabinetmaker, and—for lack of a better term—the gambler, Emmet.

"There's my hero!" A smile burst across Clancy's face as he saw Gillian seated at a corner table. Emmet tipped his cap. Katonah struggled to give a smile and lifted his palm in Gillian's direction

"Good evening, boys," Gillian exclaimed. "Let me just say, spirit and *victuals* are on my dime tonight." He enjoyed getting mileage out of the new vocabulary he'd learned from Mary.

All three smiled in delight. Emmet hooted.

"Many thanks, Robert. You're most generous, my friend," Katonah stated warmly.

"Well, look at you, throwing money around like that on us," Clancy said with delight. "Let me guess, ye found out you's kin with royalty? Or you robbed a bank?"

"Clancy, I told you already, I am kin with royalty. I'm descended from the tribe of Brian Boru, the last great High King of the Celts. An honorable warrior he was."

"Oh, yeah. I forgot, Your Highness," he said with a laugh-cough.

"Truthfully, the Lord has been kind to me of late. I've been promoted to a dock supervisor, and my employ as a fire marker man has proven to be most healthful for my coffers."

"Listen to you, fancy words, Robert. Good for you anyways and good for us too." Clancy turned to his son, face splitting with pride. "Now, Emmet here has something to say."

"That's right, Mr. Gillian, Robert, sir," Emmet said. "I'm an apprentice now at Mr. Barnum's American Museum. I help build exhibits for the new attractions. I'm the only colored man there except on colored days when they let Negros in the place as visitors. It's okay work."

"Damn better than okay, son," Clancy said. "You're a proud contributor to the Carver household now."

"My best wishes to you, boy," Gillian said. Katonah nodded in agreement.

The men feasted on roast pig, chicken legs, and sourdough bread. Satiated and drunk, they stumbled to the street about eight p.m. They had several blocks to walk before parting ways. Clancy put an arm around Gillian's shoulder—quite a stretch—and whispered in his ear. "I know what you up to, Robert Gillian. You just be careful of that Fire Marker Man."

The shock Gillian felt at being called on his secret was dulled by the recent merrymaking. They continued walking slowly side by side, Emmet and Katonah gaining distance ahead.

Clancy stopped and turned to face Gillian. "You see, Robert, you a hero because you rose to the occasion. You didn't let your fears get in the way, and you saved that lady from certain death. Nobody knows if they have that in them till the situation come up. But when you have plenty of time to think about whether something's right or wrong, and you ignore your better thinking, you ain't no hero."

"But... " Gillian was about to defend his actions, but nothing came out.

"And what do you really know about this John Mahon anyways? Just be careful is all I'm saying, Robert." Clancy gave him a light and friendly punch in the arm. Then they noticed that Katonah and Emmet had stopped ahead, waiting for them to catch up.

After the group parted ways, Gillian thought about his friend's remarks, and the vexing questions returned to haunt him. *Just who is this Fire Marker Man? And why has he chosen me for this opportunity? Maybe it's more a curse than a blessing?* Then he thought, *How odd this situation is. Fire marks that give a good name to the company protecting a building from fire are being used to mark a building for a fire? It's all wrong, this Mahon betraying his own employer. Then again, these are controlled fires, and who better than a fireman to control a fire.*

Just as he arrived at the corner of Grand and Mott Streets, he imagined Aileen and Roger waving a finger at him.

CHAPTER FORTY-FOUR

JOHN MAHON'S OFFICE
September 1858

"I suppose you think it my fault, Mr. Denny, that you spent all your reserves on business ventures around the Crystal Palace. Were you drunk when you entered these deals or just dimwitted? Perhaps both, aye?"

John Mahon was pacing back and forth in his little office on the third floor of the spindly building at the corner of Broadway and Duane Streets. Denny was seated in one of the two King George chairs, in front of Mahon's desk. He was hunched forward, head down, his waistcoat buttons bulging as if any second his belly would burst out for a grand appearance. His face was red and mottled, with a scraggly graying beard that partially hid his thickening neck. Over-fed and over-spirited, Brian Denny barely resembled the well-chiseled man of his younger years.

"You disgust me so, Mr. Denny. Twere it not for Vorhees's request, I would have passed you on a long time ago. But I gave you a chance. You botched things over and over again until the distillery fire. That was your crowning achievement! Cost my company a fortune, and we were that close to getting an outside investigation pushed on us. It could've been the end, Denny. It would've been the hangman's rope if more than a bunch of sick cows were cooked." Mahon let out a sigh and leaned against his desk. Despite the verbal torment, Denny couldn't help but observe that the wiry figure was even more hideous when he was angry. Veins bulged from the side of his head where hair wouldn't dare grow anymore. His half-nose quivered, and his one good eye seemed to convey enough contempt for both. Denny was sure that the taut scar on the man's neck must pain him as he thrashed and raged.

But now Mahon had vented his piece. He sat back down at his desk and began twiddling his pencil. "Don't you have a retort, Mr. Denny?"

"Yes. I'm sorry that some things went awry," he said. "But how was I supposed to know that the Crystal Palace would be a flop? Two hundred thousand square feet of iron and glass, a brilliant creation, a World's Fair right here in our city." He shook his head. "But nobody accounted for what they'd do with the fuckin' thing after the World's Fair."

"Well, that's one thing you're right about, Denny. Just five years old, and the Great Crystal Palace we insured for half a million is wasted space. I hear they brought in P.T. Barnum to run the place, bring in new events and such. We'll see what happens there, I guess. But what do you want from me?" Mahon gave Denny a hard glare as he drummed his fingers on his desk.

"I need to get back on my feet, Mr. Mahon. I'm just asking for my job back, you know, placing fire marks on the new buildings. I'm sure Robert Gillian does a fine job, but there's plenty of work to split, maybe a little more for me, you know, until—"

"No. I've given you enough chances, Denny. You....." Mahon stopped himself mid-sentence. "I never told you to buy up saloons and whorehouses off Sixth Avenue and 42nd Street."

"It was to become a beautiful neighborhood!" Denny raged. "We were planning restaurants, dance halls and the like. Not my fault the Palace went bust."

John Mahon started to peruse a newspaper on his desk, signaling that, for him, this conversation was done.

Denny sat back in his chair and looked up at the skinny creature. "You know, Mr. John Mahon, it would be a terrible shame for all of us if our little charade came to an abrupt end, like you're holding over me. 'Your honor, Mr. Mahon wouldn't give me any fire marker jobs unless I played his game, hmf?'" Denny stopped talking and began tapping his fingers on his lap, not sure what to expect of his bluff. He had no intention of committing himself to prison for his previous actions—unless he was certain he could plead a deal.

The good side of the hideous man's face began to twitch and turn the same color as the wretched side. He slammed his uncooked fist on the desk and stood. "You won't do that, Mr. Denny! Not even you would stoop that low. A drunken scoundrel you are, yes, but blackmail, extortion! After all the chances I've given you!"

Denny was expecting such a reaction, but he assumed that after giving it some thought, Mahon would throw him a bone, perhaps a few marker placement assignments, given business was booming so.

"Why don't you think about it, sir? I really don't ask for much."

Mahon sat down again, gazed in the direction of the window, and sighed deeply. After a pause, again drumming his fingers, he replied, "Okay, Denny. I want you to wait outside. Let me mull this over a few minutes."

"Very well, sir." Brian Denny stood and returned to the waiting room.

Mahon walked over to the third-floor window, where he could observe the brightly colored autumn leaves on the few trees below. He'd noted just the other day that there were fewer to view each year, trees of stone and brick busy crowding out the green. On the other hand, more and more of this new variety of tree had his company name implanted into their brick-and-stone bark. No, he was not going to let Denny bring them down.

He retrieved Brian Denny from the waiting room, knowing that Mrs. Grimble would have her ear to the door now.

"I will give you some marker assignments," he said. "But first we have a *special event* at the Crystal Palace. You will save the great edifice from calamity. Twas a five-hundred-thousand-dollar policy, and we are bound to get several thousand dollars from Chelsea if we save it from ruin." Moving to a small safe, he unlocked the door and withdrew a tattered ledger book. The page edges were browning, and the writing showed the quivering lines of an aged man's penmanship. "According to my schedule here, the Palace isn't due for a fire, but we need to move this up. I became quite familiar with the building when we underwrote the policy five years ago, and I hold a set of the architectural plans."

"My sincerest thanks to you, sir. I'll not let you down, you'll see. Bless you," said Denny. "You'd be helping a desperate man, sir."

"Fine, fine. Come by my office after church this Sunday, say half after noon. We'll start then."

The sarcasm of "after church" flew over Denny's head. Denny wasn't a churchgoing man. Neither was Mahon, and he was certain they'd both be going to hell anyway.

Denny sprung from his chair and gave his good hand a hearty shake. Then he opened the door and tipped his top hat at Mrs. Grimble, who was pretending to be busy tidying up for the day.

When he was gone, Mahon wiped his good hand on his trousers, fearing he had caught some pestilence. He walked across the room to the oak filing cabinet where he kept the drawings and plans for the Crystal Palace. The thought of being done with Denny once and for all brought on a rare smile.

Chapter Forty-Five

No Sputter, No Flutter

"Yoohoo, Mary!" Clara Bidwell called. "Can you come here for a moment? I need your advice on which hat I should choose for your father's visit."

"Coming, mum." Mary tucked the rag on the stove handle. She was almost done polishing the silverware and hated having to stop for such silliness. The last thing her father cared about was the type of hat his hostess was wearing.

"Ah, there you are," Clara said when she appeared. "What do you think of this one? Ostrich feathers are the latest style, but they're not so colorful."

Mary just hummed in agreement, having learned that her opinion was less important than the affirmation she would provide once the woman made up her mind.

"Now the peacock is much more colorful but a bit older," Clara continued. "I think some of the feathers are tattered. Which do you think your father would prefer?"

"Either one is fine, mum. Father is not particular with these things, I assure you." Mary just wanted to finish up in the kitchen so she could turn her attention back to the gentleman caller from the previous evening. A nice man, a bit plain, but not at all an interesting sort. She needed to figure out how she would let him down easily and without her father discovering the matter. Should he learn that the man was a successful Wall Street accountant, he would certainly be dismayed at her attitude. *And why does she need to wear a hat in the house?* popped into her irritated mind. Then she sighed. *Well, perhaps I shouldn't be thinking so rudely. Mum promised to keep hush about my caller last night.*

"Oh, there's the bell! Your father's early," Clara said as she glanced at the grandfather clock in the hallway.

"I'll get it, mum."

"Don't be silly, sweetheart. You are the guest for this visit," Clara Bidwell insisted. She pinched Mary's cheek and smiled, showing off her full set of yellowed teeth, then turned to the banister. "Lovey! Mr. Bidwell! Our guest has arrived."

No answer.

"Shall I find him, mum?"

"No, you're a guest, remember? He heard me, but as usual, he's always at some far corner of the house. Why don't you prepare the tea, and I'll greet your papa."

"Yes, mum."

I thought I was a guest. Nevertheless, Mary hurried off to the kitchen.

When Mary returned, Clara was wearing neither the ostrich nor peacock hat but a white hat with blue sequins. She watched from the doorway as her mistress exchanged pleasantries with a man in a new stovepipe hat.

It was odd to see her father in this new setting, with his new wardrobe. She felt he could be a stranger until hearing his familiar Gaelic brogue.

He bowed to her in jest. "Mary, I presume?"

"Greetings, Papa," she said.

"Can you seat him in the parlor?" Clara said. "I'll finish up with tea."

As Mary guided him to the parlor, he did not seem aware of her discomfort, he was so taken with the surroundings.

"Please, take this seat before the cat gets it," she whispered, then settled herself opposite him on the Louis XVI sofa.

An uncomfortable silence fell as Gillian cleared his throat and resumed glancing about. The Siamese cat scampered into the room and appeared disappointed that a giant had seized her throne.

"Tea and crumpets for all," Clara called out merrily as she entered the parlor carrying a silver serving tray. She gently placed it on the marble coffee table and began pouring and talking until Enoch Bidwell made his grand entrance.

"Ah, Mr. Gillian! I thought I heard a male companion about the house," he stated loudly, then smiled so broadly that his waxed handlebar stretched from cheek to cheek. Gillian began to rise. "Sit, sit, dear guest. Let me shake your hand. Mary has told us so much about you and the family journey from the Irish Isles. Terrible, terrible thing that happened there." He shuddered before seating himself next to Clara on a second French provincial sofa that was even plusher and more elegantly carved than the one occupied by Mary.

"Aye, er, yes, it was a tough journey, but most made it through, and here we are twelve years hence. I've been working my way up in the shipping business."

Just then, Mary had the urge to laugh. But she quickly considered, one could say being a dock supervisor is part of the shipping business. *Very clever, Papa.*

"And I'm second to the foreman at the very respectable White Flag Engine Company, with a commendation for saving two lives—one before I even had my feet wet. I also have a few side jobs. More than enough to keep bread on the table."

Both Bidwells were smiling and nodding.

"Well then, you have much to be proud of," Enoch Bidwell stated as he reached for his second crumpet. "Perhaps Mrs. Bidwell told you, we have been delighted with your Mary. You reared her well, sir. She's a hard worker, well spoken, clean appearance."

Teacup to her face, Mary attempted to hide her blushing.

"The credit goes to her mother, except for the 'well spoken' part."

"Ah yes, Mary's initiative," Bidwell expressed. "Lessons in proper grammar, very wise girl." He smiled in her direction.

Clara was determined to get her words in. "We've always had colored servants in this neighborhood. Fine workers, but different, you know. It was quite refreshing to get one of our own. Times change, I suppose." She sighed with a faraway look. "Why, Mrs. Rutherford, right next door, had to dismiss her Negro help when the young ones were freed. Poor woman had to convert her townhome into a boarding house. Our shared friend, Clancy, wanted to stay on for a modest wage, but she was certain the boarders would take issue. A real shame."

Mr. Bidwell cleared his throat. "I believe it's time for you ladies to retire elsewhere. We men have some business at hand." He smiled pleasantly at both, which Mary knew to mean "Leave now."

* * *

"Now, let me get to the point of your call, Mr. Gillian," Mr. Bidwell said. Clearing his throat again, he settled back in his chair, teacup in hand. "A group of my associates is seeking investors for a rail line project. It's to be an elevated train that will travel right down the center of Broadway—from Bowling Green all the way to the countryside above Bloomingdale Road! This is where our majestic city's will expand, my friend, up to the planned Central Park, then through the lands near the Hudson River. The advances in elevated trains are moving at a rapid pace now, Gillian. It'll be here sooner than you can imagine. Just think, we'll be able to move passengers swiftly up and down, from the nascent hinterlands of Manhattan right down to the heart of our city and back again. And the tracks will not interfere with street traffic, which will lessen in any case with the new trains carrying much of the load. Think about it, Gillian. A cleaner Broadway, with fewer omnibuses, fewer horsecars."

He stopped to place his cup on the table, his lap crumbs falling to the plush carpet. Then he reclined back in his seat and gazed about the room with a dreamy look, probably musing over the grandeur of the plan.

Gillian nodded, taking it all in, a type of conversation he'd never engaged in. He knew a business proposition was coming along somewhere.

"Oh, and there're more benefits here," Bidwell continued. "An elevated train, in contrast to a surface one, will mean less noise from the engine, and the coal soot will be far above the buildings."

Gillian was about to inquire where he fit into this project when Bidwell moved on to that point.

"We need to raise two hundred thousand dollars in capital to get this off the ground. We've just completed formation of the Broadway Rail Company, and we will be issuing shares of stock at ten dollars apiece. These funds will go toward the engineering plans and to purchase the land where the extension of Broadway will be. It'll give us a right of way to run our trains just above the center line of the new boulevard!"

This last bit was said with prideful delight as if Bidwell were the plan's sole originator. Then he leaned forward and gave Gillian a hard look.

"This is a tremendous ground-floor opportunity for you, Mr. Gillian. I share this with you as we are very fond of Mary, and I can tell you are worthy people like us. You've struggled as a young man, and now you have success, if not riches... yet. But you need to let your money work for you now. You see, once this project gets off the ground, the city will want to buy all our shares. They won't want a private rail line controlling movement on Broadway. There'd be no competition. We could charge whatever we desire. They will pay a fortune to get us out of the way. You see?" Bidwell poured himself more tea and sat back again.

"Yes, I believe I do, Mr. Bidwell," Gillian said, nodding vigorously. "I'll have to think about the number of shares to purchase, but I am certainly interested." He could not believe this was rolling off his tongue. *First time for everything, I guess.*

"That's fine. You are indeed a wise man. You'll be paid a spiff, too, for any other investors you bring to us. Now, there's still much to be done. These things are complicated. Thanks to our friend at Tammany, the state legislature is on board for significant funding, so the city knows they will have to act soon. Indeed, they will want our shares to control the whole thing. I'm thinking profits tenfold at the least!" Bidwell opened his eyes wide and smiled broadly.

"Well, kind of you to invite me, sir. I shall give you my word... shortly," he said, not certain when, and began to rise.

"Where are you going, Gillian? You can't leave yet. I must show you my latest collection. I'm sure Mary has made mention of it. Exquisite ceramics brought to my attention at the Crystal Palace exhibit in London. And I must say, it was a far superior World's Fair than ours in New York. I keep that quiet, though, around town."

Bidwell was bubbling with the enthusiasm of a child as he led Gillian to a dining room almost as large as the Irishman's entire Grand Street flat. He then walked the perimeter of the room, lighting each candle.

"These, my friend, are the finest candles one can buy, made from spermaceti oil found only in the brain matter of a specific breed of whale. There shall hardly be a *sputter* or a *flutter*, you'll see."

Less interested in the candles, Gillian took in the dazzlingly colorful ceramics sitting atop an array of low cabinets. Elegant curio cabinets were mounted on the walls above, all housing smaller pieces behind fine beveled glass. Tiny candles disbursed throughout these curios provided the additional illumination needed to show off the smaller treasures. Gillian, never having been to a museum, walked slowly about the room in awe.

"What do you think, Mr. Gillian?" Bidwell asked, walking behind him.

"Truly striking. Do these porcelain curiosities have a name, sir?"

"Porcelain! Oh no, Gillian, and they're not curiosities. This is English majolica, faience as it's called on the main continent. It's made from a softer earthenware material, twice fired. After the first firing, the artist paints the sculpture with glazes of the most brilliant colors you see here, a very expensive process, I'm told. But these are not curiosities. Each is made for a specific use. Take a closer look."

As Gillian looked at the large pieces on the low-topped cabinets, Enoch Bidwell proceeded to describe each. "One cannot serve lobster to guests if not from a lobster tureen," Bidwell exclaimed as he grabbed hold of a perfectly formed ceramic lobster, serving as a handle applied to the cover of the dish. He moved on to the next piece. "One cannot serve fish to guests if not from a fish tureen." The lid of this piece was modeled as a large fish displayed on its side with fine detailing of the scales and fins. Surrounding the fish were ceramic wedges of lemon and other dressings. "Now, look here, Gillian. This item is a cheese keeper, and here, a butter dish, and this is a George Jones strawberry server, complete with two delicate ceramic spoons—one for cream, one for sugar. All placed on an elegant table setting to be enjoyed by our guests!" Bidwell smiled proudly at the conclusion of his lecture.

"Simply amazing, Mr. Bidwell."

"Since the London Exhibition in 1851, majolica is all the rage in Europe, so Clara and I couldn't resist. In fact, some of these pieces came directly from Mr. Herbert Minton himself, produced at his manufactory in Staffordshire." Bidwell did not appear concerned that Gillian would not know who Minton was or where Staffordshire was located. "In fact, some of our grandest pieces will be on display next week at the Crystal Palace right here in New York."

"Well, congratulations to you, sir!" Gillian remarked, not sure what to say.

At that moment, the grandfather clock in the hallway struck one. "Oh, I do believe we need to conclude our meeting, Gillian. I have a call to make at two, and I can't be late. Ladies!" he called out to the kitchen. "Our visitor is departing."

Clara scurried out to the hallway, Mary right behind.

"Oh, it was so pleasant having you, Mr. Robert Gillian. Let me get you some crumpets for your journey," she said, and then scurried to the back parlor to retrieve the remains on the tray.

"Good to see you, Papa." Mary reached for his cloak and hat in the closet. "Keep well."

Enoch Bidwell escorted him to the front stoop. "Think about our talk, my man."

"Certainly, sir," Gillian replied as Clara rushed to him carrying a bag with the remaining crumpets. He took the bag, tipped his hat to her, and bowed. "Thank you, kind lass... er... madam."

The Bidwells returned inside. The big red door closed. Mary was no longer a guest.

CHAPTER FORTY-SIX

October 5th 1858

Two events were planned that day at the grand Crystal Palace on Sixth Avenue and 42nd Street. That didn't include the ceramics exhibit featuring Enoch Bidwell's dazzling majolica pottery. Nor did it include a fire.

Brian Denny was sober, as this was his final chance at redemption with the Fire Marker Man. He would be both stager and arsonist, so he knew a windfall would be in this for him. Just a small fire in a boiler room on the north side of the property, first floor. The foreman of Engine Company Seven was lying in wait. The fire station was merely two blocks away, and Mahon said the foreman had called a "mandatory training session" so as to have men already at post with the engines prepped.

Denny dressed as a well-heeled visitor to the exhibition. He paid his twenty-five-cent admission and began exploring the ceramics exhibit on the first level. His eyes were immediately caught by the unusual and colorful majolica pottery, particularly a life-sized peacock of striking luster and detail. The engraved plaque read: *On Loan from the Gentleman Mr. Enoch Bidwell.*

So taken was he by the treasures, he almost lost track of the time. He pulled the chain on his watch, just enough to grab a glimpse of the crystal—quarter to five. Fifteen minutes to prepare. One might assume a building of iron and glass would hardly be flammable. Not true, as the vast flooring was of varnished pine board, and the thousands of iron-framed glass panels were first set in wood sashes. Recalling the drawings in Mahon's office, it was easy to locate the boiler room near the 42nd Street side of the building.

Ten minutes to five, and a fly in the ointment. A child and his keeper were resting on a bench not less than ten feet from the target destination. Denny's mind scrambled for an idea as he walked over to the giant main-hall window overlooking the newly paved 42nd Street. A line of carriages was stationed in front of the great edifice, their coachmen conversing in a group as they waited patiently for their masters in the low-angled sun. Their serenity was to be short-lived, a knowledge that gave him an odd feeling of power. *How can I distract this boy and his keeper? Suggest that ice cream is being served in the second-floor lounge? But then, they would have a better chance of remembering me.*

Then luck came his way. The boy insisted on viewing the men's toilet with running water on the second level. The keeper was reluctant to comply until the boy said he needed to tinkle. And then they were gone.

The heavy door to the storage room made a low squeal as it opened. Without a lantern, Denny needed to leave the door ajar to allow in some form of light, so he wedged his coat in the gap. In the room, he found brand-new cast-iron and brass piping leading to the state-of-the-art furnace. The cause of the fire would be attributed to a malfunction of some sort in the new equipment. The manufacturer would surely claim that was not possible and insist it was an act of arson or sabotage. But it would be hard to prove—and hopefully harder to identify a culprit. In the end, Engine Company Seven would save the day, and the insurance company would handsomely reward the firefighting team.

Denny opened the small glass bottle of camphene, which he'd sufficiently diluted to avoid extreme combustion. The vapors were pungent, their odor filling the room as he saturated the paper mound he'd laid on the pine board floor near the furnace. He was about to check his time-piece, but he heard the church bells nearby ring five. Striking a match on the side of the boiler, he set his little fire.

A brief burst of flame, but then it appeared to smolder. *Did I dilute it too much? Surely, Mahon will have my head this time.*

Just then, the heavy door slammed shut. Startled, Denny stumbled through the dark toward the entrance, now just visible—illuminated by a small flame taking hold of the pine board under the furnace. He'd made it halfway across the room when he heard a voice call out somewhere in the vicinity.

"Five o'clock, boys. Start the gas!"

Panic set in. He pulled hard at the door, to no avail. It must have been locked from the outside. He heard the grating sound of the iron wheel turning, opening the valves that would supply gas to the new boiler and to the vast array of lamps throughout the Crystal Palace. The dawning of a new age. Central heating and lighting. Something Brian Denny would never see.

The explosion was deafening as the heavy storage room door shot like a projectile across the main floor and through the windows fronting Sixth Avenue. But that was just the start of the hellish event. Fire raced across the varnished pine floorboards and up the perimeter walls, igniting the thousands of wood frames that anchored the glass plates to the iron form. The atrium and dome served as a chimney flue, allowing the formation of a whirlwind of fire that shot up to the second level.

Five fire companies arrived within fifteen minutes of the onset. Their job was to help the visitors escape, as it was apparent the structure would be a colossal loss.

* * *

Mahon had gained twelve blocks distance before hearing the fire bells. He was overheating in his high-collared coat and earmuffs, but shedding his outerwear was not possible. Although his clothes must have appeared odd, his disfigurement would've certainly drawn more notice. In twenty minutes, he would be safely at his modest flat on 13th Street.

As he neared home, he reflected upon the successful day. *A job well done, sir!* He was certain the Crystal Palace would be no more. His claims adjusting would guarantee that the investors recouped their five hundred thousand dollars for the ridiculous building that had little use after the World's Fair. He would get his twenty-thousand-dollar cut of the deal, and he'd disposed of the vile Brian Denny. *Killed two birds with one stone, my man. And I was feeling so giddy. I don't want to think about Denny. But now it's too late. The man deserved what he got, the double-crossing thief he is... was. First, he gets me scorched to disfigurement, then he makes a deal behind my back with the distillery owners. Burns the fuckin thing to the ground for a kickback. Thinks I'll be taken for a fool. Bites the hand that's been feeding him. 'Oh, I made a terrible mistake, Mr. Mahon. Overslept and missed relaying to Spanky. I mixed my agents wrong, not enough dilution. Never happen again, sir. No, never, sir.'*

Denny, you stupid fool! Didn't think I'd know something was wrong when the distillery owners didn't even want an investigation of the fire. 'Never happen again, sir. No, never.' Well, never is right. You see, two can play the same game, Mr. Denny.

He climbed the three steps and unlocked the green door of his flat. Starting a fire was the first order of business, as the nights were growing colder. He'd have his supper, then read a novel in front of its warmth before retiring at the stroke of nine. Reading was difficult with one good eye, but he'd had many years to grow accustomed, and now, with gas lighting, it'd become a bit easier. He surely must read tonight, distract himself from thoughts of tomorrow's events. The early paper would carry the story of the fire and the fate of the Crystal Palace, which he felt assured would be a total ruin. Then he'd be in contact with the London office via the wire service. They'd want an investigation, which he would *conveniently* control.

John Mahon had no idea how far he could carry this game. But he didn't care. At fifty-eight, he was a wealthy man. He was still alone, disfigured, and with an insatiable desire for revenge. Chelsea Surety Company had paid and would continue to pay for what they'd done to him.

* * *

Half hour from the start of the blaze, the Crystal Palace of New York collapsed onto itself, a pile of melted iron and glass, pieces to be scavenged and sold as souvenirs. One newspaper reported that angels were seen flying high above the raging fire, and so every soul in the doomed palace made a miraculous escape. Only one man in the entire city of New York would know that was not true. And Brian Denny's body—or parts of such—were never retrieved, reduced to ashes.

Mahon had the event staged before Denny's arrival on the scene. Cast-iron pipes carried gas throughout the great structure, except for a small pliable section of rubber tubing hiding under the boiler. Earlier in the day, the stager had cut the tubing, a simple and effective assignment that would immediately flood the boiler room with odorless gas at exactly five p.m. Denny had sealed his own fate with his little fire.

Chapter Forty-Seven

February 1860

There'd been many rumors as to the whereabouts of Brian Denny. Most assumed he'd met his end, but some said he'd fled the city for nefarious reasons. His shipping employer and the White Flag Engine Company men held fast to the notion that he didn't vote right—or maybe not at all.

Regardless, there were few tears. And the fire commissioner hadn't forgotten Robert Gillian's heroics. This, combined with his popularity at the firehouse, led to his promotion to foreman of the White Flag Engine Company. Though still a volunteer department in 1859, this position paid a small stipend. Adding to the fortunate news, he heard the company would be relocating to a new larger firehouse and would be equipped with two state-of-the-art steam-pump engines. The men would finally have a clear view of the fire bell tower and watchman's lantern!

It was a busy—and lucrative—few years for Gillian. His sources of income now were his wages as a dock supervisor, a fire marker man for Chelsea Surety, a stipend for his foreman responsibilities, and of course, his unofficial position as a stager of "special events." But it was the sale of his shares in the Broadway Rail Line Company, at a ten-fold profit, just as Enoch Bidwell had predicted, that he credited for his wealth. His nine-thousand-dollar profit was used to open a new account at the Emigrant Savings Bank, and to start Patrick on his path to becoming a druggist.

The twenty-four-year-old showered his father with praise, and Gillian was happy to no longer need to fabricate explanations for their increasingly comfortable lifestyle, though they would still maintain modest residence at Grand and Mott Streets, just "outside" of the Five Points. But this was a lucky outcome for Robert Gillian. Bidwell's shrewdness had adverted a near disaster for the investors.

A week earlier, he'd dined with Bidwell at a fine establishment just around the corner from the Astor House. There, he was encouraged to join in the sale of the company shares. But the sale was not to the City of New York; it would be to other Wall Street investors, apparently a less sophisticated group.

"We need to sell now, Gillian," Bidwell said emphatically in between slurps of turtle soup. "We've increased the value of the stock perfectly, what with the engineering plans and the purchase of rights of way." He paused to slurp down a raw oyster, and a few drops of juice dripped on his bow tie.

"Well, that's all good, no? Why ain't... excuse me... are we not holding out for more money?"

"It goes like this, Gillian. There is a movement among property owners on Broadway to push for a rezoning to allow for much taller building heights along the roadway. With Otis's elevator and the political pressure of powerful Broadway landowners, they very well may concede to this. And bigger buildings mean more taxes for the city."

"I'm not sure I completely follow, sir," Gillian said while noting that his pâté tasted much like liverwurst, just had a nicer-sounding name.

"With taller buildings, Robert, no owner wants a steam locomotive passing just outside their fifth-floor windows. The noise, the soot." He dropped his last oyster shell in the bowl provided and toweled off his perfectly waxed mustache. Then he leaned forward. "Gillian, this is not going to be built, ever. The city will never buy our shares with the rezoning on the horizon. So, we must dispose of them before the papers get wind of this." He looked around the room for the waiter. "Are you ready to order our main fare?"

Gillian and the other investors unloaded their shares in time to make a handsome profit.

* * *

Six years now, and Gillian had never made the personal acquaintance of the Fire Marker Man. Given his few encounters with the man's visage—and temper—he frequently thought this was for the best. Still, it was odd. All those jobs, placing fire marks, staging *special events*. How simple it was to just follow the man's instructions and get paid handsomely. At times, he even felt that the Fire Marker Man was being overly generous. Then he'd conclude that his thoughts were absurd. "Look at the risks I'm taking," he would tell the mirror lining the inside of the closet door. *Besides, Mahon prefers it this way. He's a man of order and efficiency, pleasantries not necessary. No reason to meet if the process is going along without fault. I'm sure he sees me the same way, efficient and reliable.*

Part VII

The War Years

Chapter Forty-Eight

April 1861

"Well, we knew it would come to this, Patrick. Wasn't enough to leave the Union."

The two stared at the bold morning headline. *Shots Fired at Fort Sumter*. Rumors had spread through the city the day earlier but reading it in the newspaper made it official.

Patrick glanced at the wall clock. "I have to go to class, Papa. We'll talk later."

"Aye, see ya, lad," Gillian said, his mind elsewhere.

Gillian was disturbed by the news. He didn't fear that the war would come to New York, but he knew many Irishmen would fight, eager to demonstrate their patriotism for their new land. They'd be lining up, forming regiments. And Patrick, he was sure, would be taken by the war fever.

Gillian dressed for his supervisory detail at the docks, where four men were under him now. It used to be seven men, but since the secession of the South, far less cotton was being moved North, which meant fewer packets to unload, and he'd had the sad job of letting three men go. But more imports were coming from the Orient now, and much to the relief of the workers that remained, these ships weren't carrying *dead* cargo.

With Patrick gone, Gillian opened the closet door to greet his full-length looking glass. He'd added to his belly recently, as he and Patrick were eating well, with frequent suppers out. Then there were the regular nights with the fire laddies, where he always insisted on paying for all. The ale would flow, and they would feast on smoked bird and ribs.

"I don't like this," he blurted at his reflection. "A little gain was healthy, but this is unbecoming. What would Aileen think? What would Roger say?" The mirror said nothing. "I shall tighten my suspenders. Aye, that will hold my belly for now."

He felt glad he'd arrived at a solution, even without input from the mirror. Then he changed into his business clothes and became dismayed that he had to struggle to close the top button on his high-collared shirt.

"The launderer's using too much starch. I'll have to have a word with him," he muttered. But inside, he knew there was no one to blame but himself for his ill-fitting waistcoat. The wood buttons were pulling as if they might burst forth and ricochet off the walls. He decided he must talk to Simon the barber about this weight gain, and for that matter, the ulcers on his feet. Perhaps the man would have some ideas, or at least an ointment to treat the latter. Simon owed him, as he had also made out handsomely on the Broadway Rail Line shares.

Realizing he would be late if he kept dawdling, he stripped down and was about to re-dress for the docks when he abruptly stopped, catching sight of his naked state. "A fat lumberjack. That's what you are!" the mirror scolded. "An old, fat lumberjack with an overgrown beard. And still no good with the numbers."

He moved his face right up to the glass and grimaced in disgust.

"No, this ain't you, Robert Gillian. She'd not even recognize you neither." At that moment he realized that his judgment of his physical appearance—deplorable as it may be—was a mere symptom of what was really troubling him.

It was clear what he had to do. He needed to meet the Fire Marker Man. Tell him that he was done with the special events, done with the good fires. But how would it be taken? He'd witnessed the man's wrath. And he still wanted the job of placing fire marks on the buildings. It was easy money, a pleasant occupation for an aging Irishman.

Then his reflection had something to say about it. "You can't live with yourself this way, Robert. It's getting harder and harder to be a fireman when you know the truth about yourself, ain't it? One day, your games will get out of control, a good fire gone bad. What would you say if one of your own laddies gets hurt—even killed?"

But the money, like I've never seen before. Maybe, I should just give up being a fireman, and just work for Mahon, no fire laddies no more.

Gillian shuddered at his thought. "Forgive me, Lord, you didn't hear that... or you, Aileen," he said to his mortified image in the glass.

* * *

"Here, boy. Deliver this note to a Mr. John Mahon, at Chelsea Surety Company. There at 125 Broadway, the third floor. You bring me back a signed receipt from him, and I'll give you a twenty-five-cent tip."

"But it's raining out, sir. We get bigger tips when it's raining," the boy stated.

Gillian smiled. "Aye. I suppose so, but ye better not be fibbing me, boy. Okay, so be gone. We figure it out when you return."

The errand runner put the envelope into his satchel and placed his soaking cap back on his head. And he was off.

Gillian had requested a Sunday afternoon meeting and for his reply to be sent to the usual postal box—he didn't want a note delivered back to the flat, lest Patrick was there alone.

Strangely, it took three days for a response. Mahon suggested the following Sunday at two, the first weekend in May.

CHAPTER FORTY-NINE

May 1861

It'd been many bountiful years now since that first Sunday visit with Denny and crew, the day the Fire Marker Man chose Gillian to be a fire marker man. And today, he would find out why.

The palms of his hands and the soles of his feet were sweating as he climbed the steps to the plush waiting room. Mahon had warned him he was alone now, Mrs. Grimble having recently passed away of causes unknown.

The waiting room was as stuffy as he'd remembered it, and Mahon was overdue. Despite his anxiety, Gillian found himself almost drifting off in one of the plush King George chairs. Suddenly, the door adjacent to the boarded-over window opened, and out stepped John Mahon. Prepared for the man's appearance, Gillian showed no sign of surprise.

The wiry man said nothing but extended his good hand for a hearty handshake. The left side of his face smiled; the other side tried.

"Well, it's a pleasure to meet you, Mr. Mahon, sir," Gillian said, hoping the man didn't notice his sweaty palm.

"Likewise, Mr. Gillian. It is about time. And here you have me, in the flesh—so to speak," he said with deadpan humor. "Please excuse the patch over my eye. Trust me, it is more palatable than the truth behind." This time he chuckled. "Shall we sit in my office?"

He didn't wait for a response. Still nervous, Gillian seated himself in a straight-backed Queen Anne in front of Mahon's cluttered desk just as a cloud blocking the sun moved on and bright rays streamed through the window. Mahon was already at the curtains, curing the situation. Then he returned to his desk and immediately began fidgeting in his seat.

"I do need a better chair for my aging back," Mahon remarked as if they were already in casual conversation. "I assume you must be about fifty or fifty-one yourself now, Gillian, hmm?

"Huh... Oh, exactly, sir. Almost fifty-one," Gillian replied, thinking the question odd.

"Well, shall we get down to business, Robert Gillian? You obviously have an urgent matter to discuss, no?" Mahon asked as he leaned forward and placed his good hand on top of his scarred one.

"Well, tis not urgent, really, but important," Gillian replied. "The point, sir, is that while your generosity has been a blessing for me and my family, and it's been an honor to serve you placing the markers on the buildings and such..." Gillian's tongue froze mid-sentence. Suddenly, he felt certain that he knew this man, John Mahon. The voice, more gravelly but familiar. He cocked his head, questioning his own senses.

"Little Gill, why did you stop?" the man said, the good side of his mouth tilting up in a smile.

"Daniel? This can't be you... Daniel Mahoney?" Gillian sat back in his chair, eyes wide, mouth slack-jawed.

"In the flesh, little Gill—well, almost." Now his smile was so wide even his tortured side had conceded to a moment of happiness. "I adopted the alias John Mahon when I arrived in America, claiming I was a Protestant Welshman. Else, I never would have landed this position at the great Chelsea Surety Company," he said with a hint of sarcasm.

"But... but what happened, Daniel? Oh, no... I'm so sorry, something dreadful... it appears," stumbled out of his mouth as he stared at the man. Then he looked down at the floor, feeling shame as if he'd misspoken or stared too long.

"You don't have to look away, Robert. I've grown used to it... sort of. Of course, you want to know what happened. That's our nature."

"Well, should you not want to talk about it, I would understand," Gillian said, forcing himself to look at the man's better half.

"If you remember, I left the farm in 1833 and made the journey to New York. Like all of us, I had many odd jobs. The worst was hauling shit across the East River to Brooklyn. Then we'd load it onto giant carts pulled by four steeds, take it out to Long Island, mix it with other manure and sell it as fertilizer." Mahoney grimaced. "But then the Croton Aqueduct project started. I thought I was in heaven, Robert. I didn't have to travel far, and the wage was strong like I'd never seen. The promise was we'd all see the freshest water from the country delivered right here to our doorstep, even in the Five Points. But that wasn't the plan, we learned later—as you may know yourself."

"I do know about the water," Gillian said solemnly, wondering how much Brian Denny had revealed of Aileen's tragedy. But this thought was fleeting. He was still in shock, a dreamy feeling. *Is this really Daniel Mahoney?*

"I was courting a fine woman from a large farming family in New Jersey, quite well-to-do people. We planned to wed in the summer of 1836. But I'd made the cursed mistake of joining the fire department a year earlier. I was told it would give me the connections to move up in this city." He paused and cocked his head. "Hmm. When I think about it, where I am now, I suppose it did."

Mahoney lifted from his seat and went to the window, glancing out at the trees below, all sprouting tiny green leaves. "Springtime. Hope for the future," he muttered. "Others' future, not mine." He sighed, then turned back to Gillian. "My other mistake was telling me lady my real name. I thought it wouldn't matter, me being a Protestant. But she told her mother and father, and they turned against the marriage. But it wouldn't matter anyway. December 16th, 1835. The Great Conflagration they called it, the worst since the Great London Fire."

"Aye, I heard lots about that, Daniel. You were involved, then?"

"I was. Young and foolish. But the way you see me here was not my fault, you must know!" Mahoney said defensively.

"I'm sure it wasn't," Gillian replied, taken aback at the vehemence.

"You see, I was new at your Engine Company Five," Mahon said. "They were calling it the White Flag Company then. We were just as fast as the others but lost time because we had to find the bloody fire first before going to the station house."

"Didn't change a bit, Daniel, even with the horses. Not until we finally moved to a new firehouse where we get a clear view of the bell tower." Gillian paused briefly, then shook his head in disgust. "Come to think of it, we're still late to the damn fires. Sorry, go on, Daniel."

"It started as a typical warehouse fire at Pearl and the Exchange Place. But it was a windy and frigid night, cold like I never felt before. That's what did us in. By the time the first company got there, the fire had spread to the buildings on both sides. The next two companies were slow in arriving—they'd been racing with their hand pumpers, stupid fools they were, and slipped on the ice and tipped their engines. And it takes time to upright those heavy things. So, we were fourth to arrive." He turned from the window as if turning away from the memory. "I'll never forget that smell, chemicals of all sorts burning, and the tar roofs. Anyway, must have been over ten buildings on fire when we arrived. The wind was kicking up fierce, and the embers kept leaping from one building to the next. But they were also landing a distance, starting fires blocks away. That was what really frightened us. There was no telling where the fires were going to go." At that moment, Daniel Mahoney stopped to open a desk drawer. "Touch of bourbon, Robert?"

"Oh, don't mind that at all," Gillian said as he watched the bottle come out and his old friend reach for two tins on the shelf behind him.

"Two stiff ones. There we go." And he poured generously. "A bit better than that mash we used to drink. You remember, Robert? Me, you, and your father with his stories."

"Aye, I remember well. His stories were something. He would insist that our family were descendants of the great Brian Boru, last high king of the Gaelic peoples. Then you'd say, 'Not with the name Gillian, you ain't.'"

"I remember, Robert. I'd say, 'Gillian came from Guilluime, a French name, probably Norman.' He'd insist not. Then he'd say, 'Well then, we

Gillians are direct relations to Saint Patrick himself.' Then I'd say, 'Naw. Saint Patrick was a Roman.' Didn't tell him the saint could've been both."

Gillian laughed. Taking a slow sip of his liquor, Mahoney continued.

"When I think about it, I should've shown more respect for your father. Your family were good tenants back when we owned all that land. Two hundred acres. One of the last true Irish landowners outside of Galway, we were." He sighed, then said regretfully, "Aye, I should've shown him more respect, but my pride was too big and wounded, losing all that land to the bloody bank. Then becoming a miserable tenant on me own land!" Mahoney took an angry swig, and a bit dribbled out the scarred side of his mouth. "I mean, we Mahoneys were not always the kindest, but that's the way ye had to be when collecting rent from so many tenants, and we had lots of expenses and taxes too burdening us. But you Gillians always paid your rent, ne'er a problem, always pleasant folk."

His friend was reverting to a heavier Irish brogue, the one he'd remembered from their farming days. The old Daniel Mahoney was back, at least for the moment. "You were a fine landlord, Daniel. Don't be harsh on yourself."

"You're too kind, Little Gill." Then he continued. "So, when they took my land, and your father let me rent that half-acre piece, I was too humiliated to be grateful. But he never held it against me. Even when I said I was leaving for America and he'd be losing the rent."

"It was no matter. You remember Roger McCleary? He rented it. We became good friends. He died during the famine. A cut on his leg finished him."

"Oh, that's a shame, Robert. I remember he had a tough lot."

There were several seconds of silence, Gillian reflecting upon the distance of those years from the present. Then he shook his head to reclaim the moment. "Tell me the rest about the fire and all."

"Yes, of course... the fire," Mahoney said. "You see, in those days, getting enough water was even more a chore, especially if the fire was far from the two rivers like this one. We had the cisterns and a few hydrants, but the water in the cisterns was frozen solid, and the water coming out of the hydrants was freezing in the hoses. Finally, the hydrants froze over. Raging fire and no water, Robert! Picture that. All the fire bells are ringing throughout the city, but you don't need them. Every soul can see the conflagration—from Brooklyn, from New Jersey, and as far away as Philadelphia, the papers said the next day."

Gillian was mesmerized, hardly noticing when Mahoney refilled their cups.

"Chief Engineer Gulick had us forming a line with the engines all the way to the East River, like elephants in the circus. We connected the back hose from one pumper to the front hose from the one behind. But the bloody river was frozen. We had men out there with ice picks breaking through the top layer. We'd get water for a while, then it'd freeze in the hoses. Now, hundreds of buildings were on fire."

Despite the chaotic scene being described, the bourbon was relaxing Gillian.

"So that's when the mayor and the fire commissioner decided we had to start blowing up buildings to make firewalls. It was the only way to slow this down. I was eager to help, but we had to take a barge over to the Brooklyn Navy Yard to get the barrels of gunpowder. Problem was, there was a lot of ice on the river, and where there wasn't, the icy wind was churning up the water onto the ice. A bunch of ice choppers were in the lead, and I went over there with a few men from our company to secure the barrels. We even had that Negro, Clancy. He'd been with us for maybe a week. We got back to New York about three in the morning. That's when everything happened so fast."

Mahoney capped off their tins. Despite the drink, Gillian suddenly felt alert now, sensing the climax of the drama. He'd been moving through each scene as described by his old friend.

"I was eager to plant the explosives—we weren't putting out any damn fires anyway, and I had a right to be involved there. After all, I went all the way to Brooklyn, across a frozen river, to get the bloody barrels. The commissioner and the mayor take the carriage around to figure out which buildings to mark for demolition. Another half hour lost. And when they get back, Chief Gulick says he doesn't think it's the job of the fire department to be blowing up buildings. Meantime, the whole city's burning, and the mayor's yelling at the commissioner who's yelling at Gulick, 'Well, you ain't putting out any damn fire, so you better do something, for Christ's sake.' I heard it with my own ears." He touched what remained of his right ear. "Of course, during all this, looters are making off with merchandise in the street, whatever owners could rescue from their buildings when they saw the fire coming their way. So now the constables are running after the looters, who are nearly getting trampled by the panicked horses."

"Now I'm imagining a circus, Daniel."

Mahoney laughed. "Yes, I suppose it must have looked that way."

A somber mood suddenly overtook the room as the realization of how this story was going to end became clear. At least for Gillian.

Mahoney continued. "So, our White Flag Company got the order to check on a fire that had broken out near the corner of Water Street and Wall Street. The old Dutchman, Voorhees, was our foreman at the time—wasn't so old back then. He commanded me and Denny to go with him. When we arrived, we saw it was one of the newer warehouse buildings of the day, three stories. And there was a lot of fire on the top floor. Voorhees said we'd be blowing up the thing, and I volunteered to plant the gunpowder and charge. I could tell he was impressed with me and thought I'd be making a name for myself.

"We're standing there waiting for a barrel of powder to be delivered while Vorhees is inspecting the front of the building. Then he comes back to the street and says, 'Mistake, men. We can't blow this here building up. It's insured, but we may get some money for saving the thing or what's in it.' Then Brian Denny chimes in. He was new to the company too, and a scoundrel then, just how he was . . ." Mahoney stopped short with a frown. "So, Denny says, 'Mr. Voorhees, sir, I believe this building is too far gone now. We shouldn't go in, but it will make a great firewall if we bring it down fast.' Voorhees replies, 'Maybe so, but it needs to be saved. We have a hydrant over there. I'll round up some men and a pumper.'" Mahoney shot Gillian a knowing look. "That was the last I heard from Voorhees. He mounted his horse and was off to the main conflagration."

"So it's you and Denny—alone—waiting for a crew," Gillian said with an uneasy feeling he knew where this was going.

"That's right. Me and Brian Denny," Mahoney said tightly. "We waited in the frigid wind until two men rode up with two white Percherons pulling a hand pumper—big for its day. I was relieved until they found out the hydrant cap was frozen shut. They yanked on that blasted thing, beat it with crowbars. Meantime, embers from the roof were landing down on the road and spooking the horses. 'Them horses are gonna run off with our pumper!' Denny yells. 'I'll unhitch them and move them down the road. Mahoney, you scout out the first floor, see what we're dealing with.' I'll never forget that last sentence, the last time I spoke to anybody that night."

Mahoney stopped to finish his tin. Gillian followed suit, not realizing just how much he still had in his cup. He coughed as too much went down at once, then wiped his chin with his sleeve.

"That bloody scoundrel, Denny!" Mahoney seethed. "Everyone knows Percherons don't run from fires! Maybe they whinny, rear up a bit, but they don't take off. Our cowardly friend knew what he was doing, as he's the one that told me about Percherons to begin with! I walked up the three steps in front, and there it was off to the side of the door, the fire mark, shiny new brass thing, fancy script writing. 'Premises Insured by the Chelsea Surety Company.'"

"Hmm," was all Gillian could say.

"I don't have too much memory after that. I know I went into the building, then there was a thunderous sound, and I heard my own voice screaming—like I was outside myself. *Who's that screaming?* I remember thinking, then that was it."

"How did you survive, Daniel?"

"If tweren't for the hose men, we wouldn't be having this meeting today." With that, Daniel Mahoney stood and walked back over to the window. The bourbon seemed to have had little effect on the man. Perhaps it was the gravity of the conversation, or the man was just a seasoned drinker... or maybe both.

"I woke up two days later in Bellevue Hospital, wrapped up from head to toe, reeling with pain. The opium helped some. But that smell—it was nearly as bad as the pain. 'What's that awful smell?' I said to the nurse. She wouldn't meet my eyes. 'That's you, sir. Your flesh, I'm sorry to say.' Then I was in delirium for days. Twice the priest came, they say, to give me last rites. Then the third time he says, 'You still here, Mahoney?' I said, 'In the flesh, Father—I think.' You see, it's hard to kill us Mahoneys, a truth I came to think about as a curse. Sometimes I wonder if my father's somewhere out there. Although, he'd be very old by now. You probably don't remember what happened to him."

"Actually, I do," Gillian said. "Daniel Mahoney the Elder, you called him. He went fishing a little too far out, and the English Navy kidnapped him."

"Good memory there, Little Gill. That's right. It was back in 1811. They undoubtedly found out he was in Napoleon's Irish Brigade and made him walk the plank. If it wasn't for one man on his boat escaping, we'd never know what happened to him."

Mahoney returned to his desk just as Gillian stood. Despite the initial calming effect of the spirits, his head was now throbbing at both temples. How could he go through with it now? How could he tell his dear old friend that he was no longer willing to stage fires but still wanted the job of placing fire marks? Daniel must be curious as to the reason for his visit. But then again, two hours had passed, and they'd drowned thirty years of reflections with a full bottle of bourbon. Or perhaps Daniel had intuited why Gillian came but didn't want to deal with it just now.

He turned to Mahoney, who was studying a chart sitting atop his ink blotter. "My, the afternoon has faded quickly, Daniel. And it was quite an afternoon at that. I need to take leave for I have several errands to run, but we shall meet again?"

Mahoney looked up from his desk, a quizzical expression on his good side. "Certainly, Robert. Can't have too many old friends in this town, aye, Little Gill?" Then he smiled. "One thing, Robert. Sometimes when a good thing comes your way, you have to take advantage of it while it's there. This one won't be here forever. Soon Chelsea Surety will have more adjusters than just me. 'Cause of fire' inspections will grow more sophisticated, and when the days of the volunteer department are over, all will change. Spiffs will be a thing of the past. And you know it's coming, maybe sooner than we think." He waved his good hand toward the door. "On that note, you better run along, my friend."

"Thank you, Daniel," Gillian said, still discomfited as he replaced his hat. He had one hand on the doorknob when he turned back to Mahoney. "I am perplexed by one thing. Why in heavens did you wait so long to move me up from placing fire marks to... well... playing the game?"

Mahoney glanced out the window. Gillian felt that the man was avoiding eye contact with him. It appeared that he needed to ponder the question. "Well, Robert. It takes a long time for a man to place his trust in another—especially in this city. I had to feel sure you would not betray me."

Gillian smiled, then quietly took his leave. But as he descended the narrow stairway, Gillian found himself doubting Daniel's answer. And there had been the strange pauses around the subject of Brian Denny. And no remorse—let alone mention—of the late Mrs. Grimble.

* * *

The afternoon was fading. He needed to return home to dress for his visit with Daisy McGill, the barmaid from the saloon off South Street. Six years was a long time to wait to court the woman, but it was only of late that her husband had taken up residence at the bottom of the East River, just near the South Street docks. The authorities claimed it was a suicide, though they found him with bricks tied to both legs.

Gillian's only issue with Daisy was her name. "Daisy" was a name he hadn't uttered in years, at least since Aileen's passing. On a few occasions, he'd intended to share the tragic story with his new Daisy, but he came upon a wall of sorts. To climb over that wall would be betraying Aileen, or so he felt. It was their shared tragedy, the pain not to be shared with strangers.

And yet certainly, after all these years, he had a right to new intimacy, and Daisy McGill had a right to expect that from him. For now, she would get punctuality, clean clothes, and a bouquet.

CHAPTER FIFTY

February 1863

"Someone of your means, Papa, shouldn't be living in the Five Points anymore. I do suppose this flat isn't too bad, but still... " and she gazed about the living room, then looked at him again. "It's still the Five Points."

"What difference does it make, Mary? And besides, Grand Street is not the Five Points. It's just north of the Five Points. When Patrick's done with school, I'm sure he'll take Helen as his bride, and I'll be alone. Why do I need a townhouse in Gramercy Park?"

The thought of being alone stung him again. His courtship with Daisy McGill had ended within a year, after much squabbling. In time, he'd found her to be pigheaded or perhaps just not his type. Which was just as well as she became involved in a scandal that almost implicated her in Mr. McGill's ending at the bottom of the East River. Last thing he needed was the attention of the news rags.

"I suppose you're right," Mary said. "But did you at least see that surgeon Mr. Bidwell recommended?"

Thankfully fibbing here was unnecessary. "I did. He said the sores on my feet should go away if I change my diet. Too much sugar, he said, and I should stick with meat and potatoes. So I've listened, but no change yet. He also said, 'If you really want to know what's wrong, you have to taste your pee, see if it's sweet.' I said, 'No, thank you. But you can taste my pee, sir, if you want.' Then he handed me an outrageous bill. For that amount, he should have tasted my pee!"

Mary's face cracked a smile for the first time since she arrived. "Well, hopefully, this surgeon will find a cure for you soon," she remarked. "On another subject, Mr. Bidwell has requested you come by for lunch. He has more business to discuss. The War Between the States has put his business in disarray, but he seems optimistic about some new opportunity. Would Sunday after the church you don't attend be acceptable?"

"Very," he said with a smile, ignoring her jab.

"I better return. Bertie is paying a visit for dinner; there's much to do."

"That's an odd Christian name."

"He was named after Victoria and Albert's first son, Bertie, actually Edward, the future King of England. I hope Patrick and you enjoy the truffles. I've become quite skilled in the kitchen, for better or worse." Mary sighed, then moved toward the door with Gillian following. "Please be punctual on Sunday," she said before turning to hug him.

"Be well till then, my sweetheart," he said as she tied her bonnet and exited to the hallway of the building—*just north of the Five Points.*

* * *

"I have to tell you, Gillian, I never imagined such a war. I assumed Lincoln would put down the insurrection within months, those states would come to their senses, and this would be over. Now they're talking draft. Bertie won't be going, I'm certain of that. I'll pay the three hundred dollars to have him taken out of the lottery."

"I shall do the same for my Patrick," Gillian said, now realizing that the delicate subject was bound to come up soon... Patrick was finishing school. The boy would be a druggist this year. *I won't let the war find him. But Patrick may decide to find the war.*

"Well, Lincoln's war has been disastrous for my mercantile business. The cotton trade is in shambles, and I have loans to plantations in Virginia that I may never see repaid. That money we made off the worthless Broadway Rail Line shares has helped a great deal, but that only goes so far."

"Yes, indeed. That was a good call on your part, Mr. Bidwell," Gillian said, feeling much the businessman now.

"Please call me Nucky, Robert. You know me well enough, and we are almost in the same social tier now. Maybe you're not a richer man, but I am a poorer man," he said with a laugh before he cleared his throat, signaling they were about to arrive at the real reason for this luncheon.

"Sweetmeats are served, gentlemen," Clara said as she burst into the grand dining room, Mary just behind her carrying a large tray of assorted desserts. Before Mary left the room, she gave him a hard glance as if to remind him these desserts were not for him. *Surely one pecan cup wouldn't hurt.*

Bidwell studied the tray while twisting one end of his well-oiled mustache. After selecting three items, he continued. "I believe that slavery is highly immoral, and I'm certainly glad we did away with it in New York years ago. But Lincoln's emancipation may have gone too far, too quickly—perhaps requiring better treatment of them would have been in order." He sighed and ate one of the pecan cups morosely. "But it is what it is. At this stage, I doubt I will fully recover from the damages, so I've been consulting with my other partners and we're assembling a new venture." He cleared his throat and fidgeted. "The plan is to invest in two new cargo ships, state-of-the-art steamers, fast and highly seaworthy. We won't be carrying cargo; we'd be leasing the ships to trading companies. They pay all operating costs. Very profitable, easy money for us. Within five years we should have our investment back. Might you have an appetite for this, Robert?"

"Well... I don't have too much to put at risk, but what do these traders do?" he asked, feeling his own lack of sophistication again.

"They trade in many items. We already have one company on board. They'll be sailing from New York to West Africa, load cargo there, Negros and dry goods to be exchanged in the Caribbean Islands. Then they'll transport rum and other spices to sell in Europe. They are very eager to lease one boat for three years. Remember, we don't own or move the cargo, Gillian, just rent the ship to those that do."

"Does sound interesting," he allowed. "I need to check with my banker first. They've inquired of my plans with funds that are sitting idle." Robert Gillian felt a surge of pride. In his wildest dreams, he never thought he'd be contemplating investment plans, let alone be courted by bankers. Though, he did wish Aileen was there as a partner in these matters, what with her numbers skills. "Let me return to you next week with my decision."

"You won't be regretful, I assure you. This will make us all comfortable with the changing times as they are. Besides, I would loathe having to divest myself of my majolica collection. I do enjoy it so, and I already lost some pieces in the Crystal Palace conflagration," he said, gazing wistfully about the room.

Gillian stood and inquired as to the location of the water closet. Peeing frequently seemed to be an inconvenient habit he'd developed lately. Then he'd be on his way home, where he would look up the word *loathe* in the dictionary Mary had purchased for him.

"Well, just have Mary let us know when you plan to visit with your word. I must admit it is convenient having her as both a servant girl and messenger. Oh, Mary!" he called. "Can you retrieve your father's belongings?"

* * *

"Yes, Master," she called down from the top of the stairs. She quickly descended, carrying three formal shirts of Mr. Bidwell's, the well-starched detachable collars dangling from each.

"Where are you going with those?" he questioned.

"Oh, I thought I'd deliver these to Chang's Laundry after my father's departure."

"But there're just three shirts, and it's Sunday. Isn't he closed?"

"Jian... uh, Mr. Chang is open a few hours on Sunday to accommodate his busier customers," she replied. "I know it's my day off, sir, but it's no worry. I will be paying a visit to a friend who lives in the area just after."

"Well, suit yourself, dear. It's your free time," Bidwell responded.

Mary felt relieved; she could tell his mind was already drifting elsewhere. But when she turned toward the hallway closet, her father was standing there, looking at her with an inquisitive expression. She brushed by him as she went to retrieve his outerwear. *I've done nothing wrong. No reason to feel this way,* she defended herself to herself.

"Here you go, Papa," she said as she quickly delivered his outer garments—accidentally including the three shirts of Bidwell's she'd been holding.

"I don't believe these are mine. Here you go," he said as he gave her back the shirts, again gazing at her, but now with suspicion, she thought. Once he was buttoned up, the two embraced, a brief and courteous hug.

"Remember, Robert. Think quickly on this. We must move swiftly!" Bidwell called out from the parlor.

"You have my word, Bidwell," he called back as Mary rushed him to the front stoop.

"Too-da-loo, Mr. Gillian," cackled Clara Bidwell from the top of the stairs.

"Phew. Finally," Mary muttered to herself, still standing on the front stoop and clutching Bidwell's shirts. *I told Jian half past one. I best get my coat.*

In a rush, she almost forgot to retrieve her tattered copy of the King James Bible. Teaching Christianity and English language, all in one lesson. She was impressed with her own cleverness, and it allowed her to maximize time spent with her newfound interest.

Jian Chang had come to America four years earlier, arriving from China's Mandarin province. He'd heard that a fortune was still to be had in gold mining, and if that turned out to be just rumor, that railroad work was plentiful in the American West. Unfortunately, he was far too late for the gold rush, and the railroad work proved brutal for a man of his slight build. Instead, he learned the trade of cleaning the railroad workers' clothes. It was equally hard on the hands, but it paid a respectable wage. His brother, already living in New York City—and well established in the booming opium trade—encouraged Jian to travel east. He'd help him set up a laundry business in the growing neighborhood of Chinatown.

Fastidious regarding the care of his shirts, Enoch Bidwell found himself in need of a new launderer, and a friend recommended Chang's business. Mary took a liking to Chang by her second delivery of the master's shirts. He had a distinctive charm that she found endearing. Perhaps contributing to this was his valiant—sometimes humorous—struggle with the English language. But he always managed to communicate what he needed to. And she quickly intuited that he was a kind and gentle man. Though her weekly visits were routine, now on Sundays—her day off—she'd steal away to mentor Jian on the Bible and the English language. On this particular day, he'd asked her to accompany him for an early supper.

CHAPTER FIFTY-ONE

WHITE FLAG FIREHOUSE
March 1863

"Clancy, I don't get how we're still late to the fires. With this new station, we have a clear view of the bell tower, and we got the finest Percherons in the department."

The two of them were standing on top of the engine platform, taking a break from their polishing.

"Beats me. Maybe we're just used to being late? That's why we're still called the White Flag Company, I reckon." Gillian's graying friend let out a hearty laugh and a fart instead of his usual cough.

"It's like we have to live up to our expectation of being late, no matter what. As foreman of this company, I need to spend time figuring how to fix this," Gillian said.

"Maybe less time on the fire marker business would do the trick," Clancy said with friendly sarcasm. "Don't miss what I'm saying, though. I know you're making good money there, and nobody's getting hurt, but be careful, Robert, and don't forget to pay attention to other things."

"I'm just fine, Clancy. Making it while I can," Gillian replied. "My boy's almost done with becoming a druggist, and should Mary finally be courting, I have dowry money for the groom."

"Sounds like you got it figured out," Clancy said. "I was wondering, though, would you consider giving some money to the colored causes?

It's hard now, harder than ever. Colored folk are coming up here in droves with the emancipation, and peoples are blaming us for the war, which is hogwash, and you know it."

The question caught Gillian by surprise. It was certainly not the type of request he'd ever encountered, although it made sense. Truth was, he had more money than he needed and expected now to be dying alone. He started to feel self-pity again, but his mood quickly rebounded. He'd never been in the position to give money away. And it felt elating.

"Aye, I believe I could," he said.

"Well, thank you, Robert. You really are a hero." Clancy gave him a warm smile and then climbed down from the engine, their polishing job complete. "We best tend to the horses," he said, with a spring in his step.

Gillian trailed him to the stables. "What'd you have in mind? For the charities, I mean."

"You know the Orphan Asylum for Colored Children?" They're up on Fifth Avenue and 42nd Street."

"I've heard of it, yes."

"If you could spare a generous donation, they'd be most grateful. And there's the colored almshouses, two up in Hell's Kitchen. And the Negro cemetery is always short of money to keep up the graves. I'm gonna get you a list of possibilities. Then you can figure how to do it. Oh, shoot, we need more hay. I'll get it around—"

Just then, a tall black man burst out of the rear door of the engine house and into the yard. "Mr. Carver, where is you, where is you!" an alarmed voice shouted. "It's about Emmet, sir."

"What happened to my son, Harold!" Clancy demanded as he rushed from the stables.

"The blackbirders got 'em, Mr. Carver, them blackbirders!" he repeated, appearing ready to collapse in the dirt.

Clancy threw his cap to the ground and ripped his bandana off. "How the hell did that happen, Harold? You give me the whole story now, you hear!"

Harold nodded while taking a few deep breaths. He bent forward and put his hands on his knees.

"We was at the cockfights, you know, at that saloon all the way over near West Street. Emmet was sure my rooster could take on the best there and we'd make good money for an afternoon."

Harold slumped to the ground as if he knew the story was going to take even more of the wind out of him. He wiped the sweat from his brow and then clutched his shaking knees. "We went down there with Big Henry in that old cage I have. We already had the spurs, nice and sharp, tied to his feet. We arrived late, so most of the men were drunk with whiskey and such."

"Get to the important stuff, boy!" Clancy demanded.

"Big Henry won four rounds, tore one rooster to shreds that was supposed to be the frontrunner. We cashed out a sweet sum. Then the owner of the frontrunner bird comes up to us. Says real slow, 'I want to see your cock, boy,' to Emmet. Emmet says, 'I beg your pardon, sir,' and then laughs. The man and his friend don't take kindly to that. The first man says to Emmet, 'You're a cheat.' Then the second one says, 'There's nothing worse than a colored cheat.' "

Clancy's eyes opened wider than Gillian ever saw.

Harold continued. "I says nothing, but you know Emmet. He says, 'Gentlemen, you can't see my cock. He needs his rest after a trying day, and we need to clean your bird's guts off him anyways.' I pull Emmet away and tell him it ain't worth it and to just give the money back. But you know Emmet. He says, 'I don't give in to anyone that calls me a cheat.'" Harold sighed and said, "I need water, Mr. Carver."

Gillian took off for a tin, then to the pump while Clancy stood there with his head down preparing for the rest of the story.

"So, the second man says, 'Boy, we're from Washington City. Negros ain't so ornery there even with Lincoln's freeing all of them.' It was something like that. But this I remember exact words, cause he says real slow, 'I can't tell, are you a Jim Crow or a Zippy Coon? What do you think, Arlis?' That was the first one's name. So Arlis says, 'I think he's a pissin' dandy, that's what I think!' He's giving Emmet the fighting eye, so Emmet takes the first swing. Then the keeper throws them out to the street. I want no part of it, but when I come out a few minutes later, they was all gone, except for the dead frontrunner lying in his cage and dripping blood."

"How do you know they was blackbirders?" Clancy said when Harold stopped to drink.

"I went back inside and asked about the men. Two fellas recognized them as bounty hunters of them runaway slaves. They said that business is dried up with the emancipation. Said nobody's gonna pay you for a slave that's free. So, they turned to kidnapping zippy coons, they'd be calling them. Then a barkeep says, 'This point in the war, blackbirders will take whatever they can get, better than nothing,' or something like that."

Harold fell silent. After another gulp of water, he splashed the rest on his face. "I'm sorry, Mr. Carver. I'm sorry," he said softly.

Clancy fell to his knees, picked up his hat, and threw it on the ground again. Then he collapsed, prone in the dirt. Exhausted, grief-stricken, he started sobbing. Gillian sat down on the ground next to him and patted his back. He'd never seen Clancy this distraught. Then he thought back to all the ill words Clancy had for his son. *But blood is blood, no matter.* Not a word was spoken.

After a minute or so, Clancy looked up at Gillian, eyes puffy and bloodshot. "Ye gotta let me take one of them horses, Robert. I promise to bring him back. Just to get down to the saloon, see what else I can find out."

Gillian nodded fervently as Clancy grabbed his hat and dirty bandana, then sprung up from the ground. Within a minute, he had a white steed saddled up. Dust kicked up about them as he charged off down Canal Street.

"You best go home, Harold. Nothing you can do now, son."

He watched Emmet's friend slowly get up from the ground, shake the dust from his clothes, and walk around back to Canal Street. Now with just three horses, Gillian hoped that the fire bells remained silent.

CHAPTER FIFTY-TWO

April 1863

"Papa, I have to join up, and it's best before Lincoln's draft. A new regiment is being formed right now, near City Hall. Besides, this whole thing's gonna be over after the draft anyways. I won't be gone long."

It was clear to Gillian that Patrick had rehearsed his reasoning.

"You must be mad, son. You don't have to go. Just look at all the corpses coming back to the docks. I see it down there every day. Good Irish lads like yourself. Patriots, they claim, but I say fools. And now you're one of them, but even more a fool. They had no idea what was coming—you do!"

"Well, my mind is made up, Papa. I'm sorry."

"Boy—" Gillian caught himself before he went further, realizing it would be best to control his temper and resort to pleading. He took a deep breath, exhaled slowly. "Son, you're a druggist now, a professional in high demand. You just finished your schooling—schooling I paid for, I might add. I have money now. You don't need to go to battle. They're saying three hundred dollars is all it takes to buy out of the lottery. Someone will replace you that doesn't have such a future."

Gillian dropped down on the sofa. The spring sun, still early in the sky, was streaming through the curtains, the new furnishings creating shadows about the room. And he gazed about, and imagined that soon he'd be taking this in, all alone. The start of the day, and he already felt weary and out of words. Patrick was no longer a boy. At twenty-seven, he'd long been making up his own mind.

It was a valiant effort, but Gillian knew throughout that control of the situation was not his. He struggled to reframe things. *Perhaps Patrick is right. The war has turned the corner, and with Lincoln's draft, it will only be a short time before the Union crushes the rebels. He'll return, become a prosperous druggist, and marry the woman he's been courting.*

Patrick sat down next to his father and patted the man's lap. "I'm sorry, Papa. I know everything will work out. You'll see."

But only a fool would be certain of that. And Gillian knew Patrick was no fool.

"Well, why don't you whip up one of your breakfasts for your old pa? Might as well get the most use out of you while I can," Gillian said. He smiled at Patrick—a sad smile.

One week later, Gillian accompanied Patrick to the army depot outside of City Hall Park. The two embraced, then parted ways. Gillian turned one last time and saw Patrick take his place in line to obtain his uniform and training gear. It was real now, and he teared up, worried about his son's safe return. And on the journey home, it occurred to him where his real fear lay. *How* Patrick came home was a far greater concern than *if* Patrick came home. He'd already seen the possibilities with the returning soldiers. And he shuddered at the thought of his son losing both legs, or arms, or his eyesight. He wondered if a corpse would be preferable, should the boy not walk through the door like he went out the door. Then he felt shame. *For whose benefit? Maybe the boy won't feel the same way. Well, tis in God's hands now, right, Aileen?*

As he approached the Grand Street flat, his sadness grew more intense. It was real now. No Patrick, no Clancy, Mary finding less time to visit him—as she'd finally told him that she'd been spending her free time with her Chinaman friend. Still no wife or prospect for marriage—though he had to concede that he wasn't even trying. And in a few weeks, he even found himself missing Brian Denny. Though this passed quickly.

Except for the periodic fire marker assignments, and less frequent special events, he spent much of his free time at the White Flag Engine House.

CHAPTER FIFTY-THREE

A Week of Rioting
July 1863

When the draft riots began in July of 1863, Gillian felt a peculiar sense of relief that Clancy was not there to see it.

Tensions had been mounting regarding the impending draft. The masses of poor Irish Catholic immigrants were tired and mournful. They'd believed Lincoln's call was to just put down an insurrection in the South, maybe a few months of duty. Now, two years later, corpses were returning en masse. But the igniting spark was when it was publicized that men could buy themselves out of the draft for three hundred dollars, an amount no poor Irishman could afford. Add the fear of newly emancipated men and women coming north and taking their jobs, and resentment had tipped over into violence.

It started at the docks, where groups of Catholic men, women, and children began gathering around the rabble-rousers. Gillian was nearly hit by two bottles on his walk from South Street to Pearl Street.

After picking up the evening paper, Gillian went back to his flat and stayed there for two days, only going out to buy the latest edition. Rocks and bottles were hurled from rooftops, raining down on the constabulary vainly trying to keep order below. Mobs marched through the streets with clubs, breaking store windows, targeting known abolitionists, and attacking Negro bystanders. It only got worse on the second day, with incendiaries alighting buildings in the black neighborhoods. And then the lynchings began. Negros were dragged out of establishments and hung from telegraph poles or even stoned.

Robert Gillian had a feeling he might not see Clancy again. But, he considered, perhaps death in a foreign land was less awful than being killed in his own New York, where slavery had been abolished more than a half-century earlier. Good-natured Clancy, a man of impeccable character, certainly couldn't imagine being betrayed by his own neighbors. And after all, Gillian concluded, Clancy had a noble reason to be down there, attempting a rescue of his own flesh and blood, even if the boy's flesh and blood was no damn good.

To cap off that tragic week, the rioters descended upon the Orphan Asylum for Colored Children, burning it to the ground. Miraculously all the children and most adults escaped before the blaze took hold. But where could they establish a residence after? A dilemma for the moment.

Finally, the Union Army marched into the city, four thousand strong, and quashed the rebellion. Regiments arrived from Pennsylvania, as they had just defeated the rebel armies at Gettysburg. Patrick Gillian was in one of those regiments and made his way home to New York. Ironically, the Civil War Draft Riot was ignited by a fire company of the City of New York. They sent flaming bottles with kerosene through the windows of the draft office. And Gillian read in the paper, *"Firemen Starting Fires? More Investigations Needed?"* This made his stomach turn.

Daniel Mahoney spent that week brooding in his 13nth Street flat.

With all these fires, a perfect opportunity had gone to waste—it would have been easy to stage an event. Then again, the new policies being written didn't pay out for 'Acts of War or Sedition,' which might include riots. But they might still give a reward for saving a building? *Hmm. I should be on the lookout for the next riot,* he pondered.

CHAPTER FIFTY-FOUR

The Burning of New York—or Not?
November 1864

But there wasn't another riot. In fact, revised draft laws made it easier for poor Irish families to keep safe their patriotic men, while new regiments of eager black New Yorkers were sent off to fight. And there was a dearth of mentionable fires, which made Daniel Mahoney uneasy. *Perhaps the new fire codes and superior construction standards are changing things.* Logic told him this would bring more scrutiny to his own special events. But he didn't have to wait long for the situation to change, thanks to the rebel cause.

Fire bells were clanging everywhere, up and down Broadway. A conflagration possibly? There was panic in the streets. Shouts of fire came from the LaFarge Hotel, disrupting the performance of *Julius Caesar* at the adjacent Winter Garden Theatre, where the famed Booth brothers—Junius, Edwin, and John Wilkes—were on stage together. Reports were quickly coming in that fires were erupting in as many as twenty hotels as well as at PT Barnum's Museum of Wonders.

"Odd? We had nothing planned," Mahoney muttered to himself while sipping tea by the fire. He placed his cup on the coffee table and picked up a novel he'd planned to finish that night. Soon, the sounds began to dissipate, one bell after another. And then there was silence. He checked his timepiece and discovered that just an hour had passed.

Not possible; there must have been fires everywhere. He felt a bit disappointed that he had missed the show, and his thoughts went to Robert Gillian and White Flag Engine Company. *No doubt they showed up too late anyway.*

The morning edition of the *New York Times* explained the events in detail. The fires were part of a fiendish Confederate plot to destroy the northern cities. But this plot was destined to fail, even before the ill-conceived fires. The Confederate leaders believed they could quickly build a new army of disgruntled anti-Lincoln Democrats—in the Midwest—who would free rebel prisoners, then go on to attack the as-yet-untouched cities in the north. New York, the Emerald City, was at the top of the list, as all they saw were the businessmen fattening their purses, supplying the Union Army with the means to destroy the rebel cause. But they grossly miscalculated the level of support from the weary Midwesterners. A grand northern front never materialized. What they did have was a small group of incompetent Confederate agents who tried their hand at burning the entire city themselves.

In the ensuing days, Mahoney was regaled by the newspaper coverage of the grand plot. He laughed, rightfully so, at the gross incompetence of the six Confederate buffoons. "You morons, you deserve to lose the war!" he cackled away at the breakfast table. "Twenty fires, and only one took hold. How stupid are you! We have lumberyards, distilleries, coal and gas works. You chose hotels. You didn't open the windows in the rooms to draw air into the fire, no matches to catch in the rooms, early evening, so plenty of security to put out the fires. And a windless night anyways. Were you even trying?"

He was shaking his head again when something in a newspaper article caught his attention. The incendiary material was 144 vials of a chemical compound they were calling "Greek Fire." Phosphorus mixed with other secret chemicals, it was said to burst into flames when the bottle was broken and the compound exposed to air. But when not used competently, it quickly burnt itself out.

"By George! This is what we need for our events, a *perfectly imperfect* material for a controlled fire. And our scapegoat for the fires? Seething

Confederate rebels." Daniel Mahoney had an urge to dance about the room, an uncommon feeling for him. But first, he needed to get a hold of this concoction so it could be refined for their needs. And then it came to him. He'd best check the older policies on some of the Chelsea-insured properties. See if they had exceptions for 'acts of war.'

"I shall place a meeting with dear Robert. Perhaps it's our turn to make some real money off this war."

CHAPTER FIFTY-FIVE

"A New Opportunity"
April 1865

As the war turned in favor of the Union Army, Gillian was now recognized as the second largest depositor at the local branch of the Emigrant Savings Bank. Still, he lived a quiet existence, mostly alone, in the modest flat on Grand and Mott Streets. Patrick visited while on leave, nursing a small shrapnel wound caused by a newfangled grenade device. "If the army's paying for your healing, maybe they'll do something about that crook in your nose," Robert quipped. Inside, he was terrified of the day his son would arrive home via another mode of transportation, or perhaps not return at all.

But this early spring morning was an especially important day for Robert Gillian. Daniel Mahoney had granted him a novel assignment, and now he was standing proudly at his full-length looking glass. He'd be acting as an assistant insurance adjuster, completely legitimate and honorable work! First, he'd take the sidewheeler ferry right up to the new pier jutting out from West Brighton Beach, which was only a short walk from the renowned Coney Island House, a grand hotel. He was to meet two gentlemen in the main dining room. The business to be discussed? A *bad fire*, as Mahoney had explained. Or a *real* fire, which Gillian thought ironically should be called a *good fire*, a perfectly legal mishap.

The clients had owned an adjacent hotel that had burnt to the ground during the off-season. Entirely an accident, one that happened when the winter caretaker neglected two kettles on a coal stove. His only task was to discuss the estimated costs of reproducing the gentlemen's hotel.

Now he stood tall at the mirror, gut sucked in, smiling at his reflection as he adjusted his high collar and tie. "This is what I've been waiting for, Aileen. Biding my time with Daniel has paid off. This is a genuine opportunity at a legitimate new trade!" He gave a firm nod to the glass as he imagined Aileen's approval of his decision. "You see, I am getting on in years, my dear, while you remain the same age. Soon I will be too old for the dock work. And it's a win for Daniel, my old friend. He cannot bear the thought of introducing his own appearance to these men in broad daylight in a beachfront dining room. And Daniel has let on that more of this work could be coming my way if I remain loyal to him."

With that, he slammed shut the closet door, then grabbed his cloak and top hat and whistled his way out the door. As he made his way to the ferry terminal, he reflected upon his first visit to West Brighton ten years earlier, when he and Patrick had joined the masses of plebs trying to escape the sweltering summer heat. First a ferry ride to Brooklyn, then a jolting ride on the rickety Gunther's Railroad through Gravesend, over a bridge, and finally the shore.

Deep in thought, he almost forgot to stop at his designated post office box to retrieve the expense account funds. *That would be quite an embarrassment if I found myself lacking the funds to pay for what will be a sumptuous and expensive meal.*

* * *

The next morning, Gillian was still reveling in thoughts about his successful business lunch and the future opportunities awaiting him when he saw the newspaper headlines. Abraham Lincoln was dead. Purely a coincidence, though for a brief moment on that April morning in 1865, Gillian revisited an ongoing story he told himself. *Whenever good fortune comes my way, there's a price to be paid.* Then he shook his head. *Nonsense!*

Why would Abraham Lincoln—may he rest in peace—have to pay the price for my good fortune.

Three weeks hence, he learned that the good fortune was not his. The hotel fire in West Brighton was not an accident, that conclusion reached by the new team of fire investigators from the City of Brooklyn. Then, a few months later, the newspapers reported that the owners—the same men that Gillian met with—had their hotel burned to the ground to collect the insurance proceeds. It was all part of a deal with the adjacent Coney Island House proprietors. They'd offered a handsome price for the property but wanted the land delivered vacant, to expand their own grand enterprise. The incendiaries were never found, and the Chelsea clients had since fled the country with their windfall.

"I had no knowledge of this *special event*, Robert," Mahoney swore. "But it does look like these new investigators are a concern for us."

So, in the end, Gillian considered, what started out as a *bad fire* turned out to be a *good fire*—but not for him.

Regrettably, more legitimate adjusting jobs failed to come his way.

Chapter Fifty-Six

The war ended, and Gillian was relieved. Patrick would be home for good. All would be fine. He'd take Helen as his bride and begin his career as a druggist. Mary was still badgering him to take a flat in the fashionable Gramercy Park neighborhood. "I don't live in the Five Points; I live just north of there!" he would insist. "Besides, it's just myself now, lass. What more do I need!"

"A man is judged by his clothes, the company he keeps, his pursuits, and where he takes up residence," she would instruct—often—as she dropped by to place meals in his new ice box.

"Hogwash," he would say. "But thank you for caring," he would murmur, and Mary would smile his way.

On one particular visit in the fall of 1865, Mary pulled a sealed envelope from her frock. Inside was a note from Enoch Bidwell. *Important business to discuss with you, Robert. Please be my guest for dinner at the Astor House this coming Friday. After dining, we may visit the men's parlor if you so wish, my treat. I hope your sealed response is an acceptance of my offer or a suggestion for a later date. Regards. EB.*

"What is it?" Mary asked, but Gillian just bid her farewell with a smile.

The invitation to meet was not a surprise. Their investment in the secret slave ship was performing as expected. Easy money, just collect lease payments, no maintenance, no responsibility. He knew this meeting would likely be about investing in the second ship.

We're not shipping slaves from Africa to the Caribbean Islands, the ship operators are, and it is completely legal, he said to himself. *Still, I will increase my donations to the Negro organizations in the city—perhaps beyond.* While it'd begun with Clancy's urging, the Civil War riots heated his passion to end the injustice.

Clancy Carver should have been chosen foreman of their White Flag Company. The man had served Engine Company Five with full dedication, risked his life numerous times, and almost lost his life as the result of Gillian's bizarre behavior, staring at an imaginary specter in the distillery fire. Yet he was not even considered as a candidate to replace the lost Brian Denny. *I did nothing to intervene, and Clancy never said a word, accepting what he'd grown used to. All was just assumed. A Negro could never serve as foreman of the White Flag Company,* Gillian realized with shame. *Aye. I will certainly step up my secret gifts to the Negro cause!*

On the morning of his meeting, he stopped in front of the mirror and stared at his physique.

"You're a disgrace," came back at him. "A little lard around the middle is something to be proud of, but this!"

He tried to plead his case. "I think as a tall fellow, I wear it well. And I am getting on in years, fifty-sixth birthday coming up, ye know."

"Of course, I know! But you're still eating like a glutton!" the mirror scolded. "And those sores on your feet are getting worse. Have you been obeying the surgeon?"

"I have. Keeping away from the sweetmeats, straight diet of beef and potatoes."

"Your chin is sagging too. Doubt you'll be able to button your newly starched shirt."

Having had about all he could take from the mirror, he slammed the closet door and proceeded to get dressed. As he did, he convinced himself that what he was most uptight about had nothing to do with Bidwell and the ships. It was shame over his physical appearance. "Call it a gentlemen's parlor, it's still a whorehouse. Why should I care? I'm paying—well, Bidwell's paying—but it's all the same," he chattered while combing his graying beard and mutton chops. *But these are whores of a higher class, beautiful ladies. Certainly, they will judge my physique. Then again, I'm sure they've dealt with worse.*

An image of Bidwell stark naked popped into his mind and he laughed.

He squeezed into most of his wardrobe, splattered on some cologne, and struggled with the brass buttons on his waistcoat. As it was an unusually warm October day, he had an excuse to leave it behind. Suspenders, necktie, and top hat, and then he was out the door. *Mary can take me shopping for some better fitting clothes*, he concluded as he sauntered down Grand Street.

Perhaps I shall tell Bidwell that I will pass on this opportunity . . .or it will be the last time. Then again, he will be displeased with me, and I have Mary's employment situation to consider. Maybe I'll just have him withhold from me the uses for this second ship. Don't need to know the operator or the details, just forward him the funds for my share. Yes, that will do.

Chapter Fifty-Seven

March 1866

"A fresh batch of coal, Papa."

"Oh, let me help you with that, lad," Gillian said as he lumbered to the doorway and grabbed a burlap sack. "These are getting heavier, it seems. Can't complain, though." The partially burnt coal they used to scrounge for weighed far less but burned for a far shorter period of time. "Just dump it in the bin by the stove."

"It looks like you've added much to the place since I've been gone. What are these porcelain curiosities?" Patrick inquired as he stood near two shelves Gillian had constructed in one corner of the living room to display his first ever collection.

"These are not porcelain, nor are they curiosities!" Gillian scolded, surprised to hear the officiousness in his own voice. "This is English majolica pottery, a twice-glazed earthenware. You see, each piece here is meant to be enjoyed for its appearance but also to be put to good use, on a fine dining table for the proper entertaining of guests. Mary's employer, Bidwell, introduced me. It's all the rage in Europe now." Gillian smiled proudly as he adjusted the glossy lobster handle atop his fish tureen.

"But you don't live in Europe, nor do you entertain. In fact, you don't have a grand dining table," Patrick teased as he began to examine the objects. "Well, they are sort of interesting, and very colorful."

"Thank you, now we best be on our way. We better get that tooth out of you before you're in real agony.

They laced up their boots to battle the street pudding.

"Simon, you remember my boy, Patrick."

"Yes of course. Greetings, Patrick. My, you look like your father." He glanced at Gillian. "Well, your father like I remember him just off the boat." He looked between the two men. "You don't look in need of a haircut, son, nor you, Robert. Perhaps a beard trim?"

"No, the boy needs a tooth out."

Patrick cringed but otherwise remained stoic. "Say, what happened to your parrot?"

"Peety? He's long since gone. Still have the cage, though."

Gillian noticed that the wig display was also gone.

"Well, son, ye made it through the war. This should be easy," Gillian coached as he tried to mess Patrick's red top, only to remember too late it was short now.

The procedure was not easy, and Gillian needed to look away from the ordeal. But after a brief period of excruciating pain, Patrick's ache was gone. Once the gauze halted the bleeding, they could head to Gillian's favorite tavern by the South Street docks.

"Simon, where's my little friend today?" Gillian asked. "I planned on stuffing my pockets with her cob corn."

Simon hesitated, shooting a quick glance at Patrick as if there was still a child in the room he didn't want to be privy to bad news. "She passed a month ago, pneumonia they said. You remember the January we had. Her damn papa shouldn't have left her out in the cold like that. They all do the same thing." Then Simon drew in a deep breath and sighed. "I'm sorry you're hearing it now."

Gillian put his head down, shaking it back and forth as if he could deny the news. The room was silent now, but he could feel Patrick's eyes on him. Simon, at a loss for words, began busying himself folding a pile of fresh towels. He glanced at his timepiece, obviously expecting another customer soon. And Gillian just stood there shaking his head.

Frustration, then rage, quickly replaced the shock he'd initially felt. "That bloody bastard. Drinking at the saloon while a little one's out in the cold making money for him so he can drink more and whore around," came out in a low seething tone. "How many is this, Simon!" he barked. And suddenly he was angry at himself for not remembering them all, for not knowing their names. He wanted to scream and throw something, but he couldn't, standing there in the middle of Simon's shop. "It's all so unfair," he muttered. He closed his eyes briefly and drew in a deep breath. Then a long sigh followed, and he replaced his hat.

"Well, we best be going, Patrick," he said forlornly. He reached for the door handle, and then came the jingle from the welcome bell above, a comforting sound. *Well, at least some things haven't changed*, he thought.

"Take care of yourself, Robert," Simon looked at him sadly and waved. "You too, Patrick."

"Aye, Simon," Patrick responded glumly as he followed his father out the door.

A light, sleety snow was falling as they exited to the deserted street below. At least whatever news Patrick wanted to surprise him with would be a distraction from Simon's more somber announcement. *No more hot corn girls,* he reflected. More evidence this was a street of sorrow he would have to avoid.

"Well, I suppose you're going to spring some news on me, lad?" he said as they negotiated the pudding on their way to the seaport.

"My plan now is to marry Helen and join the paid fire department. I know what you're going to say, but there will be time to become a druggist," he said quickly. "My foreman says I'll be a shoo-in for a very respectable position, over seven hundred a year they'll be paying. And old man Hennessey says I can work with him part-time. With my license, I can mix powders and elixirs you know, all legal. So, he'll pay me more, and with my savings I will eventually start my own business." Patrick had somehow managed the speech all in one breath.

Gillian sighed in resignation. He knew there'd be promising careers with the new municipal department, good-paying jobs based on merit, not patronage. Well, maybe some patronage. Truth was, he knew Patrick would do just fine at any endeavor for which he had a passion. Though he was tempted to show his scarred arm to remind Patrick of the hazards. But he was tired now, and the ulcers on his legs were more than a nuisance. Besides, his mind was preoccupied with the sad fate of the lone hot corn girl.

"Okay," was all he said. And it occurred to him, both of his children had long since moved on with their lives. He needed to accept that, and maybe do the same.

* * *

He awoke with a start that night.

That damn dream again.

The specter in the fire.

Only this time it had begun differently. This time he arrived home at their old flat, opened the door, and found the apartment ablaze. Entering was impossible, but he heard Aileen in the next room gently crying. He wanted to go to her, but it was not possible. He was calling out, "I'm sorry, Aileen. I just can't. I'm sorry." At the center of the living room, the blaze began to swirl, and then it took its usual course. First the black tornado, tightening into a rope, then that chilling creature, part man, part insect. This time the creature had beckoned him forward, turning toward Aileen's cries and waving for him to follow. "I can't go in there. Leave me alone!" he pleaded.

Then he awoke. For a few moments he thought, *Could the specter have always been a dream?* "Certainly not!" he barked, forgetting that Patrick was sleeping in the next room. My long-lost friend's burns bear witness to that." Which started him thinking about Clancy's whereabouts, or if the man was even alive.

He lay in bed listening to the wall clock and Patrick's gentle snoring in the next room. And he grew angry. *They shouldn't have died!* he wanted to yell. *Not Daisy and Daphne. Not Aileen. Not the little girls selling corn.* He rolled over onto his stomach and began punching his pillow, five times, harder with each blow until he heard Patrick's rustling in the next room. Then he buried his face in the pillow, and moments later new thoughts came to mind. *I will leave New York. But first I will make all the money I can, then flee on the finest white steed. Purchase a sprawling farm in New Jersey, hire farmhands, find a mistress, and have Mary and Patrick pay visit each and every week. Dinners will be served at the grandest of tables, set with game pie dishes and fish tureens, my brilliantly glazed majolica! And only the finest spermaceti candles will light the room.*

"Never a sputter or a flutter," he murmured and then smiled. "Yes, this will be the plan."

He repositioned himself on his side and smoothed out his pillow.

I will finish my work with the Fire Marker Man, leave the docks, but continue investing wisely with Enoch Bidwell.

PART VIII

THE FINAL EVENT?

Chapter Fifty-Eight

January 1868

"Papa, take a look at this," Patrick said while finishing his breakfast. Gillian took his seat at the far end of their newly purchased dining table, oversized for the room. A plate of ham, potatoes, and jellied bread awaited him.

"I don't know what I'll do when you and Helen are wed, lad. You're too good in the kitchen to leave me," he said with a smile as Patrick tossed the *Herald* in his direction.

There it was, on the front page, lower right corner.

Alvin Farragut, President of Farragut and Son LTD, Arrested
Knowingly Supplied Shoddy Military Uniforms to Brooks Brothers
Actions Led to Weakening of Union Forces, Prolonging the War

There was a pleasure that came from knowing that there was some justice in the world. The greedy little man who insisted Mary be his mistress was getting his due. He'd contracted with Brooks Brothers to supply army uniforms and boots for the soldiers. Then he subcontracted with the cheapest slop makers in town, those with little or no experience in making durable military-grade clothing. He enriched himself wildly, to the detriment of the troops, the country, and the reputation of Brooks Brothers. Uniforms that had come apart after a week's use; dyes bleeding off when it rained; boots whose soles would abandon a soldier in the middle of a battle, glue used in place of stitching, melting in the heat of the deep South.

"Hah, Patrick! The fool is bankrupted. We must tell Mary. She'll see that revenge can be sweet."

"She probably read it in Bidwell's paper already. Maybe she'll pay call to you about it."

"Your mother would get comfort if she were here," he said, reflecting on how many years it had been since the cholera took her. "Well, you better be off, lad. I'll get another ice slab today. Just remember the Jersey milk to come home with you tonight."

"Aye, Papa, I'll bring the whole cow."

They both laughed as Patrick laced up his boots.

News of Farragut's fate was a welcome distraction, for Gillian was to meet with Daniel Mahoney at twilight in front of a building on West Street. This was to be the site of the next *good fire,* keeping within the man's meticulous schedule. For Gillian, it would be the final event, the last time he'd be an accomplice to a crime. He just needed to convey this to Daniel in a palatable way. His own finances were secure for life, and after all, Daniel himself had said that the days of this game were swiftly coming to an end. What would it matter if Gillian's ended a bit sooner? And then he wondered, when will Daniel decide that the risks are exceeding the reward? More independent investigations? Or will he take this to the end, pay no mind to risk? When the volunteers are done, and Chelsea stops paying rewards for saving a building

In front of the full-length glass, he rehearsed. "Daniel, you owe me nothing, my friend. You've been more than generous, far exceeding my family's aid to you in your time of need all those years ago. Besides, you were a good landlord to us, so we let you just a half-acre until you got back on your feet."

Yes, that is what I'll say, after this last event.

* * *

The note, holding the address of the West Street property, was found in the usual post office box. Now, this was to be a big job, somewhat complicated, but the prospects of a bountiful reward were great. The victim of this event? A hulking manufactory. Perhaps that was the reason for this unusual meeting, the reason Daniel Mahoney would leave his safe haven and venture out in the cold and dark.

Gillian's hands were perspiring under his wool gloves. What began as a brisk walk in the cold morphed into a painful experience as the sun dropped below the horizon and the wind ratcheted up off the Hudson River. Gillian increased his pace, which only made the cold worse, as he was now confronting the wind head-on. Finally, he saw the bundled-up stick figure at the end of the block, lantern light swaying back and forth, reminding him of his first view of the Fire Marker Man after the Great Distillery Fire. Strange how he had seen him as a hideous creature then, before the "hideous creature" was revealed to be an old friend. He waved to Mahoney now, just as a city lamplighter completed his task of illuminating the gas lamps along the block.

The marked building was even larger than he'd imagined. A massive brownstone, a full four stories, reportedly with two Otis lift systems.

"Ah, little Gill. Good to see you again." Their gloved hands met for a hearty shake. "We underwrote the policy on this building five years ago. She's a fine one, isn't she?"

As they moved to the opposite side of the street for a fuller view, Gillian's eyes rose to the top cornice, and then down to the company lettering just below. *Farragut and Son, Textiles LTD.*

"Oh my," he muttered. "Do you know who owns this building?"

"Indeed I do. Name's been in the papers all day. A despicable fellow. Could have cost us the war," Mahoney said, with no real tone of sympathy for the pawns who suffered firsthand from Farragut's piggish deceit. "But it doesn't affect us, Robert. We have a big policy on this. A major fire averted will pay a sizable bonus."

Gillian surveyed the street. New loft-style warehouses lined both sides of the block, built atop the tenements of years past, razed to make way for the growth of industry. But a smattering of wood structures remained, including a white clapboard building immediately adjacent to the Farragut property. In the short time of their meeting, candles were lit one by one in each room of the four-story wood structure as twilight slipped to darkness. Suddenly his attention was caught by a second-floor room. A young Negro boy was seated at a desk, reading a book by a fluttering candle.

"Robert? You're distant tonight, my friend. Let's go over one possible plan. The back of the building has a good staging point... Where are you going?"

Gillian had crossed the street to scrutinize the white frame building. The closest streetlamp provided just enough light for him to decipher a makeshift sign above the door. *Orphan Asylum for Colored Children*. He almost gasped as he covered his mouth, and then he rejoined Daniel on the opposite side of the street.

"What is it, Robert?"

"It's an orphan home. I remember now. During the riots, the mob torched the Asylum for Colored Children up on Fifth Avenue. By the grace of God, all two hundred children escaped. But no building large enough to keep them was made available, so they scattered about the town for now. Several churches helped them locate temporary housing, like this building."

"Oh yes, I do recall. They're to locate to Harlem. The city and some charities are funding a new home up there. Well, good for them, I cheer. But let us focus on the job here, Robert."

"No."

"Hm?" Mahoney turned his good side to Gillian. "No? What does that mean, my friend?"

The word "friend" stung this time. "We can't do it... I won't do it, Daniel. The risk is too great, being next to a home." He stamped his foot down on the sidewalk and stared at Mahoney with resolve. He was aware that anger was ruling him and fear would take its place later, but *so be it*, he concluded. "And I pray you don't say, 'They're only nigger children.' Not even you would be so callous—"

"Not even me, not even me! You insult me to the core," Mahoney hissed, then lowered his voice, a strange note of desperation entering it.

"One last fire, Robert, I beg of you. We can control this. Much stone and steel in this place. All will work out, you will see."

Mahoney, begging? He'd never seen this side of Daniel Mahoney. Not now, and certainly not back when they were young men on the other side of an ocean. Gillian stood resolute and forced himself to stare at the man's entire face. "I made a vow, Daniel, when I entered this game with you. Never would I knowingly put a soul in harm's way, especially not children. Besides, a fire here is complicated."

A cold gust hit them both at that moment, then a fine snow began to fall. Mahoney turned toward Gillian and held his lamp an equal distance between their faces. Gillian stifled a cringe. He'd never been this close to the tortured scar tissue.

"You disappoint me, Little Gill. I had thought you wouldn't, but I trust you won't betray me like others have."

Gillian had the urge to run but couldn't seem to communicate this to his feet. He met the man's stare with deadpan expression. "I'm sorry, Daniel. I truly am."

Suddenly Mahoney's anger appeared to vanish, and he smiled warmly. Could it be the man was about to concede?

"Robert, meet me at my office this Sunday at two. We'll discuss this more," he commanded. "Adieu for now." And he flipped his scarf around his neck and departed.

Gillian, alone on the cold, dark street, turned toward home, disappointed that this storm was not over. Just as he tossed his scarf around his neck, he heard an odd sound from what appeared to be an alleyway between the factory and the orphanage. He crossed over and lifted his lantern.

Nothing was there, and so he was on his way home.

* * *

"What happened to poor Daniel?"

That question kept returning to him as he readied himself for work, when he lay awake in the dark, and even at times when he was barking orders on the dock. He had to get away from the Fire Marker Man, yet he owed much to the Fire Marker Man. And there the problem lay, one causing him heart flutters as he stood in front of the mirror in his night-clothes, only four hours out from the meeting.

He tried to distract himself with other thoughts. Perhaps he would be seeing Aileen again soon. After all, he didn't know what the Fire Marker Man had in store for him. *Silly, silly me. Daniel would do me no harm.* The days would be getting longer soon, and he would take the ferry to Brooklyn, returning to her tomb. She would forgive his misdeeds, for certain, but she'd insist he confess his sins to their pastor at the church he seldom attended.

The mirror chimed in. "An upright thing to do, but don't you think a risky proposition, Robert?"

"Yes, too risky."

He and the full-length glass were finally in full agreement.

CHAPTER FIFTY-NINE

The Final Meeting?

Men and women sporting the latest fashions crowded both sides of Broadway as Gillian navigated his way toward the spindly building. It seemed as if he was the only person with a mission that Sunday afternoon, the only person lacking a happy façade. Dodging one last pile of the pudding, he arrived at the peculiar edifice and made his way up the stairs.

The door to the office suite was open, as was the door that separated the cozy waiting room from the sun-splashed inner office. *Daniel surely wouldn't be planning my end here with these entrances wide open.* He smiled nervously at his thought, dismissing it as silly as he stepped into Mahoney's lair.

"Good afternoon, Daniel!"

He was just in time to catch Mahoney closing a pair of blue crushed-velvet curtains, something Gillian had not noticed before.

"Greetings, Robert!" Mahoney said. "Sit. Rest your feet. I know it to be a long walk for you. Why in heaven's name don't you hire a carriage? Money surely isn't the issue now."

"I don't know. Never gave it much thought, just used to it I guess," he said, pondering the valid question.

"Well, what do you think?" Mahoney asked.

"Regarding?"

"The new curtains. What do you think?"

Mahoney was shutting the last heavy curtain, snuffing out the last of the bright sun, putting the room into an eclipse-like twilight.

"Oh. I thought they were new. Very nice, Daniel. Indeed."

"They benefit me greatly. The sun makes my skin feel taut and my good eye tear up. I really should only venture out at night, you know," Mahoney said with a grin.

There was a brief silence as Gillian fidgeted in his chair. "Daniel. Please understand. This must be over for me. I made a vow to myself and my dear wife. Never would I endanger the lives of others, certainly not children."

Mahoney sat down at his desk. "Your wife, Robert?" Your wife is dead," he said flatly. "The foul water did her in, as it did in many others. Remember, the water that was promised you from the Croton Reservoir, the reservoir I helped build when I first arrived here?" The gravelly voice grew louder as the Fire Marker Man moved forward in his seat. "They promised us fresh water in the Points, but it was a lie. The Croton water went to the plumbing in the finer neighborhoods, to the businesses that bribed the politicians, to the new hydrants. The fires get the fresh water, but not our people!" Mahoney paused, then chuckled at his last statement. Gillian found this truth absurdly laughable, and if not for his extreme discomfort, he too might have chuckled at the irony there. Mahoney's good hand was clenched in a fist, and he was in deep contemplation as he knocked rhythmically on the desk. Gillian assumed that the man was developing a new angle of persuasion—that or he was devising a plan to dispose of his old friend.

Then Gillian thought back to the advertisement in front of the new row of tenements across from his Grand Street flat. *Fresh Croton Water* and the word *nearby* in smaller letters at the bottom of the sign. He had to admit to himself, a similar sign was found in front of their building when the agent escorted them to the property. "I know how you feel, Daniel," Gillian said. "But perhaps I should have read the sign more carefully, Aileen too."

"That's not the point, dammit!" Mahoney slammed his fist on the ink blotter. "You don't know the full story!" With that, he drew a bottle from his desk's bottom drawer—whiskey would be the drink today—and delivered a tin for each of them. He poured heavily, then sat back in his chair. "It was my father's dream to own a fleet of hookers and a herring plant right near the Galway Harbor. We Mahoneys were strong farmers, and we were to be fishermen now too. I was just ten years old when he disappeared, summer of 1811. He'd been exploring the idea, went out with two farmhands and was kidnapped, impressed into the service of the bloody Royal Navy. But you know this story from back when I was your tenant, and we'd talk late into the night. You remember, Little Gill, don't ya?"

"Indeed, I do," Gillian said.

"But there was more I didn't tell you, just how I lost the farm. We were not over-mortgaged, Robert. And it wasn't the tenants not paying the rent or the crop losses. I wanted to carry out my father's dream. You see, there was much talk at the time. The powers in London were to help finance the rebuilding of the harbors along the western shore of Ireland, part of growing the fishing industry there. But without good transportation across the isle back then, it was hard to get fresh fish to market, especially in the summer." Mahoney gave a quick pinch to what was left of his nose as if smelling the stench of un-iced fish. "But that was okay because we would be salting and curing the herring and sturgeon. That's when I mortgaged our two hundred acres, borrowing the money from a London outfit... Chelsea Surety Company!" he abruptly shouted. "Perhaps you've heard of them?"

"Oh my," was all Gillian could utter. Then he finished his tin and promptly handed it to Mahoney, knowing a replenishment was in order.

"You see, the worst of it is that Chelsea knew the wind was changing in the English Parliament. The Treasury's purse was being diverted to Scotland to pay for the expansion of their harbors and fishing industry. And Chelsea was aware of new tariffs coming on imported salt and curing materials! That's exactly what we needed in large amounts! So, we got in over our heads. Then bad times hit, making matters worse. Our product was too costly to bring to market."

All was becoming clear now as Daniel paused to finish his tin. Then he slammed the cup on the desk and fixated his eye on his visitor.

"Chelsea was privy to information we had no knowledge of, so they knew we'd fail. But—they—lent—us—the—money—anyway!"

Each word came with such rage that Gillian had to fight the impulse to cringe. Then, as quickly as it came on, the rage seemed to disappear. Mahoney's good eye was staring at empty space now.

"Perhaps they were after my land," he said calmly. "Although who can guess why—times were already hard, and then there were the crop failures. Some of the land tenants couldn't make the rent, except your good father. Somehow, he managed, probably at your family's expense. But it was not near enough to cover my debt to Chelsea Surety. Couldn't sell the land off, so they took it. Then Lord Bartholomew bought it for next to nothing. Right out from under me in a flash. Now, you probably didn't know this, Little Gill, but the great lord was also on the board of directors of Chelsea." Mahoney sat back in his chair and let out a tired and defeated chuckle.

"Aye, Lord Bartholomew," Gillian chimed in, reflecting aloud. "Who can forget that scoundrel? He had an agent, Gelding, doing his dirty work. Threatened to throw us in the workhouse if we didn't take his offer for passage to New York."

Mahoney didn't respond, but his eye wandered about the room, his head cocked just a bit. "Strange how life can be, Little Gill. I came all the way across an ocean to another world, supposedly a better place, and I'm damn near burned to death in a fire to save a building insured by no other than the Chelsea Surety Company!" Suddenly alert, he slammed his good fist on the desk again, causing such vibration that his newly filled tin jumped off the ink blotter and spilled its contents on the desk. "But I needed to prove myself as a fireman, a noble citizen of the City of New York, so I listened to that bloody coward, Brian Denny! Let me ask you, Robert. Did you ever see Denny put out a fire? Always appearing on the front lines, but never really jumping in. Then when I'm feeding him *event* work and filling his bank account, he double-crosses me to enrich himself. Well, he didn't get away... "

Mahoney trailed off.

"Away? Away with what, Daniel?"

"If a man develops a dishonorable reputation, it comes to bite him one day," Mahoney said blithely. "I'm sure he didn't vote as he was supposed to. Tammany Hall doesn't put up with that." Then he sighed, sat back in his chair, and closed his one eye. "I am a tired man, Robert. Wealthy but tired. I will die soon, but at least I exacted revenge on the powers that destroyed my life."

Then there was silence, only the ticking of the wall clock in the waiting room marking time. Gillian felt anxious again, despite the spirits, and thoughts ran through his mind in rapid fashion. *Who is this man with two faces? Surely not the man I once knew. And which is the spiteful side? The tortured side, or his birthright side?* Then he pondered the fate of Brian Denny. He'd intuited all along that Daniel Mahoney had been involved with the man's disappearance. *And what about that assistant, Mrs. Grimble, an odd death there?* Anxious but oddly not afraid for his life was how he felt at that moment. He had more to say to his old friend but wouldn't dare push things now.

Still with eye shut, leaning back in his chair, Mahoney spoke. "Well, I guess your silence spells it all, Robert. I have lost my case with you," he said softly, white flag apparently raised. "That's fine, Little Gill. You and your family helped me out, and I have helped you gain comfort in the new world. You should go now. I have others who can set the stage for the final event."

Relief swept through Gillian's body. But the feeling was fleeting. After a small hesitation, he decided to press. "Daniel, I beseech you to let this go. You have enough, a spacious townhouse in a fine neighborhood, money in the bank, more than you can use. Don't risk it all!"

Mahoney opened his remaining eye and stood. The left side of his mouth smiled; the right side tried. "Farewell, my friend," he said, and offered his good hand for a shake.

"Farewell, Daniel," Gillian replied as he stood and buttoned his cloak. He walked toward the door, then paused, and fumbled with his hat. He had the uncanny urge to ask Mahoney if he could still be trained in the honorable work of insurance adjusting. But Daniel seemed cut off already, busying himself with the architectural drawings of the Farragut manufactory.

* * *

Spirits in the afternoon exhausted him, and he welcomed the fresh air on his walk home. Late afternoon, Broadway was still crowded with the well-heeled but less so than earlier. He felt glum, not because he might never see the Fire Marker Man again, but because he couldn't bring himself to say what he really wanted to, dangerous perhaps, but from the heart. *"Daniel, what revenge did you get? Money in the bank you have no use for—no one to share it with? A company that doesn't even miss the dime you stole from them? You're lonely, bitter, old, and still deformed. You need friends, you need other purpose. No man should die alone."*

That night he dreamed of the blight again. The entire family was strewn throughout the potato crop, flies covering their bodies, and Daniel Mahoney cowering and crying—alone—in a part of the field nearby. But he was unburned.

When he awoke, Gillian did something he hadn't done in a very long while. He got down on his knees by the bed and prayed. He prayed that Mahoney could control this fire, and he prayed for the man's soul.

CHAPTER SIXTY

The Final Event?
February 1868

Gillian awoke in the middle of the night every single night for the next two weeks. But the bells were always silent.

Then it happened.

One bell, two bells, three bells. Something was clearly wrong here. White Flag Company shouldn't have to respond to this distant event at Farragut's manufactory. "Perhaps it's another fire," he muttered.

But by the time he was dressed and booted, a fourth bell, then a fifth bell came.

"Oh lord! A conflagration it must be."

When he got to the firehouse, he prayed the information that came over the new telegraph wire would contradict his fears. Instead, Gillian's heart sank when he saw the address of the fire.

* * *

As they approached West Street, the wind was gusting fiercely off the nearby river. Gillian was riding the sideboard of their first engine. Still a distance away, he saw embers taking flight into the night sky, and he knew they were drifting down a distance from the main event, perhaps onto rooftops of wood frame buildings. The glow of the fire was illuminating a patch of billowy clouds marching across the sky. *Daniel, you scoundrel, you didn't account for the winds off the Hudson River!*

With other companies present, they halted their steeds a block away, too far for a hydrant hookup. The men grabbed equipment and hurried down the street. Gillian heard Spanky's voice shouting through the speaker trumpet. *Could Spanky be my replacement as stager or the arsonist himself?* He had a hard time imagining this, as Spanky was the expert at arriving in a flash and extinguishing the fire. *Who failed here?*

At this point it was no matter to dwell on. Alvin Farragut's four-story manufactory was ablaze from the third floor to the roof. Two steam pumpers were already providing steady streams to the fire from their hydrant hookups. One was dedicated to the hose men who had already entered the first level and were progressing to the second floor, just below the fire. Two other hose men were tackling the warehouse fire from the alleyway adjacent to the Orphan Home for Colored Children. Just behind them, Gillian could see that embers from the main fire had already ignited the roof of the wood frame home. His thoughts immediately went to the window where he'd seen the boy sitting studiously at a desk. He ran to the men in the alleyway. "Stop your hoses!" he shouted. "You're wasting time and our water on the fucking warehouse!"

"We're following Spanky's orders, sir! This here building's insured!"

"There's no puttin' out this fire, boys! We need to bring it down so we have a barrier!"

As the words left his mouth, the truth flew back in his face. *The building's insured by Chelsea Surety. First job is to save the building or at least rescue the contents.* He also knew that it would take precious time to get the okay from the fire commissioner and the mayor, and to round up the explosives.

"You need to save the orphanage," he insisted. "Get up to the roof there to put out the embers!"

"Not till Spanky tells us what to do!"

"Oh, bloody asses!" Gillian yelled, and then he threw his helmet on the ground and raced in search of Spanky. Gillian was winded, and his sore legs were aching, but he ignored it all, squeezing through the firemen gawking at the blaze.

It was not certain who found who, but Spanky patted him on the back.

"Gillian, just the man we need! Tryin to pull a Brian Denny on me, are ye?" the aging little man said with a quick smile before getting down to business. "Listen, the pressure's going down, and we need to do something about that orphan home—or whatever it is. River's just two blocks away, we need to make a train with the engines, ye know—the old way."

"That'll take too long, Spanky. We might have enough time to get up there to the third floor and nip this out. Who's rescuing the children?"

Spanky shrugged. "I just assumed they'd come out already."

"Yeah, but they'll freeze—" Just then, a thunderous sound grabbed their attention. The roof of the Farragut manufactory was caving in. A wave of heat hit Gillian square in the face. Then a burst of embers shot skyward and dispersed, raining down on surrounding buildings, including the orphan home. The distressed horses began pacing. A whinny came from one as an ember glanced its side.

To Gillian's surprise, the hose men in the alleyway managed to escape to the street, unscathed, an amazing feat considering their proximity to the collapse. But now the steam pump they'd been connected to made a telltale sound, indicating that air was being sucked through the machine. The water supply was dwindling. They quickly closed the hose nozzle, but the truth was clear. They had no idea how long the water supply would hold up.

Just then, several children emerged on the orphan home's front porch. At the end of the line was their caretaker, coughing and wheezing. Some of the children were crying, some appeared remarkably calm, but all were clothed and wrapped in blankets. Gillian called out to several volunteers to set up a fire in the street, knowing it would take quite some time before they could get the children to shelter.

The hose men restored the water stream. Again, there was the strange sound from the engine pump. The water sprayed in a pulsating fashion, then the steady stream returned. There was no time for a sigh of relief.

Without waiting for a command, they climbed to the top floor in hopes of nipping the fire there.

Gillian sat on the stoop with the caretaker. Her breathing was less labored now. "How many children in your charge, madam?"

She turned to him, eyes wide. "Twelve. I have twelve. And we have two cats. I don't know if they made it out . . ." She broke in mid-sentence. "Bless you. Bless you for saving—" She stopped, panic overtaking her face as she stared at Gillian. "No, I don't bless you! I know who you are. You started this fire!"

Gillian's heart began to race. "You are mistaken, madam," he said sharply. "I had nothing to do with this fire!"

"I saw you—and that creature—from over there." She pointed to the alley, and then lowered her head in a coughing frenzy.

"You are mistaken, madam," he said again in self-defense. "I had nothing to do with this fire!" even as his mind pieced things together. It was the noise he had heard before departing. She had witnessed him and Mahoney arguing. He swallowed hard and began to tremble.

"I saw you. I heard you... and it."

Both were suddenly distracted by a rumbling sound. The manufactory was giving way.

Grabbing the woman, he pulled her to the middle of the street. He didn't know whether the brave firefighters had made it out of Farragut's building, but they shouldn't have gone in there in the first place. The fire was too advanced; they had arrived too late—every single resource should have gone to saving the orphan home. But it was Farragut's manufactory that held the brass marker, the gold prize to the first responding team.

Fire bells were ringing again. More companies would be involved, perhaps even Patrick's.

The hose spray that had iced on his beard and side chops dissolved as he stood near the street fire with the children. Gillian had an odd sensation, terror, but with a touch of relief packaged together. The game was over, no more burden of a lie to endure. *But then again, exactly what does this woman know? And surely Daniel will speak for me, that I was not involved in this event. Now, perhaps she knows very little? But then again,*

Daniel and I did discuss other "events" that night. Was she privy to that? If so, she must be dealt with before it's too late. He shuddered. *How could I even think such a thing? How? I'd be facing charges for arson, insurance fraud, perhaps murder. Yes, she must be dealt with fast.*

His obsessing was suddenly broken by a shriek from the caretaker.

"We're missing two of the children! Two are missing, dear Lord. Two are missing!" she shrieked as she turned and shook Gillian's shoulders. They ran back to the porch, one of the younger children following.

"I knows what happened, Miz Willmot," a little girl said as she tugged on the caretaker's coat. "They went back for the kitties, ma'am. That's what they do."

She grabbed the child, hugged her quickly, and hurried her back to the safety of the street fire. Just as she was returning to the porch, a thunderous sound hit the street. Gillian raced to her side, pulling her back to the roadway as the roof collapsed down to the second level of the orphan asylum. Embers reached the group huddled by the makeshift street fire, igniting one child's blanket wrap. A fireman rushed to smother the nascent flame. Suddenly, one of the two hose men appeared on the porch. He was holding a wet cloth over his nose and mouth and was coughing violently. He threw the remains of a charred cat into the street. Then he sat down on the porch and hacked out a wad of brown sputum. Gillian rushed him to the other side of the road, and they sat on a mound of frozen slush.

"They're all fuckin dead," the hose man said in between raspy wheezes.

"Are you sure?" Gillian asked desperately.

"If they weren't before, they are now. Look," he said, pointing at the flaming carnage.

Gillian looked back at the building in time to see the fire engulf the porch, including the makeshift sign he'd seen on that earlier frigid night, identifying the temporary use of the building as an Orphan Asylum for Colored Children.

The fire was quick to extinguish once the final collapse reduced the building to a pile of rubble. Somewhere in the ashen heap lay the remains of two children, a hose man, and another cat.

Three carts arrived to deliver the children and their caretaker, Elsa Willmot, to an almshouse near City Hall.

* * *

The fire commissioner arrived on the scene, absent the new mayor. All attention was on the destroyed textile building.

"Spanky, come see this!" the commissioner called out, pointing to a partially scorched can of camphene. "I don't know if this has a proper place here in a manufactory," the commissioner stated. "We need to contact Mr. Farragut himself, find out what this is doing here. I want a thorough investigation of this fire, Spanky. What do you think?"

"Sounds like a good idea, sir," he responded.

"Well, let's wrap this up. Another night of sleep lost," the commissioner complained. Just then, his eagle eyes caught a weak reflection of light off a piece of rubble. "Spanky, see what that is. I don't want to burn my new gloves."

Spanky retrieved the brass plaque. Even with gloved hands, the soot-covered object was hot to the touch. He dropped it on a pile of roadside slush. The melt water quickly cooled it, and he wiped it clean. The engraving was clear.

All Peril Protection Provided By
Chelsea Surety Company, London-New York

"We've seen this fire mark before, Spanky, haven't we? More than one occasion, I think," he said, wearing a perplexed look.

Spanky swallowed hard. "Aye, I think so, sir."

CHAPTER SIXTY-ONE

The morning edition of the *Herald* was full of theories, mainly that arsonists had set the Negro orphan home ablaze, and the fire had spread to the adjacent textile manufactory. *Perhaps a heinous crime perpetrated by those angered with the South's defeat. All focus will be on finding the ways of the arsonist, and those, or the one, responsible for the dastardly act.* The article opined that before the war, punishment for the perpetrator(s) would be a moderate prison sentence. But now, the gallows would be certain destiny unless a judge could find reason for leniency.

Gillian's hands began to tremble as he clung to the edges of the paper sprawled out on the table. Not for fear of death, but for the disgrace and shame he was sure he'd experience. He saw himself standing on the scaffold in front of an angry mob, newsmen all about, perhaps even a photographer to capture the moment. Oddly, he wondered what the inside of the head covering would smell like, and would that be his last sensation? He shook his head and finally let go of the paper. Then he began pacing in front of the looking glass.

"Get control of yourself, man!" he barked abruptly at the figure. "They'll get the story straight. Besides, this was not my doing. Daniel will identify his accomplice."

Unable to contemplate work that day, Gillian sent a messenger to relay word that he'd taken ill. He would use the day to sort out the situation, figure out how to escape his predicament. *Perhaps a brisk walk up to that new Central Park to first clear my head? No. That would be a waste of precious time. Maybe I should pay a visit to Daniel, the man that brought this on me, the one who destroyed my life. Yes. That would be the intelligent thing to do, make sure Daniel clears my name should the authorities come for us.* Then, he realized, it was not *should* but *when.* "And, indeed, they will come for us, Daniel," he muttered as nausea overtook him.

Returning from his retching episode at the privy, he remembered that Patrick couldn't have been at the fire. He was tending to his bride to be, his Helen, as she had taken ill. Then he thought of the wedding in the spring, the one he surely wouldn't be attending. And Mary, well, she was taken up with her new romance, the Chinaman she'd grown acquainted with. "An idiot I must be, of course, they will all know in due time," he muttered. Panic set in again, and he dropped onto his bed. There would be no venturing out. Perhaps his last day of freedom would be spent alone in his flat, his full-length mirror out of sight, the closet door firmly shut.

* * *

The following day he again dispatched a message to the docks that he was ill. He only ventured out for the morning paper. As he'd expected, the story was far more accurate now. And they had retrieved the remains of the unfortunate ones. The children would be given a simple ceremony, followed by a burial in the Negro cemetery. Gillian wished he could pay for their caskets, then it occurred to him that he'd done so already. All those anonymous donations.

A second article included the constable's interview with a Miss Elsa Willmot. Her account was damning. She'd accurately described much of the conversation he'd had with Daniel that night. She spoke of their meeting, saying it erupted into an argument. And that one of the men looked like most of the Irish sort in town. "Usually, I don't think I could describe him, but this one was different because I saw him the night of the fire. He's a firefighter himself." Her description of Daniel Mahoney was of a wretched thing, perhaps a character from a wicked tale. Then, the nail in the coffin. She had heard their talk of previous events and Gillian's claim that he didn't want to play the game anymore.

Now he had to lie down. Nausea returned, but there was nothing left in him to regurgitate. A pillow suffered a beating, white and gray feathers strewn about the room. Finally exhausted, he lay on his stomach and dangled one arm off the side of the bed, swinging it like a pendulum. He imagined it to be a noose—the one awaiting him.

A pint of grog put him out for the night. Then, at the crack of dawn, there was a loud knock on the door.

Chapter Sixty-Two

"So, this is how it ends. A Negro woman has done us in. I'm sorry, Robert. I truly am sorry for dragging you to this point."

Tears from Daniel Mahoney's one eye dropped to the floor, more tears than most could release from two eyes.

"If only I could have reached her first, a chance to at least clear your name of wrongdoing." Then he sniffled and let out a brief laugh, almost losing his balance, if not for placing his hand on the wall just behind him. "And to think, we didn't do anything wrong here."

"There are two notes atop my sideboard. The first carries instructions for my funds, should any be left after Chelsea Surety claws back my ill-gotten gains. The remains to go to various charities. The second note carries the truth on why I waited five years to reveal myself to you. You begged to know the reason. I said that you needed to prove your trustworthiness to me first. But I never doubted your trustworthiness, Robert. I was too proud for you to see me this way, too ashamed for how things turned out. And finally, you insisted on our meeting—which I'm glad you did, my friend."

Mahoney's rambling was interrupted by a second sharp knock on the door.

"I will be with you gentlemen in a moment. Please be patient. I am not a well man!"

Daniel Mahoney kicked the stool out from under his feet.

* * *

One week later, the City of New York was greeted by a startling revelation regarding the Textile Orphanage Fire, as it was being called now. The early edition of the *Tribune* broke the story first.

Alvin Farragut, the now-bankrupt textile man indicted on charges of supplying the Union Army with shoddy uniforms and boots, has released a confession from his prison cell on Blackwell Island. His statements to the constabulary were as follows:

'My dear son, James, has been missing since the fire at my plant eight nights ago. I am certain the boy is deceased, and my now estranged wife is aware of this fact too. I know this to be true since, at my direction, James ignited the fire. It's apparent that something went terribly wrong, and I am sure his remains must be found in the rubble.'

The article stated that Farragut broke down at that moment and was unable to continue for a full ten minutes while he regained his senses.

'I am a penniless man. The insurance proceeds would have provided funds for my appeal but also charity for my loyal needleworker ladies, who have found themselves without employ through no fault of their own after the great Farragut and Son LTD was forced into bankruptcy by its creditors.'

At that point, the wretched soul asked for the public's pity and to be returned to his cell.

Baffled, though relieved, would be the best way to describe Robert Gillian's thoughts as he lay in his new home, the Tombs.

"Why would Daniel take his life?" he muttered as he paced about his cell, listening to the wailing of his neighbors. "It makes no sense, Daniel! You didn't do it! I didn't do it! So why didn't you fight this!" Then Gillian laughed. Not a laugh born of sarcasm, but a good-natured laugh. "You see, after all, you were a good man, Daniel. I knew, in the end, you wouldn't endanger the lives of those children. Rest in peace, friend. You've been tortured enough in this life."

Gillian dropped onto his cot, immediately feeling the worn-out springs beneath. He wept until Phinney brought him supper and told him that he was to be moved the next day to the finest cell in The Tombs, the deluxe accommodation usually reserved for death-row inmates.

And there it was, on his tray. "Oh no, not swill milk," he babbled. He'd thought he'd never have to see the chalky bluish liquid again. For years now, it was only the best milk and cream for his family, delivered from New Jersey, chilled on blocks of ice as it crossed the mighty Hudson River.

Disgusted, he cast the solution onto the wall of his cell.

Chapter Sixty-Three

June 1868

The trial came swiftly, which meant his freedom on bail was also swift. Charges of murder had been dropped after the authorities located the remains of the lecherous—but dutiful—James Farragut. Robert Gillian, heroic volunteer firefighter, twenty-year veteran and foreman of the White Flag Engine Company Five, was convicted on multiple counts of accessory to arson and insurance fraud. The top brass of Chelsea Surety Company were already in the midst of investigating the irregularity of certain fires at its insured properties in New York City. A slew of investigators as well as a young crop of underwriters descended upon the city.

The office of John Mahon—as they knew him—was raided, and a *New York Tribune* reporter who had the privilege of accompanying the crowd eloquently described their findings.

A lone box of brass fire marks lay open atop the center of the adjuster's desk, a stained ink blotter beneath. The low rays of the setting sun, at just the perfect angle, caught the reflection of the newly polished brass, brilliantly illuminating a room that should have been in twilight. It's expected that they will still adorn the entrances of the new heaven-bound edifices, construction all made possible by Otis's elevator contraption.

Another short article—"Possible Inquiry into The Fate of Mahon's loyal assistant, Miss Marlene Grimble"—lay at the bottom of the page, as it was less than grabbing.

Seven years was a long sentence for fifty-nine-year-old Robert Gillian, a man in far less than perfect health. A lighter sentence could have been granted had he cooperated by revealing the others invested in the game. He couldn't bring himself to snitch, despite the urging of his attorney, Mr. Thurgood, a man recommended by Enoch Bidwell.

CHAPTER SIXTY-FOUR

THE TOMBS
November 1869

With one cuff dangling from his right arm, Robert Gillian approached his usual chair across from Mary. Her head was down, so he knew it was bad news. Jian Chang also had his head lowered.

"Hello, Papa," she said softly, forcing a smile.

"Hello, my lass," he replied solemnly, reading the situation. "Don't despair, my love. I'm sure Chang's brother did his best."

"Well, yes. I'm sure he did."

Gillian felt it his obligation to break the ensuing awkward silence. "So, how is the new laundry business faring?"

She smiled broadly. "Oh, wonderful, Papa, wonderful. Better than expected." She had tears in her eyes, and he knew they were not tears of joy regarding the new business.

Chang looked up and smiled weakly at Gillian, perhaps grateful too that the conversation was moving in a joyous direction. "God must have blessed us, Mr. Gill," he said. "And Mary, she expert in running old business, good with numbers you know. And she lift heavy irons too." With that, he smiled lovingly at her.

"And the Astor House has given him a contract for laundering the men's uniforms, and he gets business from the City Hall crowd," Mary chimed in with delight.

"Splendid indeed! Your man has a flair for this business, it seems."

"Yes... yes, he does."

Then an awkward silence filled the room.

A rumble of thunder came from outside, and Mary's expression darkened.

"Are they going to move you to the Sing Sing, Papa?"

"I'm really not sure," he said, wishing they could leave this alone.

"That would be a terrible thing, indeed. It's too bad Clancy's away. He'd be able to vouch for your good deeds."

Away was far too optimistic of a term to define Clancy's whereabouts for the past six years. At this point, Gillian didn't want to know the truth. All he knew was that Clancy was a man of impeccable character, and he could always remember him that way. A loyal father to a disloyal son.

"Patrick is to visit me this afternoon," he said. "That Brooklyn Bridge opportunity is going well, from what I hear. He may just get his wish to move to Park Slope."

"That would be grand," Mary said, sounding far away while glancing out the window. Suddenly she jerked her head in his direction, her eyes locking with his. "Why did you do it!" she hurled at him. "Why did you do it!" And she pounded her fist on the table.

Chang winced and lowered his head. Maurice glanced through the little window in the door, assessing the commotion.

"I should hate you!" Mary said.

Gillian put his head down and started weeping, the iron cuff gently clanging against the table. He couldn't bear to look in her direction. "I don't know. I really don't know," he said almost inaudibly, and he meant it. But he was aware that she'd said, "I *should* hate you," not "I hate you."

Though their time was not up, Mary stood to leave. It would be the first time she didn't stay the maximum period allowed. "Come along, Jian," she whispered, still glaring at her father.

Maurice quietly entered the room and escorted the visitors away. Then he returned for Gillian.

"That's the way it usually goes, Robert. That's the way it goes," was all he said—but softly, not mockingly—as he re-cuffed the prisoner.

* * *

"Patrick, my lad, you're in unusually good spirits today."

"And you will be too, Father, when you hear the news. Like I told you before, the city's going to buy our interest in the Brooklyn Bridge project, and it includes that spit of land on the Manhattan shore they'll need for a tower. You remember, the land owned by the Lenape peoples?"

"Aye. They do let me see the papers at times. A windfall for you and the others. Congratulations, my boy." Gillian had the urge to embrace Patrick in a bear hug. But that would alarm Maurice and possibly end the visit. Then he recalled the chowder parties at the firehouse in the old days. That spit of land. That's where Katonah would gather the clams and oysters for the stew. Now it was the golden key, the final piece in a puzzle needed to complete the grandest of endeavors: a bridge to the City of Brooklyn at last.

"But bragging of my good fortune is not my reason for my visit, Father. Last week, when the deal was being finalized, Katonah informed me that he had an idea that might help your appeal for leniency."

"Pray, tell me."

"You said that all your anonymous donations were in coinage or bills. But you would sometimes attach a note of some sort, albeit without mentioning your name. So, your handwriting, Father, that could be your ticket! With your list of some of the charities and a sample of your handwriting, he can prove you were the anonymous benefactor to those charities."

"You think these charities kept my attached notes all these years?"

"Papa, all it takes is a few. And Katonah is willing to make all the enquiries. He feels certain that your note would be cherished. And I agree. A gift from an anonymous donor is the highest form of true generosity. And your counselor, Thurgood, said the judge will take that into consideration, even if your sentence is not reversed. You could be out... in as little as three years." Suddenly Patrick seemed uncomfortable.

Three years was still a long time for Robert Gillian, and then what? Would Chelsea Surety come after him for the ill-gotten gains, leaving him a destitute old man? "Well, Patrick, three's better than four, or five, or six!" he said, trying to make light of the obvious. "And besides, I've already done almost half of that."

* * *

Back in his cell, staring at the peeling paint on the ceiling above his cot, Gillian was struck by the irony of it all. Katonah, Clancy's loyal friend, a man of few words, a man he struggled to communicate with, might buy him four years of freedom. And how ironic, he thought, *a man belonging to a people whose Manhattan Island was snatched from them, perhaps through deceitful means, delivered the last piece of the puzzle, that spit of land in Manhattan needed for a bridge to Brooklyn. But this time, the Lenape people will make a handsome profit from the deal!*

CHAPTER SIXTY-FIVE

In the end, his case could not be appealed. But with Katonah's success in proving Gillian's generosity to the poor, the sentence was reduced considerably. Robert Gillian would be eligible for release in eighteen months and would remain in his spacious cell in The Tombs.

Many a night, he lay awake asking himself the same question. *Why did I do it?* Perhaps the specter in the fires was trying to stop him, give him a message? The specter he would see no more. On many a day, he would seek answers from the mouse that taunted him, scampering back and forth from his cell to the corridor, making it seem that freedom was so easy. No answer.

Then, one night, in those seconds between consciousness and sleep, it came to him so clearly. *To be in control!* The thought startled him. That's what it was about. As Daniel had said, "All fires are *good events,* if they are meant to be, if they accomplish an intended goal. A fire in a hearth is a controlled fire for warmth and for cooking. Our fires are events that we have the power to control, Robert. And the goal? Rightful financial gain to compensate for the bloody injustices done to us!"

"Was Daniel right? After all, I am an expert in controlling fire. And I rescued many a person from a *bad event,* risking my own life. So, I deserve this." Then he looked about his cell and laughed at what he'd just said.

"But life isn't fair, is it, Aileen?" Gillian stood and began pacing his cell.

"Roger, my good friend, you cautious to a fault, die from a stupid sore on your leg! Just a goddamn sore! Aileen, you survived the Typhus that snuffed out our little ones. Then, you brave thousands of miles of ocean, a journey with limitless perils, only to die from bad water because we were lied to! Cheated out of Croton water by the powers that be! Our lasses buried without dignity of caskets because our own country abandoned us! 'An Irish problem should be solved with an Irish solution,' they said. So, what was so wrong with helping myself to a slice of the pie! I deserved it! We deserved it!"

But stealing is stealing, he knew the mirror would say if it were in his cell now.

Tired, he lay down again on the straw mattress. "Well, at least I can rest knowing I did good with the money. Patrick will be a druggist. Mary will have a dowry. Her soon-to-be Protestant Chinaman—not what I envisioned, of course—seems to admire her, and he is a successful businessman. So what if he reads the King James Bible? And the charities I supported, many dollars to the Negro charities. Aileen, can you forgive me, my dear, for these transgressions?"

I believe she would, he concluded.

Robert Gillian finally found a comfortable position for sleep, avoiding that hard clump of straw in the mattress. It was a cold, late-autumn night, and a crescent moon outside the little window in the corridor provided faint light to his cell. The hearth down the hallway provided meager warmth, being such a distance away. But Phinny had supplied him with a handful of blankets. Nights like these, he would imagine himself at the West Brighton shore on a warm summer day. And on this night, he dreamed of just he and Aileen arriving via the paddle wheeler, landing at the pier near the Coney Island House. No rickety railroad for this well-to-do couple. Aileen was wearing a splashy sundress and holding a pink parasol. She was healthy, her skin glowing like it had in their early years. Now they were walking along the shore, all the other bathers slowly vanishing as the setting sun grew brighter and brighter, blinding them so that sand, sun, and sea became one.

And then Robert Gillian was all alone. His eyes filled with tears, and he was about to cry when he saw a little girl running toward him from the direction of the setting sun. Her curly blond hair bounced about as sand kicked up from her pattering feet. She was wearing the white dress he'd seen so many times before, only now the whiteness was pure, as the dress was fresh and clean—as was her face. Her rosy cheeks and blue eyes arrived at his feet.

"Oh, my little hot corn girl!" he cried out, tears of joy now streaming down his cheeks.

She smiled at him, and without a word, extended her hand for him to follow.

CHAPTER SIXTY-SIX

Tomorrows Later

Robert Gillian knew that there was no shame in just being lucky. But it had been twenty years now since the planes flew into the World Trade Center, and he still experienced pangs of guilt. Surely, he was not at fault for being in Hawaii at that moment, on a perfectly planned honeymoon. All the firefighters he knew who lost their lives that day—was he carrying the torch for their sake all these years? Is that why he remained a firefighter at Engine Company 220, Prospect Park, Brooklyn?

He'd planned to retire long ago. The plan had been to move to New Jersey, find another line of work, and perhaps serve as a volunteer firefighter somewhere. Maybe he just didn't know what career path to follow? Annie and the kids certainly wanted him to "hang it up." But firefighting was in his blood. Dust-covered family albums his father kept in the attic told the story. It was the old volunteer Brooklyn Fire Department back then, before the City of Brooklyn became part of a consolidated New York City. The story was that Patrick Gillian had settled his family in the new Park Slope neighborhood, where he'd become a well-respected pharmacist while also working for the local engine company. In some form, his ancestor was even involved in the building of the Brooklyn Bridge.

But despite the family allegiance and Robert's career uncertainties, he knew there was another reason he held on to the badge. Perhaps it was the ghost he would encounter in those rare conflagrations. The image none of the others could see, so he learned to keep silent about it. He'd put on that loathsome heavy gear that made him look like a human-insect hybrid, the respirator mask protruding like a long proboscis. And he'd carry out his brave duties. At least until he saw that strange hulking figure in the flames. A tall, burly man, bushy beard and overgrown sideburns, wearing what appeared to be a fire uniform of yesteryear. Oddly, he had no fear of the image, but then fighting the blaze was enough of a distraction. And despite the commotion about him, he had an uncanny urge to communicate with this ghostly form. As though he had an obligation to convey something but was unsure what that message should be.

Robert Gillian would keep fighting fires until he figured this out.

Epilogue

May 1872

*A*n *elderly man was shuffling down Barclay Street, an injury from a farm tool hampering his gait. "Not many houses left on this block," he mumbled, as he dodged warehouse workers moving goods in and out of large overhead doors. With so few homes left on the block, it was easy for him to spot the white townhouse, still with a majestic red door—twice his height, just as he remembered it. Strange, he thought, most things from long ago appear smaller than you remember them, but not this here.*

He climbed the three steps and reached for the brass knocker. A shiny new brass knocker, he noted. Before he'd even given it a tap, with a loud creak the door suddenly opened. Standing there with eyes open wide and a hand across her chest was an elderly woman. Her gray hair was pinned up in what he assumed to be a new style. He wasn't surprised, as so much had changed in the nine years that he'd been gone. But what was familiar to him was the colorful feathered hat she was holding by her side.

"Greetings, madam," the man said with a smile as he tipped his cap and bowed in her direction.

"Oh goodness, you startled me, sir," she said still with her palm to her chest. "Not at all good for my heart, dear god. I was just leaving for the market when..." and she paused. Then came a perplexed smile.

"My apologies, ma'am," Now he smiled at her, seeking a hint of recognition.

"You do look so familiar. Have we met before, sir?"

"We sure have, ma'am... er... Mrs. Bidwell. I recognize you with that hat for certain! It's me, Clancy Carver!" and his smile broadened so that his eyes almost closed, being pushed up by his cheekbones.

"Well, goodness gracious, Clancy Carver!" Again she rested her palm on her chest. "It must be almost twenty years. My. I should have recognized you. It must be the beard."

"Maybe. I might have had it back then but only it wasn't gray when you saw me last. And I had more hair then—a lot, and no mustache. I think it was when I called on you and the master about Mary Gillian, looking for a domestic situation."

"That's right, I do recall now. Well, look at me, not being proper. Come inside, Clancy. I was about to go to the market but that can wait—"

"Oh, thank you ma'am, but I have a lot of errands to run myself, being I just got back in town a few days ago. I've been living in Virginia since the war ended, became a sharecropper— that's like a farmer if you don't know. Finally bought my own place with a few others, part of an old plantation they broke up. We were doing fine until they came along—that's the men with the sheets."

She cocked her head. It was obvious to him that she didn't understand what he was getting at. "Oh... sounds dreadful, Clancy."

"Well, anyways. I know about poor Robert Gillian, a good friend of mine he was." Clancy lowered his head. Clara said nothing, but he felt certain that she wasn't harboring bad thoughts about the man. Then he looked up at her with a fragile smile. "But I wanted to pay my respects to his children, Mary and Patrick, that is. Does Mary still work here?"

"No. It's just me and Mr. Bidwell now. Mary is wed, a Chinaman, very successful in the laundry business. It's Mary Chang now. You can find her at 30 Mulberry Street, that's Chang's Laundry. Patrick too is wed, and with two children. He lives in Brooklyn."

"Well, I'll be! A Chinaman, of all things. Hmm." There were a few seconds of silence as they both smiled and nodded in tacit agreement that times were indeed changing. "Can I say hello to Master Bidwell before I move along?"

"Oh, I'm afraid he's away. You just missed him by a day. He took the coach down to Princeton, New Jersey, to pay his respects to an old friend that just passed. Ninety-five years old. Mr. Bidwell knew him from his navy days, the war back in 1812. Daniel Mahoney was his name. Nucky's ship sank an English vessel. Daniel was the only survivor, and it turned out that he was an Irishman, kidnapped by the British Navy. Mr. Bidwell thinks his friend may have been the father of that man they were calling the Fire Marker Man. He went by the name John Mahon. But the newspapers said his real name was... .Well, I'm sure you heard the story," she ended, *looking a bit uncomfortable.*

Clancy lowered his head slightly and nodded. "And they stayed in contact all these years?"

"Just once in a while. Daniel became quite a successful farmer in New Jersey, very busy, you know. But sometimes we would receive a crate of fruit with a note attached.

"Hmm. Well, I better be off. It was a fine thing seeing you today, Mrs. Bidwell, and please give the master my regards."

"Yes, Clancy. I will, and don't be stranger once you settle in again."

"You have my word, ma'am." And with that, he smiled broadly, tipped his hat, and was on his way

Made in the USA
Middletown, DE
23 November 2022

15397770R00198